WINTER MEN

JESPER BUGGE KOLD

Translated by K.E. Semmel

Text copyright © 2014 Turbine DK & Jesper Bugge Kold

Translation copyright © 2016 K. E. Semmel

Previously published as *Vintermænd* by Turbine DK in Denmark in 2014. Translated from Danish by K. E. Semmel. First published in English by AmazonCrossing in 2016.

Published by AmazonCrossing, Seattle

www.apub.com

Amazon, the Amazon logo, and AmazonCrossing are trademarks of Amazon.com, Inc., or its affiliates.

ISBN-13: 9781503954755

ISBN-10: 1503954757

Cover design by Turbine DK

Cover photograph by Ronny Rischel Photography

Printed in the United States of America

To Karina, Malte, and Elvira

He who dares not to choose his path will end as the stair upon which the powerful tread.

Carl Scharnberg, Danish poet (1930–1995)

PROLOGUE

Coroico, Bolivia, May 6, 1983

The city lay in the deep slumber of siesta. Only wild dogs and cats, on their eternal quest for food, could be seen wandering the streets. The dusty village rested on the crest of a small mountain, with a view of the lowlands a quarter mile below, its angular ravines, and a roaring river, whose thorny temperament could make it seem both inviting and terrifying. The warm currents of air from the citrus groves and the coffee plantations down in the valley wafted effortlessly up the slope, then fused in a tart aroma on the rooftops, right where the fog usually settled like a thick cap. But on this day the sky was clear. Before entering their houses early that afternoon, everyone had noticed with some astonishment the absence of the fog.

In the city square a mirage made the summer heat visible. It shimmered uncertainly above the cobblestones, where a man in a loose-fitting cotton shirt was shouting curses at one of the emaciated mutts. The dog skulked off with its tail tucked between its legs. Outside a decrepit tavern with shuttered windows stood three wooden tables. One had served as the Padilla family's dining table for several generations; another, its tiles cracked, had once stood in one of La Paz's most luxurious homes; the last one, the most rickety of them all, had been made by the owner of the tavern. There were a few faded umbrellas around the tables, their original colors nearly impossible to determine. A window in the little apartment above the tavern was wide open. The curtains followed the rhythm of the gentle breeze, fluttering slowly back and forth with a kind of affected indolence.

The man who lay on his bed was old. His hands were folded on top of his blanket, and his glasses rested on the nightstand, where they kept company with a glass of water. His skin had turned yellow from many years spent in the piercing sunlight, and his wrinkled cheeks were sunken. He had an untroubled look about him. From his bed, the old man had a view of Cerro Uchumachi. The green mountain with its soft curves might very well have been the last thing he saw before he died early that afternoon.

His family would not miss him, for he had no family. Nor had he any friends left. He had called himself Hector Morales, but everyone knew that was not his name. They called him, simply, the German. Although he had arrived in the city more than eight years earlier, very few people had ever spoken with him. No one knew where he was from or where he had been before he'd come. No one knew his story, but in Coroico you kept your stories to yourself, and the only foreigners who lived here had something to hide.

The few who had exchanged pleasantries with him described him as a friendly, educated man, and the women said that he always lifted his fedora and nodded if he passed them on the square. He always followed the same route, and his slow amble—cane in hand—conformed to the pace of the city. People hurried only when summer's powerful rainstorms came.

After his daily stroll through the city, he always sat on the same bench on the square. There he sat year after year, watching. He never made any attempt to strike up conversation, and the residents grew used to him the way they would a lamppost or a fire hydrant.

He was buried in the dry red soil of the cemetery behind the little stone church. The ceremony was held without fanfare, its only participants a priest and a grave digger. A wooden cross, which would soon be discolored by the sunlight, was placed at the gravesite. It read, "Hector Morales, ?–1983."

Salzburg, Austria, March 10, 1947

The harder it rained, the heavier his jacket became. Huge drops soaked the coarse fabric, which thickened at the shoulders. A raindrop trickled past the protective shield of his collar and slid down his neck. It continued down his shirt and between his shoulder blades, where its progress was finally checked by the edge of his undershirt; an icy sensation spread through his body. He shivered. The cold made him impatient. As he took a long drag on his cigarette, the drenched paper unraveled in the rain, and the wet tobacco landed at his feet. He scowled and glanced reproachfully at the dark sky, whose color answered his question: the rain had no intention of ceasing anytime soon.

He looked around. The once-beautiful train station was still in disarray. Bombs had destroyed the waiting room, and debris and twisted iron lay in disorderly heaps beside the tracks so that it wouldn't disrupt the trains. The weather was like a response to the melancholy of the place. The scenery reminded him of the nightly alarms, of the wrenching blasts of sirens that had knocked the wind out of him, of the bomb bays that had rained death down onto them, and of the panicked waiting when everything grew still. And of the awful relief of finding yourself alive while people who'd lost their loved ones crumpled to the ground or the stairs or into his arms in despair. It had been the same here. The same terror, another city.

No one had noticed his cigarette fall apart. The few others on the platform were focused on themselves. A junior officer in the dusty green uniform of the Americans was engrossed in kissing his companion. He uttered a couple of bungled German phrases and made her laugh, and they kissed again. An older, official-looking man, his suitcase between his legs, stood rocking on the balls of his feet like someone who believed it helped to make the wait more productive. Behind him stood a corpulent woman clutching a child's hand. He noticed how tightly the woman's coat was cinched around her waist, flattening her bosom. The buttons were about to burst, and when she moved, the seams creaked. The boy, who was licking a lollipop, stopped abruptly, his eyes widening at the sight of the approaching train.

Smoke from the steam boiler enveloped the platform, and the locomotive's screeching brakes drowned out the silence. He waited as passengers disembarked through the smoke. He stepped onto the footboard and took his place in the compartment, where an elderly man was already comfortably seated; they nodded at each other with the cool reserve of strangers.

He regarded the train car's shabby appearance without concealing his revulsion and decided that it would have been better if the train had been abandoned on a sidetrack. The paint was peeling, the leather seats were split and missing armrests, and some of the windows were cracked. He noticed the stench. He recalled it from his childhood—the unmistakable odor of decay, the same smell that rushed at him when he lifted the heavy lid of the chest in his grandparents' attic. Inside was his grandfather's old uniform, from a war no one talked about anymore.

Though he knew he should close his eyes and let his exhaustion overcome him, he'd planned to enjoy this trip. He lit another Gauloises and leaned back in his seat. He watched through the window as the train rolled past the Austrian landscape: Bad Gastein Waterfall, Böckstein Church, Our Lady of Good Counsel, the entrance of the long Tauern

Railway Tunnel. He absorbed his impressions along with cigarette after cigarette.

His left arm jittered up and down like an impatient child. The ruined nerve had started its daily revolt, and though he was all too familiar with the nerve's behavior, he studied it. The arm had become a storyteller. Not one that told fairy tales with happy endings, but one that should be kept well away from children and the fainthearted, one that chronicled the horrors of war—and who he had once been.

He still regarded himself with a certain level of astonishment. In his mind, he did not see himself as a man wearing an SS uniform. But others had seen something different. What people had seen was a Nazi. But he was no Nazi, and he'd never been one. Before the war, he had dissociated himself from everything remotely connected to Nazism; he had been respected and popular, and everyone had considered him an educated man. A uniform had changed all that. If you were a member of the SS, you were guilty. That's how they thought, the ones who owned Germany now, but they didn't *know* him. He wasn't guilty—or at least he didn't feel guilty—but he'd had the standard SS tattoo of his blood type on his left upper arm, and that had amounted to an admission.

He carried many sensory impressions from the war that he'd gladly forget. One was the smell of charred flesh—the stench of his own skin the time he'd put the heated blade of his hunting knife against his upper arm. The tattoo had to be removed. The skin had sizzled and bubbled like something in a saucepan. He came close to fainting but continued resolutely down his arm despite the pain coursing through every inch of his body. The small blond hairs on his arm disappeared faster than he could see, and the awful stench of burned hair and flesh assaulted his nose. An explosion of agony jolted from his arm to his chest, as though shrapnel were being pressed upward until it bored into his brain. He fought to maintain consciousness as a scream filled his throat. To relieve the unbearable pain, he'd leaped into a nearby pond in the woods, and there he had remained for several hours, until his body temperature fell dangerously low.

He pulled a flask from his inner pocket. His eyes darted toward an oncoming train. The sharp taste of alcohol met his tongue, and the aftertaste lingered in his mouth. He weighed the silver flask in his hand and estimated that it was half-full. He ran his fingertips carefully over the engraving on the side of the flask. The tiny inscription in the metal made him feel lonely, as the two letters formed the initials of his brother, the dead man.

His life had changed so much. The war had blown a deep crater in the center of his existence, leaving behind a city without houses. Although the war was in the past, it was never far from his thoughts. But everything else in his life felt distant. He missed Hamburg; he missed Sunday trips on Jungfernstieg, sailing on the Elbe, and spending days with his family in their large white house beside the Alster.

He returned the flask to his pocket. The elderly man across from him had fallen asleep and now buzzed like a honeybee, his nostrils quivering with each breath. He wondered whether he had been a victim or an executioner during the war. He searched for any sign that might give him an answer, but all he saw was an elderly man in a shabby tweed suit.

The trees' leaves had changed color several times since he'd begun his flight. His was a journey without a destination; he still didn't know where he would end up. There would be more cities, but the only place he wanted to be was the only place he could never see again. He'd set off from Hamburg just as British tanks were rolling into the city and walked south without any destination.

He remembered Germany right after the war as a confusion of soldiers: Russians, Americans, Brits. And Germans who just wanted to return home to their girlfriends, wives, families, and friends—if any remained. They marched across the country in endless columns—though they'd lost the war, they continued to display discipline. Most of them hung their heads, disillusioned, but a few officers held their heads high, proud of their war. For those who'd not yet been taken as POWs, it was another story. Before, they'd stuck together and fought together, but now every man fended for himself and many fought internal battles against themselves. He'd managed to make it through the war without firing a weapon, and yet he, too, was fleeing, trying to hide from the various armies of the world.

Now and then, he felt that death would have been a good solution, an acceptable solution. He often wondered why he wasn't dead. Like so many others. Why was he alive, and how could he actually live with what he'd seen and done? A long life lay ahead of him, but his desire to live it was minuscule. Yet he was too cowardly to die. Which was why he was sitting on this train.

A young, delicate-looking woman entered the compartment. She acknowledged the others the way a servant girl greets her master. He couldn't help but notice the large birthmark stretching across one cheek, from her ear down to her chin. She turned her head; she'd dealt with this kind of inquisitive gaze before. She removed her red rain jacket, whose color reminded him of Christmas. Suddenly he was a child again. Thinking about Christmas Eve. The smell of pine needles and oranges mixed with frying food in the kitchen, the memory of an out-of-tune music box and his brother's joy upon seeing the flash of a pair of skates beneath the wrapping paper. A lump formed in his throat at the thought of his brother, and he gulped a swig from the flask to wash it down. He would never see him again. A Luger's bullet had been his escape route. He envied his brother's courage in choosing that path.

His journey had brought him to Munich, and there he'd ceased to exist. Thanks to false papers, he became Stefan Mohringer, a traveling salesman from Mannheim; the surname "Strangl" would not be passed on. The name stopped here. No one wished to utter it any longer; it was a shameful name. Its laying to rest in the very city where Hitler had set into motion Germany's march toward hell went unnoticed.

His escape hadn't followed any predetermined plan. He'd hidden in a safe house with so-called friends, then crossed the border into Austria during the winter, alongside two other former SS officers. While the others had continued on to Italy, he'd decided to head to Linz.

He stayed in Linz for only a short time, changing residences regularly. He—who'd always lived in the same city—had now become a rootless nomad, a man without a home, a man without a trade. Most recently, he'd spent a few months living in Hallstatt, where he worked as an accountant and did paperwork at a small joinery. The joiner hadn't asked him any questions, and the idyllic city had been a perfect place to plan his future. And try to forget the past. He'd rented a basement room from a widow who was not yet thirty. She didn't call herself a widow, but he guessed that's what she was. Her husband had been on the eastern front and hadn't been heard from since 1944. Even several years after he left, she still leaped to her feet every time the creaky garden gate announced a guest and thrust open the front door with hope in her eyes, only to be disappointed once again.

The train ground to a halt. He was startled by the opening of the compartment door. A conductor asked to see his ticket. He grew fearful—as he did at the screech of a door, the ring of a telephone, a person walking too close to him—and the feeling lingered for hours afterward.

Beyond the city of Spittal an der Drau, the terrain dipped into a valley, and he could discern the river Drau through the cracked window. That meant they would soon reach Villach, fittingly called the "gateway to Italy." Here he was to meet a man by the name of Mr. Dubak, who would arrange temporary lodgings for him and get him a new passport for a price.

As the train rolled into the station, he stood and nodded kindly to the elderly man, who had opened his eyes in confusion every time the train had come to a standstill. He was supposed to meet Dubak that evening at Café Leopold. He had arrived in town early, so he sat beside the window in a restaurant and ordered beef soup and a Stiegl beer. As he ate, he watched the activity in the cobblestone square. The bronze statue in the center of the circular plaza was a gathering place for the city's doves, and they had made their presence known, shelling it with yellow excrement. He couldn't tell who the statue was supposed to depict, but he guessed it was one of Austria's many composers. Wasn't that what the country was known for? Mozart? Haydn? Strauss? Schubert?

He placed a few bills under his plate and crossed the plaza to Café Leopold. Kaiser Joseph II was the name on the bronze plate beneath the doves' decoration.

Anton Dubak was right on time. He, too, had served in the SS. Now he made a living helping people with the means and the need to flee the country.

"Mr. Mohringer?"

"Yes, I'm Stefan Mohringer," he said softly, still unaccustomed to his new name.

"Yes, of course." It was impossible not to notice the enormous gold ring on the hand Dubak offered him.

They sat in a booth in the back corner of the establishment, and Dubak gestured to the waiter for two beers.

"So you'd like to disappear?" Anton Dubak asked, leaning over the table.

"I want to get out of Europe."

"And you have the cash?"

He laid the envelope on the table, and Dubak counted its contents with the air of a man who'd done this many times before.

"Wonderful." Dubak smiled broadly, revealing two gold teeth in his lower jaw. "In a week you'll be across the border in Italy. Until then, I've found a place for you here in the city."

He checked into an old family hotel near the city's center, close to the train station. The bellhop ushered him to a room that appeared to have been furnished a century earlier. He lay on the bed, sinking deep into the soft mattress. He was exhausted and fell asleep quickly.

He awoke with a start to the sound of a car careening down Bahnhofstrasse, its tires squealing. He sat up abruptly, uncertain where he was. The car came to a halt, and from the window he saw four police officers rushing into the hotel. Though he was in nothing more than his underwear, the sweat began pouring from him, as if it wanted to expose him to the police as a guilty man. The officers thundered up the stairs. Then suddenly everything went silent. He held his breath. His escape had reached its end. Maybe Dubak had gone straight to the police and told them of his whereabouts, the money thrust deep in his pocket. The dirty bastard. Then again, maybe getting caught and enduring his punishment was for the best? Several minutes passed. They felt like hours. If the police were searching for him, why weren't they here yet? He put his ear to the door. Maybe they were on the other side, a breath away, their weapons loaded, ready to kick the door off its hinges. Time was measured in degrees of fear now. He returned to the window and pulled the curtain slightly to one side. The car was still there, idling. Still nothing. Someone shouted in the hallway, and he went rigid. Several more minutes passed before the policemen exited the hotel, dragging a man who clearly didn't want to go with them. The car spun around and raced at breakneck speed back down Bahnhofstrasse. For the rest of the night, he tossed and turned on the otherwise comfortable mattress, startling at the slightest sound. The next day Dubak moved him to another hotel.

Ten days later he crossed into Italy through a quiet border post. The bribe in the border guard's pocket made the trip easier. He crossed Brenner Pass on foot and was on the verge of collapse when he finally spied the Tower of the Twelve in Sterzing. By the time he strolled into the town, he'd walked eighteen miles. Dubak had told him to go to the Goldene Kreuz, where they were expecting him. He wasn't the first German to hide there, and he wouldn't be the last.

He remained at the hotel until his new passport and identification card were processed. Normally he would've enjoyed his stay—bought grappa on the main street, gone shopping in the boutiques, and dined at the town's many restaurants—but he kept to his room. After fourteen days, Dubak knocked on his door.

"Everything's ready." Dubak handed him his false papers.

The two men shook hands and parted ways, knowing their paths would never cross again.

He stared at his identity papers for some time. He knew he was the man in the photo, and yet the man staring back at him seemed a stranger. His eyes were distant, there but unseeing. His cheeks were hollow, and his mouth was nothing more than a narrow slit in his face. Next to the image was his new name.

In Genoa, his new papers were stamped with a permit allowing him entry into Argentina, and on May 15, 1947, he stood on the pier taking the measure of the steamship *Carmen Polz*. The harbor air was thick with petroleum, and the smell brought back memories—again of Hamburg.

He gathered his courage and boarded. A uniformed man studied his travel documents. Like the hands on a broken clock, time stopped, and every hair on his body stood on end. Blooms of sweat formed on his armpits, revealing his unease. The man looked up and smiled.

"Welcome aboard, Mr. Bock."

The journey across the Atlantic was uneventful. One month later he stood at the harbor in Buenos Aires and beheld the wide La Plata River. Someone—he didn't know who, just that it was one of his countrymen—had arranged a residence for him in the Florida district. With a suitcase in each hand, he headed toward his new home, noting with a slight smile that his house was on a street named Libertad, the Spanish word for freedom. Since most everyone spoke German in the Florida district, he had no need to learn the local language. He found a position in a German export firm. It was a mindless job, but that was just what he wanted.

In this German colony in the center of Argentina's capital, Reinhold Bock longed to find peace, but after many years spent repressing his past, he was suddenly wrenched out of his quiet life. In 1960 the Israeli secret service kidnapped Adolf Eichmann in plain sight on a Buenos Aires street, and Reinhold Bock and many others felt the ground suddenly shift under their feet. He left Argentina in haste, his rudderless journey not yet concluded, and moved on to Uruguay. His journey then brought him to Santa Cruz, Bolivia, his last stop before Coroico.

PART ONE

Hamburg, Germany, November 10, 1938

Gerhard glanced around the empty assembly hall. The lecture had gone as planned, but he wasn't as elated as he normally was. He retrieved his coat from his office, then biked slowly through the streets of Hamburg. From the university he headed toward the botanical garden, where the remains of the city's old ramparts were still visible; Bastion Casparus had been unable to keep the French out of the city and was now converted into parks and gardens. The botanical garden was abandoned, and the huge, bare weeping willow leaned threateningly across the moat—as if, in all its loneliness, it considered throwing itself into the ice-cold water. He continued past the grand justice buildings and Laeiszhalle, a neobaroque concert hall that had made its mark in music history thanks to visits from Strauss, Prokofiev, and Stravinsky. As he rode past the building, he hummed a piece from *Arabella* and thought of Emma.

Although he didn't view the city with the gaze of a visitor, he nonetheless studied it with a critical eye. Of course he could see that Hamburg lacked architectural beauty—in spite of singular pearls like Laeiszhalle—but new buildings here were constructed for practical reasons; and in this there was, perhaps, an aesthetic quality, a practical beauty. The city lacked the towering cathedrals, ostentatious castles, and fortresses so common in other large German cities. Widespread fires had destroyed the city's center several times, so all the history contained in the old houses was gone, and, as if to spite the people who'd chosen to live in this inhospitable lowland region, the Elbe often overflowed its banks. But Hamburg's residents were proud of their city, and Gerhard loved Hamburg's tenacious character just like everyone else.

In Alter Elbpark, a woman pushing a baby stroller stood on the gravel path, studying the enormous Otto von Bismarck monument, which cast long shadows in the afternoon sunlight. He slowed his pace to steal a glance at the stroller. A small, round-headed girl, swaddled in a wool blanket, smiled up at him. All at once he felt a surge of sadness flood him like the Elbe, a heartrending feeling he'd never come to terms with. He'd had a child once, but he was thirty-eight now, and he knew that he would never have another.

He parked his bike near St. Pauli Piers, where only the tall clock towers could compete with the two impressive ocean liners docked in the quay. Magnificent ships like the *Cap Arcona*, *Monte Rosa*, and *New York* ensured that North and South America, Africa, and the Orient were no longer inaccessible points on a map. A cacophony of sound suddenly filled the emptiness inside him as he watched the small, industrious tugboats putter off with one of the many oceangoing steamships that would soon set sail for some exotic destination. Tugboats with spluttering motors chugged up and down the Elbe pulling barges, and ships large and small were loaded and unloaded. The odor of diesel fumes hung like an invisible cloud between the jumble of cranes towering above the shipyard; on the harbor's edge, freight trains shrouded in smoke clattered back and forth, whistles shrieking as they set off with coffee from Brazil, spices from the Far East, and wood and cotton from North America. The harbor was like a beating heart, pumping products through the blue veins of the globe. It was the heart of Germany.

Gerhard sat on a bench watching his breath steam in the air. The temperature was below freezing, despite the few rays of sunlight. Feeling Bismarck's eyes on his back, he turned around. As he studied the iron chancellor gazing out over the city from his high vantage point, he thought about all that had transpired since Bismarck united the country. Germany was a ticking bomb, and he wondered when it would detonate. Gerhard's black horn-rimmed glasses steamed up. He removed them and polished them with his handkerchief. Shivering with cold, he considered his day.

His lectures in the assembly hall had begun to sound increasingly hollow as fewer and fewer students attended. Some had enlisted in the army, others had left the city, and Jews had been forced out of the university altogether. It was a lamentable sight to look out over all the empty seats in a place that represented the cradle of wisdom.

Everyone seemed to just accept what was happening. The eradication of the individual, the reduction of the people to a faceless gray mass shouting *"heil"* on command. It was as though everyone in Germany had become paralyzed. They'd screamed for change until their voices were hoarse, and they'd gotten the change they'd clamored for. But what happened when that change wasn't for the better? He no longer recognized his country. And how could they change anything now—now that they were up against forces like Goebbels, the master of agitation? With his plainspoken manner, the man had a rare talent for working his way into people's brains and hearts, circumventing their reason, and homing in on their emotions. First people were seduced by the marches, parades, and flag waving; once they were thus hypnotized, the speeches followed, and the words became gospel. By nature, Gerhard wasn't a man consumed by hatred, and yet he felt nothing but contempt for Goebbels. Of course, he never voiced his feelings aloud.

A voice startled him out of his reverie. "They've got that figured out!"

"Sorry?" Gerhard hadn't noticed the old man who'd sat down on the bench.

"Marching. They certainly know how to do that. They're everywhere you go."

The man nodded at a regiment of Hitler Youth marching past in their black winter uniforms and laced boots.

Unsure how to respond, Gerhard simply smiled. The man sliced an apple into wedges with his pocketknife so that his few remaining teeth could masticate the fruit.

"I always expect to see a bear riding a unicycle when I see their goose-stepping—it's all a ridiculous circus act." The man cackled with delight.

Gerhard kept silent and thought about his fifteen-year-old nephew. He'd noticed how indifferently August wore his Hitler Youth uniform, with its sand-colored shirt, leather cross strap, and long white knee-high socks. He wore it because he had to, because a 1936 law forced him to. On the streets, uniforms were everywhere: SS, SA, *Luftwaffe*, *Wehrmacht*, *Kriegsmarine*, Hitler Youth, and so on. Everyone was part of the same club now, except Gerhard.

"The Nazis are a bunch of idiots, if you ask me," the old man said suddenly.

"It's dangerous to say that kind of thing to strangers."

"At my age a fellow has nothing to lose." He spat an apple seed onto the ground. "At my age a fellow has already lost." Another seed flew from his mouth. "Allow me to introduce myself. I'm Theodore Weinhardt."

The old man offered Gerhard a gnarled hand, and Gerhard squeezed it cautiously so that he wouldn't crush the man's brittle bones.

"Gerhard Strangl," he said, looking the man in the eye for the first time. He had a friendly face. Two bushy gray eyebrows jutted in every direction. His nose reminded Gerhard, both in form and color, of a clown's nose, and his eyes were nearly impossible to see through his thick eyeglasses. In his lap lay a soft felt hat, one of those types of fedoras people wore in Tyrol.

"If only I were younger. Why don't you young people do anything?"

The sentence sounded more like a reproach than a question, and Gerhard shrugged. He knew he had to consider his words carefully. Though it was hard to imagine, Theodore Weinhardt could be an informant. They came in all shapes and sizes, so why not an old, hunchbacked man? And why such brazen questions?

"Hmm," he said neutrally.

"Then I'll answer the question myself: no one dares. Everyone's so damn cowardly now. The communists weren't afraid to fight," said the old man. Maybe this Weinhardt was a communist himself, Gerhard thought. Then the man continued. "I'd have gladly gone to war for that man up there. He was worth fighting for." He jerked his finger over his shoulder at Bismarck without turning around. "Not like Hitler. He's no statesman. He's just some bumpkin with a silly mustache. Don't you agree?"

The old man folded his knife and returned it to his pocket. From the opposite pocket he pulled out a pouch of tobacco and a pipe, which he carefully began to plug with almost ritualistic precision.

I agree completely, Gerhard thought, *but I won't admit that to a stranger.* "I'm not really sure," he mumbled.

The old man lit his pipe, took a satisfied puff, then blew the smoke out of one corner of his mouth. "You don't look like one of them. What do you do, Mr. Strangl, if I may inquire?" The old man leaned toward him, and Gerhard smelled a strange mixture of bad aftershave and pipe tobacco.

"I teach at the University of Hamburg. I'm a mathematics professor."

"Don't you mean Hanseatic University?"

"I'll never get used to the fact that the Nazis have renamed it," Gerhard said following his intentional slip of the tongue.

"Aren't you rather young to be a professor?" Weinhardt asked, scrutinizing him.

"I'm thirty-eight."

The old man studied him. "Now that you mention it, I can see that you've got a little gray on your temples." He gave a dry, chuckling laugh that caused his bushy eyebrows to flutter. There was something infectious about it, and Gerhard soon found himself laughing, too.

"Be careful! The Nazis are afraid of bright people like you." He pointed at him with the stem of his pipe. "If the citizenry is too intelligent, they'll just burn their books."

Again Gerhard laughed along with the old man, whom he'd begun to like.

Like a wave, laborers began flooding the harborside by the hundreds. The whistles had sounded; it was quitting time. Numerous small boats carried the longshoremen back to the residential districts along the Elbe's many tributaries. Workers in overalls and wool sweaters, dockhands in boiler suits, office workers wearing fedoras and suits, and secretaries in skirts and high heels were all rushing home after another workday. Only Gerhard and the old man were not part of the hustle and bustle.

Gerhard and the old man remained seated, silently watching the throng. Gerhard pulled a cigarette from his green pack of Ecksteins.

"I feel bad for the Jews. But it's all about finding a scapegoat who can't fight back," said the old man. "Consider this: an entire family disappeared from my building last night, and this morning all of their possessions were strewn about the street. Even the cemetery in Altona has been vandalized. And this is happening all over Germany."

"It's terrible." Gerhard studied the old man, who was now cleaning his pipe with the point of the pocketknife he'd used to slice his apple. He enjoyed speaking with Mr. Weinhardt, and Gerhard was convinced he was no informant. Nowadays, one felt safe only among family and good friends. His experience was that people were divided into six groups, and everyone belonged to one of them, whether they realized it or not. There were the fanatics, the supporters, the opportunists, the fearful, the doubters, and the resisters. The final two categories were thinning in number, unfortunately. More and more of them would soon be categorized among the fearful or the detained resisters. He thought of a seventh group: the dead.

"Are you married, Mr. Strangl?"

Gerhard shook his head, discreetly covering up his wedding ring. He didn't have the energy to talk about Emma.

"I am. A pleasure it is. Sometimes." The old man chuckled again. "That's why I come down here to the harbor so often. To get out of the house for a while."

Gerhard smiled. "Yes, Goethe was right: 'He is happy, be he king or farmer, who finds peace in his home,'" he said.

The old man considered a moment. "Or Socrates: 'Once made equal to man, woman becomes his superior,'" he said. "There's no doubt a kernel or two of truth in those words."

"Wasn't it Nietzsche who said, 'Woman was God's second mistake'?"

"That's correct. Listen to us," Weinhardt said.

"You seem like a very well-read man," Gerhard said, almost quizzically.

Weinhardt answered in a tired voice: "I was a schoolteacher in my younger days. I'm glad I'm no longer teaching, because nowadays the teachers are told what they must teach the children. All that rubbish about race. I'm sure you'll agree."

"Very much so." Gerhard briefly considered what he could allow himself to say, then continued. "We were told to remove everything written by Jews from our syllabi, and all the Jewish professors were asked to leave the university. Two-thirds of the students are gone, either because they're Jews or because they've joined the army." Gerhard stamped out his cigarette. "All discussion between students and professors has become completely meaningless, since no one dares to state their opinion anymore. People hardly dare describe what they have in their lunch box."

And that wasn't even the worst of it. Whole branches of research had been removed, and new branches had arisen in their place. The curriculum was now thick with subjects like the biology of race and national socialistic ideologies. History had become military history, just as law now dealt with the military penal code. And the transformation wasn't evident just in the curriculum. In 1933, the Nazis had taken control of the university, and the few who had risked speaking out against them were gone. Now the flags that fluttered from the buildings were adorned with swastikas.

"So you come down here to relax like I do?" Mr. Weinhardt asked.

"You could say that the harbor has become my window onto the world."

The old man smiled. He offered Gerhard his hand. "It has been a pleasure speaking with you, Mr. Strangl."

"Likewise, Mr. Weinhardt."

Gerhard watched as the old man rose, stiff backed, clutching his cane. With his other hand he briefly lifted his hat, then staggered off down the pier.

Gerhard remained seated on the bench, thinking about their conversation, while a paddle steamer splashed down the Elbe. There was something he hadn't told the old man. He was actually a member of one of their clubs—the Nazi party's, that is—but not because he wanted to be. He would never have been considered for a professorship at the university if he hadn't joined. It had been his lifelong goal to become a professor, a teacher of a higher order, so he had joined in 1933, and in 1937 he got his reward. What did it actually matter that he was a member of the party? It didn't do anyone any harm, and he took solace in that.

The old man had reminded him of the book burnings in 1933, when he'd watched in horror as many of his favorite titles were thrown onto the flames for being considered un-German. The thought still made Gerhard angry: How could an Austrian be allowed to decide what was or was not German? Hitler's propaganda minister, Joseph Goebbels, had told forty thousand enthusiastic supporters in Berlin that the book burning was a breakthrough in the fight against moral corruption. Great books by writers like Franz Kafka, Erich Kästner, Thomas Mann, and Marcel Proust burned to ashes. Heinrich Heine, who had once watched his own books burn, had written, "Where they burn books, they will also ultimately burn people." But the Germans would never, thank god, fulfill Heine's pessimistic prophecy. Of this Gerhard was certain.

A tugboat lined with tires berthed at the dock across from the bench, causing a few irritated gulls to fly off the nearest mooring poles. He guessed that the tugboat had been at the free port, because it had lowered its smokestacks, which was something tugboats did only when they had to sail under the low bridges that linked the free port with the rest of the harbor.

A large cargo ship rebuked a smaller ship with a loud blast of its horn, and the smaller craft quickly moved out of the way. At first glance the traffic in the harbor appeared to be an incomprehensible jumble, but he'd begun to work out who gave way to whom and which boats were so huge that they didn't cede to anyone. Lowest on the hierarchy were the tour boats, which the others didn't even seem to consider real ships. The tugboats were the perennial outsiders, the anarchists among the river's ships.

He was freezing now and stood up to retrieve his bicycle, which he'd leaned against one of the bald trees on the promenade. It occurred to him that the tree resembled a wicked old witch, maybe Weinhardt's wife. He smiled at the thought and biked home to his apartment in Neustadt.

He filled his copper bucket in the coke room, then went up to his apartment, tossed a few shovelfuls into the stove, and lit a few sticks of kindling. He sat in his chesterfield recliner, his favorite piece of furniture. He'd traveled the world through classic works of literature in this chair, and it stood as a visual—albeit secret—testament to Kafka, Kästner, Mann, Proust, and all the other authors whose books had gone up in flames. He inched his chair closer to the stove and held his cold hands over the mint-green tiles. The warmth flowed from his fingertips to his arms, then down through the rest of his body.

He thought of Weinhardt. His frail body housed a strong mind. He wished more men possessed his courage, but he was a dying breed. Although Gerhard had all the prerequisites, the people of his generation were doomed to be cowards. The young had to be mobilized, and there was no better place to do that than the university, where he had a voice. He should educate them, give them the courage to voice their opinions. Should, should. If only there were more people like Weinhardt, because it would take a large choir to rile up the country. He cursed himself. This was where he always got stuck. Courage. He simply lacked the courage. All his dreams of saying "enough is enough," of going away, of making a difference were a delusion. When would he learn? When would he recognize himself for who he really was?

He looked at the clock. It was time to go.

Neugraben, Germany, November 10, 1938

It wasn't fair to the city of Neugraben to call it ugly. It was a typical German city, and it didn't call attention to itself in any way other than by being typical. It wasn't the sort of place that attracted landscape painters and aesthetes, but it had a few interesting features, such as the old, red, half-timbered houses, the stout St. Michael's Church, and the great forests south of the city. From the high Falkenberg hilltop—which strove in vain to be considered a mountain—one could see the entirety of Neugraben and its environs, all the way down to the Elbe, which slowly wound its way toward Hamburg.

In the district around Waltershofer Strasse, smokestacks spewing black smoke stretched toward the blue sky like monuments to industrialization. Behind them, an extensive network of railroad tracks ensured that the rest of Germany could enjoy Neugraben's productivity. The clothing factory was here in a brick building with tall, curved windows that allowed daylight to penetrate even the farthest corners of the vast factory floor. The chairman's office was located on the second floor near the entrance.

Karl Strangl sat behind his desk talking on the telephone. Behind him hung a portrait of his father, Reinhardt, whose illness in 1932 had forced him to hand off control of the factory to his elder son, Karl. Reinhardt Strangl had started the business with two seamstresses in 1895 and grown the company to the point that it now employed more than six hundred.

Karl hung up the phone and went out to the receptionist. When he asked her to find Mr. Müller, the familiar tapping of the typewriter ceased, and Mrs. Meissner adjusted her already meticulously coiffed hairdo with both hands. The middle-aged secretary smiled and replied that Müller was already on his way.

Karl returned to his desk and removed a cigarette from his silver case. After lighting it, he scrutinized the cherry as if it concealed a secret he hoped to uncover. He always smoked Gauloises. It was a holdover from the First World War, when they found the packs on dead French soldiers. Maybe *he* himself was the secret? How many people looked at him and thought, *that man is a killer?* No one, because he never talked about the war. Not even to August and Maximilian. But who was interested in an old war anyway? He ran his hand through his hair, which was getting a little too long. His elder daughter, Hilde, often teased him that he was starting to resemble one of the young boys who danced to swing music down in the St. Pauli district. He still felt like a young boy, and aside from the emergent gray hair on his temples, he could still deceive himself whenever he glanced in the mirror.

"The chairman wished to speak with me?" Hans Müller stood in the doorway.

Hans Müller was fifty-two years old and managed the factory's day-to-day operations. Müller, who had worked his way up from the bottom under Reinhardt Strangl to his current position as the chairman's right-hand man, was well liked by everyone. He was a loyal, vigorous man who had forsaken marriage for a life wedded to the factory, and Karl couldn't imagine being there without his efficient assistant. He never said out loud that Müller patched over his own deficiencies as chairman.

"Please come in, Hans, and have a seat."

Müller sat down, crossed his legs, and pulled a stack of papers from the black leather folder that he always carried under his arm. "I expect the chairman wishes to review the order one last time."

"You always know what I'm thinking. Do you have a spy in the reception area? Maybe you're having an affair with Mrs. Meissner, who gives you information." They laughed as the unsuspecting secretary entered the room with two cups of coffee on a tray.

When she'd left the office, Karl leaned back in his chair and clasped his hands behind his head. He savored the moment. He'd been looking forward to sharing this news with Hans; it was the kind of news that should be shared with those who'd done the most to make it come about.

"The order is confirmed, Hans. We are to deliver 250,000 uniforms to the army over the course of the next two years." He tried to sound relaxed, but his voice came out as thrilled as a boy's.

Müller's entire face smiled, even the deep cleft in his chin. "Wonderful. And what about the SS uniforms?"

"Hugo Boss and the others are still hogging those."

"So we didn't get any?"

"No, still just ten thousand annually," Karl said without showing any sign of disappointment. He leaned across his desk, accepted the papers Müller handed him, and examined the order. Until now the factory had mostly made work clothes. They had produced thirty-five thousand of the Wehrmacht's uniforms annually since 1934, but now they would have to convert their production to manufacture primarily uniforms. As long as Hitler continued to expand and equip the army, there would be growth at the Strangl Clothing Factory.

He spun the small stamp-holder rack on the table and removed a stamp. He moistened it on the square pad and pressed it carefully onto the paper. From an elegant wooden box in a desk drawer, he pulled out a Parker fountain pen. He brought it out only on special occasions, and he'd carefully filled it that morning, hoping to use it later in the day. Concentrating deeply, he wrote the date and applied his signature. Karl gave Müller a proud smile and handed the stack of papers back to him. Müller stood and turned to leave. Then he stopped in the doorway.

"Congratulations again. That's a fine piece of work, Mr. Chairman."

"Don't be so modest, Hans. It's your doing as well."

Karl set the fountain pen gently back in the box and returned it to the drawer. There his gaze fell upon the party pin. It didn't look like much, but it opened more doors than a ring of keys, and it conferred advantages that the uninitiated were forced to do without. He had joined the National Socialist German Workers' Party in 1932, not out of any conviction but because his father had advised him that it would benefit his business to do so. He wore the pin only during meals with select contacts and business connections and, as he had recently, whenever he needed to negotiate a big contract for uniforms. The little emblem with the swastika had proved very useful in such situations.

He walked back out to reception and asked Mrs. Meissner to have Albert bring around the car. He retrieved his jacket from the coatrack, then nodded pleasantly at the secretary, who was transcribing on her typewriter.

It was his custom to walk through the factory at closing time. First into the cutting room with its long storage tables littered with rolls of fabric, where people were busy cutting the fabric with patterns so the seamstresses could quickly sew a sleeve, leg, back, or whatever it was they specialized in. Then he entered the huge factory floor, where all the seamstresses sat in long rows behind humming sewing machines, which they tried to drown out with chatter. Beyond the floor was the stockroom, where the completed garments were bundled. He imagined the shelves bulging with uniforms, as they would be soon; he could already hear the trucks pulling up to the loading docks and the freight trains whistling.

By the time he walked out to his waiting car, darkness was descending, as if the smoke wafting from the stacks had finally managed to turn the blue sky black.

"Good afternoon, Mr. Chairman," his aging chauffeur said. He was, as usual, right on time. Karl always said that Albert was as reliable as a Swiss watch.

"Good afternoon, Albert. Or is it evening? It is already getting dark."

The chauffeur opened the rear passenger door of the glistening Opel Admiral, which hadn't been driven even a thousand miles since its maiden voyage.

Karl slid inside, and the chauffeur closed the door behind him. A copy of the day's newspaper lay on the backseat. It crinkled when he unfolded it. He was instantly disgusted by what he saw on the front page. A large photograph of an angry mob on a Berlin street filled the entire page beneath a headline that read "The Righteous Anger of the People." He thumbed through the newspaper until he found the article, which explained in bombastic prose how the German people had taken the bull by the horns and driven out the scheming—the writer had used that very word—Jews from several of the city's districts. The newspaper glorified all the violence that had erupted across the country during the night, then went on to state that the rebellions were understandable. Karl sighed in frustration; it was impossible to find a neutral newspaper anymore.

It had all started with the murder of German diplomat Ernst vom Rath. A few days earlier, a Polish Jew by the name of Grynszpan had visited the German embassy in Paris and pulled a pistol on vom Rath. Though vom Rath had taken five rounds to the belly, he'd died only yesterday. All hell broke loose in Germany. Jewish shops and synagogues were smashed and burned to the ground, and Jews across the country were assaulted and beaten; thousands were arrested and taken away. The factory workers hadn't been able to talk about anything else all day; many, it seemed, were proud of what had transpired. He shook his head, put the newspaper down, and wiped the ink from his fingers with his handkerchief.

The drive home usually took half an hour. The Opel crossed the Elbe on the North Elbe Bridge, which reminded him of a poor man's version of London's Tower Bridge. Then the car drove through Hammerbrook, whose gloomy gray streets were lined with cheap workers' housing. Albert turned left down Grosse Allee. A trolley and a double-decker bus with an advertisement for Juno cigarettes on one side raced toward the Opel. Outside of a secondhand bookshop, an elderly Jewish man was busy sweeping up shards of glass while a flock of boys shouted obscenities at him; no doubt the same boys were the reason he was now sweeping. The enormous central station soon appeared in view, looking like an anthill as streams of laborers and soldiers came and went. The car then headed toward the posh neighborhood along Harvestehuder Weg. Boastfully calling attention to their inhabitants' wealth, the small mansions and luxury villas with their manicured lawns stood in stark contrast to the deplorable conditions in the workers' district on Hammerbrookstrasse.

The car turned onto Heilwigstrasse, then down a large stone driveway. With Alster Lake in the background, the whitewashed villa resembled a postcard. From the southeast-facing balcony, there was a great view of Krugkoppel Bridge, the small marina on the other side of the bridge, and Alster Park on the western bank. The villa had been built in a neoclassical style characterized by symmetry, a mansard roof, windows divided by muntins, and a tall plinth foundation.

From the backseat, Karl acknowledged Albert with a pat on his shoulder. "Thanks for the ride. Your wife feeling better?"

"Much better, thank you. And thank you for the flowers. That was very kind of you."

"No need to thank me."

Albert climbed out and opened the rear passenger door. Karl paused a moment in front of his enormous house.

The entrance, with its wide front steps and embellished wrought-iron railings beneath a large gabled roof, always reminded him of a small palace. He'd known he would buy this house the moment he laid eyes on it. He'd stood on the semicircle drive and imagined Ingrid waving to him from the front steps as he drove off to work, imagined August setting sail from the little pier at the edge of the garden, and the twins on the lawn splashing each other with water as Hilde sunbathed on the balcony. He'd had to admit since then that dreams and reality seldom cross paths—in fact they intersected only a few times—but whenever they did, he was happy.

He figured they were all home because they were expecting guests for dinner tonight—or rather, a guest. As the plump young servant girl Karin took his coat in the hall, he made a wisecrack that bounced right off her. If only she were pretty, he thought. She curtsied dutifully and disappeared into the kitchen, from which wafted the scent of roast duck. He heard the housekeeper setting the table in the dining room, the silverware clinking softly each time she set a fork or knife beside the Rosenthal service. When he walked through the living room, she greeted him pleasantly, and he saw how carefully she was polishing the silverware with her white apron—even though the girls in the kitchen had no doubt just washed them. She held each glass up to the light, and if she wasn't satisfied with what she saw, she put it back on the silver tray. He wondered why an even number of chairs encircled the long table but didn't think anything more of it.

The big woodstove in the living room crackled, creating a stuffy heat that he didn't care for; it reminded him of those scorching days in the north of France in stiflingly hot uniforms. His wedding photo rested on the mantle. He'd been twenty-one, Ingrid twenty. She was sitting on a chair with her bridal bouquet in her lap, and he was standing behind her, his hand resting on her shoulder. They were smiling—dream and reality had indeed met in that picture frame, and their happiness was visible. A horseshoe meant to bring them luck was tied to the bouquet, and they'd always marveled at how well it had done its job. She was twice as old now, but remained just as beautiful as she'd been that day.

The living room led to the sunroom, where Ingrid sat in a wicker chair with her back to him. A teacup rested on the glass table in front of her, and he noticed the steam rising from the cup and spiraling dreamily up toward the white-caulked ceiling, blending with the gray smoke of her cigarette.

She hadn't heard him enter, so he studied her surreptitiously, savoring the moment. She wasn't beautiful in the conventional sense, but with her oval face framed by nearly black hair and a sober expression that lent her face a touch of sadness, she had a distinctive appearance. Her green eyes often appeared to be gazing off into the distance. Though she was sitting just a few feet away, she seemed very far away.

Ingrid wasn't like other society women. Not because she didn't care, but because she didn't seem to belong. She was bored, he knew, but she had her garden, her books, and her children. He knew she was acting when she beamed like a radiant hostess or played the part of a curious guest asking about the interior design of another host couple's home, and he appreciated her for this. Though she was the daughter of the mayor of Binz and thus part of the city's upper crust, she radiated an almost childlike joy in the simplest things, like spring flowers in bloom, a hedgehog on the lawn, or a good book. And then there was her rose garden. Mr. Nikolaus, the old gardener, tended the entire garden with loving meticulousness to ensure that it was presentable year-round, but he was forbidden to lay a finger on her rose garden. Alluding to the gardener's Dutch roots, she often told Karl in her characteristically caustic tone that the only thing people from the province of Friesland understood were Friesian horses and tulips. That said, Karl often saw Ingrid and Mr. Nikolaus engrossed in conversation in the rose garden, and he knew she was fond of the old gardener.

When he finally stepped forward, she raised her cheek to accept his kiss, her gaze still fixed on the indeterminate distance. He kissed her softly, then left the room to review the mail. One letter's formal appearance caught his attention. He unfolded it slowly and read it in astonishment. The last rays of daylight fell through the window onto the swastika at the top of the page, as if the paper was illuminated from behind. He shook his head and tucked the letter in his pocket.

In the living room he sat down at the shiny black Steinway. He ran his hand gently across the lid before lifting it. The full-throated sound of the first key strike always surprised him, and he enjoyed seeing the hammers work against the strings as they produced the softest notes, as if to justify the human sense of hearing. It was like stepping into another world, one in which time, place, past, and future fell away, leaving only the present.

"Could you please change your clothes, dear? Our guests will be arriving soon."

Ingrid's voice brought him back to reality.

"It's just my brother," he said.

"No, Heinz is coming, too."

His sense of serenity dissolved. How he wished he could have postponed the moment when Hilde had met that young policeman. She was nineteen years old now, and they'd been seeing each other for six months. Although Karl had grown accustomed to the young man, he still wasn't enthusiastic about him. His cheeks were red as apples and stuck to either side of his face like two halves of a tennis ball, giving him a childlike appearance. Both Hilde and Ingrid seemed to find him charming, but Karl thought he resembled an oversized schoolboy with his clear blue eyes and short, combed-back dirty-blond hair.

And he called his daughter Hildegard. Karl was always startled to hear her full name. Everyone had called her Hilde since she was an infant. He doubted that Heinz was the right man for her, but if Hilde liked him, well, then Karl would just have to accept it.

Karl went upstairs. Hilde was the most positive person he knew, and there was no question that she had inherited that quality from him. She had the same blue eyes, the same long, straight nose that would make a Roman envious, and a mouth that always seemed ready to smile. They had the same outlook and the same approach to life. August had gotten his mother's withdrawn and brooding nature, as had Sophia. Maximilian was an odd mixture of them both but resembled his grandfather most of all.

After washing up in the bathroom, he put on a clean undershirt and removed a slender bottle of Farina from the shelf. *"Kölner Wasser"* had become "eau de cologne" because it sold better—though the Germans were hardly Francophiles. He wondered whether Hitler would change its name back to cologne water.

He opened his wardrobe to find an appropriate suit. Instead he pulled out his officer's uniform and stood before the mirror holding it against his body. On the collar of the gray-green uniform jacket were the officer's epaulets with their insignias that indicated he was a lieutenant. The light-gray background behind the insignias identified him as a reserve officer—or weekend warrior, as his brother teased him. An eagle was embroidered into the fabric above the left breast pocket. At the end of 1937 he'd applied for admission into the reserves and entered with his rank from the First World War as an officer cadet. By October 1938 he'd reached the rank of lieutenant. He'd had the uniform customized, which was visible on the pants' tailoring. He regarded the little tag on the neck with pride: Strangl Clothing Factory. Though the factory filled his days, he still felt like a soldier. Once a soldier, always a soldier.

Karl hung his uniform back in the closet and selected a pinstriped suit, a single-breasted affair from Burberry in London. He came down the broad stairwell to the hall just as Karin let Gerhard in.

"I see you still swear by your bicycle," Karl said, shaking his brother's hand. "Why don't you get yourself a car instead of freezing? I can help you get a good price."

"No, thanks. I like to ride my bike," Gerhard said as he handed his scarf and coat to Karin, who waited awkwardly nearby. The servant girl took the coat and disappeared into the cloakroom.

"Good god, come inside and get something to warm you up."

In the living room he poured two glasses of sherry and handed one to Gerhard. They watched Hilde and Heinz chatting in the sunroom.

"They're happy together," Gerhard said, nodding toward the young couple.

"Yes." A moment passed before Karl continued. "Yes, they are."

"Come on, now, that's how fathers always feel. How do you think old Friedrich felt when you stole his eldest daughter?" Gerhard gave him a friendly pat on his shoulder.

"You're right. Maybe I'll learn to like him."

"My dear Gerhard," Ingrid said as she came into the room and shook her brother-in-law's hand. She was wearing a short-sleeved red shirt and matching skirt. Around her neck she wore a white silk scarf. "Dear, would you be so kind as to call the two turtle doves. We're ready to be seated."

The twins, Maximilian and Sophia, were positioned at either end of the table, a measure their parents were forced to take if they wanted any peace at the dinner table. Karl had recently visited his good friend Ernst Grabner at the Blohm & Voss shipyard, and he told everyone about Germany's new battleship, the *Bismarck*, that was currently under construction. Heinz told a rapt Maximilian about when German giant Max

Schmeling handed American boxer Joe Louis his first defeat in New York City in 1936 and returned home a hero in the airship *Hindenburg*. He neglected to mention the rematch two years later, when Schmeling was defeated and then mocked for losing to a black man.

Sophia stuck her tongue out at Maximilian, who in turn crossed his eyes. Karl cast an amused glanced at the pair.

"I got a letter from Berlin today," he said, pulling the envelope out of his pocket and unfolding the paper. "I've been invited to meet the führer."

"Well now, what could he possibly want with my brother?" Gerhard asked.

"Hitler, Himmler, and Goebbels are looking for a fourth man to play bridge with." Karl smiled impishly at Gerhard.

"I thought that was Göring's spot."

"No, he doesn't play, drink, or go out with women." Everyone around the table laughed except the twins and Heinz. Karl waited until everyone fell silent. "It says that I'm to be honored, along with other industry leaders, at a ceremony in the Reich Chancellery."

"You must be proud to have the opportunity to meet Hitler," Heinz said with reverence.

"Well, I don't know about that." Karl looked at his wife. "But it'll be nice to take a trip to Berlin, won't it, Ingrid?"

"I won't say no, and this time I'm making you go to the theater."

"Fine. As long as I don't have to see one of Wagner's operas."

"We'll see," Ingrid said with a mischievous gleam in her eye.

Karl had been wondering how to respond ever since reading the letter. Although he wanted to decline the invitation, he knew that would only hurt the factory. He would have to consider the trip to Berlin as the cost of doing business. It annoyed him that he was being drawn into this, but maybe they just wanted to thank him for his work. He folded the paper and stuffed it back in his pocket. He looked at Heinz. Hilde's boyfriend clearly admired the führer, but why? Karl couldn't see what was so special about meeting Adolf Hitler.

He watched Heinz gulp down an unseemly large swallow of red wine, his Adam's apple bobbing as the liquid glided down his throat. He sensed that his gaze was making Heinz nervous.

"What about you, August? What will you do when you're done with school?" Heinz asked Karl's elder son, who hadn't said a word during the meal. Karl could tell that he'd asked the question only to divert Karl's attention away from him.

"I plan to—"

"He'll be a soldier like his father. Isn't that right?" Karl broke in.

"Yes."

"Good choice," Karl said, raising his glass to toast his son.

"Choice is hardly the right word," August mumbled, low enough that Karl couldn't hear.

August then withdrew into himself and glanced at Gerhard, who noticed how uneasy the boy looked. Like a frightened child.

"Hitler will probably have conquered all of Europe before you're even fully trained as a soldier. So you'll be able to sit in Paris and drink red wine or flirt with the girls in Rome," Gerhard said, smiling at the young man, who returned a shy smile. He knew that August was no more a soldier than he had been himself. And yet the boy pulled on his Hitler Youth uniform every day. Weinhardt was right: it was a circus act, and poor August was its casualty.

"Wonderful meal, Ingrid," Gerhard said as he wiped his mouth with his napkin.

"I'm glad you value my talent at putting my servants to work." She smiled. "I can also boast that I did not make the dessert." She knew Gerhard appreciated her sense of humor.

"Uncle." Maximilian seemed alarmed by the strength in his own voice, which cracked in a falsetto. His voice had only recently begun to betray him. "Can you tell us your Hitler joke again?"

"Now's not the time," Gerhard answered evasively.

"Please, Uncle," the twins shouted in unison.

Gerhard glanced at Karl, who shrugged.

"All right, then." He eyed the two expectant children. "What does the perfect Aryan look like?" He glanced around the table. "He's blond like Hitler, tall like Goebbels, and skinny and fit like Göring."

Maximilian howled with laughter, even though Gerhard had told the joke many times.

Sophia said sourly to her uncle, "I don't get it."

"Hitler thinks we should all be tall and muscular Aryans with blue eyes and blond hair, but Hitler has dark hair, Goebbels is a small man with a clubfoot, and Göring is fat."

"That's not funny at all." It was clear that Sophia still didn't understand. She sat back, sulking in her seat, and rested her head in her hands, both elbows planted on the table. The room went quiet.

"In school they say the Jews deserve it," Sophia said to break the silence.

"Let's not discuss that now," Ingrid said.

"I'm curious. Aren't you a policeman, Heinz?" Gerhard asked, knowing full well that he was.

The young man nodded.

"Then maybe you can answer a question that's been spinning around in my head all day. Why didn't the police intervene yesterday, when the Jews were attacked?"

"It would have been impossible to control such an unruly mob. Everyone was out on the streets, and they were angry. The German people are sick of the Jews," Heinz said, making sure not to look directly at Gerhard as he spoke.

"The people weren't behind it. It was the SS and SA," Gerhard said.

"Is that what you think?" Heinz asked. "It was a spontaneous rebellion. It's in the police report."

"You can say many things about the Germans, but if there's one thing they are not, it's spontaneous. It all seemed too planned. If you ask me, it's the Reichstag fire all over again."

"They're tired of the Jews and their endless fraud and deception. The people have spoken, and can you blame them?" Heinz said sternly, more loudly than he'd intended.

Gerhard raised his voice. "Have you ever seen a Jew treat anyone poorly? Has anyone at this table?" He glanced at the others. "No, it's propaganda, a pure fabrication, something the Nazis made up. The Jews are no worse than the rest of us. That's just what Hitler wants us to believe."

"That's a very dangerous position to express," Heinz said, though his demeanor suggested that he immediately regretted his remark.

"Are you threatening me?" Gerhard leaned over the table.

Karl rose. "Why don't we drop it and give thanks for an incredible meal?"

"I'm sorry. Thank you for inviting me here tonight." Heinz gave Ingrid an ingratiating smile as he pulled the chair out for Hilde.

Gerhard remained seated after the others had left the table and tried to reproduce the conversation in his head. Did Heinz really believe what he was saying? Or was he covering up the truth? Gerhard couldn't figure him out. Something was going on behind his smile and his blue eyes—he was certain of it—and even though he hadn't said as much directly, Gerhard detected a clear warning in his words.

He looked in on August, who'd grudgingly begun playing a game of dominoes with Sophia at the round mahogany table in the living room. His blond hair was carefully parted and combed from left to right, and like his blue eyes, it lacked luster. Combined with his mournful mouth, his face occasionally appeared glum. When he looked at the boy, Gerhard saw himself. He too had been introverted and shy at age fifteen. Soon August would turn sixteen; in two years he would finish high school, and then he would undoubtedly continue on to the university. Unless, that is, he joined the army.

It was obvious that August wasn't listening to Sophia and that his mind was elsewhere. Gerhard noticed him turning his head as though listening to something happening in another room. When Sophia finally got his attention, August's face lit up in a smile, or what Karl called "the rare smile." Gerhard could see Ingrid sitting in the sunroom with her back to them. An open book rested on her lap, and she was biting the bookmark absentmindedly. Before dinner, Maximilian had asked Heinz whether he wanted to see his room, and Gerhard could hear Maximilian timidly showing Heinz around upstairs. He went into his brother's office.

Karl closed the double doors. He poured two glasses of brandy, and they took their seats in the dark leather recliners. Among the many things imposed on the Germans in the Treaty of Versailles, the oddest was that they weren't allowed to use the word "cognac." So they drank brandy instead.

"It's not like you to get angry," Karl said, handing Gerhard a glass. He knew that his brother had no interest in politics. He was interested in injustice and always had been. Maybe it was because he'd been teased for being smart—and different—when he was a schoolboy.

Gerhard accepted his glass, then looked at his brother. "Don't you see? Something's wrong. People don't ask questions anymore, and they take whatever's written in the police report to be the indisputable truth. That's just not the case," he said, growing agitated.

"Of course I can see that, but you should keep those opinions to yourself. It could be dangerous for you if the wrong ears heard them."

He stared at Karl. "People don't have convictions anymore! The Nazis have convictions, and the Jews have to live with the consequences of those convictions. How many people do you think died last night on account of those convictions?"

Karl refrained from answering, instead saying in a resigned voice, "They've dubbed it 'Kristallnacht,' the Night of Broken Glass. We've had the Night of the Long Knives and now Kristallnacht. I wonder, what will be next?"

"I'm starting to lose all hope in democracy. I thought Hitler was just a provisional figure. I'm not saying democracy's the right path, but . . ."

Karl interrupted him. "Now you almost sound like a communist. Germany has never had a democratic tradition."

"You can call me a socialist if it stays between us," Gerhard said drily.

"If people heard you say that, you'd be off to Dachau with all the other socialists . . . and communists."

There was a brief lull in conversation. Gerhard twirled his wedding ring. He'd long wondered whether or not he should remove it, but he'd decided to leave it on. Technically he was still married, after all.

"Have you ever even asked August what he wants to do?"

The question surprised Karl. "Come on, it'd be good for him."

"August is a thinker; you've got to respect that." Gerhard glanced around the office, whose walls were paneled with dark wood and lined with books. He doubted that Karl had read any of them. He looked at his brother, who seemed enormous in his recliner. Karl was tall, nearly six feet two, with broad shoulders and a body still marked by all the training he'd done in his youth. He peered up at the display cabinet on the wall, where Karl's track and field and rowing medals were visible through the glass.

"A soldier can think, too, you know."

"Were you allowed to think when you were a soldier?" Gerhard asked. He recalled his own military training, which, for someone who liked to use his head for more than just holding his helmet in place, had provided no intellectual stimulation at all. Karl said nothing, so Gerhard continued. "He's different. He's not fit to be a soldier. He's like me. And he's only in the Hitler Youth because all the other boys in his class are."

"But he's a fine athlete."

"Because you want him to be."

Karl eyed Gerhard in silence for a moment as he considered what his brother was telling him. Gerhard stood and went to the window. Outside it was dark, but the outline of the lake was visible by the light emanating from the houses around it. "How can you concentrate in here with such a view?"

Karl grunted. If only Gerhard knew how little work he actually did here. "You think I'm a strict father?" he asked.

"I think you're a good and fair father, the kind of father I would've liked to have been. But I think you expect too much from August," he replied, with his back to Karl.

"I don't agree." Karl concentrated on his glass, which suddenly seemed more interesting than the conversation. Others might see such a comment as an invitation to continue the discussion, but Gerhard knew all too well that when Karl spoke like that, there was no reason to go on.

Gerhard's eyes gradually adjusted to the darkness outside. At the edge of his vision he made out the tall, wide crown of the copper beech whose silhouette swayed threateningly in the breeze. It was a handsome tree. Its oval leaves had changed from summer's purple-red to orange, then autumn's bronze, before dropping away, leaving the tree in its current bare and scruffy state. He glanced toward Krugkoppel Bridge, whose streetlamps formed halos of light in the air like fireflies. The marina was behind the bridge. During the summer the place swarmed with children who covered every square foot of the Alster in their skiffs, but during the winter the harbor resembled a ghost town. All the boats were up on land, and everything was packed away. Only the mooring poles remained, like stalks on a stubbled field, and the ice lay like a solid cap across the entire lake. Gerhard returned to his seat. The two men said nothing for some time before Karl broke the silence.

"Weren't you happy in the army?"

"The army wasn't for me, and I'm glad I didn't go to war like you."

"You were lucky."

Gerhard completed his military training in the late summer of 1918, but just before his regiment was ordered to the western front, he broke his leg in a training exercise. As he lay in a hospital bed, his leg in a sling, the Germans surrendered.

"I'm not like you. I can't shoot at other people. I don't have it in me."

"I don't have it in me, either. I just did it," Karl said slowly, as if it were the first time he'd allowed himself to think about the war.

"Oh, that's right. Sometimes you do things without thinking." Gerhard smiled disarmingly at his brother before he went on. "What about your Nazi connections? Have you considered that? And now they're even tighter."

"What do you mean?"

"You're collaborating with them. Doesn't that make you feel lousy?"

"Come on, Gerhard. We've talked about this." Karl stood to fill his glass.

"Right, but the SS thugs were wearing your uniforms last night. Doesn't that bother you?"

"Just because their clothes come from my factory doesn't mean I get to decide what they do. And besides, we don't produce many SS uniforms." He saw no reason to tell Gerhard about his disappointment at losing out on the order for more. He sipped his brandy. "If a man sells an ax to a lumberjack, is it his fault when the lumberjack plants the ax's blade in another man's back?"

"Nice parallel, but you're taking money from the Nazis."

"And I'm okay with that. You worry too much about something that's out of your control. Do as I do and make the most of it. Try not to think too much about it."

"We can't all stop thinking. It's bad enough that our leaders have," Gerhard said, putting down his empty glass. "I won't judge you, Karl. Just be sure not to get too mixed up in something you can't control."

Karl surveyed the chessboard that rested on a little table between the recliners. An unfinished game. If Ernst Grabner chose to move the black bishop from E7 to F6 in his next move—the most obvious choice—Karl would checkmate him four moves later. He knew Ernst well enough to be certain that his friend would overlook that detail. He studied the pieces to see if there were any possibilities he hadn't considered. He picked up his remaining knight. It was made of heavy, hand-carved ivory. The more he studied the handsome pieces, the more he noticed their intricacies. He ran his index finger over the knight's mane. It was a pleasure to touch—cold, but pleasant nonetheless. He . . .

"Are you even listening to me?"

"Yes, of course."

Gerhard stood and offered Karl his hand. "I should go home now. Thanks again for an exquisite meal." He walked into the hallway and got his coat.

After Gerhard had gone, Karl stood in the large hallway, glancing around as though he might discover something new there. He looked at the stairwell leading to the upstairs rooms, where his family lay asleep, and the telephone. The black device that portended bad news. He'd been sitting in the wicker chair beside it when he'd gotten the call about his father.

He could still recall the stretch of time from when the telephone had rung to when he had entered the hospital at the Henneberg Hospital—the terrible medicinal odor in the hospital's long hallways and the nurses' white smocks with their indeterminate stains. The farther he'd gone into the building, the more the smell blended with the stench of illness, which hung like a nauseating mist beneath the cracked ceiling. The gloomy atmosphere radiating from that place was capable of smothering the last spark of hope in even the most optimistic patients and their families. He'd come to console and be consoled. His mother, Anna, had been confused and agitated, but she'd gradually settled down.

By the time Karl walked into the room, his father had had another stroke. His hulking body shuddered, then fainted, as though life and death had met in a battle of gladiators. They fought over the poor figure caught in the center of the arena. Death lunged, and again his father's body shuddered. Life parried the blow, and Reinhardt opened his eyes. Death struck again, and froth formed around his father's gaping mouth. Doctors rushed in and shooed Karl and his mother out of the room. They stood in the hallway, blind to Reinhardt's fate. A conversation with a doctor, waiting, another doctor. *Good-bye, Father.*

After several hours they were granted permission to see him. He was in a semiprivate room. A doctor stood writing notes in his file, which was fastened to the end of the bed when not in use. When he was done, a stout nurse pulled the curtain closed. The wall of fabric ensured that the room's two patients could only hear each other's pains, not see them.

The man in the other bed hadn't moved since Karl arrived. His facial muscles had curled the corners of his mouth upward into an unnatural smile, and his eyebrows had settled about half an inch above their original position. Karl didn't know what was wrong with him, but the way he lay there smiling, he looked like someone waiting for death to arrive. His father seemed no better; he looked exhausted and spent most of his time sleeping, occasionally grunting like a wounded animal. Now and then, after seeming far away, he would open his eyes and begin shouting incoherent sentences. Anna, who stood beside the bed holding her husband's frail hand, watched him with pleading eyes. Then he'd doze off again, his sizable belly causing the blanket to rise and fall in rhythm with his breathing.

Reinhardt had been a shadow of his former self ever since his strokes in 1932. Once he'd been a hard man. A man who'd forged his own path from peasantry to prosperity and never felt that he owed anyone anything. A man a son would fear. They'd never said it aloud, but Karl knew Gerhard felt the same hatred toward his father that he himself did.

And yet Karl was dependent on Reinhardt, because what would he do if his father died? Reinhardt hadn't really been in charge of the company these past six years, of course, but Karl always asked his advice and never opposed his father's recommendations. Most people saw Karl as a confident man, but he wasn't sure he could lead the clothing factory without his father's assistance. Thank god he had Müller. He was probably the best thing Karl could inherit from Reinhardt.

He didn't know how long he'd been standing there staring at the telephone on the little table below the mirror. Everything around him was quiet, an intense silence that was present only late at night when Ingrid and the children slept. This was his time. The time when he felt alive. In the living room he opened the lid of the gramophone and carefully removed a record from its thick cardboard sleeve. He held it between his index fingers as he placed it on the gramophone, then gingerly put the needle down on the shiny shellac disk. He poured himself another glass of brandy and relaxed into the soft recliner. He studied the expensive Telefunken apparatus, whose beautiful sounds always aroused his excitement. The piece was made of marbled walnut and had a loudspeaker shaped like a flower. Zarah Leander's voice emerged from it:

> *I am alone in the night, my soul keeps watch and listens*
> *O heart, do you hear how it sounds? How it sings and*
> *soughs in the palms?*
> *The wind has told me a song of a fortune*
> *that is impossibly beautiful*
> *He knows what my heart is lacking, for whom it beats*
> *and glows*

He knows for whom. Come, come. Ah!
The wind has told me a song of a heart
that I am missing.

He couldn't decide whether the song made him sad or happy, but Zarah Leander's intimate voice moved him deeply. All Germans sang along to her latest hit, *"Bei mir bist du schön,"* though he suspected it would never have been so popular if they knew it was written by two Jews.

He massaged his fingers. They were swollen again, and his joints hurt. Dr. Strauss had told him that it was *gicht*, or arthritis. He'd explained that the word "gicht" was originally an old German word meaning "bewitched"; then he'd gone off on a tangent about how the medical appellation "rheumatism" came from Greek and meant something or other that Karl had already forgotten.

The seamstresses were often afflicted with arthritis, but he'd never worked with his hands, so why was he coming down with it? It disappeared for weeks at a time, only to return with renewed vigor. He cursed softly to himself.

He hadn't told Ingrid. There was no reason to worry her. He believed she should be shielded from ailments and troublesome news. That's why he'd never told her anything about the war. He preferred not to ruminate on it—however impossible that was—but Gerhard had brought it up this evening. He was still bitter about the way the war had ended. Frontline soldiers had been left in the lurch by the military's leadership, and when they were told it was over, no one in the trenches believed that they'd lost the war. That's why he'd joined the reserves. If another war came, he would fight for his country. And this time they would win. He tried to guide his thoughts elsewhere, but like an unwelcome guest, the war kept knocking on the door of his memory. Though he rejected it politely but firmly each time, it returned day after day and knocked again. If he invited it inside, it would remain for the rest of the day and then usually stayed the night.

Amiens, France, August 8, 1918

It was bitterly cold when the regiment arrived in France at the beginning of November 1916. The winter's unavoidable chill had already set in, and the battle at the River Somme had entered its decisive phase. Karl had joined the army when he'd turned eighteen late that summer, and after basic training, the Seventy-Sixth Infantry Regiment had been sent to northern France. At the train station in Altona, his father had shaken his hand and said, "Good luck, my boy," while his mother bade her elder son good-bye with tears running down her cheeks. Gerhard had been silent and withdrawn, but Karl understood, and the two brothers had parted without unnecessary words.

Two weeks later the regiment was sent to the front. The sudden transition from childhood to manhood had been like a religious confirmation, albeit without all the Christian rituals. He hadn't initially noticed the change, but one day all of his childhood innocence was gone, replaced by something that he couldn't define: the western front. This was where Karl had met Ernst Grabner. Although he was an officer cadet, and Ernst only a private, Karl looked up to him because he'd already spent two months on the front line. They'd been born on the same day in the same year—July 28, 1898—and they quickly discovered that they had even more in common. Both were sons of well-to-do manufacturers—Karl of a clothing manufacturer and Ernst of a boatbuilder, whose firm had been bought many years ago by shipping giant Blohm & Voss. Ernst was assured of a good position with them as soon as he returned from the war. They soon became each other's confidantes, and they helped each other get through the war as best they could. Afterward Karl often said that he would have gone mad in

France without Ernst. Early on, their conversations were mostly about family, friends, girlfriends, and Hamburg, but before long they moved on to whether the British Vickers machine guns went *ta-ta-ta* or *te-te-te* and which type of artillery grenade they would rather be struck by.

No one thought much about the new recruits when they arrived. The tacky slop at the bottom of the trenches made each step a challenge, and suddenly they couldn't even walk. They were as helpless as newborns. Which was precisely how the others regarded them. They were new, and until they proved otherwise, they were of no use to anyone.

The day after they arrived, Karl stood in one of the trenches surveying the last vestiges of a forest. Every single tree had been blown away, and splintered stumps were all that remained. He imagined how an officer might start barking orders once he discovered a cluster of trees trying to hide in the morning mist. Suddenly the dead trees became too much for him, and Karl was overcome with emotion. It was then he realized that he had a lot to get used to if he was going to survive this war. But he also discovered that there were some things he would never get used to: the stench of urine and all the lice that had taken up residence in his crotch, his armpits, and the elastic of his pants, robbing him of sleep because of the constant itching. And the fat, well-fed rats that seemed to thrive in the trenches. Karl noticed how the others hung their rations in the shelters so the rats couldn't reach them, and he was soon following their lead.

He spent his days with Ernst, Alois Konrad, the Blacksmith, and Jochen Weber, who was never called anything but Weber. They drank a sour, brown liquid that was supposed to be a coffee substitute, while their breakfast consisted of day-old bread. The Blacksmith was big as a house, but his skull and brain had been arrested in development. As a result, his head was disproportionately small, and there was something similarly infantile about his behavior. He was a replacement, and either you had to teach that kind of person to behave or you had to ignore them. To pass the time, Weber used to entertain the men with jokes and raunchy stories about a wild female variety singer he knew, but he was suffering from shell shock, so he was nothing more than a uniform without content now. His hearing was gone, and he sat like an invalid, his eyes open and vacant. They'd urged the lieutenant, Kleist, to send him to the field hospital several times, but the lieutenant insisted that Weber was just faking it. Those suffering from shell shock were seldom taken seriously, but Karl had seen too many cases to believe they were all faking it.

Karl dipped his stale bread into his coffee to help ease it down his throat. "Put your socks against your skin so they can dry out," he said to the Blacksmith, who'd removed his boots.

"No way. You'll just laugh at me again."

"I'm trying to help you."

"You ever hear of trench foot?" Ernst asked. When the Blacksmith shook his head, he continued. "If you have cold or wet feet all the time, you'll get trench foot. At first you won't be able to feel a damn thing on your feet, then they'll swell up, and soon you can forget all about wearing boots."

The Blacksmith looked down at his stocking feet.

"Maybe you'll wind up with gangrene, and the only cure for that is a doctor sawing off your feet," Ernst said, clawing at his mustache.

"Then you'll be hopping toward the enemy on stumpy legs with a bayonet in your hand. Picture that, Strangl!" Konrad grinned.

Karl shrugged. He didn't think the Blacksmith would last more than a week or two. Men like him might be big and strong, but many of his ilk ended up cracking like dry twigs. The Blacksmith wouldn't be the first. Before him there had been Wangelin, and before Wangelin, Lauth.

"Shut your trap or *I'll* saw your feet off," the Blacksmith said angrily. "Then you won't be able to escape with your stolen merchandise."

Nobody knew exactly what Alois Konrad had done before the war, but the widespread belief was that he was a common thief or a professional conman, an appellation he'd given himself one evening.

"Is it going to rain?" Karl asked, hoping the question would put an end to the two men's bickering.

"I think it's going to be a fine day," Ernst replied.

Weather was a frequent topic in the trenches because it marked the thin demarcation between a bearable and a horrible day.

They'd been promised more replacements in two days, but out on the front line two days could seem like a lifetime. He looked forward to being relieved, to removing his boots and eating a warm meal. The soldiers alternated between the trenches on the front line, the reserve position—which was far more peaceful—and a rest position well behind the front line where they could regain their strength. But how much rest they got depended on the enemy.

Karl knew for certain that he'd killed two people. He didn't recall the precise dates, but both occurred a few months after the regiment had arrived in France. The first time, he'd had the late watch that night. Convinced it would be a quiet night, he'd begun to meticulously rearrange the sandbags stacked on the edge of the trench so that they would provide better cover. The soldier who'd put them there couldn't possibly have ever stood sentry because they'd been tossed down heedlessly. Afterward he'd felt well protected and relatively safe. He had a view of no-man's-land and mulled over that term, unable to determine whether it was called that because no one occupied that chunk of ground or because no man made it out alive. The merciless strip of land had been transformed into a wasteland of sludge. No one—not the Brits, the French, or the Germans—had been able to bury the dead who lay between the two trenches, because anyone who ventured out there was mowed down. A thick stench of rot and decay hung over the entire area, a smell that no one ever got used to. It was nearly impossible to find a wedge of earth for the few bodies that could be buried because everywhere they dug, they came across arms, legs, and other body parts.

Karl loathed the birds. Though they'd once been satisfied with nuts, insects, and larvae, they'd morphed into ferocious scavengers, and his dead mates had become exquisite meals. The larvae were still there—more than ever—and species of birds that Karl had never even heard of circled like vultures over the beleaguered terrain. All other animals had long since retreated to more hospitable places, and you could hardly blame them. Even the landscape itself had been drained of color—except for an occasional burst of blood red, which then washed away in the rain or sank into the mud. About a quarter mile away, on the other side, the British sat in their trenches keeping an eye on them and the same depressing sight.

The waning moon was barely visible that night. There was about sixty to eighty feet between the guards, and they were forbidden to speak to one another. Time slowed to a crawl. After a few uneventful hours, Karl's senses were abruptly sharpened when he spied something crawling behind the barbed wire fence. He listened, suddenly tense, hoping an animal had blundered between the two fronts. Food was scarce, so an animal of any kind made for a good meal.

If only his heart would stop hammering in his chest. His eyes scanned the muddy wasteland. Nothing moved. Soon he began to relax again. He stamped in place to keep his feet warm but never stopped scanning for him—that's what they called the enemy: "him." They never referred to them as the British, the French, Canadians, or Australians, but simply "he" or "him."

A figure rose into a half-seated position less than seventy-five feet away.

"Grenade," Karl screamed, though the person had yet to throw anything.

Karl reacted swiftly. He felt the give of his trigger and watched as a bullet from his Mauser M98 bore into one of the man's shoulders, spinning his torso around before he dropped to the ground. The wounded man stumbled to his feet, still determined to toss his grenade into the trench. Karl loaded his rifle and pulled the trigger again. This time, his shot blew the top of the man's head off along with his helmet, which flew several feet before skidding across the frozen mud with the same clatter as a pan lid falling on the floor.

The man had managed to pull the latch on the grenade, which rolled out of his hand. Karl ducked as it exploded, and judging from all the screaming and groaning that ensued, he knew there were others out there. Other silhouettes stood and ran for cover, but a volley of machine gun fire to Karl's right ripped at the stumbling bodies. The following day he saw the corpses of eight British soldiers on the other side of the barbed wire. When he later wondered aloud why they'd attacked with eight men, Ernst guessed they'd been trying to bring captives back for interrogation.

The second time Karl had taken someone's life had been much easier, even though it was in hand-to-hand combat. During the German spring offensive in 1918, he had jammed his bayonet deep into the chest of a Frenchman. It was as if a barrier inside him had been broken. "Once you've taken one life, it's easier to take another," an officer had told them before they'd been sent to the front in 1916. What was his name again? It didn't matter anymore—he died shortly afterward—but whatever his name was, he'd been right.

"Do you think they'll attack today?" The Blacksmith startled him out of his daydream.

"What?" Karl said absentmindedly.

The Blacksmith repeated his question.

"No, they would've already set off their fireworks display."

Usually you knew when the enemy would attack because he would initiate a massive artillery bombardment several hours before in an effort to weaken their defensive position. Karl saw no sign of an imminent assault on that early dawn.

Ernst pulled a cigarette from his nearly empty case. He managed to light it, then passed it around. It was the waiting time. Karl knew he should enjoy the waiting because it meant that no one was dying, but everyone hated it. The waiting time was like a good friend you took for granted but missed as soon as he was gone.

Suddenly it was as if the entire world exploded around them. The earth shook; the sky rained down metal, gravel, and rock; and the air grew thick with smoke.

"They're coming!" the Blacksmith shouted unnecessarily.

Advancing behind the cover of tanks and mist, the British opened fire on the trenches and the German artillery positions. An infernal series of grenade explosions erupted all around, and a dense cloud of gas began to spread over the trenches.

"Let them come." This was the lieutenant's first actual confrontation with the enemy, and his words lacked conviction.

"Weber, gas mask!" Karl signaled to his friend while strapping on his own.

Weber gazed at him blankly, his eyes glassy. Though the bell indicating a gas attack had sounded, he evidently didn't understand the order. Weber began to cough, and Karl abandoned his position to search feverishly for Weber's gas mask.

"Damn it," he mumbled as Weber crumpled up, gasping for breath.

The lieutenant lifted his gas mask for a moment. "Back to your position, Strangl!" he shouted, gesturing with his rifle.

The tanks rolled right over the barbed wire fences, rendering them useless, and all around Karl soldiers were falling victim to the intense barrage. Two German soldiers crawled out of the trench and raised their hands in surrender, but a machine gun salvo blasted through their chests. Things didn't go any better for those who chose to scramble up the back of the trenches to flee the melee. The noise—the machine gun fire, the explosions, the tanks, the planes—was deafening, and coupled with the gas masks they wore, shouting orders was impossible. The British were well prepared, and they'd struck the German line of defense where it was weakest.

The bullets peppered the edge of the trench relentlessly. Karl and Ernst manned a machine gun position and answered the fire with their MG 08, which sprayed projectiles across the field of battle until there was a loud click.

"We're out of bullets," Ernst screamed, pointing down at the empty wooden box.

"I'll get some more," Karl shouted through the noise.

Normally it took four soldiers to man the position, but the Blacksmith was gone, and Weber had an excuse. The machine gun wasn't supposed to stay quiet for long because the attackers would exploit the weak point as soon as they realized it had gone silent.

Karl sprinted down the narrow pathway, trampling over several of his dead and wounded companions, who were getting pushed deeper and deeper into the mud. The Blacksmith sat against the wall drawing rattling breaths, a gaping hole in his temple. Karl couldn't believe he was still alive with such a wound. The pop of handheld weapons mixed with the screams of the wounded, and the medical unit ran about in a confused frenzy, not knowing where to start. Karl grabbed the ammunition from an abandoned machine gun and dashed back. He couldn't help but notice that the Blacksmith had sunk into the mud with the others. As he returned to his position, he saw the lieutenant, who had turned his back to the battle.

"Drop your weapons," the officer roared, lifting both hands above his head.

"Listen to the lieutenant, he's right. This is pointless," shouted Konrad. The others followed their order.

Damned cowards, Karl thought before a rifle butt struck his jaw and he fell to his knees.

"Get up." The soldier thumped Karl roughly with his gun.

Slowly, Karl stood. His head ached, and his legs wobbled beneath him. Ernst clutched him in an effort to steady him.

The British marched their prisoners across no-man's-land, which had once again grown colorful. The Brits had lost many men, and the dead lay everywhere. Dismembered limbs clung to what remained of the barbed wire fence and were scattered across the battlefield.

Once the prisoners were corralled, many of them dropped to the ground in exhaustion or sat down listlessly. Karl glanced around at the others. Filthy and reeking, with sunken cheeks and bloodshot eyes, they all looked like old men—though few were older than twenty. He himself had only recently turned twenty, and he was exhausted, hungry, and defeated.

He didn't see Weber or Konrad. The lieutenant sat a few feet away staring vacantly into space. He was smeared in blood, but Karl couldn't tell if he was wounded. He'd urinated in his pants and was shivering despite the heat of the rising sun.

"Kleist, are you injured?" Karl whispered as quietly as he could.

The lieutenant slowly turned his head. Tears trickled down from his eyes, washing the grime down his cheeks in two thin stripes. He looked away.

Ernst pulled a cigarette from his case, the last one. He'd been saving it, no doubt to celebrate a victory, but now he would use the strong tobacco for consolation.

"Give me your case," Karl said.

Ernst handed it to Karl, who rubbed it on the filthy sleeves of his greatcoat. He looked at it, using the case as a mirror, but he didn't recognize the man he saw.

"What will they do to us?" Ernst asked softly.

"I have no idea, but I've heard they treat their prisoners well."

"Even if the prisoners have shot their friends?"

"We can only hope."

A soldier next to them began to sob uncontrollably. The sensory overload could cause a man to lose his mind. They'd seen and heard too much to ever be normal again. If they wanted to maintain their sanity, they would have to fill their minds with something other than the horrors of war. He thought of Ingrid. If he made it back to Germany, he would marry her.

Hamburg, Germany, November 10, 1938

He sidled up close to Ingrid. She lay with her back to him, her hair smelling freshly washed. He imagined her climbing out of the bathtub, a towel wrapped like a turban around her head. Imagined her slathering her body with lotion, her legs gleaming from the aromatic ointment, her hands gliding along the curve of her breastbone and down her belly. To many, Ingrid was a mystery, but Karl loved her small oddities, from her outward-facing belly button to her dry sense of humor. He inched closer to her.

He slipped his hand under the wide sleeves of her nightgown and found his way to her breast. He caressed it, then nipped it softly, the way she loved. He traced her perfect shape, worked his way farther, and enclosed his hand around her other breast. He pinched her nipple between his middle and ring fingers. He could feel her skin pimpling with gooseflesh. When she pressed herself against him, heat radiated from her inner thighs to his groin. His finger slid along the edge of her panties. He carefully forced the blue silk aside and entered her. He pushed in as far as he could, and though the edge of her panties rubbed against the shaft of his penis, he didn't pay it any attention. He thrust slowly and deeply, as Ingrid pushed back against him. He pulled her nightgown up to her shoulders and ran his hand along the arch of her back; it was smooth and muscular, but still somehow soft. They made love languidly, taking their time. Ingrid's small, soft moans and scent brought him to a swift climax, and he came with an extended groan. She always told him he sounded like a hungry bear waking from its winter hibernation. She rolled over and gave him a wet kiss before turning her perfect back to him once more.

"Good night," she said sleepily.

She fell asleep immediately. Karl couldn't relax; his thoughts resisted his desire for sleep. Whenever he recalled the war, his thoughts would inevitably return to the one that was imminent. Because it was coming—and it put Karl in a difficult position.

Why was he thinking about this at all? He already knew the answer. For a long time, he'd imagined that he would have a difficult decision to make, but he'd already made his decision. He'd made it in an English POW camp back in 1918. It was then Karl determined that, should Germany ever go to war again, he would fight. So he would have to fight, even if that meant fighting for the Nazis. He wouldn't be fighting for them anyway, but for Germany. He would stand by his decision. If Germany called, he would answer.

Gerhard hung his coat on a hook in the narrow hallway. He brushed his teeth at the kitchen sink. Then he went to his bedroom, undressed, and laid his clothes on a chair. From his wardrobe he removed a clean shirt, a cardigan sweater, and a pair of pants, which he set on another chair. He'd come to think that going to bed was pointless; he rarely slept well. He crawled under the heavy duvet, sighed loudly, and then his mind began to roam. He hated lying alone in bed, because then his thoughts had free rein, and that meant they circled around Emma, even though it had been more than seven years since she'd passed.

He often imagined himself standing in the harbor. *He's carrying a suitcase. He has foregone clothes for his notes, but wherever the big steamer is taking him, he will have enough money to be properly outfitted. The gangway creaks under his wavering steps. Halfway up the gangway he turns, bidding Hamburg farewell. But he catches sight of them on the pier. They are both present. One waves. She's beautiful and whole. Her body is full of life, and once again he feels the forgotten desire. The other is just weeks before her burial. He glances up at the smokestacks that are issuing thick columns of smoke into the sky. The engine's exhaust system causes the entire ship to vibrate. Everything's ready for departure. They're just waiting on him. He hesitates. Deliberates without words. His feet are stuck in place. He hears the splash of his suitcase as it breaks through the surface of the water. He walks back to the pier.* The journey was only a dream, and that's all it could ever be. He'd promised Emma that they'd always be together. A promise he intended to keep, even though that now meant it would be in the grave.

Tuberculosis had claimed her. The disease had snuck up on her. At first she'd tried to hide it, but eventually she began leaving a trail of bloody handkerchiefs around the apartment. In February 1931 her body gave up. In her final months she'd been isolated from the world at a sanatorium, and when Gerhard visited her, a glass window partitioned them. He remembered the stench. The clinical odor mixed with rot. Patients in decline and medicinal products. Emma's thin hand on one side of the cold glass and his against the other. An impenetrable wall preventing a married couple from having a meaningful farewell. From here he could do no more than glimpse the remnants of the person he loved.

Emma had been filled with courage and joie de vivre, but even standing up had become an immense obstacle. She'd been beautiful, very beautiful, and that was how he chose to remember her. Her long, dark hair pinned back in a bun, her kind face with its small upturned nose, and the freckles scattered across her nose and cheeks beneath brown eyes sparkling with life. A life that slowly leaked away, a face that had become an unrecognizable mask of skin stretched taut over her skull, and a few remaining tufts of hair that she no longer had the energy to fix. Her eyes had, in the end, implored him not to come, so he visited her only when he knew she would be sleeping.

She was the only woman he'd ever loved. And the only woman who had loved him. Sure, he'd held hands with Hanna Zickler, but that was during the years of innocence. He wasn't a man women loved, not like Karl, who'd always been the object of women's adoration. They found him handsome and charming when he, in his man-of-the-world style, expounded on a subject that was only of any interest because it was coming from him.

Emma had thought Gerhard was interesting. At first he'd had a hard time believing that her interest was sincere, but gradually, as he got to know her, he saw that she was genuine in all that she did. He liked the man he was when he was with her. They talked for hours; she asked questions and he answered. He asked questions and she answered. They'd laughed and danced—even though he was a terrible dancer. They'd made love and fallen asleep in each other's arms. That was how he remembered it. But the woman he missed so terribly had never existed. It was as if someone had taken an eraser and wiped out parts of his memory. Blotted out the arguments, removed the constant nagging doubts about how much she loved him, and obliterated all the heartache with Laura, their daughter. He knew that his memories were an idealization of all that was good.

After her death, he had moved out of the big apartment in Eimsbüttel. The small apartment in Neustadt was a better fit for him, and from his office window he had a view of the tall tower on St. Michael's Church. The office became the center of Gerhard's life. He eventually pushed his bed into the room so that he could throw himself into his work as soon as he opened his eyes on the days he didn't lecture. In 1937 he'd published his first book, an algebra textbook, which had taken him four years to write, and now he'd begun jotting notes and creating an outline for his next one. His central thesis was that numbers were the starting point for everything. A kind of mathematical creation story. The idea was taking shape in his mind, and he looked forward to finally getting started.

He thought of his childhood. He and Karl had grown up in Hamburg. As the sewing factory grew, the Strangl family had slowly risen from the lower middle class into what could be called the upper class. Reinhardt had been strict and uncompromising, and he approached fatherhood the same way he approached his business. Their mother had been soft and indulgent, and later they would often say that she had been everything a mother should be. When Karl returned from the war, it was expected that he would train in his father's company—though he'd never been asked—and Karl did so out of a sense of duty. Whether Gerhard would join the family business had never even been discussed. A decision he greatly valued, actually. While the other healthy, strong boys—as Reinhardt described them—were out playing in the yard after school, Gerhard sat, to his father's great dismay, in his room doing calculations or reading books. He found numbers and letters to be good company, and they'd stayed by his side through thick and thin throughout his childhood. In the end, the straightforwardness of numbers had attracted him more than the secretive nature of letters. Not that he didn't like letters, words, and language, but the meaning of numbers was immediately clear, while letters had a way of hiding the actual, the essential. That was why he had chosen mathematics over literature for his livelihood. Even the most complicated number combinations were logical to Gerhard.

The bed creaked when he rolled over. Thinking of his father didn't help. So he turned back to thoughts of his book. That was better. Maybe that's why he wrote—to flee from his thoughts? Finally his swirling, busy brain came to rest, and he fell asleep.

It took him a long time to register the knocking on his door, despite the fact that the person on the other side was doing his utmost to make his point. He picked up his black horn-rimmed glasses from the nightstand and noted the strip of light that had found its way into the room through a slit in the curtains, though he'd tried to pull them closed. He went into the hallway, still uncertain whether someone had really knocked or it was just a lifelike dream that had wrenched him from his sleep. A voice removed all doubt.

"Gerhard Strangl?" The voice was deep.

Gerhard hesitated. "Who's asking?"

"Ulrich Grabel and Siegfried Schauer, Gestapo. We would like to ask you a few routine questions."

He'd heard about the Gestapo's routine questions. The Gestapo was the ideological police, and one thing was certain: when their people knocked on your door, it wasn't to bring you good news. Gerhard slowly opened the door; outside stood two men in the Gestapo's unofficial uniform—fedoras and trench coats.

"Please come with us to headquarters. We won't take up too much of your time; it shouldn't take more than ten minutes," said the taller of the two men.

"What's this all about?" Gerhard glanced down at himself but saw no visible sign of the quivering sensation he felt in his entire body.

"As I said, routine questions. We need to clarify a few minor details and you can help us," said the policeman amiably.

He invited them inside, and they waited patiently in the little entranceway while he dressed and ran a comb through his blond hair. A black Mercedes was parked down on the street. He'd heard stories about people being picked up by the Gestapo and then thrashed behind drawn curtains before being tossed out at some random spot in the city. He was glad there did not appear to be any curtains in the car. And yet his mouth was dry, and he continued to quiver within as he climbed into the backseat.

The drive took less than five minutes. On the way the two Gestapo men chatted casually with the driver about traffic and the weather, while Gerhard did everything in his power to hide the fear growing inside him. He'd ridden past the huge yellow building on Stadthausbrücke— the Gestapo's headquarters—many times, always hoping that he'd never see the inside of it.

As the car pulled up to the main entrance, Gerhard thought that this must be the first step in the Gestapo's scare tactics. An enormous coat of arms embellished with swords that jutted out like fangs hung threateningly above a tall archway, reminding him of a mouth ready to devour its prey.

A uniformed guard opened the door for the small group. In the hall they turned left and entered a lobby so vast and high ceilinged that the echo of their footsteps vanished into nothingness. He was ushered to a teak bench, where Grabel and Schauer bade him good-bye. He followed them with his eyes as they departed. Suddenly he was alone in the gigantic room; he felt like an insect that might, at any moment, be crushed underfoot.

He tried to appear calm, but his nervous quivering had now become a rumbling volcano inside him. The questions, like lava, forced themselves upward. What did the Gestapo want with him? Was this a mistake? *Do they think I'm someone else? I haven't done anything—or have I? I'm too cowardly to do anything that would irritate the Gestapo.* Everyone had heard stories of the Gestapo's brutality. He chewed at his lip, shifting again in his seat.

He'd been waiting for close to an hour when a door at the other end of the hall opened. A short man in a blue suit walked resolutely toward him and stopped before the bench. He pursed his lips. "I'm Detective Superintendent Kögl. Come with me, please."

The way the detective superintendent rolled his *r*'s indicated to Gerhard that he was from southern Germany.

Apart from a large oak desk, all of the furniture in the detective superintendent's office was made of dark wood. Behind the desk was a large window, but the curtains kept out the light.

"Do you smoke?"

Gerhard accepted the cigarette with a slightly trembling hand, hoping that it would bring a measure of calm to the chaos raging in his head. The man on the other side of the desk appeared to be around fifty years old. Most of his hair was gone, and there wasn't quite enough left to cover his crown—though he'd certainly made a valiant effort at doing so that very morning. His jowls hung loosely on either side of his cheerless mouth, and his pointy chin jutted out belligerently, like a fencer on the attack.

"Your name?" His voice was flat.

"Gerhard Strangl." Gerhard removed his glasses and cleaned them, a nervous habit. It was as though he thought he could think more clearly by blurring his vision.

"Your profession?" the Gestapo man asked, though he certainly already knew the answer.

This ritual, with its trivial questions on formalities, continued for ten minutes. Like a cunning boxer, the detective superintendent danced around his groggy opponent, deftly avoiding those questions he most wanted answered. To Gerhard, the uncertainty was unbearable. His face flushed, and he was struck by a sudden, feverish sensation.

"Let's get straight to the heart of the matter." The man paused for a few seconds to draw out the tension, and Gerhard held his breath.

"Mr. Strangl, I understand that you have made negative statements about the party and our führer, and that is very upsetting." He hurried to add, "Before you deny it, I should tell you that I have confirmed your subversive activities with several sources." He paused again as he scrutinized Gerhard. "Otto Freier, Petra Schimmelmann, and Peter Stolz can all testify to this, and all three have reported you for treason."

Gerhard tried in vain to say something, but nothing found its way across his lips. On a few occasions, he'd said too much or mentioned things he shouldn't have, but only in the company of people whom he trusted. And he'd never heard of Otto Freier, Petra Schimmelmann, or Peter Stolz.

Kögl continued: "You're probably sitting there thinking that we're going to take you out in the courtyard and shoot you, and that is indeed a possibility. But let's chat a little more before we decide what to do with you."

"I don't understand. You have the wrong man. You must be mistaken." Gerhard heard his voice tremble.

"There's no point in proclaiming your innocence. I am the one who decides whether you are innocent or not." The detective superintendent leaned back in his chair.

"I've never said anything about the party or the führer; I . . ."

Kögl interrupted him. "There is no reason for you to raise your voice, Mr. Strangl." The Gestapo man leaned across his desk, his hands folded, as if he were about to reveal a secret. "Imagine the Gestapo as a pack of wolves. If you keep your nose clean, they have no tracks to follow, but if you don't, we'll find you. And we bite." He was clearly very satisfied with his little analogy.

"You have committed an offense against the laws of our country, and when one does that, the hammer drops. You've probably heard many stories about the Gestapo. Some are true, and some are not. It's even possible we've made up a number of them ourselves, but we can't say—in any case, not to you."

While the detective superintendent was warming up, Gerhard sat on the edge of his seat. He should stand up and leave, because this had to be a mistake. They would figure that out soon enough. He was innocent. The heat in his head was almost unbearable now. What had he done? He'd told a harmless joke a few times, but that couldn't possibly be the reason he was here. But were there other reasons? Although he despised Nazism and the Nazis, he'd kept his nose clean. He'd been careful to keep his views inside the four walls of his home. But now he was sitting here.

"The wolves have found you. You are guilty. Now, we have a few options, and these are what you and I need to discuss. But first I want to ask you a few questions, and I need you to really consider them before you respond."

The policeman exited the room and returned a short time later with a young, flat-chested secretary who would record the minutes of their conversation. Kögl took his seat behind the large desk and planted his elbows on the surface.

"Have you ever spoken disparagingly of the führer?"

Gerhard slowly removed his glasses and swallowed a lump in his throat. When he put his glasses back on, Kögl's eyes were resting impatiently on him. *How does one answer in such a situation? Is there a right answer? What should I say? Yes or no? In every decision there is a right choice and a wrong choice.* If he answered yes, what would they do to him? He already knew, but wasn't it always best to tell the truth? Kögl hadn't taken his eyes off him. Gerhard cleared his throat, but his answer was almost inaudible.

"Yes."

"Have you ever talked disparagingly about the party?"

"Yes."

The detective superintendent and the secretary left the office. Gerhard was alone, his hands resting in his lap. They were gone a long time, and the wait seemed interminable. But he already knew what the verdict would be: a firing squad. Pimply young boys with rifles would fill his body with lead before the day was through so he wouldn't take up space in one of the Gestapo's prison cells.

His hands shook as he tried fishing a cigarette out of his pack. He succeeded but dropped his lighter before he could draw a flame from it. He gave up.

Kögl returned, this time by himself. He sat down and rifled through the papers he'd carried back with him.

Gerhard watched him. For god's sake, he couldn't just sit there and accept a death sentence. He had to fight back. He would challenge the Gestapo's guilty judgment. He would exit this building today a free man. And then he would keep his mouth shut until the Nazis disappeared and everyone realized what a farce this all was.

"I understand that you are a member of the party, and that undoubtedly puts you in a better light, but we nevertheless consider you an enemy of the state, and I'm sure you know what we do with such people. There are thousands of people like you sitting in Dachau—socialists, communists, Jews, and other scum—and it would be very easy for me to make you a number in a striped prison uniform."

Of course Gerhard had heard about the concentration camp just outside of Munich, which had housed since 1933 opponents of the Nazis and those whom the Nazis simply considered unworthy of freedom. And he had heard how those people were treated. He wouldn't let that happen to him. Swallowing another lump in his throat, he looked pleadingly at the detective superintendent, who continued.

"I would like to ask you a question, and I believe I know what your response will be. But I don't want you to come to me later and say you weren't given the opportunity to choose." He eyed Gerhard inflexibly and made another of his long pauses, which Gerhard had grown tired of. The detective superintendent reminded him of a caricature of the evil police chief in a bad film in which the actor histrionically overdramatized his role.

"We can send you to Dachau, and you'll probably be dead within the year, or . . ." Another long pause. "Or you can work for us."

Gerhard was struck dumb. Work for the Nazis? That was the last thing he could imagine. But if the alternative was death?

"We need smart people," the detective superintendent went on, interrupting Gerhard's rumination. "I've got plans for you, but in the meantime, you will be the Gestapo's eyes and ears. We'll have more challenging assignments for you down the road." The detective superintendent smiled for the first time; then he continued. "Now, remember. It's your education we need, not you personally. You should be glad you're not a grocery clerk because you'd already be dead by now." He paused. "So, what have you decided, Mr. Strangl?" Kögl said in an unnecessarily loud voice.

By the time Gerhard was dropped off in front of his building an hour later, he was completely spent. He had difficulty grasping what had just happened, and his head swirled with snippets of his conversation with the detective superintendent. Gerhard replayed the interrogation again and again. It was as though it hadn't happened to him at all, but he'd instead observed someone pretending to be him. A clever, trained actor who'd practiced Gerhard's movements and gestures; on the big stage he had mimicked him to a tee without anyone recognizing that it wasn't the real Gerhard Strangl—it was a facsimile.

He sat in his recliner in a daze. How dare they touch him? Didn't they know who his brother was? Didn't they know that his brother manufactured uniforms for the Wehrmacht and SS? That he was a good citizen? All this time he'd thought he was safe thanks to Karl, not that he'd ever done anything that should give him reason to fear the Gestapo. But it seemed that no one was safe anymore. They didn't care about anybody. Power was what they craved, and once they got it, they did everything they could to keep it, even if it meant trampling on people like him. Usually he was strong, but he'd fallen apart during questioning. He was disgusted with himself. It wasn't like him, but there was something about the building—about Kögl's office and Kögl himself—that had made him feel like a very small and inconsequential man without any free will. Normally he was not the sort of man to lie down without a fight, but Kögl had had a psychological power over him that he couldn't explain. He had become a hapless dog. "Yes, Mr. Kögl. No, Mr. Kögl. Certainly, Mr. Kögl." He cursed his cowardice. He had turned into a man he hardly recognized. A man who had cracked, a man stripped of the willpower he ordinarily possessed. He hated himself in that moment. Gerhard Strangl wasn't someone who kowtowed to others. But wouldn't everyone have done the same? Everyone feared the Gestapo, after all.

"Think rationally. There must be a reasonable explanation. This is all just a mistake. There's no other way to explain it. Everything will be resolved soon," he said softly to himself. Though it wasn't even ten in the morning, he poured some schnapps in a wine glass. After three gulps, he refilled his glass. He lit a cigarette and inhaled deeply. The strong tobacco made him cough. Before long his coughing turned to nausea, and he dashed to the bathroom, where the schnapps came back up; he retched until his stomach was empty. If only he could empty his head the same way, he thought. He collapsed on the bathroom floor in despair, and there he remained.

Hamburg, Germany, November 18, 1938

"Why are you telling me this only now?" Karl asked, stepping past Gerhard into his apartment without so much as a hello. Moving too quickly, his brother missed the coat hook, but he didn't even notice the smacking sound his coat made as the wet material hit the dark, lacquered wooden floor.

"I thought . . . I hoped that it was all just a mistake," Gerhard said as he followed Karl into the living room.

Karl turned to Gerhard, who remained indecisively in the doorway.

"But you should have—"

"I know," Gerhard said, looking down.

"Goddamn it, Gerhard. What have you gotten yourself into?" Karl dropped into the chesterfield. He obviously didn't expect an answer to his question. "Even if the Gestapo did make a mistake, they'll hardly admit such a thing." He pulled a silver case from the inner pocket of his coat and put a cigarette between his lips. It juddered up and down as he spoke. "Tell me everything. Start at the beginning."

Gerhard told Karl about the interrogation, from the time Grabel and Schauer knocked on his door until the detective superintendent made his surprising offer. He told him about the false accusations made against him by three people he'd never heard of. He told him about the assignment the Gestapo had given him at the university, as an informant, and about his growing desperation.

Karl shook his head. "Why didn't you lie?"

"I don't know."

Gerhard went to the window and glanced down at the street. Wasn't that what he'd learned: It's always best to tell the truth? His mother had stamped that principle into both of her sons. That's why he never lied, and why he considered lies the weapon of the weak. If you couldn't trust the truth, what could you trust?

An Opel Blitz, its truck bed laden with coke, stopped at the entrance to the building across the street. A man in a hat leaped from the cab and began dragging heavy canvas sacks down the steps. The white letters on the truck's door were nearly covered in black dust, so Gerhard figured that it had brought its load directly from the harbor. "The poor man's fuel," that was what people called coke. Although Gerhard wasn't poor, he burned coke just like everyone else on the street because it was cheap. His upstairs neighbor Hannah appeared from behind the truck, tugging her children Jakob and Rachel along by their hands. They crossed the street and entered the building. Gerhard rubbed his forehead, then turned to Karl.

"Can you pull some strings? You've got so many connections. What about Ernst Grabner?"

"SS and Gestapo are very different things. Ernst can't do anything about it."

Gerhard looked down at the floor and said softly, "I can't work for the Gestapo. I can't."

"I wish I could help you, but . . ." Karl didn't finish his sentence, as if he didn't want to put his own inadequacy into words. He'd always held a protective hand over Gerhard, and even though they were adults now, his desire to protect him had never waned. Karl recalled how he'd saved Gerhard from pranks like the wet pants trick—and worse—whenever Horst Prohl and the other boys decided that the bespectacled bookworm would be the day's victim. Gerhard was, once again, surrounded by the bigger boys, but this time Karl could do nothing. He looked at his brother, who seemed so weak standing there with his glasses in his hand, like someone who'd just received the news that he had only two weeks to live. But maybe that's how Gerhard felt. He was being forced to work, against his will, for one of the country's most feared organizations.

"For Christ's sake, Karl. We're the good guys. I'm not a damn informant, so what am I doing among these fiends?" Gerhard buried his face in his hands.

"We've got to keep a clear head, Gerhard. Keep a low profile. You hear me?" Karl stood, gently removed Gerhard's hands from his face, and looked him in the eye. "Do you hear me?"

"I hear you." Gerhard slowly put on his glasses, then straightened up.

Karl gave him a compassionate smile, hugged him, and patted him clumsily on the back. The brothers searched for something to say. Finally Karl said, "I've got to go to the factory. You going to be all right?"

"I'll be all right."

Gerhard stood in the entryway watching his brother's shadow vanish behind the frosted windowpane. He was exhausted. The night before had been one of those nights when he'd woken up wondering whether he'd slept at all. He kicked off his slippers and lay down on the bed. He could feel a headache smoldering just below the surface of his skull that made his eye sockets ache. He closed his eyes.

He'd long since stopped asking questions about how life worked. After Laura died, his and Emma's life had centered on why and how, and when Emma got sick, his head had been filled to the brim with why and when. If life had taught him anything, it was that those kinds of questions were futile. One had to just accept the way things were, regardless of how unjust it felt. He simply had to continue to think rationally. Otherwise he'd crack.

A familiar feeling overwhelmed him. He'd never said it out loud—it wasn't the sort of thing one admitted—but he was lonely. He missed Emma terribly. Loss was a ruthless, merciless feeling; he'd been able to live with it whenever they'd been separated for short periods because release was in sight, a joy that wiped all the pain from his memory. But when his longing wasn't relieved, it grew into a knot that filled his chest until he was close to bursting. No matter which path he followed in his mind, he came upon Emma. The laughing Emma wearing a swimsuit at the beach, the dancing Emma at their wedding, the naked Emma lying outstretched on the bed, and Emma the corpse with her untidy clumps of hair and unrecognizable face.

Over time he had developed a fear, a fear of his own thoughts, which he'd tried to flee by no longer reflecting on anything. He couldn't stop thinking entirely, but he chose to focus on just a few areas: his lectures and his books. He tried to repress all the thoughts that brought him pain. It was, at its core, contradictory: a university professor who'd stopped thinking. Part of his job was to think, to leave no stone unturned. How could he suddenly fear his own thoughts, fear what images his head chose to show him? He had always viewed himself as a thinker, and so had others, but if he no longer was, then what was he? He knew perfectly well that it was all an illusion—of course he'd never stopped thinking—but if he repeated it to himself often enough, maybe his brain would finally begin to cooperate and bar all those unwanted thoughts.

He heard Jakob's and Rachel's small feet running through the rooms in the apartment above, and he opened his eyes. He liked those two, but since they were Jews, he never said that aloud, of course. People in the building no longer associated with them, and he'd noticed that he was the only one who said hello. The Grünspan family—father Aaron, mother Hannah, and children Samuel, Esther, Jakob, and Rachel—had been lucky to be out of town during the terror of Kristallnacht, but Aaron's clockmaker workshop had been nearly obliterated. It was said that more than thirty thousand Jews had been arrested that night, and the concentration camps at Buchenwald, Dachau, and Sachsenhausen now teemed with people. Germans joked that there wasn't enough room in the camps for all the long noses. Rumors circulated that another concentration camp would be built soon. Although no one considered that unusual anymore, this one would be located near a former brickworks in Neuengamme, only fifteen miles from Hamburg's center.

Although he felt terrible for the Jews, his countrymen derived a certain sense of security from knowing that the Jews were the ones being subjected to the clampdown. But it seemed that Germans also treated Germans badly—he himself was now living proof of that.

Hamburg, Germany, February 15, 1939

Gerhard biked through the white, ivy-covered gateway. The main entrance—with its high, majestic columns, flagstone mosaics, and well-groomed grounds—made up the university's presentable half, but on the other side, ivy reigned. Founded in 1919, the university was located in the Rotherbaum district close to downtown. The large lecture hall was housed in a beautiful, square building with a towering dome. The roof of the hall was shaped like a woman's breast and covered in verdigris, just like those in Fritz Klimsch's statues.

Gerhard had begun to study mathematics here at the age of nineteen. The science faculty, which included mathematics faculty, was housed in the west wing along with the medical faculty. Gerhard's office was on the second floor.

The office that came with his professorship had once belonged to one of algebra's masters, Emil Artin. Artin, however, had been forced to leave because his Russian wife, Natascha, was half Jewish. The last he'd heard about him was that the family had boarded a steamship bound for the United States. When Gerhard heard about Emil's unfortunate circumstances, he hadn't rejoiced, but he did feel a kind of intoxication. He knew this was a once-in-a-lifetime opportunity for him. When Gerhard was offered Emil's position, he pretended that he felt bad about accepting the job, but in a secret moment he thanked Natascha's parents for bringing her into the world. When people asked him about it, he made a sad face, shrugged his shoulders, and said glumly that one man's death is another's bread. His conscience demanded that he write Emil a letter. He was delighted and relieved when he got a reply at the beginning of 1938. Emil had accepted a good position at a university in the United States. Gerhard felt happy for him—but mostly for himself.

He arrived at his office early this morning. The space lived up to the prevailing image of a professor's office. Two of the walls were lined from floor to ceiling with mahogany shelves filled with books. Although some books stood upright and others lay flat, they were all arranged in a system that allowed him to find whatever he was looking for, and he knew exactly what he'd find in each of his books and on which page. Stacks of papers and opened volumes rested on his mahogany desk. He liked his heavy writing desk a great deal, especially the soft rattle the brass handles made when he opened or closed the deep drawers.

Behind him hung a map of the world as it appeared in Galileo's day. He admired Galileo, regarded him as a colleague; he'd been a professor of mathematics, after all, at the University of Padua. Whereas other professors and lecturers had photos of their wives and children on their desks, Gerhard had no personal objects, not even a picture of Emma. Those who knew the story didn't ask him about her, and he dodged questions from those who didn't.

This morning he was scheduled to hold a lecture on the beauty of algebra. He'd spent much of the night preparing the lecture, and now he wanted to scan his notes one last time. It was to be a memorable lecture that included rising tension, a climax, and denouement. He'd worked it out like a piece of theater. He hoped that his students would be drawn to algebra in the same way he'd been hypnotized by the world of numbers as a student. He wanted to challenge the view that algebra was constricted by rules and enable them to see the beauty in the abstractions concealed behind the rules.

When he opened his door, he nearly knocked the young adjunct Ralf Cullman to the ground. Cullman had been at the university for a year, but the two men hadn't ever really spoken. Gerhard had noticed the adjunct; his odd appearance—a high forehead that seemed to rise interminably, a narrow mouth with thin, almost invisible lips, clear blue eyes behind round glasses, and red hair parted down the middle—made him impossible to overlook.

"I'm sorry, Mr. Strangl. Do you have a moment to talk?"

"Of course." Gerhard sat at his desk while Cullman took a seat opposite him. The adjunct seemed nervous, so Gerhard offered him a cigarette, which he politely declined. "How can I help you?"

The narrow mouth smiled vaguely, and it seemed to take great effort—an effort he clearly would have preferred not to make. "I have enormous respect for your work."

"Thank you."

"And I consider you a very sensible man."

Gerhard wondered where this conversation was headed and what Cullman even knew about him and his work. He sucked on his cigarette as his eyes automatically gravitated toward the man's high forehead.

"I'm honored, Cullman, but to what do I owe the pleasure of your visit?"

Cullman's eyes flickered before they settled on some object on Gerhard's desk. "It's hard for me to say this, but I believe you are the right person."

Gerhard leaned toward the adjunct and smiled broadly in an effort to help the man relax. His curiosity was piqued, but he didn't want to press him.

"You see," Cullman said hesitantly, "some of us in the faculty are of a different political bent, if you understand what I mean?" He regarded Gerhard with an apologetic expression.

"You'll have to explain." Gerhard tamped out his cigarette.

"We meet regularly to debate how we can improve the political situation in Germany." He looked directly at Gerhard now. "We believe there is a need for, well, let's call them changes, if things are going to get better."

"And where do I fit in the picture?"

"We believe that you share our views. We would like to invite you to participate in our secret meetings. I hope you won't turn us down, but if you do, I hope you will be discreet and not expose our activities."

He studied the adjunct. Either he was courageous, Gerhard thought, or he was foolish. "Who are the others?"

"I can't tell you that you until you've given us your assurance."

Gerhard gave him an understanding smile and slowly removed another cigarette from his pack. "I can't give you my assurance, but I will consider your invitation."

He had no intention of getting involved in anything so dangerous, and yet he was curious to learn more, so he didn't wish to categorically reject Cullman's invitation.

"We meet every Thursday evening at nine o'clock in the university library, if you are interested." Cullman stood and offered his hand. "Thank you for your time."

"That's quite all right. I will consider your offer."

After Cullman left his office, Gerhard sat staring out the large window. A few minutes later he watched the adjunct stroll across campus and continue down Edmund-Siemers-Allee. The redheaded man glanced over his shoulder several times, as if he was being followed or could feel Gerhard observing him. Then he vanished from sight. During the conversation it had struck Gerhard that something was amiss. No one in today's Germany would express such a dangerous suggestion so explicitly. But what was he to do? One thing was certain: he wouldn't go to that meeting in the library on Thursday. But what would actually happen if he showed up? There was no reason to follow this train of thought, however, because he knew himself well enough to know that he didn't dare. But he was curious who the others were. No, he couldn't do it. *But should I report this to the Gestapo? Should I call Kögl immediately and tell him what I just heard? Then I would put Cullman and the others in jeopardy. My sympathies are with them, but how could they actually know that? How can Cullman be so sure that I won't tell the police? What the hell just happened?*

He shook his head, disconsolate. It was a terrible situation to be thrust into, and he'd done nothing to deserve it. What should he do? He considered his options and decided that he would pretend it had never happened. He would pretend Ralf Cullman had never entered his office, that he had never sat in that chair. Bad things might just go away on their own if you ignored them. He wished their conversation could simply be deleted from history, never to be thought of again.

The pleasure he'd felt anticipating his lecture was gone now, but it returned once he stood in the lecture hall.

"Good morning." Gerhard glanced around at the students in attendance. His voice always trembled slightly whenever he began a lecture. He didn't love the prospect of speaking in front of large groups, but he was rarely nervous; still, his voice always made it appear as though he were.

"Today I would like to tell you all about the wonders of algebra," he said with a smile.

Hamburg, Germany, April 14, 1939

From his window Gerhard gazed toward St. Michael's Church. The sun had tinted the morning sky with a pink brushstroke. Like a migratory bird that had been away on a journey, the sun had finally returned, he thought.

It was Friday, and he was planning to take one of his increasingly rare days off. He felt guilty about it, but he needed to rest his mind. The development phase for his next book had lasted an inefficiently long time, and even though he felt the core idea was leading him in the right direction, he was having trouble getting the actual writing under way. He would have to begin eventually, just not today.

In the kitchen he placed a zinc washbowl in the sink, filled it with water, and washed his face. He heard a knock on his door. Not expecting to find anyone on the landing, he took his time drying his face with the towel that hung from his shoulder before he went to open the door in pants and an undershirt. The upstairs neighbors' two youngest, Jakob and Rachel, were often bored, and it wasn't uncommon for them to rap on his door only to run away. Those two had had far too much time on their hands in the last year since all Jewish children had been forbidden to attend school. He always played along; he couldn't yell at those curly-haired kids when they looked at him with their big eyes.

On his way out of the kitchen, it occurred to him that Weinhardt had perhaps misunderstood their agreement. Theodore Weinhardt was supposed to stop by for coffee that afternoon, but Gerhard knew him well enough by now to know that sometimes his memory betrayed him. Gerhard enjoyed the old man's company. They shared the same interests; Theodore was a learned man, and he said things Gerhard didn't dare to. And he felt that speaking to Weinhardt made him smarter. In truth, the old man was probably the closest thing he had to a good friend. Theodore and his wife lived in a small apartment. When he visited them, he'd seen only the entranceway, living room, and tiny kitchen, but he got the feeling that their bedroom was just as cramped as the other rooms. The furnishings were old-fashioned but cozy. When Theodore had opened the door and smiled with his nearly toothless mouth, a pleasant aroma of coffee and something indefinable greeted him. Once inside, he discovered Mrs. Weinhardt's passion for orchids. There were orchids everywhere, making the living room look like a tropical forest. The air was heavy and moist, but the older couple didn't seem to notice. Mrs. Weinhardt, whose first name was Greta, was a buxom woman with a big heart and a talent for baking cookies. Every time Theodore made some sarcastic remark in his high-backed recliner, she'd smile at him. Gerhard's impression of her was much different from what the shrewd Theodore had described. But again, that was part of Theodore's charm: you never knew if he meant what he said.

Gerhard opened the door. Ulrich Grabel and Siegfried Schauer stood on the landing. "Come with us." Their tone was sharp.

"Let me finish getting dressed. One moment," Gerhard said, surprised.

"Hurry up, we don't have all day," Schauer responded gruffly.

Gerhard quickly closed the door behind him, and they descended the stairs. Mrs. Zimmermann always responded to the slightest sound on the stairwell, and the curious blabbermouth came out of her first-floor apartment to the stairwell; she had apparently realized that if she wasn't the building superintendent's wife, then she was nothing, and so she continued playing the part, despite the fact that her husband's health no longer allowed him to fulfill his duties. Broom raised, she stood now at the bottom of the stairwell, ready to give Rachel and Jakob another tongue-lashing. She hated those two children and the disruption they caused among the otherwise decent folk, as she called the residents of Jakobstrasse number 7.

They climbed into the black Mercedes. Gerhard had worked for the Gestapo for five months. Work probably wasn't the right word, since he'd made no attempt to find out anything useful for them. Kögl had described the university as a breeding ground for troublemakers and political dissenters, but Gerhard wouldn't betray his colleagues or the students. He just didn't have it in him. He'd reported to Kögl once, but that was only to tell him he had nothing to report—and that when it came right down to it, he didn't know anything about troublemakers and political dissenters at the university. His lack of information had garnered him a head shake from the detective superintendent, and now Gerhard stood to be reprimanded by this little man once more. There was Ralf Cullman and his little group, of course, but if Gerhard didn't mention them, no one in the Gestapo would ever know about them. Besides, there was something strange about Cullman, though he couldn't put his finger on what it was. They hadn't spoken since, and that amazed Gerhard as much as the man's peculiar inquiry in his office.

They drove to headquarters in silence, and he was ushered into Kögl's office, which was empty. Only now did he notice the family photo on the detective superintendent's desk. Kögl was surrounded by his wife and son and two daughters, and they looked happy. Kögl himself even looked amiable enough standing there with a smile on his face. Gerhard turned and saw some kind of war medal in the shape of a cross hanging on the wall. He was surprised that anyone still cared about such things, that there could be prestige in a war they'd lost.

The door opened, and Kögl and a man in an SS uniform marched in. There was something comical about the sight of the squat Kögl and the towering SS officer together. On the right side of the latter's jacket collar were two SS symbols—symbols of power—and on the left side was the badge that identified his rank, a captain.

The detective superintendent sat down, and the other man stood behind him, his arms behind his back. He was nearly six feet five, Gerhard guessed, and his penetrating eyes made Gerhard nervous, so he concentrated on Kögl instead. Gerhard noticed that the policeman's hair didn't quite cover the crown of his head this time either. He felt sorry for Kögl: every morning he tried combing his hair over his head, and he never succeeded. Over time, he'd have less and less hair, never more. It was a battle he could only lose, and yet he kept fighting the good fight.

"Sit down," Kögl said through pursed lips.

"Do you know who I am?" The tall man's voice was deep and authoritative.

Gerhard shook his head.

"I'm Captain Lorenz, Erich Lorenz."

The name meant nothing to Gerhard, but the fact that he was from the SS didn't bode well, especially when he took into account the mood of the two men. The skin on Lorenz's face was tight like a mask, and Gerhard felt certain he'd never develop any wrinkles from smiling. He noticed a ring on one of Lorenz's long, slender fingers and wondered whether the man had smiled on his wedding day.

"Do you know why I'm here?"

Gerhard shook his head again.

"It's my job to make sure that you're in Dachau the day after tomorrow."

"But . . ." A bolt of pain spread from his neck and throat to his entire body, buzzing through his limbs like an electrical current. He put his hands to his temples and squeezed, as if that would make the pain go away and—with it—the news itself. He tried to protest, but suddenly found himself in a silent film, or, more accurately, watching one. The scene blurred before his eyes, the colors vanishing. The plot was already written, and no matter what he did, nothing could change the outcome—they were sending him to Dachau.

"But I work for you," he screamed shrilly.

"Do you, Mr. Strangl?" Kögl took the lead now. He clearly seemed to think that things were moving too slowly. "You are a foolish, foolish man." Through his round glasses he stared intensely at Gerhard, who collapsed back into his chair.

"Don't you realize that we check up on our informants? And although you had ample time to do so, you did not share this information with us. It has been nearly two months!" He slammed his fist on the tabletop so hard that a coffee cup next to him sprang up, almost toppling over before settling back on its saucer. "It was a test, Strangl, a test." As he spoke, spittle flew from his mouth. "And now we have no choice but to send you away. It's a shame because we could've used you." He made an irritated face, like an actor training before a mirror. "What do you do with your students when they fail a test?"

"I give them another chance," Gerhard said almost inaudibly as he removed his glasses.

"Louder, I can't hear you," sputtered Kögl. A red blotch began to spread across the detective superintendent's throat, as if he'd been seized by a sudden flare-up of eczema.

"I give them one more chance," Gerhard repeated.

"You would like that. The Gestapo wants nothing to do with you. What about you, Erich? Can you make use of such an untrustworthy and disloyal shit?" The detective superintendent looked up at the tall SS officer, who continued to stare at Gerhard.

"No," Lorenz said.

"Maybe he wants to request a short period for reflection," Kögl said to Lorenz as he scratched vigorously at his throat.

"Maybe." The tall SS officer articulated the word very slowly.

A long pause followed, during which none of the men moved. They'd evidently agreed on the course of the conversation beforehand, Gerhard thought, but now they seemed to have both forgotten what was on the next page of the script. They had him right where they wanted him, so this show was superfluous. The detective superintendent seemed to start when he realized that it was his character's turn to walk onstage. He pressed the intercom and told the secretary to send Gerhard away.

Gerhard was taken to the prison cells in the basement. Two policemen he'd never seen before clutched his arms—which had grown numb from the rough treatment. He was so wiped out that he flowed down the stairs as if he'd been reduced to liquid. His vision was blurry, and the guards' faces vanished. Where were Grabel and Schauer? Not that he was particularly fond of those two, but in some bizarre way they felt like acquaintances. These new men seemed brutal and indifferent and lacked Grabel's and Schauer's manners.

They went down a long white hallway that could just as easily have belonged in a hospital. He noticed the ceiling, where pipes crisscrossed like an underground intestinal tract. They'd taken the trouble to hand-cuff him as if they feared he would run. If only they knew how feeble he was.

A guard ushered them through a heavy cell door, which then slammed shut with a deafening crash that startled Gerhard, causing the policemen to further tighten their grip on him. He feared he was being guided to an ice-cold cell with bars, where the wind would whistle all night as he lay on the rock-hard bed, where a bucket in the corner would serve as his toilet and rats would dart across the floor and fight to have the first go at the fresh meat.

They stopped at a counter fitted into a rectangular hole in a wall, behind which was a room.

"Deposit your things there," said a stout officer on the other side of the counter, pointing at a metal box. "Watch?"

Gerhard slowly removed his watch, a gift from Emma.

"Wallet, belt, lighter?"

He reluctantly put them all into the box.

"Anything else?"

"No."

"Shoes."

"What?"

"Give me your shoes," the officer said, holding his hand out impatiently.

Gerhard bent down and unlaced his shoes, then put them on the counter. He walked down the hall in his stocking feet, still flanked by the two policemen. They halted before a massive metal door. His hands shook uncontrollably, and he could barely hold his arms up as they removed the handcuffs. One of the policemen, a ruddy-faced man in his twenties, grinned at his colleague before shoving Gerhard so forcefully into his cell that he fell on the ground. His cheek scraped against the hard floor, and he lay there motionless as pain spread like heat across the right side of his head.

What the hell was this? Had the entire world gone mad? He squeezed his eyes shut, expecting to wake up from this nightmare soon. In a moment he would wake up, open the curtains, and look over at St. Michael's Church; he would go into the kitchen, make a cup of coffee, and quietly enjoy his morning.

When he finally opened his eyes, he found himself gazing at the leg of a chair. He lifted his head a little and saw that the rickety chair was pushed under a narrow table against the wall. He got up on all fours and glanced around the cell. Along the wall opposite the table stood a cot with a tattered mattress, at the foot of which was a folded blanket. High up on the wall was a small rectangular window that allowed only a narrow sliver of light into the cramped room, which was illuminated by a dim bulb on the ceiling. In the corner nearest to the door was a toilet bowl; next to that was a sink that had turned brown.

He sat down heavily on the bed and watched as the sliver of light floated impossibly slowly over the room, as if the room were a sundial, until it disappeared. The click of a metal bowl of soup being inserted into his cell through a hatch in the door built expressly for that purpose brought him out of his catatonic state. He figured it was now evening. As he slowly ate the transparent soup, he grew overwhelmed by how unreal everything seemed.

He pushed the chair under the window and stood on its leather seat. He could just barely see out the window, but the view was nothing more than a brick wall a couple of feet from the thick glass. There was an iron grate on the window, and he could tell despite its sturdy mesh that the sky had begun to darken.

He lay down on the bed and examined the bare walls and the knots on the wooden ceiling. Over and over again he wondered who had reported him to the Gestapo, and little by little the answer came to him. Why hadn't he thought of it before? It had to be Theodore Weinhardt. The old man had won his trust, but it had all been a trap. He'd seemed so harmless, but now Gerhard understood that he was truly wicked. How could Theodore do this to him? He had thought they were friends. And what was he guilty of? Everyone makes mistakes—some larger than others—but could they really throw people in prison for simply voicing their opinion? Hammering his fists against the heavy metal door, he heard himself shouting, "I demand justice! I demand justice!"

He shouted again and again, his chant echoing in the cramped space until he collapsed in exhaustion onto the bed. He was afraid of himself. He'd never heard himself shout before, and he didn't realize that his voice contained such power—even when he felt so weak. He awoke to the narrow sliver of light striking his face. He followed the sliver of light's slow march across the floor five times, and he supposed that five days had passed.

Berlin, Germany, April 19, 1939

The luxurious express train the *Flying Hamburger* had conveyed Karl and Ingrid from Hamburg to Berlin in just a few hours the day before. They'd enjoyed a meal in the dining car of the lavishly furnished train, whose ticket prices frightened off the rabble. Karl had been summoned to the new Reich Chancellery, where he was to meet the führer. They'd checked into the Kaiserhof Hotel, where Herman Göring had celebrated a wedding worthy of a king when he married Emmy Sonnemann, an actress from Hamburg, in 1935.

Lying on the bed's soft silk sheets, Karl savored the moment. He gazed up at the opulently decorated stucco ceiling and the chandelier that converted the sun's rays into dancing speckles of light on all four walls. The room was the size of their dining room, and he needed to remember to tell Hilde that even the bars of soap had been imprinted with the words "Kaiserhof, Berlin." It would make her laugh.

Ingrid came out of the bathroom wearing a robe, her hair swaddled in one of the hotel's towels. They'd been to the opera house to see a production of Georges Bizet's *Carmen* the night before, and now she hummed a few bars from the opera as she waltzed across the woven carpet. She lay down on the bed, her arm behind her head, and looked at him. He knew what was coming—Ingrid was obsessed with Hilde and Heinz's upcoming wedding—but Karl was doing his best not to think about it.

"Come on, Karl. He's not so bad," she said, as if reading his thoughts.

Karl mumbled something incoherent, and Ingrid laughed and gave him a little tap on the shoulder. He tried sneaking a hand beneath her bathrobe but got another tap.

"Hilde's so fond of him," Ingrid said as she fought to still Karl's hands. "You can only envy them for being so in love. You remember how we were?"

Binz, Germany, July 16, 1915

Karl's parents had spent their summers in Rügen when they were young and in love. This had continued year after year, and though Karl was very fond of the island—with its white sandy beaches, steep chalk cliffs to the north, and numerous bays—he dreamed of visiting the French Riviera, Switzerland, or Italy. He knew, however, that the timing wasn't right due to the war.

Although the Great War had erupted the year before, Reinhardt and Anna Strangl insisted on going ahead with their annual summer vacation on Rügen as planned, and since the western front was relatively calm, the war didn't get in the way of this family tradition. As always, they stayed in Kurhaus Binz, an architectural gem whose inhabitants could live a fairy tale life. Indeed, the stairwell leading to the lavish main entrance resembled the very one on which Cinderella lost her shoe late one night.

The Strangls had been there only four days when Karl began to feel restless.

As he let sand run through his fingers, he wrinkled his nose at the odor the onshore wind carried with it. He watched Gerhard. He envied his brother, who was never bored; his suitcase was always packed with books. His mother called them back from the hotel terrace, and they ate lunch in silence. His mother smiled at him every time he looked at her, while Reinhardt never lifted his eyes from his plate until it was empty. Karl set down his silverware on his plate, as he'd been taught, at three o'clock. During yet another fit of boredom, he began to count the green and yellow parasols on the beach. When he'd confirmed that they were equal in number, he started counting the ships out at sea. That's when he saw her. She was alone. She wore a white summer dress that clung to her body, and she was very pale, practically translucent. She sat on the edge of the pier, dangling her legs over the edge like a schoolgirl.

He couldn't take his eyes off the pale girl. Her gaze was fixed on something in the water, and she hadn't shifted her eyes away from whatever it was for some time. Even from a distance, he sensed her sadness. He racked his brain to recall the last time he'd seen so enthralling a vision as this sad, translucent girl.

She mustn't leave. She mustn't stand up and walk away, he thought to himself, just as the girl got to her feet. She strolled to the edge of the pier, which jutted far out into the water. He hurriedly wiped his mouth with his napkin and asked for permission to leave the table. When his parents and Gerhard could no longer see him, he began to run. Only when he had come to a halt in front of her did he realize that he hadn't considered what he'd say to her. For the first time in his life, he was utterly speechless.

She turned toward him, studying him. Now he saw how beautiful she was. Her green eyes seemed to have complete power over him. He felt her eyes upon him, and in that moment all he wanted was to meet her gaze. He looked down. She appeared self-confident, and he blushed as he searched for something to say. The moment stretched on interminably.

"Do you know how to ride a bicycle?"

"Yes," he replied hesitantly, surprised at her question. "But I don't have one."

"You can borrow my brother's. I want to show you something."

They bicycled out of Binz along withered rapeseed fields and were soon engulfed by a large forest. She rode ahead, and he couldn't help but notice the slender body beneath her dress. The fabric fluttered in the wind, hugging her angular shoulder blades, which moved every time she pushed down on the pedal.

They hadn't exchanged a single word since getting onto their bikes. Once they exited the forest, he guessed they'd gone about two and a half miles. They continued along the coastline, below which lay the bay at the bottom of a cliff formed by chalk deposits. A road sign indicated that they'd reached a town.

The girl stopped, and he followed her lead. Before them stood the strangest building he'd ever seen. It looked like a cross between a wooden castle, a spider perched on the water, and a train station standing on legs and dipping its toes into the water's edge. The beach surrounding it was thick with people in recliners, none of whom were paying any attention to the odd building.

"What is it?"

"Sellin Pier. Isn't it beautiful?"

"Yes."

"At low tide it stands on the beach, but at high tide it stands in the water."

As they returned through the forest, he pedaled up alongside her and smiled at her. She smiled, too, then took his hand. An unfamiliar sensation rushed through him, and all the hairs on his arms rose at once. He felt as though his bicycle was pedaling itself, and if he let go of the handlebars, he would continue to follow the pale, green-eyed girl. He was like the blind man who could suddenly see. Colors, scents, sounds—everything was intensified. His senses were overwhelmed by so many impressions, and he felt he might faint, but he didn't care. He was filled with melancholy when they got back to Binz.

"May I see you tomorrow?" he asked as they put their bikes away.

"Yes." Without a word of farewell, she left him standing, bewildered, on the sidewalk.

As Karl trudged back toward the hotel, his heart thumping, he couldn't tell whether he was sad or exalted.

The next day, he combed the city, full of anticipation, hoping to find her. After a few hours, he was close to giving up when she appeared before him wearing a sunflower-yellow dress with a matching bow in her dark hair.

"My name's Ingrid."

They walked around the town. The tree-lined Main Street was rimmed with restaurants and pubs housed in squat, whitewashed houses, most of which had small turrets with rounded cupolas. Looming above the rest of the buildings was the Hotel Loev, whose needle-sharp towers stood in stark contrast to the rest of the city's architectural softness. The huge hotel's columns and balconies reminded Karl of paddle steamers, and he recalled a trip he'd taken on the Elbe with his family when they'd traveled in just such a vessel, which had once plied the Mississippi. He recalled the splashing and grating noise the paddle wheel made as it slowly urged the riverboat forward while people on the bank waved at them.

Ingrid and Karl walked around all day, as though neither dared to stop. When evening arrived, they headed down to the sea and sat on the edge of the pier.

"Do you see the clouds dancing on the vanishing point?"

"What's the vanishing point?" Karl felt silly having to ask such a question.

"Do you see over there where the sky and the sea come together? It looks like a black line. That's the vanishing point."

"Oh, yeah. I see that," he lied.

"When there's no wind, powerful ground swells cause the ships and the clouds to appear as though they're dancing. If the sun didn't set in the west, it would appear that way, too."

"I didn't know that."

"Doesn't it look like you can almost touch it?"

"Yeah." He wasn't quite sure he understood what she meant.

They sat in silence for some time. Then she nestled her head against his shoulder. He stiffened, not daring to move, not wanting to lose this moment. He tried coming up with excuses to stay there for the rest of the day. His arms, which he'd been leaning back on, began to quiver, but he didn't want to move them—even when they started going numb. He wanted to put his arm around her bare shoulder but couldn't bring himself to do it. He tried to summon his courage and touch her soft skin with his palm, but his arm didn't budge. He tried again and couldn't do it. She got up, and he stumbled to his feet, too. They stood before each other uncertainly, and Karl cursed his own awkwardness when he offered her a formal handshake in parting. She gave a short laugh and kissed him on the cheek—he knew he wouldn't wash his face that night—and then she was gone.

They saw each other the next day, and the day after that, and the day after that, and so it went until they took their leave at the station, when the Strangls boarded the train back to Hamburg.

Berlin, Germany, April 19, 1939

Although the hotel was within walking distance of the chancellery, a Mercedes convertible picked Karl up and brought him there. The enormous complex had opened in January of that year. Among the many buildings were the Marble Gallery—which made the Hall of Mirrors at Versailles look like a dollhouse—the massive government buildings, Joseph Goebbels's Ministry of Propaganda, and the Court of Honor where Karl and the other businessmen were to meet Adolf Hitler. The führer's private chambers were housed in the old Reich Chancellery. On the other side of the vast central lawn were the soldiers' barracks, where Hitler's personal SS elite corps, the First SS Panzer Division, was billeted. Albert Speer, Hitler's chief architect, was the brain behind the complex, and it was impossible not to be impressed by the immense compound. Karl had never seen anything like it.

Along with other industry leaders, he was guided down the wide staircase to the Court of Honor. The four imposing columns that marked the entrance were flanked by two sculptures. A military orchestra played marching music, and he made use of the time they spent waiting by studying the Greek-inspired bronze statues of naked men. To his right stood *Wehrmacht*, whose sword in hand symbolized the army, and to his left stood *Party*, whose torch represented the party's fighting spirit. He noted that—unlike their Greek sources of inspiration—the two statues' faces had Aryan features.

Karl had difficulty understanding why he and the others were to be honored, but he assumed Hitler was courting them so that they'd support him financially and with increased production. You didn't say no to Hitler, and that's why he was at this parade now. He had to admit, however, that he was also curious.

As they stood waiting, he snuck a glance at his watch. More than an hour had passed. He surveyed the SS troops positioned in two long columns on the opposite side of the flagstone courtyard, facing each other like pieces on a chessboard ready to begin the game. They all wore black uniforms and carried flags and stared straight ahead. His first move would be to push his pawn forward to E4, anticipating that the SS troops would respond by moving their pawn two spaces ahead. Then he would sacrifice his pawn by moving his F-pawn two spaces; if they chose to rebuff his king gambit with the classic defense, pawn to G5, he'd advance his H-pawn two spaces. It would be an open exchange, and the struggle for the four middle squares would be anyone's to lose. He looked forward to continuing the game, but a hush fell over the crowd just then, and his fantasy burst. The massive oak doors were thrown open, and the führer appeared in a sand-colored uniform jacket. With him was a long retinue of officers.

The orchestra stopped playing, and everyone turned their gaze upon Adolf Hitler. From the topmost step, he gave a short, energetic speech in which he declared that all Germans needed to support the country's leaders; it was everyone's duty to take part in the development of Greater Germany, but above all, to support the military. Karl forgot to listen. Instead he wondered about Hitler's short stature, which was impossible to ignore—despite the fact that he stood on a higher step than everyone else.

After his brief, staccato speech, the führer made his way along the row of industry leaders, greeting each one of them personally. Every time he came to a new businessman, an officer whispered a name in his ear. The führer smiled courteously, asked a few questions, and nodded attentively as the responses were nervously given. He was now only five men away from Karl, whose hands suddenly began to sweat. He wondered what the führer might ask him. He glanced at the man by his side, who discreetly wiped his hands on his pants. Karl followed his example.

When it was Karl's turn, he gave the führer a firm handshake. He feared that he'd squeezed too hard, but the smile beneath the narrow mustache remained.

"Mr. Strangl. We greatly value the work you do for Germany."

"Thank you, *mein* führer." The words came to him automatically, as if his mouth had decided to cover up his anxiety.

Clearly, the man had no idea what he did for a living, but one could hardly expect the führer to have heard of Karl Strangl from Hamburg. Standing opposite the Reich's chancellor, he confirmed the man's short stature. It felt strange talking down to the mightiest man in Germany, maybe even the world. Karl felt rather awkward until Hitler thankfully broke the silence.

"I understand that you provide the German army with uniforms?"

"Yes, *mein* führer, and it's an honor," Karl heard himself say.

"Perhaps you will deliver my parade uniform tomorrow?"

"No, *mein* führer."

"I see." Hitler nodded his head slowly and rocked forward on his toes; his gaze grew distant until the officer whispered once again in his ear. As the führer moved on to the next businessman and began asking him questions, Karl couldn't help but notice how well prepared the chancellor was.

When the ceremony was over, Hitler and his entourage wandered down the row saluting the attendees. Then they vanished through the same oak doors through which they'd entered earlier. The crowd exhaled, having seemed to collectively hold its breath in the führer's presence.

Karl hung back, filled with an indeterminate sensation. He wasn't the least bit impressed by Hitler, but he recalled the long unemployment lines before his rise to power. Throngs of hopeful people had lined up day after day, though they hadn't the slightest chance of getting work. Hitler had eliminated the unemployment line, and now everyone had work, just as he'd eliminated the despair following their defeat in the last war. That was all good, of course, but he couldn't forget all the terrible things that came with the Nazis. They'd even opened a concentration camp just outside the city, in Neuengamme, which was surely already packed with unfortunate Jews.

He thought of the Robinsohns. Whenever Ingrid or the children had to buy new clothes, the family had gone to Robinsohns Brothers on Neuer Wall, Hamburg's best shopping street. The three-story department store was well stocked with the latest fashions for women and children. Karl remembered their trips with a mix of joy and irritation. Doing things together as a family was pleasant enough, but he hated the unavoidable waiting that came with outfitting a woman and four children.

He remembered one trip to Robinsohns in particular. The year was 1933, and it had been one of those days when spring seemed right around the corner. It was cold, but the sun was shining, and so the family had headed out to do some shopping.

From a distance they saw a man on a ladder leaning up against Robinsohns' tall storefront windows who appeared to be decorating the building's façade. As they approached, Karl noticed that it wasn't a man but a boy in uniform. And he wasn't decorating. He'd just finished writing the letter "E" in "Jew"—a word the entire country had come to despise, the people whom Germans had been taught to hate. The boy drew a meticulous triangle, then an upside-down triangle over the first one, so that it became the Star of David. Another young man in uniform had been watching him from the sidewalk, and when the boy was finished, they both regarded his work with satisfaction, as if they'd just produced a great work of art. Karl had fumed inside. But he knew all too well that he'd only be inviting trouble if he got involved.

That was the last time they'd shopped at Robinsohns. An official boycott of all Jewish shops was launched on April 1, 1933, and since then it had become a punishable offense for Aryans to do business with Jews. In 1938, after years of being boycotted and harassed, Robinsohns was sold for well below market price to Franz Fahning—who had Aryanized it by changing the name to Hirschfeld's House of Fashion.

As Karl and the others left the Court of Honor, the SS troops remained standing at attention, their chests puffed up. He glanced again at the two sculptures. Everyone was now working to strengthen the party or the army, including himself. Though sewing uniforms for the war machine seemed innocent enough, he was still contributing to the war effort. Should he have declined the uniform order? Should he have declined the invitation to Berlin? He consoled himself by reasoning that no one in their right mind defied Adolf Hitler.

Hamburg, Germany, April 19, 1939

Gerhard counted them again and again and came up with the same number every time: 666. It could hardly be a coincidence. Maybe the knots in the wooden ceiling were trying to send him a message, but what message? The room must have once served another purpose—he doubted that anyone would build a cell with a wooden ceiling—but it did provide him a diversion. He divided it into sections. The first section covered an area that ran from above the door to the toilet and over half of his bed, ending at a board that was darker than the others. The next section ran to the outlet, from which hung a whitish-yellow cord attached to the bulb. The third and fourth sections were separated by another differently colored board. He began to count again but grew distracted by his own thoughts.

The devil's number was 666, but what did it actually mean? He knew that if you were to add up all the numbers on a roulette wheel, it would come to 666. Was that a hidden message to players that roulette was the work of the devil? Hardly. But that meant that the sum of the first thirty-six whole numbers added up to the devil's number. Was it in the Gospel of John? In Revelation? He didn't remember but recalled Tolstoy's *War and Peace*, in which the count's son Pierre Bezukhov developed a mathematical proof that Napoleon was the devil himself. By taking the French alphabet and giving it the same numerical values as the Hebraic alphabet—that is, *A* was 1, *B* was 2 . . . *L* was 20, *M* was

30, and so on—he showed that the sum of the letters in "l'Empereur Napoleon" came to 666. Gerhard tallied the numbers and reached the same conclusion. Not that he'd doubted it, but just to pass the time. He imagined that time—much like the moisture on the stones in a dungeon—ran down the wall. Time had become visible, something he could reach out and touch. It was cold and clammy. It was a time of waiting, but what exactly was he waiting for? Or was it wasted time? The words "wasted time" suggested that one got nothing out of the lost minutes, hours, and days, but could this waiting time be used for something constructive? Or was it just wasted time in disguise?

How had Pierre Bezukhov come up with the idea? he asked himself. *And did it only apply to Napoleon? Maybe there were multiple devils?* He tried it with Attila, who'd conquered most of Europe with a mixture of evil and greed, but came up with the number 211. Ivan the Terrible didn't get 666, either, and he pondered whether or not it should be spelled in Russian. He didn't speak Russian so moved on to Hitler instead. What about him? He came up with 222. So Hitler could be the devil, but only if you multiplied the original sum by three. He decided to find a simple formula that would show that Hitler was Satan in all his glory. He had time, after all—whether it was wasted time or waiting time—and when it came right down to it, Hitler was the reason he was here at all.

He paced in his cell, which he'd long ago counted as five times seven steps wide. What was the key to Hitler's evil? Prime numbers? Irrational numbers? The Fibonacci numbers? He gesticulated with his arms and counted on his fingers as he trudged from the door to the window, then back to the door, then to the window and back. He paused beneath the window and peered at the sky through the iron grate. So simple. It was so simple. If A was 100, B was 101, and so on, then the proof was right in front of him. He added the numbers again. Talking to himself now.

"If H is 107, I is 108, then T is 119. That's 334." His voice trembled now in anticipation as he counted excitedly. "L is 111, E is 104, and R is

117, and the total of that is 332. That makes the grand total," he shouted, "666!"

He'd found his proof! Gerhard Strangl had proved that Hitler was the devil himself. It was a mathematical breakthrough on par with the Pythagorean theorem, Euler's formula, and Gauss's Theorema Egregium. He snapped out of his euphoria as he realized that what he'd just postulated was useless. If he ever got out, he couldn't tell anyone. He would just end up back here again, or worse. But what might he use it for, then? He fell onto his bed, and his heart—which only a moment before had been pounding eagerly in his chest—grew calm. He grinned at himself. *Are you going mad, Gerhard?* No, it would take a great deal more for that to happen. Then he'd wind up in some institution just like Emma and Laura. There was a noise in the corridor. Steps and subdued conversation. He stood. He could tell that whoever was out there was coming closer, but he wasn't able to decipher what was being said, even when he put his ear against the cold door. A ring of keys clinked and one was inserted into the lock. A ruddy-faced guard opened the metal door.

"Strangl, you have guests."

It's Karl, he thought. *He's come to get me out of here.*

Kögl appeared from behind the guard's broad back and entered the cell. He was wearing a pullover and a pair of gabardine pants, and he seemed relaxed. "Well, have you learned your lesson, Mr. Strangl?" He spoke firmly and precisely.

"I don't understand what you mean." Gerhard smiled absentmindedly at the detective superintendent.

"Listen to me." Kögl's clear eyes tried to capture Gerhard's flickering gaze. Gerhard relaxed. "You must give us names, addresses, something. You are a spy for the Gestapo now, and we just want you to do your job. Everyone knows something."

"But I don't have any names or addresses," Gerhard pleaded. "How can I give you something when I don't know anything?" he said, the despair rising in his voice.

"That's a shame. Since we have big plans for you." Kögl rapped three times on the heavy door, and the guard opened it from the outside. In the doorway he turned. "Think hard. We'll talk in a few days."

The metal door slammed shut with a bang. The detective superintendent said they had big plans for him. What could he mean? He dissected the possibilities. How might the Gestapo use a mathematics professor? He could think of only one thing: code breaking. He couldn't say no to that—the work would be both exciting and challenging. It had to be code breaking. Of course it was code breaking. But that meant he had to give them a name.

Berlin, Germany, April 20, 1939

On September 30, 1938, Germany, Great Britain, France, and Italy had signed a pact that forced Czechoslovakia to relinquish the Sudetenland to Germany on October 10. That same day, Hitler and British prime minister Neville Chamberlain signed a peace treaty, and Europe drew a breath of relief. The threat of war had been neutralized.

Then, in the middle of March 1939, German troops occupied the rest of Czechoslovakia. As the German Wehrmacht marched through the streets of Prague, Hitler declared that Czechoslovakia was no more. The country was divided. The Sudetenland was annexed by Germany, the regions of Bohemia and Moravia were declared a German protectorate, and Slovakia became an independent state that wagged its tail like some lapdog every time the big dog barked.

Shortly afterward Hitler turned his attention to Poland, pressuring it to return Danzig and the Polish corridor to Germany—a region that had provided the country with access to the Baltic Sea following

World War I. Poland rejected German demands, and on April 6 entered a mutual agreement with Great Britain to assist each other in case of attack. To the south, the Italian dictator Benito Mussolini rattled his saber, and on April 7 his forces occupied Albania. To the southwest, the Spanish Civil War had just concluded, and General Franco had defeated the Republicans' lawfully elected government. February 1939, when the Republicans lost Catalonia, was the beginning of the end of the Spanish Republic. Göring's Luftwaffe had been especially active in the war, which the inhabitants of Guernica had felt in both their bodies and souls.

But no one in Germany was thinking of Guernica on April 20, 1939. The day had been declared a national holiday, and everyone had the day off from work and gathered in the streets. They'd donned their Sunday best—large-buttoned dresses, broad-brimmed hats, and starched collars. And it wasn't just Berlin's residents; people from around the country had made the trip to the city to celebrate Adolf Hitler's fiftieth birthday. Nazi flags fluttered from every window and balcony. Doric columns had been erected along Unter den Linden—adorned with swastikas, of course—on top of which sat the national eagle symbol. Confectioners had made cakes in tribute, and shop owners had placed portraits of the führer in their windows—the reason for this jubilee was in evidence wherever you looked.

For the occasion, Albert Speer had unveiled the new east–west axis, which connected the city's center with Charlottenburg, where the black American Jesse Owens had won four Olympic gold medals three years earlier, to the Nazis' great chagrin. The Berlin Victory Column, constructed in 1873 to commemorate triumphs against Denmark, Austria, and France, was given a new, central placement so that the goddess of victory could peer out across the city from atop the tall granite pedestal.

In the evening, they lit flames on top of each of the boulevard's Doric columns, and the Brandenburg Gate was illuminated at the end of the boulevard, its flags fluttering in the breeze.

Karl contemplated the amount of fabric used in all the banners across the city and thought it all a waste of good material. He looked at Ingrid, who was staring straight ahead beneath her wide-brimmed yellow hat. The white hatband wrapped around the crown fluttered, and although there was no breeze, she clutched her hat as if she feared it would blow off. She took in all the commotion, wonderment etched into her face. From their excellent seats on Siegesallee, they had a great view of the procession, which exceeded even the Roman victory marches that had once meandered through the streets of Rome following a successful military campaign. An honor once reserved for the likes of Julius Caesar, Marcus Antonius, and Caligula was now given to Adolf Hitler, and he hadn't even won his first victory. While the old Romans had subjugated most of Europe and northern Africa, Hitler had had Austria served to him on a silver platter, and, like the playground's biggest bully, he'd done nothing more than threaten Czechoslovakia to get what he wanted.

Karl thought of Heinz. His future son-in-law had been envious of their trip to Berlin during Adolf Hitler's birthday celebration. Heinz always talked about the führer the way a little boy talks about his father—with awe, submission, and reverence. Karl had seen Hilde looking unhappy one day, but she refused to confide in Karl. Ingrid told him later that Heinz had volunteered with the SS. He possessed an almost childlike enthusiasm for national socialism; just like so many others, he'd told Karl that one couldn't reject it until one gave it a chance. That was how people in Germany thought, and so they were sucked in. Karl tried very hard to understand Heinz. He was from the small city of Wehrden and had experienced nothing but his hometown, the police academy in Fürstenberg, and Hamburg, so he took everything at face value. Which was inaccurate, Karl knew. Heinz was the type who got swept along with the tide, but wasn't that true of everyone in Germany these days? Wasn't that why the Nazis had come to power in the first place? In a certain sense, Karl had to admit—though he was loath to do so—that they were right: national socialism had to be experienced. Besides, he couldn't help but be impressed by the enormous military arsenal on display in the parade. Never-ending columns of soldiers, paratroopers, motorized divisions, cavalry, tanks, and cannons rolled down the avenue, and the tanks' thunderous caterpillar tracks made the ground tremble. The Luftwaffe's planes were in the air all day, and the masses cheered every time a Messerschmitt, Stuka, Heinkel, or Dornier whipped across the sky.

The rhythmic clop of jackboots had a hypnotic effect, and when applause erupted, it was as if all of Berlin was clapping in unison, accompanied by the beat of marching drums and brass and wood instruments. Karl had difficulty imagining Germany ever losing a war—no country could withstand this army and this people. England and France must be quaking in their boots watching this well-oiled war machine, this triumph of military industry, this deathblow to the Treaty of Versailles.

Karl couldn't help but feel a certain fascination; while he saw very plainly the grandeur of the spectacle, something deep within him rejected it. A man behind them, a tall man with a long, thin face who appeared to be about the same age as Karl, whistled and eagerly pumped both fists in the air at the parade. When Karl turned to casually study the throng, he noticed the man's eyes radiating joy as the führer's motorcade passed with Hitler standing beside his chauffeur in the Mercedes convertible. Those eyes displayed the same wholehearted elation he recalled from when his children were born. Karl recognized the unconditional surrender to an emotion. But he couldn't bring himself to submit to national socialism—not voluntarily, in any case.

They finally walked back to their hotel, Karl guiding Ingrid through dense crowds, past buildings decorated with endless bunting. She continued clutching her hat as if she were afraid to lose it.

"I can't take any more," Ingrid said tiredly, throwing herself onto the bed. She'd dropped the yellow hat on the chair and kicked off her shoes. "Much can be said about Hitler, but he sure knows how to throw a party." She grinned.

"I'm glad we don't live in Berlin," Karl said as he laid his jacket over the back of a chair and rolled up his sleeves. With a practiced movement, he loosened his tie. "The people here seem spellbound."

He pulled his silver case out of his jacket pocket and removed two cigarettes. He lit both and handed one to Ingrid. She patted the bed with one hand, gesturing for him to lie down beside her. He arranged his shoes at the foot of the bed, lay down, and took a deep drag on his cigarette.

Hamburg, Germany, April 22, 1939

"What did you say his name was?"

"Theodore Weinhardt."

"Theodore Weinhardt." Kögl jotted this down in his notebook while rhythmically pronouncing the letters in the name, like a schoolteacher trying to imprint the first rules of orthography in his pupils.

There was a knock on the door, and the secretary entered. The detective superintendent glanced at her hungrily through his round steel glasses, then turned back to Gerhard.

"Good." He made one of his familiar pauses. "Now that Miss Kehl is here, you'll have to repeat what you just told me, so we can get it into the report."

Gerhard shifted nervously in his seat and began. He explained how he and Weinhardt had often met at the harbor, and how they'd discussed the situation in the country. He told them that Weinhardt lived in Altona, and that every afternoon he walked along St. Pauli Piers. He told them that the old man was especially sarcastic when he talked about Hitler, Goebbels, Göring, and Himmler, whom he referred to as national socialism's useless breeding stallions. But Kögl must've been aware of that already. He was, after all, the one who'd sent Weinhardt to test Gerhard in the first place. Just like he'd sent Cullman. Like a puppeteer, Kögl stood behind the scenes directing and conducting.

"Do you hear what I'm saying, Mr. Strangl?"

Gerhard snapped to attention and met Kögl's squinting eyes.

"Do you hear what I'm saying, Mr. Strangl?" the detective superintendent said again, raising his eyebrows.

"I'm sorry, I . . ."

"I understand. The first time's not easy, but let me assure you that Weinhardt and his ilk have earned their punishment." The Gestapo officer smiled warmly. "Go home and take a nice warm bath. Tomorrow you'll return to the university, and our little matter will be forgotten." Kögl offered his hand. Gerhard knew that if he accepted it, it would exonerate Kögl from all the days Gerhard had spent in the basement under these offices. He shook the detective superintendent's hand.

"You'll continue your work for us as before, but soon you'll have more interesting assignments. I promise you," Kögl said, closing the door behind Gerhard.

It had been eight days since Gerhard had last seen the light of day, apart from the sliver traveling across the floor of his cell, and now the sun scorched his eyes like the bonfires on St. John's Day. The guard at the entrance nodded pleasantly to him as he began making his way down the street. Usually, Gerhard hardly ever noticed his own breathing, but like a diver who'd believed he would never see the surface again, he gasped for breath. He sat down at a small café table at Bomhoff's Bakery and ordered a slice of marble cake and a cup of coffee. With unaccustomed deliberation, he savored every morsel in the same way a man condemned to death enjoys his final meal. Afterward he bought a pack of Eckstein cigarettes and headed down to the harbor. The day was still young, and he had no plans other than to empty his pack.

From a distance the cupola-topped clock tower near St. Pauli Piers resembled a wizard sporting a mint-green hat. Just as Gerhard reached the harbor, the ball dropped on the Zeitballturm, which stood at the entrance to Speicherstadt and its endless warehouses filled with tobacco, spices, tea, coffee, silks, and blankets. The buildings towered over both sides of the narrow Zoll Canal like tall bluffs. The ball fell every twelve hours to enable seamen to set their chronometers; without the exact time, it was impossible to estimate the degree of longitude and thereby the ship's exact location on the sea. He'd wondered what the rasping croak of the ball meant for many years, until Weinhardt explained the connection to him one day. He snorted at the thought of the old man.

A dense, smoky mist hung over the petroleum harbor's many fueling terminals, and the whaleboat *Walter Rau* was drifting slowly past. He walked westward past the old Elbtunnel. At the fish market, where the fishmongers barked loudly behind their booths, peddling fresh fish, chickens, geese, bread, cheese, and vegetables, he turned north. In St. Pauli he found a movie theater and watched a stagecoach try to escape from Geronimo. He stayed on for *The Wizard of Oz*, which featured the clock tower at St. Pauli Piers. By the time he exited the theater, the evening sun was shimmering like a red ball, and he decided to head home.

> *Clear the street for the brown battalions*
> *Clear the street for the stormtroopers*
> *Millions are already turning to the swastika for hope . . .*

The words from the "Horst Wessel Song" were coming from a tavern, sung by a drunken men's choir. *That damn song,* he thought. As he passed the tavern, he imagined what it might look like inside. He pictured a large wood-paneled pub with giant, sturdy-handled beer mugs set on long tables in which many had inscribed their initials. On the benches around the tables sat short-haired men, their arms around each other's shoulders, bawling along with the song. Cigarettes had left black splotches on the tabletops, while a dense cloud of cigarette smoke hung below the ceiling. He could almost smell the odor wafting off the place. Two drinking buddies in SS uniforms stumbled toward him, holding each other up. He tugged his hat farther down his forehead and crossed the street.

"Hello, friend."

Gerhard stiffened.

"Yeah, you in the gray coat."

He turned and looked at the two SS men. One was flushed and clearly being held up by the other. If he started to run, they wouldn't be able to follow him. They were too drunk for that. But what if they were armed?

The man who'd shouted at Gerhard did his best to appear sober. "You have a cigarette?"

"I do."

The man accepted the Eckstein Gerhard offered him. "Thank you. You wouldn't happen to have another? Wouldn't want the first one to get lonely." He smiled broadly, revealing a handsome set of teeth that would make any actor envious. His friend spluttered with laughter and nearly lost his balance.

Gerhard breathed more easily once he'd turned his back on the two drunks. He glanced back. The one with the great set of teeth tried in vain to light his cigarette, while his buddy began throwing up on a poster for a variety show that was plastered to the wall of a house. Gerhard's nerves were frayed. He couldn't take it anymore. All he wanted was to get home.

He closed his door and methodically locked it. There was no food, so he found the little grinder in the cupboard and ground up some coffee beans. A cup of coffee and a few dry cookies would have to suffice for a meal. He needed a compass for his thoughts, which were spinning every which way. It was as if they too had been locked up, because they were now pushing to get out. In spite of the other thoughts' persistent attempts, one particular thought kept emerging on top: Why?

He put the kettle on the stove and lit one of the gas burners. He sat at the table. Tears welled up in his eyes, and his jaw muscles tightened. He balled his hands into fists and sat rocking his head back and forth. Why had he been forced to get mixed up in all this? Why couldn't he just be left in peace? That was all he wanted. He'd been naïve to trust strangers at a time when no one could be trusted. The hiss of the kettle became a shrill whistle, and he cursed himself. His cowardice, his goddamn cowardice.

Had he shouted? His outburst startled him. Usually he was in control of his emotions. One didn't display such emotions publicly, and there was no reason to do so inside the four walls of one's home, either.

There was a knock on his door.

"Mr. Strangl, is something wrong?" Another knock. "Mr. Strangl?"

He recognized the sharp, obdurate voice. He stood and went to the door, but didn't open it.

"No, Mrs. Zimmermann, nothing's wrong." His voice quivered.

"But I heard a noise in your apartment."

He knew that she would remain where she was until she got an answer that fit with the story that she'd already begun composing in her head. "All is well." *All but my life,* he thought.

"But I heard a noise. We haven't seen you for days, and then suddenly this commotion," she continued.

He threw open the door. "What concern is it of yours anyway, what happens in my apartment?"

"As the super's wife—"

"You aren't the super's wife. Herbert isn't the super anymore, so stay out of it."

He slammed the door with such force that the door frame nearly gave way. He heard her talking to herself on her way down the stairs. Still in shock over his outburst, he undressed and began to clean himself feverishly at the kitchen sink. He scrubbed and scoured his body with the hard brush until his skin burned. If he put enough force into it, he might be able to wash away the experiences of this past week, as if they were a stain that could be removed. Water splashed onto the kitchen floor. All he could think to do was get himself clean, put on his newly washed pajamas, and crawl under the fresh linen sheets—and then, of course, apologize to Mrs. Zimmermann.

Hamburg, Germany, June 4, 1939

He was back in his office again. Actually, it was misleading to call it an office because he didn't do much work in here. But he couldn't call it his sanctuary or his refuge. He came here often, claiming he had a lot to do, because this was where he could find peace and quiet. Peace and quiet from his family, peace and quiet from his life. In this room his thoughts could wander, and he could be a different Karl from the one who ran the Strangl Clothing Factory. He felt like an imposter, one who'd deceived his family and cheated his way to wealth, and now sat in his big house—in his room with the misleading name—waiting to be found out.

Of course he could never have refused to take over the factory. His father's illness had forced his hand. Although he reasoned that he didn't owe his father anything, he hadn't been able to bring himself to turn him down. He often asked himself what was wrong with him. He had been offered a tremendous opportunity at a time when people in Germany were going hungry and dressed in rags—and still he wished that it had never been offered to him. An illogical hope had caused him to believe that his father would survive him, so that taking over the company would never come up for discussion. He'd never grown accustomed to the title and never felt like the chairman. While Gerhard had forged his own path through life with mathematics, Karl had effectively become Reinhardt. He'd become the man he couldn't say no to, the man he'd never had the courage to admit he hated.

One day he would sell the factory. When the time was right, it would make him a fortune, and he would visit every corner of the globe with Ingrid and the children. He'd read about the Great Wall of China, and he couldn't believe such a thing could possibly exist unless he stood beside it. They would travel to Easter Island like Captain Cook and journey to Africa and see animals they'd never dreamed existed. When they returned from their long trip, he would find a house in the country, where they could live in peace and quiet, away from all the Nuremberg Rallies and military parades in Berlin. But the time wasn't right. If he were alive, his father would never have accepted a sale.

He removed a pack of cigarettes from his writing desk and opened it with his letter opener. He carefully placed his cigarettes in the silver case Ingrid had given him on their wedding day. He put the last one between his lips, then leaned toward the table lighter and lit it. The smoke stung his eyes, and it irritated him that he was still bothered by it. There was a sheet of paper on the desk that he would pick up and study with concentration if anyone were to knock on the door. It was always the same sheet. He glanced at the bar, which was set inside a globe. One had to lift the northern hemisphere to get at all the delights lined up in the southern. The little voice inside him said once again, *You drink too much, Karl.* Today he had to admit that it was right. His mouth was still dry after the night before, and he had no desire for a drink, at least not yet.

He went out to the garden. The still dew-damp grass made his bare feet wet, and blades of grass stuck to them. Normally he would brush them away, but he didn't have the energy to do that today, and his laziness defeated his sense of order. He fell into a folding chair that someone had set on the pier. Maybe one of the guests, or maybe he'd done it himself; he couldn't remember. He polished his sunglasses with his unbuttoned shirt. August, up early as usual, had been out on the lake since dawn, and Karl couldn't see the skiff anywhere. Up at the house, everyone was busy cleaning up after the party. He would have preferred to hold the wedding at a restaurant in the city, but Ingrid had insisted that they not spend the money on such an extravagance.

It was pleasant to sit in the morning sunlight. The wedding had been beautiful, and most importantly, Hilde had been happy. And Ingrid had been happy. He'd had too much to drink. Not so much that he'd been visibly intoxicated, but enough that he was now getting his punishment. His head was heavy, and his temples throbbed. He wasn't sure whether it was because he had a hangover or because Hilde would now be moving away. Or because of Heinz. But it was rude of him to think like that.

Karl had always thought that Hilde would fall in love with a young, ambitious businessman or a doctor or, at the very least, someone who earned double what Heinz did. Someone who could protect her, someone about whom one could say, "He's a good man." No one would ever say that about Heinz. Karl had this impression confirmed when he met Hilde's new in-laws. They were simple people. In fact they were a low-class family in their shabby Sunday best, which they probably pulled out of the closet each week so that the priest could make them feel guilty with yet another sermon on sin. They certainly weren't sinners, just country people who feared God, change, and the big city—in that order. They'd arrived in Hamburg via train and departed the same day, so that they could return to their town that Karl had never heard of, home to their secure life among other familiar parishioners. They hadn't offered to help or pay for any part of the luxurious celebration, leaving Karl with the entire bill. Not that it mattered, but it was the principle of the thing. They'd been so disengaged, so uninvolved. In that sense, he understood Heinz a little better now.

Normally he loved weddings, but to him, this one had been a good-bye party. A sad farewell both to Hilde and to a time that would never return. Soon she would move to the loft apartment on Brennerstrasse that he'd procured for them, where she would share a bed with Heinz. No doubt she'd be pregnant before long.

Would they one day hang a gold, silver, or bronze medal around Hilde's neck? In May, they had awarded the Cross of Honor of the German Mother for the first time, an honor instituted to reward women who gave children to the Third Reich. Bronze was awarded to mothers who gave birth to four children, silver for six and seven, and gold for eight or more. The cross was white and blue with a black swastika at the center of a white background. Around the swastika was the inscription "The German Mother." Ingrid had accepted the cross, but no one in the family ever saw it. Karl had suspected that she'd tossed it out until he found it one day in Sophia's room hanging from the neck of a sad-looking bear with a red bow tie.

The twins were twelve years old now. Sophia was part of the Young Girls' League, the younger sister, so to speak, of the League of German Girls, and Maximilian wore the uniform of the German Young People. Loyalty to Hitler, community before the individual, and physical strength were the central tenets in the upbringing of the fatherland's children. Karl had once described the youth organizations to Gerhard as Nazi factories, but membership was compulsory, and so he had resigned himself to receiving lectures on the führer and the greatness of the Third Reich from his children at dinnertime. It was as though they had been brainwashed. Thank god the Hitler Youth hadn't had the same effect on August and Hilde, who still seemed capable of thinking for themselves.

Karl suddenly recalled a story that Hilde had shared a year ago when she was in the League of German Girls, a girls-only branch of the Hitler Youth that had been compulsory since 1936. He vividly recalled her sitting at the dinner table in her white blouse, dark-blue wool dress that fell to the middle of her shins, and black cotton scarf held together by a woven leather knot on her chest. It was a Saturday, and she'd just returned from a social evening with the other girls in her group. A seventeen-year-old girl had announced that she was expecting, and all the girls had squealed and cheered. She had reached the ultimate goal toward which they'd been taught to strive: motherhood. Hilde had been shaken by the girls' reactions, and he remembered her observation that night at the table: "The only thing league girls fear worse than death is being unable to bear children." She'd barely been able to contain her sarcasm, which could just as easily have come from Ingrid's lips. Ingrid hadn't wanted Hilde to be part of the league, but Karl had insisted. "If everyone has to participate, then she has to do her duty," he'd said, and Hilde had been happy to be involved. He hoped the same would be true for August in the Hitler Youth; he hoped it would put some hair on his son's chest and toughen him up. He could use that.

August waved at him from the little skiff. Karl suspected that his many forays on the lake were, in reality, a way for him to be left in peace, to be alone. The lake was August's "office."

August had begun to remind him more and more of Gerhard. Both were withdrawn, and both were more comfortable alone. Karl sometimes got the sense that he didn't know either of them.

Gerhard had seemed unhappy at the party. In fact Karl couldn't recall when he'd last seen his brother smile. And this whole interlude with the Gestapo had only made things worse. Seeing Gerhard suffer like that was difficult. Karl would go pay a visit to the Gestapo sometime soon. There must be something he could do. If nothing else, he could bribe the detective superintendent.

Hamburg, Germany, June 6, 1939

Gerhard sat at his writing desk in a gloomy frame of mind. *Another one*, he thought, tamping out his cigarette in the ashtray. Yet another lost soul pulling on a uniform and giving up what he did best. What a waste. He'd had great expectations for Rudiger Riemer, but he'd just walked out of his office for the last time. Riemer could have gone far. He was driven by the same curiosity to understand numbers as Gerhard himself had been at his age. He sighed loudly. Soon, only members of the Hitler Youth would remain in his classroom as they were the only ones granted stipends anymore. Gerhard had begun to feel that lecturing to half-empty halls was pointless.

The telephone rang insistently. The call was from a Miss Reinfeld, a secretary, inviting him to dine with a Walter von Amrath that evening at Restaurant Savigny. Anyone with even a modicum of interest in literature knew who Walter von Amrath was. He was a professor of literature at Friedrich-Wilhelm University in Berlin who'd written two acclaimed books, *The Great Literary Works of the Nineteenth Century* and *The Muse of the German Poets*—both of which were admired in literary circles—and he was greatly respected for his research.

Gerhard hung up the telephone with equal measures of curiosity and pride. Though he and Dr. von Amrath didn't share the same field of study, the professor nevertheless wished to meet him. When Gerhard had asked his secretary whether others would be attending, she'd said no. Von Amrath had, in other words, explicitly asked to meet with him. A distinguished literary scholar had requested his presence, and his alone, at Restaurant Savigny. He couldn't help but wonder what the reason for this unexpected call might be, but he eventually gave up.

It began to rain as he turned down Mönckebergstrasse. He checked his wet summer coat in the restaurant's coatroom, wiped the droplets of water from his glasses with a handkerchief, and smoothed down his side part. A distinguished-looking waiter with a little mustache guided him to a table, then stood nearby awaiting his order. Gerhard thumbed aimlessly through the menu, glancing up at the door several times. Only now did it occur to him that he didn't know what Walter von Amrath looked like. A well-dressed gentleman who appeared to be around forty-five years old—the age he assumed von Amrath to be—checked his hat in the coatroom and scanned the restaurant. His eyes rested on Gerhard for a moment before moving on. His face lit up in a smile, and he sat down at a table beside a man and two women, whom he greeted amiably. Gerhard's gaze had followed him across the restaurant, so he hadn't realized that a man of medium height now stood before him. The man cleared his throat.

"It is a pleasure to meet you, Mr. Strangl." Von Amrath had a kind voice.

"The pleasure is all mine," replied Gerhard.

The waiter pulled out a chair for the new arrival, and Gerhard studied von Amrath while the man conferred with the waiter about their order. Von Amrath spoke with his chin held high, and his cheeks and throat were flushed pink from a recent shave. His face was open and affable, and there was something reliable about his looks. He seemed like the sort of man you would confide your deepest secrets to, knowing they would be safe in his possession.

"Let's order the house's finest Mosel wine," he said, glancing quizzically at Gerhard, who nodded. The waiter jotted it down in his notebook.

Von Amrath turned back to Gerhard. "It is said that it takes five times longer to harvest the grapes along the Mosel than those in the best French wine districts because of the steep slopes." He formed an incline with his hand. "That's why I prefer wine from Untermosel, out of respect for the enormous work that goes into it. If the grapes had to grow in the same conditions in France, they would never be harvested. The French are simply too lazy."

Gerhard smiled. It hadn't taken long for him to get a good feeling about the man sitting opposite him. He was learned, he was articulate, and they had shared interests. But he still hadn't the foggiest notion why they were meeting. Now he would find out.

"Dr. von Amrath . . ."

"Walter, call me Walter," von Amrath said just as the waiter returned with the wine. They tasted it fastidiously.

"Wonderful," von Amrath said, smacking his lips. He leaned back in his chair, looking satisfied. "You're probably wondering why I asked you here."

Gerhard nodded. Von Amrath explained that he'd moved to Hamburg three months ago. He wanted to be close to his mother, who had become a widow five years earlier. Now she lived in Ahrensburg, northeast of Hamburg, but was old and sick and had no one to take care of her. Gerhard recalled hearing of Walter's sister, Birgitte von Amrath. She'd been one of the country's most talented harpists. Not many women were allowed to play with the Berlin Philharmonic Orchestra, and Birgitte had been among the chosen few in the male-dominated orchestra pit. But in 1935 she had followed the example of leading figures like Fritz Lang and Rudolf Carnap and emigrated to the United States. Last he'd heard, she was playing in the New York Philharmonic.

Von Amrath leaned back as the waiter set a plate of appetizers on the table. He scrupulously unfolded his white cloth napkin and laid it in his lap before continuing his story. He was paying a housekeeper to take care of his mother now, but he wanted to be close to her. Gerhard asked about what would become of his job at the university in Berlin, and von Amrath explained with a smile that his job wasn't going anywhere, and that he had plenty to keep him busy in Hamburg.

Before leaving Berlin, he had received several new assignments unrelated to his university work, and he would continue that work in Hamburg. Without going into further detail, he let Gerhard understand that it was especially important work. There was a pause and the two men smiled at one another, each waiting for the other to speak.

Gerhard noticed a party pin identical to his own on von Amrath's lapel. "National Socialist DAP" was written on the small, round emblem, with the imposing swastika dead center. In and of itself there was nothing strange about it, but he'd never imagined that a man like Walter von Amrath would publicly advertise his membership in the party. That's why he hadn't considered wearing his own pin this evening. As with his own party membership, it had no doubt paved von Amrath's way to a leading position at the university. Though it was easy to overlook, it opened doors.

"May I ask the reason for this meeting?" Gerhard asked finally.

"Of course," von Amrath said, patting his mouth with his napkin. "I know you work for the Gestapo." He ran his tongue across his upper front teeth to remove any remaining bits of food. "Those fellows aren't a particularly nice bunch, so I imagine you would like to get away from them." Before Gerhard could respond, von Amrath continued. "The younger ones are the worst. They think they can treat people like shit. The older ones at least know how to communicate without shouting and carrying on like idiots. They started out in the real police, so they're used to that line of work." He smiled as he uttered the words "real police." "The younger men have no past, and without the Gestapo they have no future, either."

Gerhard made a questioning face to try to get him to finally declare his purpose.

"I'll come to the point." Von Amrath cleared his throat. "I want to recruit you for my department."

"Department? But I'm a mathematician."

"I mean my SS department." Gerhard's expression turned to one of disbelief. "Allow me to introduce myself properly. SS Major Dr. Walter von Amrath." He offered Gerhard his hand with an accommodating smile, and Gerhard took it, his mouth agape.

"SS?" Gerhard clawed involuntarily at his chin. He picked up his glass of Mosel wine and took a long, slow swallow as he tried in vain to think of something to say that couldn't be viewed as a criticism of the decorated doctor of literature. What the hell was a man like him doing in the SS? Gerhard had always believed that SS members came primarily from the lower classes, and now here was this well-educated man telling him he was part of it. Not only that, he was the leader of an entire department.

"I can see that you're shocked. But I assure you I'm not a national socialist."

"Then why the SS?"

"Hmm, why SS?" Von Amrath paused to consider, though it could hardly be the first time he'd been asked that very question. "The Nazis may not be the best people, but they need assistance, and instead of sleeping in the passenger compartment, you can, like me, help drive the train. Or at the very least shovel coal." He laughed tersely. "Democracy is a beautiful thought, but it's utopian. Look at the Weimar Republic. If you ask me, technocracy is the way forward. Let he who is capable lead. It won't do to put responsibility in the hands of the people; they are too emotional, and one cannot steer a country with emotions."

Gerhard had never thought of it that way. The more he thought about it, the more it made sense. He studied the literary scholar as the man sliced off a small chunk of his steak. He raised the meat to his mouth and chewed carefully, then pointed at Gerhard with his empty fork.

"My department is in charge of transportation," he said, and went on to explain that it was a vital department, responsible for conveying troops, materials, and supplies. He added that they would also be handling logistics—which was not a simple assignment at all. That's why he wanted the best and only the best in his department. He'd been granted carte blanche authority to assemble his own team, and he'd immediately thought of men like Gerhard Strangl. Gerhard didn't know if this was true, but he couldn't help but feel a little flattered all the same. Von Amrath continued. When the war came, they would need every man, and dynamic men in particular. That's why he wanted Gerhard. Von Amrath ended his little speech by appealing to Gerhard's conscience, pointing out that if he chose to work for his department, he would be allowed to fulfill his war duty by doing something as innocent as transportation. He wouldn't ever have blood on his hands.

He gave Gerhard a kind look, and Gerhard said nothing. They ate in silence for some time. When Gerhard laid his silverware down on his plate, the waiter removed it almost before the clinking of the silverware had faded. If von Amrath worked for the SS, then it couldn't be that bad. He was in every respect an intelligent man, Gerhard thought, so he'd probably entertained the same concerns as Gerhard himself. And Gerhard had, of course, often wished that someone would rescue him from the Gestapo's embrace. Here was his opportunity to make a choice. The Gestapo hadn't given him that possibility—well, they had, but given that it had been a choice between life and death, he didn't really consider it a choice. A thought struck him.

"But what about my work at the university?"

"You may, like me, put that on hold for a while. If every young man must go to war, there's nothing for you there anyway." He smiled with his eyes. "In fact it's quite liberating. Even though I work for the SS now, I have a lot more time to work on my next book. As will you. Are you currently working on something?"

"I am."

"Good. People like us shouldn't waste away. We need to keep busy. Sitting in some dusty office is no good when your skills are needed elsewhere." He gestured with his hand and added, "There are many advantages to being in the SS, and besides, we'll make sure your book is published. Consider that a mere formality."

Gerhard had feared that his next book would never be published; after all, there was no place in Germany for literature that deviated even slightly from the Nazis' strict ideas. Although his main thesis was in no way provocative or experimental—at least not to him—the Nazis might see it differently. It was impossible to know with any certainty what they thought, and now von Amrath was promising him something close to literary amnesty. How could he turn it down?

Von Amrath seemed to sense Gerhard's dilemma. He filled Gerhard's glass with more of the dry Mosel wine and tried to soothe his anxieties by describing his department as a group of decent people who would have to tip the balance on the scale if Germany was to reach the greatness the country deserved. Gerhard had heard that cliché before, but it carried more heft when it came from this man's mouth.

"You won't have to begin with the privates at the bottom of the ladder. You're much too valuable for that. For god's sake, you are one of the country's leading mathematicians. We'll give you the title you deserve," von Amrath said as he reached for the wine and then waved the bottle at the waiter. "May we have another bottle of this wonderful beverage?" The waiter went off at once for a new one. Gerhard had grown woozy but was unsure whether it was due to the wine or the conversation.

After dinner the two men stood. Von Amrath patted his belly with satisfaction.

"That's another advantage—these wonderful dinners on Himmler's tab." He laughed but quickly altered his expression to one that inspired more confidence. He laid a hand on Gerhard's shoulder. "It's quite simple. Say yes and you won't have to give the Gestapo another thought." He smiled as he squeezed Gerhard's hand. "Can I count on you?"

"I need to think it over."

"Of course."

It was no longer raining when they exited the restaurant. The fresh air that always followed a summer rain made Gerhard's head feel better. A gleaming Mercedes 500K pulled up to the restaurant, out of which climbed a man in uniform and a stylish young woman with a fox fur slung around her neck. The man offered the beautiful woman his arm as they walked into the Restaurant Savigny. Von Amrath saluted the man with a "heil Hitler," then turned to Gerhard.

"Meeting you has been quite a pleasure, and I look forward, hopefully, to working with you in the future. Good night."

"Good night," Gerhard said, and turned toward home.

He gazed absently into the shop windows as he walked. Through a cobbler's newly cleaned windowpane, he caught sight of his own reflection. He raised his hat a little and stared into his eyes. Gestapo or SS? He was caught between a rock and a hard place. What if he couldn't avoid going to war? What if every German man had to fight? He was still young enough to be called up by the Wehrmacht, and he had military training. Wasn't a transport division preferable to the front line? He let his eyes roam down the window, studying himself. He tried to imagine how he'd look in an SS uniform, but his mind refused to create such a picture. He pulled himself away from his reflection and walked on, his head bursting with questions. If he joined the SS, would it turn him into someone else? Would he no longer be the mathematician he was? He wouldn't have time for his work at the university, but hadn't Chancellor Schenk recently called him into his office to inform him that his lecture hours would be drastically cut next semester anyway? There were no longer enough students to justify his present course load.

Von Amrath was a sensible man. He didn't seem like a brainwashed Nazi, more like a pragmatist. *His new job description probably has not changed him, so why should it change me?* Gerhard thought. Agreeing to the job in the transport division would mean that Kögl would no longer have any control over him. It was a pleasant thought. He didn't feel comfortable within the unpredictable Gestapo, but in von Amrath's division he would be among likeminded men. As it unfolded in his head, it seemed like a vote between good and evil. Kögl, who'd put him in some miserable jail cell, versus von Amrath, the guardian angel who'd treated him to a meal in one of the city's finest restaurants. He paused. *Have you already forgotten all the stories about the SS? Has the Mosel wine completely erased your memory? Can you be bought for a good meal and some intelligent conversation? It's not a choice between good and evil; it's a choice between evil and evil. You've let the articulate professor blind you. Big words and eloquence don't make the SS a desirable place to work.* By the time he inserted his key in his door, he was at a loss.

Hamburg, Germany, June 12, 1939

"Perhaps we can agree on a price." Karl put his checkbook on the table and gazed questioningly at the two men. "What would you like?"

He wasn't able to catch any of what they were saying as they conferred softly between themselves. He couldn't imagine a sum that he wouldn't be willing to pay to wrest Gerhard free of the Gestapo, so he felt quite confident. He glanced around the very ordinary office and waited patiently for the men to agree on a figure. He'd already forgotten the tall man's name. Karl wasn't familiar with SS ranks, but given the three stars on the man's collar, he assumed that his rank corresponded to that of *Hauptmann*, or captain. He didn't respond when Karl flashed him a forced smile, so Karl shifted his attention to the smaller man, who had to be Kögl. The man with the comb-over didn't look as dangerous as Gerhard had described him. Karl noticed that the detective superintendent had unusually small ears, and was impressed that they managed to keep his glasses in place. On the wall he spotted a brass cross inlaid with silver, which suggested that Kögl had apparently been a brave soldier. Karl turned back to the detective superintendent, who promptly cleared his throat.

"We want you."

"I beg your pardon?" Karl stared in confusion at Kögl, who looked back rigidly.

"Our price is you," the detective superintendent repeated.

"I'm not sure I understand."

The tall man explained, "It's quite simple. If you voluntarily join the SS, the Gestapo will release your brother."

"Join the SS?" Only a moment ago he'd felt that he had everything under control, but now he had no idea where the conversation was going. What could he give them that they didn't already have? He turned from Kögl to the SS officer and back to Kögl again. Both men seemed to be enjoying the situation. When he'd entered this office a short while ago, he'd felt brazenly certain that he could bribe these two men, but now they'd flipped everything on its head.

"Correct. Join the SS," said Erich Lorenz in his deep voice before adding, "As an honorary member, of course."

"That's out of the question."

"Consider your brother," Lorenz said.

Karl had no idea what membership would entail. No, actually, he did: a horrible argument with Gerhard. He wouldn't want Karl to sacrifice so much for him. But Karl knew his brother would do the same for him, so Gerhard would have to understand. No, he couldn't even consider the proposition. But it wasn't as though all the SS members he knew had horns growing out of their heads. They were just regular people. Ernst Grabner was in the SS, though he was more focused on blood and honor than Karl. The SS weren't real soldiers. They were more of a brotherhood, with secret handshakes and that sort of thing. It amazed him that Ernst was even involved with such an organization. He bit his lower lip.

"Let me see if I understand you correctly. If I become an honorary member of the SS, my brother will no longer have to work for the Gestapo?" Karl said following a lengthy pause.

"Correct," Lorenz replied.

"And what does honorary membership entail?"

"Nothing. But we would be greatly appreciative if you wore your uniform on official occasions."

His eyes roamed to Kögl. What did the detective superintendent get out of all this anyway? He lost an informant but would be on good terms with the SS. But he already seemed to be on good terms with them.

"What does the SS get out of it?" Karl asked.

"Prestige. You're an industrious businessman, one of the city's elite, and you will be a good representative for us," Lorenz said in a friendly tone. "Your colleague—or perhaps it would be better to say your competitor—Hugo Boss supports the SS, and his business has only benefitted as a result."

Karl was irritated that Lorenz used such a cheap ploy, but this was about his brother. Lorenz removed a sheet of paper from his attaché case and placed it before Karl, who looked at Lorenz, surprised. Had they planned this from the start? He could hardly believe it. Or did Lorenz carry these documents around with him should he ever meet some lost soul?

"So let me sign the damn thing," Karl said peevishly, but he paused right before signing the paper. "I want it in writing that Gerhard no longer works for the Gestapo."

"You'll get that," Lorenz replied quickly.

"And I want to know who ratted on Gerhard." He glanced up at Lorenz, who turned to Kögl.

"That would be a family matter," the detective superintendent said.

"A family matter?"

"Don't give it another thought. Just sign."

His hand cramped as he squeezed the pen. Now only his arthritis could stop him from becoming part of the SS.

Outside, Karl stood on the sidewalk for a moment, trying to light his cigarette. Though the day was windless and summery, his attempts were futile and he gave up. He climbed into the backseat of the waiting car and felt the heat at once. The leather seats were scorching hot, and he saw dark splotches under the armpits of Albert's shirt. After finally lighting his cigarette, he pulled out a handkerchief and wiped his forehead with it.

Lorenz came out of the building and scanned the area with a look of satisfaction on his face, the way a king regards his kingdom. He started down the street, his steps so long and measured that his protégé—a subordinate in the SS—struggled to keep pace. Karl watched them until they were out of sight.

He saw the concern on Albert's face in the rearview mirror. "Mr. Strangl." The chauffeur turned his head to study him. "You look like you've just seen a ghost."

"It's much worse than that," Karl said very softly. "I've just joined the SS."

"You're joking," Albert said, chuckling.

"I wish I were."

Albert scrutinized him. Karl knew what the chauffeur saw. Albert saw a tired, gray man, a weak-willed and apathetic man whose confidence had crumbled. He must have looked like a child sitting on his shiny leather seat. A child who had hunched down in his expensive suit to hide from the world.

Karl didn't respond to Albert's question about where he wished to go. He just stared straight ahead, his forehead furrowed as though he were trying to solve a difficult equation.

"Where to, Mr. Strangl?" Albert said again.

When Karl got home, he went directly to his office, where he could be left in peace, alone with his thoughts. He sat at his desk. He might have to go off to war again. He glanced at the cabinet hanging on the wall. Through the small, square glass panels he could see his medals. Though he'd earned them many years ago, he was still proud of them. Truth be told, he was prouder of his sports trophies than of the Iron Cross Second Class, which lay inside. Perhaps because they reminded him of his carefree childhood.

It had been a long time since he'd given the Iron Cross any thought, and now it languished inside a small lined box while his other medals remained visible. There was his bronze medal from 1911, the gold medal from 1912, and the silver medal from 1913. There were two gold medals from rowing and two academic achievement awards from his school days. They all looked like coins minted in antiquity. And like some proud numismatist, he displayed them in his glass case.

One particular medal had a special place in his memory. It had been 1912, a hot and windless day at the end of August. The yearly school championships were to be held at the small, dilapidated athletic stadium beside the old water tower in Stadtpark. His goal was to improve on his bronze medal from the spring and get a silver. No one could defeat Bernd Beukelmann, and no one even hoped to—including Karl. Bernd, a sinewy boy whose body was covered with freckles, was in a class by himself. His entire body worked in rhythm, each movement carefully calibrated for optimal speed, and Karl had been seven or eight feet behind Bernd at the sixty-meter dash all year long. He'd only glimpsed the boy's freckled neck and the backs of his white knees.

But this August day would prove different. Karl wasn't nervous. All he was thinking was that he would shake Bernd's hand this time, and he wondered how he might introduce the idea of training with him without sounding pushy. Before the race Bernd seemed focused, as always, and Karl studied Herbert Wankel, his closest competitor for the silver. But the pale boy who sat behind him in school was tense and dissatisfied with his shoes, and he kept taking them off and putting them back on. The entire school was sitting in the bleachers, and the mood was festive—if for no other reason than none of the pupils would have to fear old Mr. Reuben's temper or Umberger's whistling ruler, which left red welts and tear-filled eyes.

Karl glanced at the bleachers. He was ready.

"On your mark!"

He focused his gaze on the reddish-brown track stretching out before him.

"Get set!"

He tensed every muscle.

"Go!"

His body lunged. The start was excellent, his best ever, and his first three steps—meant to bring him near his top speed—only made him feel that he had much more to give. Out of the corner of his eye, he noticed that Bernd Beukelmann, in the lane to his right, wasn't ahead of him; they were neck and neck. His legs moved by themselves, as though he were running downhill, and Bernd soon disappeared behind him. When he crossed the finish line, Karl felt as though he could've kept running. He glanced toward the bleachers, where all the pupils stood cheering.

Disappointment radiated from Bernd as he pressed Karl's hand and uttered a guttural congratulations. Karl was on top of the world, and so he asked Bernd if they could train together as if it was the most natural thing in the world. But that turned out to be Bernd's final race. He wasn't used to losing the sixty-meter dash, and now that he knew what it felt like, he didn't want to experience it again. At least, that was what Karl reckoned later. Karl's victory qualified him for the district championships of 1913, where he brought home a silver medal behind a long-legged boy from Bergedorf.

That same year, he won gold in rowing on his home turf, Alster Lake. Karl was a good rower, but his partner, Ulrich Ahlendorf, was a force of nature; every stroke he took was so powerful that it seemed the shell might split in two from the force of it. The other competitors claimed that Ulrich would have won with anyone as his partner, but Karl knew it wasn't true. Unfortunately Ulrich later succumbed to polio, and his legs stopped growing. Karl used to visit the boy at home, but Ulrich began to believe all the chatter that he could've won the medals by himself and insisted on reminding Karl of that every time he visited. Karl didn't bother to correct him since Ulrich could no longer win even with supernatural powers. He had stopped visiting in 1915, when the Ahlendorfs moved to southern Germany, and he never again heard from Ulrich.

Karl tried not to think about what had happened today. An honorary member of the SS. It sounded like something he should be proud of, but he wasn't. It wasn't the first time the SS had tried to recruit him. Ernst Grabner had once lectured him on the benefits of the SS, but he'd laughed it off, and Grabner knew him well enough to realize his efforts had failed. Now he'd signed up without any urging from his friend. Ernst would be pleased, but Karl feared Gerhard's reaction, and he already knew what Ingrid's would be. Why hadn't he taken some time to think it over? What would happen to him when Hitler started the war that he so badly craved? Karl had made a promise to himself—he would go to war for his country again if he was needed. But would it be with the SS or the Wehrmacht? Would he be allowed to decide for himself? Of course he would, and of course he would choose the Wehrmacht.

He went to the bar, grabbed a bottle of port, and poured some into a long-stemmed glass. He put the bottle back and sniffed his drink. He swirled his glass in the air, spinning the fluid faster and faster until a hole formed in the liquid at the center of the glass. It fit his mood. He stood now in the middle of a maelstrom that was pulling him in every direction. What until just a few days ago he'd had complete control over was now out of his control. The liquid licked up the edge of the glass, and when some of it landed on the parquet floor, he abruptly stopped rotating the glass. He tried to mop it up with his shoe, but managed only to spread it around more. He looked at the dark stain in despair, then plunked down in one of the two recliners.

What had he been thinking? He rubbed his palms roughly against his face. What had he actually signed up for? Honorary member of the SS. He didn't know what that meant. They had explained it to him, of course, but one could hardly trust the Gestapo or SS to tell the truth. He'd been so busy trying to save Gerhard from the Gestapo that he'd forgotten to save himself.

Hamburg, Germany, June 13, 1939

Gerhard placed a blank piece of paper in the typewriter and spun the roller. Over the course of the last few days, he'd written fifteen or twenty pages; he didn't know the exact number, but now that he'd finally begun his book, he felt a great sense of relief. His ideas fell into categories, connections, and logical conclusions, and the words found their way onto the paper. Earlier, he'd almost given up. At times it had seemed pointless to fight his way through. More than once he'd asked himself whether it was worth the effort, whether he had other books in him, but now his thoughts flowed right onto the paper. The pleasant, rhythmic sound produced by the swing arms of the typewriter as they hammered against the black ribbon and struck the paper had a calming effect on him. He'd purchased his Continental in 1933. It was a handsome tool, with gold letters on the keys, a shiny black chassis, and tabulators that reminded him of a sliding weight scale. On each swing arm sat two letters, one lowercase and one majuscule, and a little bell gave off a tiny ping every time he reached the right margin. As with Pavlov's dogs, his response was conditioned: when the bell rang, he raised his hand and automatically changed lines with the handle fitted for that purpose. His left hand found it without his having to even take his eyes off the paper.

The typewriter symbolized something good, a place he liked to be; when his work was going well, all his thoughts funneled through his fingers and the swing arms to become letters on the white paper, which in turn went on to become complete sentences and paragraphs. His mind felt clear and sharp as his ideas took shape across the page. He hadn't been this energized in months. Which was why he couldn't help but feel irritated when there was a knock on his door. He decided to ignore whoever it was until they gave up and left. He listened, hoping to hear footsteps retreating down the stairwell, but the insistent rapping against his door continued. He recognized the voice at once.

"Guess what I've got?" Karl said, almost before Gerhard had opened the door. Karl waved a sheet of paper as he entered.

"Oh, don't make me guess," Gerhard said as Karl followed him into the kitchen. "Coffee?"

"I'd rather have something stronger." Karl's face glowed like that of an eager boy who'd just witnessed the season's first snowfall. "Guess."

Gerhard rummaged in one of the cupboards and finally found what he was looking for—a bottle of Tullamore D.E.W. In another cupboard he found two stout glasses, which he handed to Karl, who trailed him like a little dog into the living room.

"Come on, take a guess," Karl said, setting the glasses on the dining table.

Gerhard filled the two glasses, then set one on the table for Karl, who was still standing. "Is it Hitler's obituary?" he said at last.

"It's something that'll make you just as happy."

"I'm in no mood for a guessing game," Gerhard said in a tone of voice that made it clear he'd grown impatient. He sat down on a dining room chair.

"What if I told you that you no longer work for the Gestapo thanks to your big brother?"

Gerhard looked at Karl suspiciously. "What have you done?"

"I've pulled you out of shit creek."

"What have you done?"

Karl pulled out a chair and sat down. "Let me tell you." Karl went on to describe his meeting with the Gestapo, then steadied his gaze expectantly on Gerhard. "You don't look pleased."

Gerhard stared unblinkingly at the table. Two or three times he moistened his lips as if to speak, but each time he opened his mouth he changed his mind.

"Coffee?" Gerhard asked again.

Karl shook his head, but Gerhard stood and went into the kitchen, and Karl heard the familiar sound of running water filling a kettle. He laid his hand on the smooth tabletop. His finger located a gouge. The width of the gouge matched that of his pinkie, and it was a good two inches long. It appeared to be a blemish in the wood or a knot that had worked itself out, and it had to be old, because it was the same color as the lacquered oak surrounding it. He ran his finger back and forth through the gouge. There was something comforting about the feel of it—something reassuring about the imperfection, he thought.

Gerhard returned to his seat opposite Karl. His breathing was heavy and labored, and it occurred to Karl that he'd never heard his brother breathe like that. Gerhard had always appeared so self-possessed; he was a master at concealing his emotions. Just then, however, Gerhard looked apprehensive. Gerhard removed his glasses, aggressively polished them, and put them back on only to repeat the motion a moment later.

"Gerhard?" he said in a questioning tone of voice. His brother didn't respond, so he repeated his name.

Finally Gerhard looked up. Karl saw the sadness in his eyes. He noticed that the corners of his brother's eyes were moist and that his upper lip quivered slightly. Gerhard wet his lips. "My SS number is 324.584. I report to Major Walter von Amrath, transport division."

"What are you talking about?"

"We're colleagues now," Gerhard said laconically.

PART TWO

PART TWO

Buenos Aires, Argentina, October 25, 1962

He got off the bus at the Plaza de la República. He blocked the sunlight with his hand and stared up at the tall obelisk in the center of the plaza. He cast a glance over his shoulder and headed up Avenida 9 de Julio. The broad boulevard was overwhelming and loud, and the scale of it frightened him. Nevertheless, he pushed on. The Teatro Colón came into view to his left. A poster announced in large letters that José Neglia was the headliner for that evening's ballet production. The blast of a ship's horn down at the harbor made him think of *Cap Arcona*. If they had all moved to this wonderful city on that great ship before the war, they could have lived without the perpetual nagging of their conscience and the constant, uneasy fear of being tracked down. They could have avoided the war altogether. But they'd stayed put in Germany, and his brother had shot himself. And so he was lonelier than ever.

His job at the German export company was mind numbing, though it occupied only four hours of his day. But time had become an odd thing. Although he was happy to have to work only a few hours each day, he didn't know how to fill the remaining hours.

He turned right and walked down Avenida Santa Fe. A group of schoolchildren blocked the entrance to Plaza San Martín as their teacher, a short woman in her early fifties, made sweeping gestures with her arms to explain the statue at the park's entrance. He studied her and decided that she'd been beautiful once.

He'd barely set one foot into the park before he caught sight of the jacaranda trees, whose flower-covered tops arched over the path like soft pillows. The subtle hue of the pale-violet flowers surprised him anew every spring. Though he'd lived in Argentina for many years, he'd never grown used to the shifting of the seasons. The only thing he lamented was that the beautiful trees didn't have a scent.

A man on a bench studied Gerhard over a copy of the *Buenos Aires Herald*. For a moment Gerhard thought of turning around and heading back the way he'd come. He felt as though he was constantly being watched—at work, in the bank, on the bus, in the square—as if a pair of eyes was resting on him forever and always. Even when he lay in his bed at night, he would search for an observer but could never locate him.

He watched the man slowly fold up his newspaper and stick it under his arm. Gerhard continued walking, but the man remained seated on the bench. Outside the busy Estación Retiro train station, he boarded a bus bound for the Florida district. At the back of the bus, he found an empty seat beside a large woman. The press of her thigh against his made him uncomfortable.

Gerhard got off at his stop; a man was standing there puffing on a pipe. It was a warm day, and his jacket was draped over his arm. He noticed that the man didn't have armpit stains on his white shirt, as he himself did. He guessed him to be around thirty years old, and he didn't look either South American or European.

Gerhard began to walk. Again he sensed he was being watched. When he turned, he saw the man was going in the same direction as he was. Gerhard picked up his pace. Eyes flickering, he glanced about, hoping to find a side street, but he knew the area and was well aware there was no place for him to hide.

It had been many years since he'd tested the limits of his body, and he was surprised that he couldn't move any faster. His pulse raced, and before long he was gasping for breath. His legs seemed stiff and his joints sore, less flexible than they'd once been. He glanced over his shoulder. The man was still there. Sweat dripped from Gerhard, but the man seemed unperturbed by the heat.

In a few hundred yards, he would be home. If he got that far. He would go through the house, into the backyard, and out the little passageway in the back. The man would have to walk all the way around and down the next side street to get to the passageway, so he might be able to get rid of him that way.

A white Ford Consul was parked on the curb, idling. As he passed it, a cigarette butt was tossed on the sidewalk in front of him and the window rolled up. The man was still behind him. Dots appeared in his vision. His body was begging him to stop, but he forced it onward. A stitch formed in his left side.

As he struggled toward his garden gate, he heard a car door slam behind him. He turned around. He could no longer see the man. The white Ford Consul slowly rolled away from the curb. He peered at its windows, but it accelerated with a roar before disappearing down a side street, its tires squealing.

He stood panting on the flagstones leading to his house. He looked down the street, imagining the car careening around the corner on two wheels. He pictured Adolf Eichmann at the gallows, captured in the same city. He'd been hanged in Israel just a few months ago. And now they had come for him! Was it Mossad? Why hadn't they nabbed him? He was a tired old man unable to defend himself. Why hadn't they apprehended him?

Relieved and confused, he put his key in the lock. He retrieved two suitcases from the small space beneath the stairwell and immediately began to pack.

Berlin, Germany, September 6, 1939

Karl sat on the train as it moved toward Berlin. His cheek against the glass, he watched as the train flew past the flat landscape. The fields, the cows, the gardens all appeared unchanged, as though someone had forgotten to tell the people here that the war had begun. He thought of Gerhard and couldn't believe his brother was so naïve. Everyone would be affected by the war; Gerhard wouldn't be able to hide in a transport division. But that's how Gerhard had always been. He lived in his own little world of numbers and books, a world Karl did not understand. Yes, they were bound by blood, but Karl occasionally thought that might be the only thing that connected them, because they often seemed like two strangers. Now they were two strangers heading to war.

Late in August 1939, a few days before the invasion of Poland, Germany had mobilized its reserves, and Karl had been summoned. The conversation with Ingrid that followed had been anything but pleasant. He recalled it almost verbatim. Irritated, he'd asked her if she'd heard him. He knew Ingrid—she would simply pretend she hadn't heard anything she didn't want to hear.

"Supply troops," he repeated.

She nonchalantly asked him when he'd be leaving, and he replied that he needed to report to his division in two weeks. She set a bouquet of roses on the table. There were many colors and varieties in her rose garden, but she'd plucked only yellow flowers that day. She asked him to hand her a vase as if they were talking about something as meaningless as the weather. He remarked on her beautiful bouquet and asked if the flowers were from the garden, immediately aware of how foolish the question sounded.

"Of course they're from the garden. No, the big one." She turned and grabbed the vase off the mahogany countertop behind Karl, who was forced to step aside. She carefully arranged the bouquet and then tilted her head as she assessed her work. She hummed softly as she set the vase of flowers in the middle of the table. Karl followed her into the sunroom, where she began to snip withered leaves from the plants.

"Say something."

"What do you want me to say?" she asked with affected wonder.

"Don't you even want to know where I'm going?"

"You're going to war. It's the same everywhere. So one place is as good as another." She stared out at the lake as she spoke.

"I'm going to Berlin. I'll be home again soon," he said, putting his arms around her shoulders. He kissed her neck. She resisted, not much, but she resisted. "I'll be home soon."

"That's nice. Bring some bread home for coffee, will you?" She pulled away from him and sat in one of the wicker chairs. She picked up the cigarette pack from the table and lit one. She looked past Karl, who sat facing her.

He shook his head despondently. "I don't understand you."

A junior officer met him at the station, and together they rode to the supply depot located outside of the city. The car came to a halt in front of an underground depot; the part of the building visible above ground level was windowless. The driver explained that the enemy's bombers couldn't detect them that way.

Karl was stationed at the supply depot outside Berlin during the invasion of Poland. Daily life there was monotonous, and the glaring light of the ceiling lamps made people either crazy or depressed. The work reminded Karl of all the boring administrative assignments at the factory that he had always pawned off to Müller. In his absence Müller had assumed responsibility for day-to-day operations, so Karl knew the factory was in good hands. His honorary membership in the SS hadn't demanded much of his time—he'd gotten a few invitations, shaken some hands, and toasted with some smiling faces—but the SS had tripled its orders with Strangl Clothing Factory as a result.

Soon he began to long for a spot closer to the war, if not on the front line. After Christmas—what was now called War Christmas—he applied for a transfer, and in February 1940 he became part of the Seventh Panzer Division's supply troops. That same month the division got a new commander. His name was Erwin Rommel.

His decision to transfer didn't sit well with Ingrid. Karl's division entered Belgium on May 10, 1940, with General Hermann Hoth's Fifteenth Army Corps. On May 13 they crossed the Meuse River, on May 18 they occupied the northern French city of Cambrai, and on June 10 Rommel reported back to headquarters that the division had reached the English Channel west of Dieppe.

On June 22 a French delegation signed a ceasefire agreement in the Forest of Compiègne. The Seventh Panzer Division was then ordered to Paris, where they were to prepare for Operation Sea Lion, the invasion of England. Herman Göring's Luftwaffe was, however, unable to dominate the airspace above the English Channel, and the operation was called off. The division experienced a peaceful interlude after that, functioning as an occupational force in the Paris suburb of Saint-Germain-des-Prés, where the German army had established its headquarters. The division was transferred later that winter to the Bordeaux region, where the ungodly cold of the capital was replaced with more hospitable southerly skies.

Although most of the men missed the city and its many jazz clubs, variety shows, champagne, and beautiful women, Karl preferred Bordeaux. In Paris food had been a necessary evil, but in Bordeaux they enjoyed an abundance of wine, cheese, bread, and sausages. Before long he was introduced to a sweet white wine that put him in a state of culinary ecstasy when it was accompanied with dry cheese—and then of course there was the red wine. Fields in all directions were packed with row upon row of bare grapevines; people in this region didn't waste their fertile soil on cattle or pig farming. Instead, they ate fish and poultry and duck. He often went to the market in the little fishing village of Blaye-et-Sainte-Luce north of Bordeaux to purchase vegetables, fish, cheese, ham, and sausages for the company cook to prepare. Karl enjoyed his time in western France, where he ate and slept well; the only thing that was missing was his family.

Bad Godesberg, Germany, April 6, 1941

Karl kicked a stone into the river. It flew in an arc and skipped once on the water's surface before sinking without a sound. The Rhine, the old border of the Roman Empire, was as calm as the Elbe. It flowed quietly past as if trying to avoid discovery. Rivers had an untroubled quality about them, as if time wasn't a part of their reality, as if the water stood still and instead the world around it was flowing past. In the water he saw the reflection of the gentle mountains on the opposite shore. His cigarette sizzled briefly when it struck the water, erasing the reflection. A filthy cargo ship carrying short stacks of coal floated silently upriver. A man in a wool cap was painting the rust-red stern as the ship sliced slowly through the water. The makeshift scaffold fastened to the hull had room for only the man and a bucket of paint. Dangling his legs like a playful child, he slowly coated the ship with black paint. At the other end of the ship, the wheelhouse rose like a watchful prairie dog, and a bald man—wearing tight suspenders that appeared to hold his belly in place—stood in the doorway gazing absently toward land. He rapped his pipe against the rail and disappeared into the wheelhouse.

A ray of sunlight cracked the dense cloud cover. The air was warm, and Karl was happy they were approaching winter's end.

A bird trilled in a tree by the roadside, and he tried to locate it. But he soon gave up and turned his attention back to the river. He felt a keen desire to shuck off his uniform and leap into the clear water, which looked particularly enticing in the sunlight. He recalled the legend of Lorelei from his school days. A young woman, it was said, threw herself off the cliff in despair because her beloved had been unfaithful. She'd been luring seamen toward the cliffs ever since, ensnaring them with her beauty and her voice as she brushed her long, golden hair, and causing countless shipwrecks.

He heard a Zarah Leander song, as alluring as Lorelei's, and turned and glanced up at Hotel Dreesen. Paul Piroska had dragged a portable gramophone onto one of the balconies and was waving down at him. Four soldiers sat playing cards at a folding table on the rocky riverbank. Coins clinked, and one of the players, a man with a low forehead and a Frankfurt accent, hurled obnoxious expletives. Karl recognized the man beside him, or at least knew who he was. Everyone knew who he was—even before he'd been reassigned to the division. Lieutenant Alfred Wasner had wound up in the hospital in Paris with two bullets from a prostitute's .22, one in his derriere and the other in his femoral artery, which had nearly taken the horny young man's life. Only a quick intervention by one of the regiment's doctors had saved him. When Karl heard the story from Piroska, he'd wondered why the doctor was there at the brothel, but that was never explained.

All the men around the table were from the panzer divisions and had that all-or-nothing attitude characteristic of the tank commandos and their men. Some were braggarts who didn't view the supply troops as real soldiers, least of all Karl, who was an old man compared with the others. Other men his age were majors, generals, and the like—but what did he have to prove? It didn't seem to matter that he'd won medals for his fighting in the last war—they had no respect for him. Until he'd been called up, Karl had harbored a romantic dream that he was still an eighteen-year-old soldier who could march sunup to sundown. He'd since realized that he was an old-timer; his legs were sore, his back ached, and his entire body hurt. And then there were his hands, but only he knew about that. They had no use for old men like him on the front line.

In February 1941 the Seventh Panzer Division had been transferred to Bad Godesberg on the Rhine, where they were to await further instructions. Erwin Rommel was called to Berlin, where he was appointed commander of the German Africa Corps. A general major with an impossibly long name—Hans Emil Richard Freiherr von Funck—assumed responsibility for the Ghost Division. The very opposite of Rommel, von Funck hailed from an old Prussian military school where battles were led at a command station a safe distance from the fighting and not, as Rommel had, from the front line.

The division had been built so that it operated almost like a living organism. Everything was controlled at the division headquarters by the top officers, with General Major von Funck as commanding officer. The division's top supply officer was Major Helmut Strunz, an upstanding man from Duisburg who, like Karl, had fought in northern France during the Great War. The supply service consisted of six smaller truck companies—also called "columns"—and three large companies that transported fuel. Karl had been promoted twice and now commanded one of the latter fuel companies.

The column was made up of more than sixty men and twenty-six vehicles. Twenty trucks for transporting gasoline—divided into four groups—two trucks for transporting other materiel, a small personnel carrier, and three motorcycles. Each of the group's five trucks had a driver and a soldier armed with a carbine. The unit also had a medical officer, a cook, kitchen assistants, staff to distribute gasoline to the panzer regiments, and personnel from the transport division to convey the column's weapons, supplies, reserve parts, and more.

Sergeant Major Paul Piroska was the supply column's second in command, and he quickly became indispensable to Karl, who viewed him as the military counterpart to Hans Müller. Administrative work bored Karl—numbers, numbers, numbers, trucks, trucks, trucks, everything on wheels—but Piroska threw himself into every assignment with an enviable eagerness. It was his job to ensure that everything functioned properly, and that's what he did. Piroska was a plainspoken, jovial man of twenty-eight, with a long, pronounced face that culminated in a strong jaw beneath a large, broad nose and smiling, narrow-lipped mouth. He tried combing back his hair, but his thick brown curls couldn't be tamed with pomade or brilliantine or Brylcreem. Although he was small of stature and build, his face gave him a commanding presence. He had a master's in law from Ludwig Maximilian University in Munich. On the day after his final exam in 1937, Paul had packed his suitcase and bought a return ticket to Passau. His birth city and a girl by the name of Liesel were tugging at him, but his hatred of Munich also played a role. According to Paul, the city of Munich buzzed with evil. The Nazis were in charge, and if you didn't say "heil Hitler" with the appropriate conviction in your voice, it was a dangerous place to live. For a lawyer who didn't work for the party, Munich was not the best place to be.

He and Liesel were married in 1939, the same year as Hilde and Heinz, and Karl often regretted that his elder daughter hadn't found a man like Paul. He took solace in the fact that Heinz was in Poland now. He'd joined the SS and belonged to some kind of special deployment group. Karl didn't know what those task forces did; truth be told, he didn't care.

Karl threw a few more stones into the Rhine. Then he walked down to the parking lot in front of the hotel, where four officers stood hunched over an ordnance survey map spread across the hood of a Kfz 15 half-track. A leather satchel hung from one of the car's side mirrors. He recognized von Funck with his small, proper mustache. The commander had a long, narrow face and alert brown eyes, and when he saw Karl he waved him over.

Karl had exchanged only a few words with the general major, but he had a positive impression of the division's commanding officer. The ambitious Colonel Ernst-Werner Sonntag, chief of the infantry regiment, and Major Hans Beyerlein, who was the division's operations officer, were standing with von Funck, along with Strunz, the division's head supply officer.

"So, Strangl, do you have your troops under control?" Strunz said, giving him a friendly pat on his shoulder. Sonntag was focused on the general major and didn't pay Karl any heed.

"Of course." Karl could still hear the music from Piroska's portable gramophone. Thank god the other officers couldn't see his unshaven second in command, who was at that moment waltzing around the balcony with an imaginary dance partner, his belly exposed beneath his unbuttoned shirt.

When the men turned back to the map, Karl noticed that it showed a section of northeastern Poland and East Prussia. Von Funck pointed to a city in East Prussia and explained that Colonel Rothenburg, the head of the Twenty-Fifth Panzer Division, was there with his regiment. He pointed at a neighboring city.

"And this is where we'll join them: Insterburg."

Von Funck briefly outlined the situation to the cluster of men. Over the course of the coming days, the divisions' vehicles, materiel, and troops would be loaded onto trains and travel across Germany and Poland. He imagined the men would be eager, after a few weeks' idleness, to get back to it, and a huge assignment awaited them there. The general major went off to put the final touches on the practical arrangements with his staff officers. Strunz remained behind with Karl.

"We'll be busy, Strangl," Strunz said, offering Karl a cigarette.

"So it's Russia, then."

"Yes, it's Russia."

Near Minsk, White Russia, June 28, 1941

A flickering candle cast restless shadows on the wall. The only light in the church entered through the large vaulted window behind the altar. The sun was setting, and through the window's frosted glass Karl could see the city engulfed in flames.

His pen had been resting on the paper for some time. He'd been unable to write a single word. He had much to tell, but his hand wouldn't cooperate. His arthritis had begun tormenting him at night. It bothered him a lot these days. Maybe it had something to do with the climate. In exactly one month he would turn forty-three, but his hands were already those of a dotard. He thought of Dr. Strauss and rubbed his fingers. The doctor had been right, unfortunately; he was having difficulty grasping things. Fortunately it didn't happen often, but one of these days Paul Piroska or one of the others would notice. He stubbornly pried open his fingers' viselike grip with his other hand, and his pen fell from his hand. He picked it up and began to write.

> *Dear Gerhard,*
> *I'm sitting in a small village in White Russia about nine miles from the capital city of Minsk. From where I'm sitting I can see Minsk burning, and I don't know whether it's the evening sun or the flames from the city that's giving the sky its fantastic glow. It's burning because of us. I don't know what you've heard back home in Germany, but on June 22 we launched Operation Barbarossa. I won't bore you with too many military details, so I'll keep this short: we are divided into three army groups. Army Group North is heading toward Leningrad. Army Group Center, of which I'm part, is going toward Moscow, and*

Army Group South is bound for Odessa, the Crimea, and the oil regions in the Caucasus. We expect to capture Moscow before Christmas. Russia will be ours, and the war will be over.

White Russia reminds me of Hamburg and its environs; it's completely flat here. There are potato fields and forests of spruce, pine, and birch; there are narrow rivers, lakes, and peat bogs. Some people are glad to see us, and many in the small towns along the route welcome us with flowers and smiles. They are apparently happy to be rid of the Russians. When the invasion began, our men were in high spirits, but the journey through White Russia has drained the joy out of many. We rode through a cabinet of horrors: corpses, dead cows, and flames. It appears the army is leaving a trail of fire, death, and destruction in its wake. We saw great columns of people heading in the opposite direction, away from the front, bearing all their possessions. The luckiest among them have carts, but the rest carry whatever they can in their arms. There are old men with long white beards, girls with scarves around their heads, and mothers and children. Those people don't give us flowers because we've destroyed their homes. We've been sequestered in a village. "Sequestered" may be the wrong word because the residents have been kicked out of their homes and our division has moved in. We sleep in the church. Despite the horrors, we sleep well and eat well. I have full faith in my men, and I hope that they have faith in me. I miss Hamburg, and I miss you. I hear that the English are bombing Hamburg, but I understand that everyone is doing all right. When this war is over, I hope that men like you and I can look ourselves in the eye and tell ourselves that we didn't abet the evil

that goes hand in hand with the war. I advise you to
do whatever you can to remain in Germany because the
front is no place for you. I have . . .

The pain in his hand caused him to drop the pen. He grimaced and turned to see if anyone had seen. Most of the men lay on the wooden pews; others sat or sprawled on the church's stone floor. He couldn't bring himself to evict families from their homes, so he'd lodged the men from his transport column in the church. The only hurdle had been an argument with the priest.

He looked at his hand, the damned cripple. Suppressing a sigh, he balled up the paper with his other hand. He tilted his head back to study the paintings on the ceiling. Frescoes on the whitewashed vaults depicted winged figures with golden halos and childlike angels floating in the air. The winged creatures surrounded three figures, which he had trouble distinguishing in the murky light. He presumed they were Jesus, the Virgin Mary, and John the Baptist.

He stood and walked down the hallway past the arms depot, then out through the heavy double doors. The church, a crudely built structure of wood and stone, sat on a hill from which he could see all of Minsk. Karl's eyes roamed up the tower to the onion-shaped dome topped with a cross that stretched toward the sky.

He saw a figure approaching. The priest, a bulky man in a black cowl, had remained nearby, but when he saw Karl, he turned and darted around the other side of the building. He evidently refused to let the church out of his sight. Karl wanted to offer him one of the benches in the arms depot to sleep on, since he'd no doubt planned to spend the night tucked into one of the church's outer walls.

The village at the foot of the hill looked no different than any of the others he'd seen in recent days. Squat wooden houses hedged in by flimsy picket fences lined a broad, dusty path. Piroska sauntered up the hill, a triumphant smile on his narrow lips. His face was sunburned, and his brown hair had grown lighter, either from the sunlight or the dusty Belarusian roads. He handed his canteen to Karl, who sniffed it.

"Honey?"

"Taste it," Paul said eagerly. "It's a kind of beer. An old man gave it to me."

Karl took a gulp and handed the bottle back to Paul, who nodded toward Minsk.

"Was that really necessary?"

"What?" Karl asked.

"Bombing the city to smithereens. They welcomed us." He held up the canteen. "If we destroy everything they have, they'll stop giving us mead."

"Yeah, well. What we destroy in Minsk won't be used to defend Moscow." Karl recognized the hollowness in his words; he'd only repeated what Colonel Sonntag had said that afternoon.

Paul gave a tired nod. The sun would soon sink below the ridge. Karl tore himself from the view and headed back toward the church. He turned briefly to study Paul, who seemed to be enjoying the sunset and his mead in equal measure.

Most of the men were asleep. He unfurled his blanket on one of the pews and shoved his boots underneath. He lay down in his uniform. He could just make out, through the window, the flickering lights from the city. He closed his eyes and recalled the day's events. There was the prison camp they'd come upon and the three men they'd lost. They'd kept a good distance from the action all day, and still Johan Phliegel and two drivers were dead. They'd stopped in Maladzyechna, a midsized city between Vilnius and Minsk, and Phliegel had noticed an unexploded artillery warhead, its tip lodged into the ground on the public square. Being one of the regiment's photographers, he'd taken numerous snapshots of the two drivers posing with the dud bomb—which was as tall as a man—until one of the men foolishly leaned against it. In the resulting crater they found only the legs of the camera tripod and a boot.

When Piroska awoke Karl the next morning, his back was sore from the hard pew. Karl stretched and looked sleepily at his next in command, who was awaiting his orders.

"Find out when they want us ready to march," Karl said, more brusquely than he'd intended.

"Yes, sir. I wonder if it'll be a short journey?"

"We're going only as far as Minsk today," Karl said as he put on his boots. He didn't need to lean forward very far before the unpleasant stench of his socks reached his nose.

An hour later, the supply column was ready to go. All the trucks were parked at the bottom of the hill, and Karl climbed into the lead vehicle, an Opel Blitz. A former state champion in light heavyweight boxing who now weighed a little more than was allowed in that class, Dirk Bongartz was a seasoned driver who'd been with them in Poland, Holland, Belgium, and France. He was known for his good-natured disposition and his crooked nose, the result of several breaks during his boxing career. He didn't talk all that much, but at least he didn't whistle. In Belgium and France, Karl's driver had been a skillful man by the name of Günter Quast. Everyone called him Tuneless because he always whistled snatches of random tunes, assembling an unbearable confusion of medleys that drove the men—and especially Karl, who rode with him—mad.

Bongartz turned the key in the ignition, and the engine sputtered to life. Karl signaled to the other vehicles that they were ready. The dispatch rider, who was so filthy that Karl almost couldn't tell the color of his uniform through the thick layer of dust, slowly pulled his motorcycle alongside the truck. As Bongartz put the vehicle in gear, Karl took one last look at the church's onion-shaped tower.

"Stop!" he screamed.

He jerked open his door and practically fell out of the cab when the vehicle behind them rammed their truck. He righted himself and sprinted up the hill. The arms depot was ablaze, and the fire had already begun spreading to the church. A soldier stood a little ways off, a gasoline can in his hand.

Karl ran over to him. "What the hell are you doing?" he yelled, tearing the can out of the alarmed soldier's hand.

"Orders from Colonel Sonntag," the soldier said apologetically as he took a couple of steps backward, terrified of Karl's incensed expression. Karl gazed down at the town, where several of the wooden houses were engulfed in flames.

"Did that fool ever consider that we might have to return someday?"

"The colonel doesn't believe in retreat."

Karl snorted. He had a hard time believing that a colonel could give such an ill-advised order. But he knew the reason. The motorized infantry had followed the panzer troops during the past few weeks, and now that they'd caught up to them, they wanted to show their balls.

He ran back to the trucks. Paul, who stood with a group of men watching the fire, rushed toward him.

"Didn't someone borrow Johan's reserve camera?" Karl asked, out of breath.

"Yes, Remmel did."

"Tell him to take pictures of the town. Sonntag's not getting away with this."

Twenty minutes later, medical officer Thomas Remmel was done, and the column trundled off toward Minsk. A dispatch rider had marked a path for them to follow by planting small flags on the edge of the road with the division's logo, a yellow *Y*. The air was stagnant, and it looked like it was going to be another hot summer day. They were so close now that they could smell the dense smoke that hung above Minsk like a storm cloud. Parts of the city had been reduced to smoking ruins, and their eyes stung as they approached; in spite of the heat everyone rolled up their windows. It was a paradox: German soldiers running through the streets putting out fires their own bombs and artillery had started.

After four days in Minsk Karl's company was given orders to leave the city and follow the combat troops, who were already on their way to Vitebsk. So the column quit the vast area that had been established only days before as the army's supply depot, laden with full twenty-liter gasoline cans. As they drove down a broad boulevard, Karl noticed that painters had begun camouflaging a number of buildings so that they would be harder to spot from the air. He figured that was probably where they'd house high-ranking officers, or perhaps those houses had been selected for the different departmental headquarters of the Wehrmacht, Gestapo, SD, SS, Abwehr, and whatever else might be there.

The central train station was teeming with people. Securing the railroad was a high priority since many supplies came directly from factories and warehouses in Germany and were then transported as far as possible on freight trains. Minsk would serve as a supply hub. Everyone in the supply troops liked the statistic that for every man in the battlefield, three more were necessary to outfit him, deliver food, secure lodging, and so on. It made them feel important, and their vital role was most apparent at the station. Supply troops were loading ammunition and other equipment onto trucks, which then drove to and from the loading docks. Somehow the military police managed to maintain order amid this logistical chaos. A band of bakers stacked loaves of bread by the hundreds, which were then loaded onto a trailer hooked to a Hanomag tractor. A pile of mail formed a small mountain on a sidewalk, and several men—with bare torsos and oval-shaped dog tags dangling from their necks—were busy sorting envelopes. Affectionate words from home, photographs of newborn sons and daughters, sad reports of a brother's passing in a U-boat at the bottom of the sea, and news of a cow that had calved were all jammed into pale-yellow envelopes. Letters often felt like moral support from home, making life at the front more bearable. Not that they needed moral support—they'd begun to feel indestructible following victories in Poland, the western front, northern Africa, and the eastern front—but letters and packages from Germany nonetheless energized the soldiers.

The column continued on past a modern government building. The courtyard in front was thick with vehicles. The apartment buildings across the street from it had been reduced to ash and mangled iron, but the government building was undamaged, and a giant hammer and sickle rested on top of the façade, mocking the German conquerors. But he knew it wouldn't be long before it, too, would be wrapped in a Nazi flag and then melted down.

As they drove across the Svislach River, he studied the opera house, a singular, pompous affair that emphasized the immense contrast between the capital's architecture and that of the villages. They were nearly beyond the city limits when something caught their attention. At the edge of a lush green park speckled with oak trees with broad crowns and gnarled trunks, a group of soldiers stood assembled around a fat officer. But it wasn't the cigarette-smoking soldiers who attracted Karl's notice—it was the spectacle behind them. A man was tied to a light pole, his head hanging at an awkward angle and a gaping hole in his chest. Behind him on the park lawn lay three tidy rows of ten corpses, all of whom had met a similar fate by the firing squad, who were now enjoying a cup of coffee as if they were having a picnic. *Give us Germans credit about one thing,* Karl thought with disgust: *Even our executions are committed in an orderly fashion.* His stomach lurched, and he felt a sudden urge to vomit. He tried to stifle the overwhelming nausea, but it didn't abate until an hour later.

On July 10 the defense of Vitebsk collapsed following a week of intense fighting. The Russians set everything ablaze as they fled the city so that the Germans couldn't make use of their new conquest. A dismal pile of ruins greeted the advancing army. One of Karl's men said they might as well remove the sign at the city limits, because Vitebsk no longer existed. Smolensk was no different. Its factories had been destroyed and the entire residential district leveled. The occasional chimney or church spire protruding here and there were the only reminders that a city had once stood there.

The Russian soldiers—the very ones who had just annihilated their own homes—marched past them by the thousands, their heads low. In their mismatched and filthy uniforms, they didn't look like an army at all. The Germans were just 250 miles from Moscow now, and judging by the endless columns of prisoners, there were no soldiers left to defend the capital.

Hamburg, Germany, August 28, 1941

Gerhard awoke with a dry mouth and a lump in his throat. Even before he'd opened his eyes, his head and body were resigned to the sad anniversary. His limbs were drained of energy, his appetite nonexistent. He pulled the duvet over his head and considered staying home. It was a day he'd rather forget.

His entire life replayed in his mind as he lay there. He and Emma had been trying to have a child for a long time, and in 1927 she finally became pregnant. They had it all planned: they would name the baby Thomas if it was a boy and Laura if it was a girl. The nursery had been ready for two years, but it was Laura who brought it to life. She had been the light switch that illuminated the room and brought the colors, sounds, and smells to life. His relationship with Emma had suffered as they'd struggled to conceive, but now it blossomed—they were capable of creating life, of creating joy. But then they discovered that they could also create sorrow.

Losing a child was indescribable. The doctors said there was something wrong with Laura's heart, and Laura was taken from them in one devastating blow. When she died, it was as if all the world's evil came together and wedged itself between them. There was nothing they could have done. Their powerlessness led to tears, and when they were out of tears, it was replaced by emptiness and then an oppressive grief that would never go away. Grief consumed them like a corrosive liquid. Their family tried to console them, saying things like "there must be a reason," "you can still have other children," and "life goes on." But to lose Laura was to lose Laura forever. The feeling would never go away; it was a feeling without beginning or end. They didn't lose just Laura; they lost a large part of themselves. They'd had her for only five months and nine days, but they would never be the same.

Afterward, they tried to hold onto the fragments of their life, but the pieces were brittle and kept splintering in their hands. They struggled, and they struggled, and in the end they struggled against each other, and their grief became a protracted fight that only ended with more loss.

Today marked precisely ten years since Emma's death. The prospect of spending the entire day alone in his own company forced Gerhard out of bed. He dressed slowly, not caring that he was putting on the same clothes he'd worn the day before.

Karl had forgotten the day's significance, but Ingrid had called the night before to invite Gerhard to dinner. He'd declined. He regretted it as soon as he hung up, but he was too proud to call back.

He dragged himself to work. Pedaling was difficult, and the bicycle seemed heavier than ever. He'd hoped to make the day feel like any other by going in to work, but he couldn't suppress his memories. They eventually turned into stomach cramps, so he went home and vomited, and spent the rest of the day lying in bed staring at the ceiling. The next day he got up and went back to work.

In August 1939, Senior Squad Leader Gerhard Strangl had begun his work in the transport division under SS Major Dr. Walter von Amrath. His escape from the Gestapo was short-lived, since his department underwent a massive restructuring just a month later. The transport division was assigned to Branch IV in the new Reich Main Security

Office, and Heinrich Müller became the head of Branch IV—also called the Gestapo.

The department was located in a three-story whitewashed building in Mittelweg. Built at the turn of the century in the art nouveau style, with ornate cornices on each story where doves liked to sit cooing all day, the property had once housed a Jewish law practice, but the owners had immigrated to the United States, so the SS had acquired the building cheaply. Gerhard knew perfectly well that "cheaply" meant "confiscated."

He'd been in the division for two years now, and the work wasn't the least bit taxing. It consisted of making logistical calculations, which came down to calculating space in cubic feet. X needs to be moved from A to B, and there can be Z number X in each Y. X was materiel, food, and sometimes troops. He was rarely tired when he sat down at his typewriter every afternoon. He had a lot of time to work on his book, and the stack of pages next to the black Continental grew daily. Soon he'd be done with his first draft, and then he'd begin revising it. He'd once gotten his best ideas down at the harbor—the entire skeleton of the book had come to him there—but the harbor had lost its appeal.

Gerhard shared his first-floor office with Norbert Seitz-Göppersdorf and Friedrich Olmo. Seitz-Göppersdorf's and Olmo's desks were shoved together in the center of the room, so the two men sat facing each other. Gerhard's desk extended out from theirs.

A portrait of Hitler hung at one end of the high-ceilinged room. His face was turned to the right, but his eyes gazed to the left, and his expression was stern. His hair was perfectly parted; his mustache emphasized the width of his nose. The Iron Cross Second Class—which he'd been awarded in the Great War—hung from his chest pocket. A dark-brown leather strap stretched across his chest. The portrait was positioned so that Gerhard couldn't help but see it every time he glanced up.

The same serious expression met Gerhard whenever he rotated his head to the left, where Norbert Seitz-Göppersdorf sat; with his slightly awkward and stiff mannerisms, he always seemed uncomfortable in the company of others. He was a withdrawn man with a narrow face that lacked any distinctive features, and his personality was just as complicated as the pronunciation of his unwieldy name. Gerhard knew nothing about him but assumed he was around thirty. He'd already begun to lose his blond hair, and his scalp was visible through the locks that remained. Every morning he sat down in his chair, then meticulously scooted it forward, gripping his seat with both hands. He would place his brown leather briefcase on the desk and open it with a metallic click, then remove the fountain pen that he always placed on the right side of his left shirt pocket. He would rake his thinning hair with a wide-tooth comb and clasp his hands, which revealed no discernable evidence that he'd ever committed himself in marriage to a woman. Gerhard wondered if he prayed. He wasn't sure what Seitz-Göppersdorf had done before this, nor did he want to know.

Olmo, on Gerhard's right, was Norbert's opposite. He was, like von Amrath, quick to smile and put others in a good mood just by his presence. Gerhard had known him at the university, where he'd been part of the science faculty. If he ignored Norbert's chronic bad mood, the division's atmosphere was pleasant. Walter von Amrath had been a transport officer in the Great War, which was why he'd gotten the job as commanding officer; it was fine by him since, as he said, "We won't get any blood on our hands here." Gerhard and von Amrath got along well. They often dined together and regularly discussed literature, philosophy, and food, among many other things. They deftly avoided any reference to the political situation in the country, and only rarely did they speak of the war.

Gerhard sat with his hands in his lap, staring out the window as Olmo entertained Miss Reinfeld with stories about his offspring. When the secretary forcefully jerked up the window to frighten the doves off the cornice, he was startled.

"Their nonstop cooing is making me crazy."

"Do you mean the men?" Olmo asked with a boyish smile.

Ms. Reinfeld was laughing as she exited the office. Olmo had told them about his youngest daughter, Martha, who'd just started walking. It always pained Gerhard to hear about other people's children, and it was unfortunate that Olmo liked to talk about his a great deal.

Just then von Amrath thrust open the door and rushed into the room. His face was beet red and he was panting. All three men turned in alarm toward their superior, who stood in the doorway gasping for breath.

"The Jews," he wheezed. "Goddamn it, they've unloaded the Jews on us." A small, fine splatter of spit arced from his lips and landed on the floor.

Stunned, they stared at their boss, who'd never been so out of sorts. Norbert always looked distressed, but that distress had intensified and his eyes were wider than ever. Gerhard's thoughts raced, but he couldn't grasp a single one: they whizzed past like a train, and his eyes flickered as he tried to focus. Olmo gathered his wits first. He stood, gently took von Amrath by the arm, and helped him into an empty chair by the desk. He poured a cup of ersatz coffee and placed it beside von Amrath.

Gerhard thought of Aaron and Hannah. He'd stopped hearing his Jewish neighbors upstairs a while back, and Jakob and Rachel hadn't knocked on his door in a long time. Then one day, he suddenly heard footsteps and the scrape of chairs in the apartment once again. He went upstairs to say hello. He wanted to show the family that he didn't consider them animals—an appellation that had become popular— and he'd purchased a bouquet of yellow and orange gerbera daisies for Hannah, her favorite. But an overweight woman he'd never seen before opened the door. A short, balding man with a mustache appeared behind her with two plump children. Gerhard handed the woman the bouquet without a word; then he nearly stumbled down the stairwell in his eagerness to return to his apartment.

Von Amrath stared absentmindedly at the coffee cup on the desk. "This wasn't part of the deal," he said to himself. "This wasn't part of the deal."

Gerhard, who'd recovered by now, got Olmo's attention. The other man understood immediately and pulled out a bottle of French cognac from a desk drawer. Gerhard got four glasses from the cabinet behind him, then set out one for each of them. Seitz-Göppersdorf, who hadn't said a word since von Amrath entered the office, gazed at the others, a terrified look on his face. Olmo, however, remained calm, and his hands did not even tremble as he poured the cognac.

Von Amrath explained—in a disjointed and confusing way—that their department was to assume practical arrangements like ordering trains and materiel, and then, together with the German Reich Railways, organize route planning so that the transports wouldn't get in the way of troop transfers and other freight traffic. "We'll begin moving them in six to eight weeks. I don't know where we're supposed to begin or what we're supposed to do with them."

"Move them? Where?" Olmo asked.

"Away, out of the country, to the east," von Amrath said shrilly, making a sweeping gesture with his hand.

"But Walter, we can't possibly do that," Olmo said. "How in the world are we supposed to move all the city's Jews? And why?"

He got no answer.

Kiev, Ukraine, September 19, 1941

He ran. His legs trembled, and he wouldn't be able to run much farther. But he had to go on. His lungs were about to explode. *Don't panic, August,* he kept telling himself. His growing despair made his head feel warm. Where were the others? Loud and insistent, his fear and a ringing in his ears drowned out all thought.

He stepped on a brick, and his foot slipped. He saw the wall just as his shoulder struck it with great force. He fell to the ground and remained there. He closed his eyes and tried to suppress the pain, but it was impossible. He listened for sounds around him but could hear nothing but his own heavy breathing.

He raised his head cautiously. He'd dropped his weapon when he fell, and it lay in front of him. He tried to reach the strap with his right hand, but it hurt, so he got it with his left. As quietly as possible, he dragged it over the cobblestones, the sand, and the dust. He glanced around. There was a small shed about fifteen feet away that appeared to be undamaged. Behind it were the remains of an apartment building that had been reduced to a few fragile-looking walls and a heap of rubble. All the windows were missing, and the frames reminded him of empty eye sockets. He crawled cautiously toward the small wooden building. The door was unlocked. He squatted inside the small room, which was no more than six by nine feet.

He tried to spit. His mouth was full of sand and blood, and a trail of blood ran down his cheek. He tried to locate where it was coming from, but the sand made it difficult to tell. When he rinsed his mouth with water from his field canteen, his tongue found the explanation: a large wound in his cheek. He must've bitten himself when he fell.

When August's eyes had acclimated to the semidarkness, he examined his hand; sand and pebbles were pressed deep into his palm, and he brushed them off to reveal an abrasion. Blood issued from the tiny scratches—which looked as though they'd been made with the fine blades of a grater. Now he noticed the smell of a latrine.

He was eighteen years old, and he'd become an adult today. Yesterday he had still been an untested soldier who'd yet to face his first battle. Now he didn't quite know what he was—and even *whether* he was. Every illusion he'd ever had about heroes and bravery had been eclipsed by the ugliness he'd witnessed over the last few hours.

The Germans' strategy had been to drive the Russians out of Kiev, so they could fight them in the open. August's regiment had been sent to eliminate the few remaining pockets of Russian troops in the city. But when he saw Peter Christian's head explode, he forgot everything he'd learned about military tactics and advancing techniques. In his panic he'd lost track of his platoon. The lieutenant had probably already added his name to the list of dead. Right below Peter Christian's.

He heard fighting, the pop of handguns. It was coming from a few streets over, but he could see nothing through the narrow slit between two boards. He couldn't stand not being able to see what was happening. He had learned how gruesome sound can be, and also that you can vomit without making a sound. More than once he emptied the contents of his stomach onto the floor of the little shed, the stink merging with the smell of shit.

For a brief moment the gunfire ceased. He heard shouts in Russian and then the gunfire began anew. A figure turned onto the street. He carried a rifle or a submachine gun in his hand and had the sun at his back, but August immediately recognized the contours of the heavy Russian helmet. He swallowed a lump in his throat.

The Russian looked frightened and was glancing uneasily from side to side. He was walking toward the shed, now around eighty feet away. August cocked his Mauser and tried easing the cartridge into the chamber as quietly as possible. Only fifty feet separated them now. The soldier stared directly at the shed, reminding August of a bloodhound that's caught a scent. The fleeting glances had been replaced by an intense gaze, as if he hoped to see through the boards. Thirty feet now. August held his breath. The Russian's footfalls grew cautious, and fear returned to his eyes. He appeared to be the same age as August. The soldier paused, slowly raised his weapon and pressed it against his cheek, then took another step forward. August would have to shoot first. He wouldn't wait until the door opened; he would fire the magazine's five cartridges straight through the door. He squeezed the trigger of his rifle halfway down. Then another soldier appeared and waved at his friend. The soldier seemed relieved, and he turned and ran after the other man, following him down an alley. The street was empty, and August vomited again.

He had to find his platoon, and soon. But which way should he run? If he remained where he was and his comrades were forced back, he would be cut off from them. He found a canister of Scho-ka-kola in his satchel and wolfed down a few chunks of the caffeine-rich chocolate that they'd been given before the operation commenced. The chocolate would give him the boost of energy he would need to make the sprint he sure as hell wasn't looking forward to. In his pocket he found the little brass compass and opened it. When they'd crossed the broad boulevard with the trolley tracks, his platoon had had the sun at their backs, but the Russian had the sun at his back just now. He tried to recall their route through the city. He heard gunfire and explosions in the area, which must mean that there were Germans nearby. He would count to ten, then run. But when he reached ten, he didn't move. He tried again, but he couldn't do it that time, either. A pain shot through his shoulder, and he vomited again. And then he ran.

There was no one in the street. He ran to the wall he'd bumped into earlier and followed it until he made it to the side street that the Russian and his comrade had gone down. He continued running, cocking his ear for the sound of battle. At the next side street, he spotted a few Russian soldiers heading in the same direction as he. He squeezed himself against the wall and tried to muster the courage to continue.

He got his legs moving again, albeit reluctantly. As he got closer to the crossfire, he halted, trying to peer down the street while staying invisible. There was no one. The body of a Russian soldier lay curled up a few feet away, his wide-open eyes staring directly at August. A bullet had pierced his cheek. Suddenly the man's chest heaved. His mouth parted slightly, and a bubble of blood emerged. When the bubble burst, the body emitted a lengthy sigh. A bullet whistled past August, boring into the wall beside him and loosening a chunk of mortar. The shot had come from behind him, and he instinctively turned to find the sniper. A figure, half-concealed behind a street corner, was taking aim. August ducked as another bullet penetrated the wall right above his head. Left? Right? He ran to the left.

He sprinted as fast as he could with all his equipment as shots were fired both in front and behind him. He had only one hope: that the shots fired ahead of him were from German weapons. He thought he recognized the pop of German carbines, Schmeissers, and MG 34s, but he wasn't sure. It was all happening so fast. Maybe he would be out of harm's way in a few moments—or maybe his war would be over. His life, too, for that matter. Suddenly he pictured himself at that moment and saw something comical about his situation: a German soldier running at full speed, unsure whether he was running toward or away from the enemy. He felt cumbersome, heavy, slow and wished he'd inherited his father's agility. This wasn't how he'd imagined his first war efforts, and it wasn't the story he would tell when he got back to Germany. If he got back. He began to feel desperate, trapped as he was just then between two armies at war.

Straight ahead of him was an abandoned trolley car. When he came to it, he leaped sideways through the door. The bottom of the car was littered with shards of glass, but he didn't pay them any mind. He gasped for breath, his chest pumping like a piston—up, down, up, down—and he didn't even notice that the glass sliced one of his hands when he pushed to his feet. He peeked out the back window and spotted a few Russians in the distance walking toward the trolley car. So he'd run in the right direction. He nearly slid on the shards as he walked cautiously through the car and out the front door. Though still out of breath and drained of strength, he bolted again. He sensed his legs were about to give out on him, and his shoulder failed him at the most crucial moment. He dropped his weapon. Suddenly he felt trapped, confined by his burdensome equipment. He tore off his rucksack, tossed the metal canister containing his gas mask to the ground, and instantly felt lighter, faster.

A grenade landed in front of him, and a dense cloud of dust bloomed over the street. He penetrated the dust cloud and entered a thick mist of sand and grit. He saw a head emerging behind an overturned horse cart. There was a whiny, metallic hiss and a bullet grazed August's helmet. *I can't die now,* he thought, as he fell to the ground. More heads appeared. Gun barrels leaned against the walls. An arm rose in the air and waved at him. It was Reichel, his lieutenant. August got to his feet and sprinted the rest of the way, faster than he'd ever thought possible.

Reichel grabbed him, but he didn't stop running. He had to get away—all he was thinking was that he couldn't die, not yet—but the lieutenant clutched him firmly, and August finally dropped to the ground behind a pile of debris. Reichel let go of him.

"Falkendorf. Get him out of here."

The sergeant picked him up. Dangling limply in the big man's arms, August began to cry. Not that he wanted to; he simply couldn't hold back his tears. Falkendorf stopped, put him down, and gave a mighty swing. August fell backward, reeling with pain from the punch. Falkendorf then yanked him to his feet and dragged him away, shouting that war wasn't for tender souls and that he'd have to get his shit together if he wanted to survive.

Kiev fell that day. As evening approached, Reichel guided the platoon to a house that seemed relatively intact.

"Go to the basement," the lieutenant commanded.

Four guards were posted on the ground floor of the house, while the rest of the men collapsed in the damp, moldy-smelling basement. The platoon had lost three men in addition to Christian, and eight had been wounded.

August sat down, his back to the clammy wall. He tipped his head back and stared at the gloomy concrete ceiling that matched his mood. Although explosions continued to rock the city, the gray mass above their heads secured them—or at least made them feel secure.

"Hotel Kiev." Rolf Mertz showed his crooked teeth as he smiled at August. "Rumor has it that our headquarters are at the Hotel Continental. I guess our officers are stuffing themselves with caviar as they gambol in comfy beds."

August wasn't in the mood to talk, least of all with Mertz. He'd mocked August, calling him a worthless soldier. He knew exactly what the others thought of his actions today, but he couldn't change what he'd done. He'd never be a good soldier, he knew that, but he was trying. He did the best he could, but it just wasn't enough. He turned from Mertz and looked at Stanislav, who was already asleep. *Impressive*, August thought. He closed his eyes but knew he'd be unable to sleep. He tried to think of something pleasant. Karin, the family's servant girl, came to mind. He daydreamed about her often.

Swiftly moving boots hurried down the stairs, and a major from the pioneer troops rushed into the basement. "Out, all of you. We need all hands on deck."

"But the men need rest," Reichel said, stumbling to his feet.

"It'll have to wait."

"But—"

"The city's burning. You'll have to catch up on your beauty sleep later." The major kicked at Stan's boots, and Stan opened his eyes in confusion.

August overheard the officer's short exchange with Reichel: One explosion after another had left Kiev in flames. Hotel Continental had been blown up, and hundreds were dead. Before the Russians left, they'd distributed mines all over the city, and the flames from the detonations were threatening to spread. The major explained that they'd lost an entire company when a bomb exploded while they were putting out a fire.

For the next five days, August and his companions became firemen instead of combat troops. Meanwhile, the fighting continued outside the city. On September 26, after ten days of fighting, the last Russian troops capitulated east of Kiev. Reichel announced that four Russian armies had been decimated and more than half a million soldiers were surrounded and taken prisoner. August found that hard to believe but soon had other things to think about; their next target was Poltava, and after that Kharkov, somewhere between Kiev and Lubny. They met a dispatch rider from the Sixteenth Panzer Division, who told them the story. German troops had captured a Jewish saboteur in Kiev as he was slashing fire hoses with a knife. From then on, the Jews were blamed for every explosion in the city. As a result, all the Jews in Kiev had been required to meet at selected addresses under the pretense of being transferred to work camps. They were asked to bring their documents, money, and warm clothing. This happened on Yom Kippur, the holiest of all the Jewish holy days, the day of forgiveness between individuals and between people and God, the day when God determines everyone's fate.

"They were led, one hundred at a time, to an enormous ravine called Babi Yar," the rider explained.

Mertz grinned. "Sounds like a Russian nursery rhyme." He began to sing: "Babi Yar, Babi Yar."

Rochus Gildehaus jabbed him in the rib with his elbow, and he stopped.

"The children." The dispatch rider had tears in his eyes, and his voice had grown unsteady. "They didn't even shoot the children. They just threw them into the ravine."

"Who did?" Gildehaus asked.

"Special task forces from the SS, people from SD, a platoon from a police battalion. And the Ukrainians."

"Were you there?"

"Yes, for Christ's sake. I watched them line up at the edge of the ravine, naked. I watched them fall into the ravine, dead and wounded alike. I saw how the soldiers beat the survivors to death with shovels as they waded around in a sea of bodies. And I saw . . ." He couldn't go on. His face was pale, his eyes vacant.

August couldn't bear to hear any more and wanted to take a few steps back. But something compelled him to stay within the circle of attentive men, a circle that continued to grow. An illogical craving. A craving that made him want to know everything about these cruelties, a craving that compelled him to stay—despite his aversion to hearing a story he didn't wish to know. It was a craving that sought a bizarre gratification.

When the dispatch rider finally continued with his story, an image of evil took shape—evil converted into unspeakable acts. The executions had lasted from dawn until late at night over the course of several days. When they were finished, the only thing that returned from Babi Yar were trucks filled with the clothing of more than thirty thousand people.

What the hell does filling ravines with dead Jews have to do with war? August wondered as the group slowly broke apart. Sure, in the Hitler Youth they'd been inculcated with the notion that Jews were subhuman. And of course the Jews had too much power in Europe, especially in Germany, but he saw no reason to hate them. Or murder them.

Gildehaus put an arm around the distraught rider's shoulder and gently guided him away. He clambered slowly onto his motorcycle. Without a word of farewell, he put his bike in gear and headed down the road.

August wanted to cry. He tried to force his brain not to think of what he'd just heard. But his brain wouldn't obey, and images of naked, frightened people and bloody bodies filled his head. No one cried or pleaded, but empty faces stared at him as if he were the guilty one. He was shaken, and the feeling spread through his body. He trembled at the thought that his own countrymen—Germans—had done such a thing. People from the same country as Schiller and Goethe. People from Hamburg, from Cologne, Stuttgart, and Munich. People like him.

Hamburg, Germany, October 4, 1941

They went outside. Gerhard glanced up at the three-foot-tall clock on the façade of the main entrance. It was quarter to two. Von Amrath lit a cigarette and offered one to Gerhard. They smoked in silence. He could tell that von Amrath was tense, and he could understand why; he wasn't particularly excited himself about the meeting ahead of them. He couldn't help but notice how von Amrath's lips tightened around his cigarette every time he took a puff. His face seemed tired, and the smile around his eyes was gone. Gerhard noted how his own hand shook when he tossed his cigarette on the ground. To draw attention away from his hand, he crushed the butt emphatically with the toe of his boot into the cobblestoned square, swiveling his heel from side to side in large arcs.

They'd arrived at the Hannoverscher Station well ahead of time. Too much time, really. Gerhard's work had once been a distraction, but suddenly it had become something concrete, an insistent reminder of what awaited. A cold gust swept across the square, and he buttoned his black uniform jacket up to his throat. He pulled up his red arm-band, which kept sliding down. It irritated him that he hadn't properly cinched it and that he still wasn't used to the uniform.

When they'd walked beneath the Roman arches at the main entrance, he had expected the place to be buzzing with activity and life. He'd imagined suitcases and other baggage stacked on the platforms that divided the various tracks, sweaty railroad workers loading and unloading cargo from the trains, signals shifting from green to red and back again, conductors blowing their whistles, and kiosks selling fruit and flowers at the entrance. But the station was terrifyingly silent and the signals turned off, and the few freight cars he saw were all empty. A man in tattered clothing had approached them carrying a bundle, and when von Amrath asked him where all the trains were, he'd shrugged and hurried on. Von Amrath looked at Gerhard with a puzzled expression on his face.

A black car parked nearby and a chauffeur stepped out. With long strides he went around to the rear door and opened it. A man of medium height climbed out; his face was pockmarked, and he looked to be about thirty years old. The chauffeur continued around to the second rear door, from which a slightly older man with a fedora in his hand appeared. He put the hat on and glanced about confidently. As the men started toward Gerhard and von Amrath, the pockmarked man remained a few steps behind the other. The elder of the two intro-duced himself as Detective Chief Superintendent Otto Glienicke of the Gestapo, before offhandedly remarking that the other man—who carried a brown leather case under his arm—was Martin Hornow. Glienicke was a tall man, taller than Gerhard, with a stiff manner and a voice that commanded one's attention. He wore black leather gloves, and both men had donned trench coats.

"We're all here, then," a high-pitched voice said right behind them. Gerhard hadn't heard anyone approaching, and they turned around in alarm.

"Heil Hitler." A hand was offered, and they shook it firmly. "Franz Fuchs, German Reich Railways."

Gerhard watched as Glienicke slowly removed his gloves. With his opposite hand's thumb and index finger, he clutched the tip of his pinkie and loosened the glove in three short tugs: one hard tug, then a gentler one, and finally another hard tug before the finger emerged from its hole. He moved on to the other fingers, then handed his glove to Hornow, who was standing behind him; he repeated this procedure with the other glove as if he had all the time in the world. It was clear that he'd performed this little routine often because he did it with the meticulous precision that comes only as the result of practice. When Hornow had received the second glove, the gray-haired chief superintendent removed a shiny cigarette case from his coat pocket.

Fuchs took the four men on a tour of the premises. The empty platforms and the large train station with its four towers reminded Gerhard of an old fortress abandoned by its defenders because of some epidemic. Between the towers curved an enormous barrel roof of wood and glass, which provided shelter for much of the platform. Gerhard noticed that it smelled of diesel. It wasn't the same smell as at the harbor, but a sharper, more pervasive odor that occasionally tickled his nostrils.

"It's perfect," Glienicke said. "It has everything we need." He had difficulty concealing his enthusiasm as he continued. "It's centrally located and yet remote, so we can avoid getting too much attention, and there's room, plenty of room, for all the people." He threw up his hands and turned toward the four men on the platform.

The man was right, Gerhard thought. The station was ideal. It was in the center of Hamburg, close to downtown and the harbor, but isolated on the small island of Kleiner Grasbrook. People didn't walk here unless they had an errand to do, and the high walls on either side of the railway tracks would keep the curious from seeing in. He glanced at von Amrath, who nodded curtly to convey his agreement with Glienicke's remarks.

"Who is in charge of this operation?" von Amrath asked to fill the silence.

"Claus Göttsche from the Gestapo's Jewish Department. But we can thank Kaufmann for the fact that they'll be removed."

"Ah, Kaufmann," von Amrath said, without revealing his true feelings about Hamburg's regional party leader. Karl Kaufmann, who had controlled the city and the entire district of Hamburg since 1933, had long been concerned about a lack of housing. Thousands were homeless as a result of Allied bombing campaigns in the residential districts, but now he'd come up with a solution. He would simply get rid of Hamburg's Jews so their homes could be given to the Germans. Von Amrath had clashed with the capricious Kaufmann on several occasions and had never had anything good to say about him when talking to Gerhard. Kaufmann was the type of man who ensured that the entire machine ran smoothly. It was men of his ilk who made Hitler's dreams possible.

Fuchs scribbled diligently in his notebook, then paused to look up. "Are you planning to move only the Jews? It's easier to recognize them now with the yellow stars on their chests." He smiled at Glienicke, who ignored his ingratiating style.

"The Jews and the gypsies," Glienicke replied promptly. He hastened to add proudly, "But we've already thrown most of the Sinti and gypsies out of the country."

And after that it'll be those with crooked teeth, then the left-handed, and then those with an overbite, Gerhard thought. He pictured people on the platform, their suitcases stuffed with all the possessions they could carry. There would be no one to wave good-bye to them, since all of their family members would be on the same train. It would be just the Gestapo and SS on the platform, and all they ever waved were rubber truncheons.

"We won't be in *carambolage* with other railway traffic here," Fuchs said, addressing each of the men.

"Excellent," Glienicke said. "Excellent." Without looking at Hornow, he extended his hand back toward him, and the gloves appeared in his palm. Following a stern "heil Hitler," the two men vacated the train platform, and Gerhard soon heard the squeal of the car's wheels on the cobblestones. Fuchs remained standing, apparently unsure whether he needed permission to go. Von Amrath intuited his hesitation and gave him permission to leave. They watched him head down the platform and vanish through a side door. Some time passed before either of them spoke.

"And when do they expect the first transport?" Gerhard said, giving his superior a questioning glance.

"In three weeks."

"Oh, we'll have our hands full, then," Gerhard stammered.

Von Amrath nodded without looking at him.

Gerhard would have to translate this experience as swiftly as possible into numbers, breaking down reality into simple figures. In his world things were easier to deal with if they were written in numbers. He would have to convert people into figures, and he would have to begin his calculations immediately.

"How many will fit in one compartment?"

"Compartment?" snorted von Amrath. "They'll be shipped in stock and freight cars."

Gerhard stared at him, dumbfounded. "But then we're treating them just like animals."

"Many people believe that's exactly what they are." Von Amrath began to walk toward the exit, and Gerhard followed him.

"And you?"

"You know very well what I think about this," he said angrily.

"Walter, we can't do this." Gerhard stopped, throwing his hands up in despair. He watched von Amrath's retreating back as it continued past the enormous "Departure" sign near the exit.

"Carambolage," von Amrath said. "When the hell did the national railway begin speaking French?"

Near Belgorod, Russia, October 23, 1941

A rusted chain stretched across the uneven forest trail. A dilapidated sign inked with black letters hung from the center of it.

"Whorehouse, 1,500 feet," Mertz said laconically.

"That's what it says?" August instantly regretted asking the question. The others laughed. He didn't know whether they were laughing at Mertz's comment or him.

"Good, my crabs could use some company." Bernd Carstens's remark now drew the laughs, and August was relieved.

Mertz put his arm around August's shoulder. "You know what people do in a whorehouse, Blondie?"

August tried twisting free of Mertz's forceful grip, but Mertz only squeezed harder. He licked August's neck. August smelled the foul odor of Mertz's yellow teeth.

"Leave him alone, Mertz. Go bother someone else," said Rochus Gildehaus, a powerfully built cabinetmaker from Bad Oldesloe, giving Mertz a shove. Laughing, Mertz tumbled forward before regaining his balance.

"You two don't need a whorehouse. You've got each other."

"Shut your mouth, Mertz." Lieutenant Reichel had come up beside them. "If this shitty map is right, then we're almost out of the woods. We should be able to see a city soon."

The city consisted of nothing more than a few abandoned houses. They weren't arranged in any kind of order, and instead looked as though they'd been dropped out of the bomb bay of some plane. The handful of buildings hardly deserved to be called a city, but they had nevertheless been given a name.

They took shelter in an old cabin. It had been a week since they'd last slept indoors. August could hardly believe the world's greatest army was sleeping under the open sky in below-freezing temperatures. It was clear that the grass-roofed cabin had once housed people, horses, and goats, and the soldiers cursed the former residents who had taken their animals with them, therefore depriving the men of a decent meal. The people had lived at one end of the house. In the center of the room was a small fireplace, a kind of clay oven that allowed the heat to spread; a dented metal pan hung from a hook above the fire pit. A table, four stools, and two beds whose mattresses were feed sacks stuffed with straw made up the sparse furnishings; one corner of the room seemed to be a shrine with religious icons on the wall, crosses, and tapers in a three-armed candelabra. On the other side of the house were three stalls where the animals had lived. Now the little cabin provided shelter to what remained of the platoon.

August lay in one of the stalls. Though it was covered with hay, there wasn't enough of it to cushion him from the hard stone floor. He tried to see out the broken windows, but they were filmed over with fine crystals of ice, turning the glass opaque. It reminded him of the Alster in winter.

He heard Falkendorf telling his favorite story, the one about the children in Kraków. He'd heard it before, and so had the others, but this time it was for Kreidl and Lohmeyer's benefit. They were new and so they listened, enraptured, to the officer's tale.

Stanislav Novak lay beside August. Stan was a Pole from Kunowice, near the Oder River. Before the war, the river had formed a natural border between Germany and Poland. Stanislav, whom Mertz disparagingly called "Polack Girl" because of his soft facial features, brown eyes, and heart-shaped mouth, was from a hardy stock not known for giving up. When everyone else was spent following a long day's march and threw themselves down in the first good place they could find, Stanislav stood back with a cockeyed grin, as if he'd been resting all day. He said it was because his family had slogged in the fields day in and day out to put food on the table, so he was used to toiling from sunup to sundown.

Stanislav was the youngest of six children. His five older sisters had married five brothers from the same family—which might make it quite convenient if they wanted to complain to each other about their in-laws. The two families were like a Gordian knot braided insolvably together. Unfortunately the family had no younger daughters waiting longingly for Stanislav to return from the front.

Stanislav didn't say much, but he and August were on good terms. They both frequently kept to themselves, but August noticed how the rest of the platoon respected Stanislav on account of his skills as a soldier, while the same was not true of him.

He glanced at the others in the stall, all of whom belonged to his squad. He smelled the rancid stench of their clothes, which for weeks had alternated between clammy and dry, making their odor practically as visible as a thick mist around each of them. They were filthy as shit. His gaze landed on Rochus Gildehaus, whose big white teeth flashed every time he smiled, and he smiled often. He was leaning against the wall next to Rolf Mertz, a short, sinewy man with yellow teeth. August saw nothing redeeming in the man. He was a nuisance, the way a fly buzzing around the room is a nuisance. August hated that Mertz had dubbed him "Blondie" because he thought August deferred to others in the same cowed manner as Hitler's dog. His gaze then fell on Eduard Hülsmann, who had a face like a professional criminal, though there was no wickedness in him. A piece of straw stuck to his cheek fluttered up and down with each exhale and inhale of breath. Bernd Carstens looked over at August, his eyes shining above his beard. Lorelei lay with his back to them. If he hadn't been such an enormous man, he would have looked like a child sweetly curled up in the fetal position, both hands tucked under one cheek. Exhaustion was etched into Martin Wander's face. His matted beard and filthy appearance made him look like an unemployed, down-on-his-luck chimney sweep. He sat with his arms around his knees, rocking gently back and forth. No one in Germany would have invited any of these men into their homes or offered them a heel of bread or something hot to drink. They looked like destitute good-for-nothings who'd stab a man in the back for fifty pfennig. August was fond of them. Apart from Mertz and Falkendorf, they were all good men.

They had literally marched into Russia. Walked until their boots felt like lead weights. Now they could travel up to thirty miles a day on their own two feet—not in trucks, half-track convoys, or horse-drawn wagons, but by putting one foot in front of the other over and over again. Of course that was nothing compared to a panzer division, which could travel between sixty and ninety miles a day, or the motor-ized divisions, which could travel as far as one hundred and fifty miles in a single day. But when it came to raw human strength, the soldiers in the stall had reason to be proud. And reason to be exhausted. August wasn't made for trudging. He could handle the first twenty miles, but after that it was torture. If it hadn't been for Stanislav's indomitable spirit driving them both forward, August would have been left behind long ago in some ditch in Ukraine. Falkendorf surely would have been okay with that.

Manfred Falkendorf was a braggart. He told all and sundry of his achievements in Poland; if even half of what he said was true, he'd be more beast than man. But his efforts in Poland had won him the rank of sergeant, and that commanded a certain respect. His favorite story involved an evening shortly after the invasion of Poland. He and two others had wandered aimlessly through Kraków looking for a place to warm themselves up. They'd ended up in the Kazimierz district on the Vistula's eastern bank, which was named after a Christian king who'd treated the Jews kindly. Jews were now the primary residents of the neighborhood, and he told of how they'd pissed on the splendid Corpus Christi Basilica before crossing the circular plaza in front.

A number of the district's houses had been abandoned in such haste that the former occupants had left behind all their belongings. With Falkendorf in the lead, they'd entered one of these empty homes, which they'd chosen because the façade's lavish ornamentation suggested that the owners had been wealthy. They'd found nothing of value inside and decided to light a fire to warm themselves up. In their search for something flammable, or even some better alcohol, they'd gone down into the basement. A locked door piqued their curiosity, and they found eight frightened children hiding behind it. They were hungry, dirty, and afraid. The oldest among them, a thirteen- or fourteen-year-old girl, kept the door key on a necklace hanging from her neck. Falkendorf grabbed the necklace and pulled her toward him. He described her as having dark, snakelike curls and a small, delicate head that fit in the palm of his hand. At first she'd resisted his overtures, but because she was hungry, she quickly lost her strength. He put a package of chocolate on a table in the center of the basement, and she set her steely-eyed gaze on it. He groped her again, and once again she resisted, but after a slap or two with the back of his hand, she'd gotten in line. He ripped her dress off her and fondled her girlish breasts with his coarse, filthy hands. Her eyes, now veiled with tears, continued to stare at the chocolate.

"Shut your mouth, Falkendorf. I don't want to hear your disgusting story." Reichel had awoken. The lieutenant was the only one who dared talk like that to the brutal sergeant.

Falkendorf lowered his voice and continued.

"Did you give her the chocolate?" Lohmeyer asked.

Falkendorf raised his eyebrows and patted his chest pocket, as he was still carrying around the same package of chocolate. He smiled secretively, then went on. His buddies had picked two other girls, and when they were done, the soldiers locked and barricaded the three girls in the basement again. Falkendorf explained that they would have something fun to play with if they ever returned to the house. Lohmeyer asked what they did with the other children, and he told him they'd tossed them into the river. As the children floated around in the Vistula, they'd used them for target practice. In the end Falkendorf had thrown a hand grenade into the water, because it was time for them to go find some booze. He was clearly proud of this story. Whether it was true or not, no one knew, but it served to guarantee that no one challenged Falkendorf.

Norbert Zollner, leader of the third squad, entered the cabin. His nose was red from the cold, and a fine layer of snow covered his shoulders. He brushed it off, and it fell to the floor, where it quickly melted into small puddles. He sat down at the table beside Reichel, who had pulled out a map and a compass. Falkendorf joined them, and August listened in on their subdued conversation.

"What about the panzer troops? Where are they?" Zollner asked.

"Who knows?" Reichel blew his nose loudly into a handkerchief, which he then rolled up and stowed in his pants pocket. "They're rushing ahead and leaving us with the cleanup."

"That's what my big brother always did, too." Zollner laughed hollowly. Falkendorf just grunted.

"They're probably in China by now," Reichel said.

The panzer troops' swift progress deep into Ukraine had left the infantry and the artillery with an almost impossible task. Large pockets of Russian soldiers still needed to be fought back as the infantry advanced, and they were falling farther and farther behind the fast-moving panzer divisions.

"Get some sleep, Zollner, you look like a sack of shit," Reichel said, patting the group leader on the shoulder. He turned to Falkendorf. "You, too, Manfred." Falkendorf grunted again, then began to roll a cigarette.

August hadn't managed to get any sleep yet when Carstens poked him and indicated that it was his turn to keep watch. Reichel had posted two guards in the hayloft. It wasn't actually necessary, since the third platoon had positioned machine guns to the east, south, and west of the little village, and a river created a natural shield to the north. But the lieutenant was taking no chances.

August crawled unsteadily up the rickety ladder and crawled up through the narrow hole. The old wooden loft was in such terrible condition that it looked like it might fall on the heads of the sleeping platoon below. At the other end of the loft, Hülsmann was staring out at the slumbering countryside. August scuttled over to the cast-iron window and peered out. The moon dangled on its cord like an incandescent bulb someone had forgotten to disconnect, illuminating the terrain below. He stifled a yawn. The firewood that was to keep the men warm was stacked just below the window, and the remains of a Volkswagen Kübelwagen sat like a naked skeleton beside a dead horse with a missing hind leg. Someone—maybe a hungry farmer or soldier—had probably cut it off before the body had become a deep-frozen lump. The rest of the poor animal now lay waiting to be discovered by the birds, its large, square teeth set in a grin as if it found the whole absurd scene comical.

He scratched his groin. The day's harvest: twenty-six lice. And there were more. It had become almost as natural to pick lice from his body as it was to piss or eat. He'd never imagined that such tiny insects could be so irritating. In fact he'd never imagined he would ever get lice or that he would have to accept it like some dog that was too lazy to get up from its nap. He yawned at the thought of a nap.

He heard Hülsmann coughing on the other side of the loft. Suddenly the servant girl Karin peeked around the woodpile. The snow had begun to fall heavily, but the large flakes melted on her black uniform. Her white, starched apron fluttered lightly in the wind, and though she was wearing only knee-high stockings, she didn't seem to be cold.

He frequently dreamed of Karin. He didn't know if it was love, but he'd thought of her constantly since the day he'd surprised her in the bathtub. That day remained vividly etched in his memory. Not like an old photo with yellowed edges, but with sharp contours and a richness of detail that most of his thoughts lacked.

It had happened one autumn morning in 1938, in late September or early October. The red, yellow, and orange leaves had dropped from the copper beech to blanket the front lawn. His mother said the leaves had turned early that year. While the others slept, he'd stood on the dock watching the cauliflower-like cumulus clouds drift across the sky to determine the direction of the wind. Satisfied with what he saw, he crawled into the moored skiff, tied the big sail to the boom, and hoisted it up on the mast. After cinching the foresail, he cast off and shoved the boat away from the dock. Using his hip as leverage, he drew in the boom, ducked under it, and made sure to get the wind astern so the boat could travel at a good clip. The city slept as he sailed around the lake, the stillness broken only by the pleasant sound of the keel slicing through the water. Everything else fell away, and he thought only about bringing the skiff and the wind into harmony and striking the optimal airstream. It was that same quest for perfection that he noticed in his father whenever he sat at his shiny Steinway playing "Clair de Lune." When he forgot all about Debussy and heard only his own music. He loved to hear his father play. When he'd been out on the lake for some time—just how long, he wasn't sure—he turned the boat around, trimmed the sails, and set course back toward the house.

He walked through the kitchen where the servants had their rooms, hoping that he might run into Karin. On Sundays they were allowed to sleep in, so there was no one around. He slathered honey on a piece of bread, which he ate at the table in the middle of the enormous kitchen. It was strange, he thought. On the one hand he wanted to see Karin more than anything, but on the other, he was afraid to see her. What would he do? What would he say? He slathered another hunk of bread with honey, then headed to the bathroom to wash his sticky fingers. He pressed down the door handle with his elbow, and there she stood.

She was naked, completely naked. Standing in an oval zinc tub, steam enveloping her. In her hand she held a porcelain jug, which she'd just emptied over herself. She didn't look startled. It was more like she'd been expecting him—or at the very least hoped he'd come.

Although it had lasted no more than a few seconds, he still recalled every detail. Her smooth hair had looked even smoother when it was wet, framing her round face and making her underbite a little more evident. One of her breasts appeared to be larger and heavier than the other. One nipple had pointed directly at him. The other had pointed straight up in a more lively way. His eyes had rested briefly on the larger of her breasts, and he'd immediately felt the blood rushing to his head. He'd never imagined that a woman's breast could be so compelling, so captivating. His gaze wandered down her abdomen, lingering on her navel, a dark cave the size of a coin. His eyes traveled farther down, along with the water slowly trickling down her body. The warm water had streamed in a thin jet from the dark hair between her legs into the tub until only droplets remained on her skin.

Her belly was plump, her hips broad and ample; she didn't resemble any of Fritz Klimsch's female statues that he'd sneaked peeks of in books at the library. He'd been fascinated by those statues, but nothing compared to what he'd seen that day. She saw him staring at her, and she did nothing to cover herself, but instead let him study her body. His eyes met hers, and he admired her shiny cheeks and her mouth with its slight underbite—which he'd since kissed thousands of times whenever he was alone.

She pulled a towel off a hook, then carefully wrapped it around herself. August had mumbled an inaudible apology before closing the door. He remembered how he'd stood by the door, his heart hammering and his body trembling. He often dreamed that he'd opened the door again, gone into the bathroom, and closed the door behind him, but he didn't know what was supposed to happen after that.

They hadn't been able to look each other in the eye after that, but then August didn't recall whether they'd ever been able to do that. Now, though they shared something, their eyes fled from each other, brushing only a back, an arm, the nape of a neck. It had been a wonderful experience, but maybe he was the only one who felt that way? He didn't dare think about what she might feel for him, for fear that he would be disappointed.

He frequently replayed the fantasy when he was awake, starting over from the beginning if he forgot a detail, as though to avoid reaching the end.

He awoke to someone thumping him on the back. The blow knocked the wind out of him, and he gasped for breath. His eyes struggled to focus in the darkness, but he saw only the outline of a figure.

Falkendorf hissed between his teeth, "You better not be fucking sleeping."

"I—"

"Shut up," he said, and shoved August toward the ladder. August crawled ahead, but Falkendorf leaped on him and sat down heavily on his chest, pinning August's arms down with his knees. He punched August. Once, twice, three times. Hülsmann turned his head and saw them, but quickly looked away.

Falkendorf put his mouth close to August's ear. "If the Russians don't kill you, I'll do it someday."

Hamburg, Germany, October 25, 1941

"Names?"

"Abraham and Gretchen Markowitz."

The Gestapo man stamped the paper and nonchalantly waved the couple on. He'd laid his cap on the table in front of him, next to two stamps and a black ink pad. Gerhard had seen him use only one of the stamps so far. He doubted the other one was ever used. He stood behind the Gestapo man and couldn't help but look down at the back of his head. The man's hair was thin and blond and wispy as a doll's and didn't conceal the tiny orange freckles on his scalp. His ears jutted out unnaturally, and Gerhard imagined that he must have been teased in school. His neck bobbed a bit whenever he spoke.

"Names?"

"Max and Elsa Bromberger."

Before people had begun to arrive at the station, Gerhard had exchanged a few remarks with the Gestapo man, who indicated that he wasn't happy about the work he was supposed to carry out. Maybe he felt compelled to say that. Or maybe he'd been speaking to himself, to justify his own involvement, and not to Gerhard at all.

"Names?"

"Kurt, Frieda, Rolf, and this one is Denny," said the man who held a little boy.

"Surname?"

"Hirsch. Are we really heading to Lodz?"

The Gestapo man shrugged lethargically.

In the middle of October, rumors had begun circulating among Germany's Jews that they were to be expelled from the country. The chairman of the Jewish Union in Hamburg, Dr. Max Plaut, had asked the Gestapo if the rumors were true, and he'd been relieved to hear them deny it. Two days later, however, he'd gotten a call from Claus Göttsche from the Gestapo's Jewish Department. A thousand of the city's Jews were to be relocated to Lodz, Poland, the following week. The detective sergeant asked Plaut to create a list with a thousand names, and the doctor refused, declaring that they could put his name at the top of the list.

So the Gestapo had constructed the list themselves. The 1,034 who'd been chosen were ordered to meet at a building near the university owned by the Gestapo the day before the train would depart for Lodz. More than one hundred of the names on the list were volunteers who wanted to leave the country and escape the fear they felt as a result of being Jewish in Germany. The next morning they were loaded onto trucks and driven to Hannoverscher Station, where the train was waiting.

Gerhard had ordered the train cars. He'd requested twenty passenger cars, unable to bring himself to ask for freight or stock cars. That meant fifty to each car, two automobiles for the SS guards who would escort them to Poland, and five freight cars for baggage. What he was given was a grand total of twelve passenger cars.

Friedrich Olmo had planned the train's route together with an employee of the German Reich Railways: from Hamburg over to Berlin via Frankfurt an der Oder, Reppen, Kutno, and Görnau to Lodz. Seitz-Göppersdorf had notified the relevant stations that a through-passing train would arrive on October 25. Troop transports and other supplies moving to the front were the top priority, and that meant the train would have to hold for other trains along the way.

"Names?"

"Eduard and Anna Beer. And this is Martin, Frieda, Lotte, and Siegfried."

Gerhard looked at the family. The father was wearing a suit. It had been a fine suit once, probably at the time of their wedding, but now it was frayed and faded. The mother held herself with grace, standing tall and proud before the table where the man who now administered their lives was seated. They'd done nothing to deserve being thrown out of their own country. It was their country, too, after all. But their lives were no longer their own. They had no rights. And yet the woman had her pride. He studied the four children. They all looked like German children, and they had traditional German names. The youngest, who was probably around twelve, had dirty-blond hair. That had to be Siegfried. It could just as easily have been Maximilian. But this boy was a Jew, and he was therefore undesirable. Gerhard shook his head and glanced around, hoping no one had noticed the disapproving gesture.

Glienicke stood, his gloved hands behind his back, beside a few other commanding officers on a small podium so that he could observe the entire crowd. He seemed satisfied.

"Names?"

"Carl, Helene, and Herbert Maidanek."

Next to the Gestapo man with the jutting ears sat a second man; he leaned back just slightly in his chair, looking pleased, then glanced at Gerhard and blinked. Gerhard shifted uncomfortably and eyed the throng. The platform was filled with well-dressed people. Everyone had donned their best clothes, but with their bowed heads and anxious body language, they resembled a burial procession. Their arms were filled with suitcases, bags, and sacks. Even the children carried all they could.

"Names?"

"We are the Kahan family. Philipp, Matilde, Gustav, Rachel, and Rosi."

That's when Gerhard saw him. His long, lanky figure towered above the others. Standing there with his soft trilby on his head, he seemed filled with sorrow. Like someone who had no idea how to act in this crowd of people. A short, stocky woman with her hands full of baggage shoved him peevishly, and Gerhard watched him apologize. He lifted his brown hat and looked shamefacedly at the woman, who appeared to repay him with a hurtful remark; the man's expression wrenched in brief, genuine pain. Everyone was nervous and testy.

Gerhard started in the man's direction.

"Aaron."

The man took a long time to react. In his profession as a watchmaker, he'd earned his living whenever time stopped. Now it was as if he himself had stopped.

"Aaron. Don't you recognize me?"

The man squinted as if the strong sunlight kept him from seeing clearly. His face revealed no trace of recognition, and a small, apologetic smile pushed at the corners of his mouth. But then all at once his expression indicated that he remembered.

"Gerhard," he said finally. "Gerhard Strangl."

"Listen up. Keep your eyes down and look remorseful. It has to appear like I am scolding you."

Aaron nodded. He removed his hat and stared at the ground.

"Where are Hannah and the children?"

"They got away," he said in a raspy voice. "Except for Rachel. She was taken from us, a lung infection." He grimaced. "What's going to happen to me?"

"I wish I knew."

"Can you help me?"

"I'm afraid I can't. I don't have the authority."

Aaron gazed at him, baffled. "Then you needn't bother explaining why you're wearing that uniform." He raised his head, and Gerhard could feel the contempt in his angry glare. "I thought you were a good man."

Just then, Gerhard noticed out of the corner of his eye Otto Glienicke watching him and Aaron.

"Go on, Aaron."

His former upstairs neighbor held his gaze and didn't move. Gerhard finally averted his eyes and saw Glienicke nodding at him as if to ask if everything was all right. The detective chief superintendent leaned toward one of the other Gestapo men and pointed down at him and Aaron. The Gestapo man leaped deftly from the little podium and started toward them. But wedging his way through the dense crowd wasn't easy. With his eyes, Gerhard tried to force Aaron to walk away. He felt the heat going to his head and Glienicke scrutinizing him. He didn't know what they would do to him once they realized he knew a Jew. The Gestapo man approached, snarling at the crowd to clear a path. For a brief instant Gerhard wondered whether slapping Aaron would make him disappear. He made a last, desperate attempt.

"Go on," Gerhard hissed through his teeth.

With defiant slowness, Aaron finally started moving. He slung his canvas bag, probably containing all of his possessions, over his shoulder and turned his back on Gerhard.

Gerhard felt that back mocking him, expressing the very same contempt that he'd witnessed in Aaron's eyes. *What could I have done?* he asked himself. *I couldn't have done a thing to help him.* But it was as if that slim back were ridiculing him, spitting at him. *Who does he think he is? I am a good man. I'm not like them.* He glanced toward the small podium. *I am a good man.*

"Is there a problem?" The Gestapo man was right behind him now.

"No. Not at all."

"Who was that man?"

"Just some dumb Jew."

An elderly man bumped into the Gestapo man, who nearly fell over. Gerhard waited for the angry eruption that would surely follow. But the officer just turned and accepted the apology from the shrinking, guilt-stricken man. These Gestapo men were completely unpredictable, Gerhard thought. Another officer might just as easily have beaten the old man with his cane. Instead the Gestapo man now helped the elderly man over to one of the tables, where he was asked to give his name. People had begun to climb into the waiting passenger cars, and the officer now helped the man onto the train.

It was immediately clear to Gerhard that there weren't enough cars for so many people. They were already crowding onto the footboards and would soon be swelling out the windows. But people continued to pour through the narrow openings until the doors were shut by a couple of soldiers.

German shepherds on leashes sniffed along the edge of the train, their trained snouts scanning beneath the cars to detect runaways. When they were finished, the soldier at the head of the train signaled to the conductor, who wiped his forehead on his sleeve, put on his cap, and climbed the four iron steps. The train emitted a shrill screech and was slowly set into motion.

Gerhard watched as the overfilled cars glided past. People were squeezed against the windows, and the frightened faces looked at him. He heard children crying inside the train, which suddenly halted, brakes whining, only to immediately begin moving again. He remained on the platform watching the train grow smaller and smaller until, finally, he could no longer see it.

Two weeks later Gerhard stood on the same platform watching Hannah help Samuel, Esther, and Jakob into the train before her own back disappeared into the stock car.

Volokolamsk, Russia, November 18, 1941

Karl sat in the cab watching the snow. It fell slowly and continuously, blanketing everything in yet another layer of whiteness. Just when he thought the sky couldn't deliver any more, the night's snowfall added another layer. But snow was preferable. He thought back on the terrible autumn. Operation Typhoon, the offensive against Moscow, had begun on October 2. By the end of the first week, they'd conquered an area the size of Hamburg and taken thousands prisoner. They felt invincible. Karl and Paul Piroska predicted that they would celebrate Christmas in Red Square. The Battle of Vyazma, a medium-sized city only 150 miles from Moscow, had successfully concluded a week later. The supply column alternated between the front—which was moving continually eastward—and the supply depots behind the front. But then came the rain.

It rained for days, making the terrain impassable. The supply column was hopelessly stuck outside of Safonovo between Smolensk and Vyazma, and the entire offensive against Moscow was bogged down in a deep quagmire.

Karl was frustrated. He knew that combat vehicles would stop working without gasoline, but the supply column was unable to cover more than three miles per day under these conditions. Loaded with heavy gas cans, the vehicles sank deep into the mud. Whenever they finally got some traction, the cars just splattered an impenetrable wall of mud on them. The men wound up spending more time outside their vehicles than inside, since the trucks were constantly sputtering to a halt. By evening, their pants were rigid with caked mud. Some cut the mud off with knives, but Karl and Paul quickly discovered that the best way to clean their pants was to soak them so the hard mud once again grew soft. After that, removing it with a razor blade was easy. Every evening they shaved their pants, and every morning they were back in mud up to their knees.

They had to leave behind several vehicles that quite simply couldn't be extracted from the mud. Karl jokingly told his men that they could just retrieve them in the spring. They continued to advance at a crawl. Whenever they reached a paved road, the jubilation could be heard through the entire column; every time they approached a larger city, the roads improved. As Karl recalled, it was the medical officer Remmel who had suggested laying hewn boards underneath the wheels on the muddier stretches of road. After that the cars could drive a little faster, albeit with long boards sticking out from under tarps in the backs, since they had to transport the "road" as well.

Winter had arrived abruptly and forcefully. The cold was everywhere, and it penetrated everything. A few weeks ago, the prodigious rainfall had been replaced by snow. The frost set in, and the mud froze. Though this meant that their vehicles could once again advance with supplies, their joy was short-lived because everyone began to freeze.

They'd spent the night in their vehicles, and Karl was still disoriented from sleep as he leaned back in his seat, feeling as though the cold were coming from inside him, freezing him from his bones outward.

He crawled stiff-legged out of the truck and staggered over to the soup truck, where two chimneys billowing smoke promised a hot meal.

The freezing men clustered around the soup wagon, or "goulash cauldron," as they called it. Several were still wearing their summer uniforms, and they would soon succumb to the cold, Karl thought. He might, too, if he didn't get hold of some warmer clothes. He exchanged a glance with Remmel and Piroska, who was stomping in place. Remmel seemed like he never felt the cold. Karl envied him.

Two hours later, the supply column departed from Volokolamsk. As usual, the horizon—as flat and colorless as a heavy blanket—depressed him. Though he'd asked himself many times what they were doing in this impassable country, he had yet to find an answer that satisfied him. Forests, swamps, mud, and now the cold had all done their utmost to stop them. They would have a long winter ahead if they didn't reach Moscow, but he still believed they would. They were only seventy-five miles from the Christmas tree in Red Square, and the German armies were positioned in a semicircle around the city.

They drove through a forested area lined with indolent spruce trees leaning across the road. He was cold as hell. He never cursed, but this situation practically called for it. If only he could get warm. He would do anything for a respite from the cold.

"Stop!"

Bongartz braked. "What's the matter?"

"Nothing."

Karl opened the door, leaped out, and ran into the woods.

"You need to take a dump, boss?" someone shouted behind him.

He'd spotted something among the trees. Now he hoped to have his hunch confirmed. Where his sights had once been trained on enemies and threats, they now focused on clothes—anything that might warm him even the smallest bit: a pair of woolen socks, a pair of boots.

It was too good to be true. He lay in a clearing, dead. His stripes indicated that he'd been a major in a panzer regiment. There was no sign of a wound, no sign that he'd died in battle. He was mostly covered in snow, but beneath that thin layer was the lambskin coat Karl had spotted from the truck—a lined lambskin coat with a fur collar and a hood. He glanced nervously over his shoulder and was relieved to see that no one else had seen the dead soldier. He wouldn't have to fight for the coat. Stripping it off him wasn't easy. The officer's arms were stiff from frost, and he had great difficulty undoing the buttons with his own cold fingers. His hands were, as usual, stiff and aching, but the prospect of a real overcoat helped him fight through the pain. How deep he'd sunk. Not so long ago, he could have purchased the finest sheepskin. In fact he could have sent people out to buy it for him. Now he was scrabbling around a corpse in a snow-covered forest. It was undignified—not only for himself but for the dead officer. Then he had an idea. He would restore the major's dignity by giving him a proper burial. It was the least he could do—now that he'd acted like some pitiful grave robber. He pawed around inside the man's pockets and found a soldier's book. He opened it.

"Fritz Heidenreigger," it said.

He felt a bit embarrassed as he returned to the vehicles. By halting the column he'd put it in danger, but what did it matter? He would no longer freeze to death now. He ordered a couple of men to retrieve the dead man. Three freezing soldiers jumped from the bed of one of the trucks and cast envious glances at his newly appropriated coat. They hadn't been among those lucky enough to secure winter clothes from the warehouse in Smolensk. Clothing supplies were but a drop in the ocean; everyone plundered everything from everyone—whatever could provide even the slightest warmth. With their sallow, unshaven faces, women's shawls tucked underneath their helmets to warm their heads and ears, and jackets, pants, and boots in every shape and size, the proud Wehrmacht soldiers now had a rather ragged look about them. One soldier from a reconnaissance unit had even gone so far as to layer a couple of flowery dresses under his thin uniform jacket. The soldiers continued to plow ahead despite their bizarre appearance, and little by little they advanced toward the Russian capital.

The three men dragged the body from the woods, then arranged it on top of the gasoline tanks in one of the truck beds. Once the column was on its way again, the driver turned to Karl, who for the first time in a long while felt an ounce of good fortune thanks to the coat.

"Someone you knew?"

"Fritz. Fritz Heidenreigger," Karl responded tersely.

Five days and one burial later, they reached Solnechnogorsk, forty miles northwest of Moscow. The division's combat troops had been lodged in a glass factory at the edge of the city, while supply troops bivouacked in an empty metal workshop. Karl figured all the machines and workers had been transferred to the east—along with the rest of Russia's industry.

In the evening they saw rockets illuminating the sky over Moscow, the searchlight's beams sweeping the sky, and glimpses of the city's air defense guns combatting the Luftwaffe's bombardiers. This was where Karl heard the song for the first time. Piroska and a subordinate from the signal troops had found Radio Beograd's powerful transmitter frequency. Every evening at 2155 hours, Lieutenant Karl-Heinz Reintgen ended his broadcast with a sad song about adoring lovers; each night, more and more soldiers clustered around the radio as Lale Andersen sensually crooned "Lili Marleen." She could never measure up to Zarah Leander, in Karl's eyes, but the sad song made an impression on the soldiers. It gave them courage and a reason to fight even more savagely, because the notes reminded them of their loved ones at home.

Solnechnogorsk was also the first place he came across bomb dogs. The dogs were trained to crawl underneath German tanks with explosives strapped to their backs, triggering a detonation when an antenna touched the undercarriage of the tank. The German shepherd—ironically a breed of German origin—had gone under an Opel Blitz in Karl's convoy, and the vehicle exploded with a deafening roar, costing him not only two men but a truck and three tons of gasoline as well. Because of the burning gasoline, they couldn't approach the vehicle for some time, so they never did bury Neubarth and Thiessen. They'd shot every dog they saw ever since that day.

On December 6 the Russians began a large counteroffensive, and Karl was told to pull his column out of Solnechnogorsk. They'd been so close to their target, but the order to pull back made Moscow seem farther away than ever. Each day they distanced themselves more from the Russian capital, the men's morale dipped lower. The temperature, too, continued to fall, with daylight temperatures reaching only ten degrees Fahrenheit. Piroska had heard there were trains in Smolensk loaded with winter clothes, but the locomotives' boilers didn't function in the brutal cold. Frostbite became an everyday occurrence, and Karl ordered everyone in the company to rub their faces and ears with snow as soon as they began to lose feeling in them. Many of his men still succumbed to the cold, but at least it was a painless death. Others had to have limbs amputated, and whenever a frostbitten soldier lost a leg or a foot, Karl felt guilty because of his lambskin coat.

The drivers started the vehicles' engines every couple of hours throughout the night to ensure that they could retreat if necessary. In the morning the frostbitten soldiers crawled into the trucks and drove across snow-covered marshlands. Four days later they found themselves in a village more than fifty miles from Moscow. On the way, two drivers had panicked when a Russian fighter plane began circling above their heads. One had driven his truck into a river and the other into a ditch, where the truck burst into flames. They had lost four men and were now down to just eight of the original twenty-two vehicles.

Karl ordered his men to remove families from a few of the village's houses, so the company could be billeted in them and warm themselves around the large fireplaces. Other families had just been ordered to cook supper for the column—under surveillance, of course—when a noise erupted.

The men who came running past them through the snowstorm looked like ghosts. Some fell into other soldiers' arms, while others continued running. They glanced feverishly over their shoulders like hunted animals. A knot formed in Karl's belly as he read the fear in their eyes. Whatever was causing the men to flee had frightened them out of their wits. A bearded corporal collapsed in Karl's arms, sobbing like an inconsolable child. Karl was just patting him on the head when he heard a truck topple onto its side close by; it was filled with wounded men, all of whom began shouting and moaning. The corporal stood up in alarm and took off running again. Karl turned and saw a mortar shell rip the man's body in half.

A captain pulled out his service revolver and fired into the air. He shouted orders to one side, then the other, but no one paid him any mind. Mortar shells began raining down on them, and Karl's men were caught up in the chaos. They fled just as a T-34 tank emerged from the swirling snow and started shooting at the column's trucks. Bongartz and a few others crawled into an Opel Blitz. His hands trembling, Bongartz tried starting the car but got only a hoarse splutter. A 76-mm grenade slammed against the truck, lifting it several feet off the ground. Then it dropped back to the frozen ground like a heap of scrap iron.

More tanks appeared, with Russian soldiers in white winter uniforms looming above and between them. Karl and the captain looked at each other. The officer gave Karl a despairing smile, and together they started running. They passed a major, who stood, paralyzed, watching the advancing Russians. He doffed his cap, greeting them in the same friendly way you might say hello on the street. Over his shoulder, Karl watched the man draw his pistol. With painstaking precision, he fired eight shots at the Russian tanks. The magazine's last bullet he planted in his own temple.

Only as darkness began to fall in the afternoon did they dare slow down. The captain, a man by the name of Julius Kruppke, was from one of the First Panzer Division's reconnaissance units; he came from Zwickau and spoke with a thick Saxon accent. Several men joined him and Karl, and the small group now consisted of fourteen soldiers. They spent the night at the edge of a forest. By the following morning, two had frozen to death. They made no attempt to bury the dead in the impenetrable ground but just covered them with snow, knowing full well that come spring they would be visible again.

The group, which had grown to twenty-seven men despite an additional six deaths, struggled through the snow for several days. They navigated by the sun and the trail of burning cities and bridges left by the engineer troops. They spent one night in a pigsty that had remained intact. Everyone was sullen, absorbed in their own dark ruminations whenever they rested. Karl sat with his knees pulled up underneath himself, rocking back and forth to keep warm. He looked at the others. There was no trace of their former confidence; gone was their certainty of victory. The bitterness had crept in, and they were close to cracking, physically and psychologically. Beside him sat a young soldier. His lips and eyes were blue, his cheeks red. He thought of Kleist, his lieutenant in the Great War: the same soldier, a different war.

Kruppke broke the silence.

"Fifteen miles. That's how close we were to Moscow. And look at us now." He spat.

"Were we that close?" Karl's voice shivered with cold.

"I saw the road sign myself. Moscow, fifteen miles." Kruppke grinned apologetically. "And while we're dying here, Hitler has found himself a new war."

"Shut your mouth." A canteen flew across the barn and clanked against the wall behind Kruppke, who leaped on the culprit and pounded the other man's face with his fist, breaking his nose with a loud crack. The captain had just raised his fist for another powerful punch when the others pulled him back.

Karl saw Kruppke shaking as he sat down. Everyone had reached the breaking point.

"What do you mean, a new war?"

"Haven't you heard? Hitler declared war against America." Kruppke scrutinized his knuckles.

The news took him by surprise. The last thing they needed was another enemy.

The next day they continued west. Many of them got frostbite, and the locals eyed them with disgust whenever the men warmed themselves by the flames of their houses. Karl knew that he should feel bad for the locals, but he no longer felt anything. For a long time now, he had felt only a pervasive emptiness. Everything had become meaningless, trivial. All he had to do was his duty. Do his duty and then go home. The only time he ever felt a hint of warmth was when he thought of his family back home. He had received letters from Ingrid after lengthy delays, but no one knew where he was right now, so it had been a while since he'd had any news from home. The last he'd heard, everyone was doing well, including Gerhard. He knew that August was in Army Group South somewhere in the Ukraine.

Karl recalled only occasional moments in recent months when he'd felt anything at all. Two weeks earlier, they'd found shelter for the night at a village school, which their army had cleared out to use as a field hospital. The classroom was remade into a sickroom with beds and mattresses, and on the blackboard Karl noticed what he presumed to be a priority list of who would require an operation first. The teacher's desk had functioned as an operating table, and an unbearable stench still lingered in the room. When Karl had opened the window, the sight outside the window had made him vomit. A towering heap of amputated legs, arms, hands, and feet lay entangled in the blood-red snow.

By Christmas, they had retreated back to Volokolamsk, only a month and a half after they'd optimistically departed the city. They were weak and irritable, sick and tired of the war. Karl couldn't stop thinking of Hamburg, of the house by the Alster, of Ingrid, and he often imagined how wonderful it would be to return home. At the same time he feared the thought. Would he be the same man? He pushed the thought aside, unable to stomach it.

Volokolamsk was a paradise after the last few weeks. Although the cold was still intense, the living conditions in the city were quite different. There were showers, and Karl shaved off his lengthy beard. Most of all he looked forward to being free of the lice. The small mites that sought out his body heat were driving him mad.

A large group of bedraggled men stood outside a house set up for bathing and delousing. The delousing took place in a kind of sauna where the temperature rose to over 140 degrees Fahrenheit. The men's faces were emaciated, and they all looked exhausted, with black circles under their eyes. No one smiled. Karl wandered among them on his way to the entrance. A broad, flat-nosed private, scratching at his lice, stared absently at him. Karl pointed at his stripes, hoping the man would step aside, but he was met with a defiant glare. The private puffed himself up. Karl didn't want a confrontation. His delousing would have to wait. A hand fell on the man's shoulder just then, and he moved promptly out of the way. A smile appeared in a dark, filthy, weather-beaten face, and Karl recognized Paul Piroska. The two men embraced. A few days later Thomas Remmel came strutting into the mess tent as if he'd just been outside taking a leak. He patted Karl on the shoulder and went right on talking as if they'd never been separated. Karl, Piroska, Remmel, and the rest of the supply column celebrated Christmas together.

Suddenly the holiday meant everything to Karl. Dönselmann found a tree, and they decorated it with whatever they could find and sang "O Tannenbaum" and "Silent Night, Holy Night." Karl wasn't the only one fighting back tears, and each man withdrew into himself as he was flooded with emotion. They thought not only of their families at home but also of the fact that they'd been to hell and survived.

The winter was endless, and it snowed daily. The division regrouped, and the supply column was given new vehicles. In March the Seventh Panzer Division was transferred to Rzhev.

Artemovsk, Ukraine, March 12, 1942

Lorelei, so called because he was about the same size as the cliff that towered above the Rhine, gestured for them to stop. Reichel moved to the head of the company, conferred with Lorelei, and drew his binoculars to his eyes. He called for the young Baumann, who ambled nervously through the ranks with his map case slung over his shoulder. Zollner and Falkendorf joined them. August couldn't hear what the lieutenant and his two subordinates were saying, but judging by their gestures and body language, they weren't in agreement. Reichel pointed eagerly away from the forest, while Zollner pointed in the opposite direction and Falkendorf listened with his arms crossed, nodding occasionally. Reichel eventually turned his back on the two men and studied the terrain beyond the woods through his binoculars for some time.

August made eye contact with Stanislav, who stood closer to them. He sensed August's question, but shrugged. Everyone was tense after a hectic morning of heavy Russian bombardments, and their discovery of an entire platoon of disfigured dead compatriots along the road had further disheartened them. Men like Mertz and Falkendorf didn't notice such things, but August couldn't get accustomed to death's daily sweep across the countryside. Like a destructive whirlwind, it sucked the life out of even the best soldiers in a split second.

August was sick. He'd been sick for weeks now, and it was only getting worse. Martin Wander had listened to his chest and confirmed he had the first signs of pneumonia. August had been his last patient.

Wander had been killed that same afternoon. It had been an otherwise quiet day, and they'd finally gotten a bit of rest—and yet they'd still lost two men before it was over. One man had been kicked in the head by a horse, leaving a clear imprint of a horseshoe in his swollen forehead. Ironically, it was this very Austrian, Lustenberger, who'd spoken proudly of the Spanish Riding School in Vienna. But he'd become the victim of a breed of horse far inferior to the Lipizzaner in grace and elegance. Wander had been just as unlucky. An inattentive driver from the supply column had overlooked the poor medical soldier, who was dragged for twelve feet underneath the heavy vehicle before the truck came to a halt. Falkendorf had yanked the unsuspecting driver out of the cab and beaten and kicked him until he bled. No one stopped him.

Eduard Hülsmann and August buried the two men, hammering up a cross made of two wooden planks and draping each man's helmet on the cross. Hülsmann used the tip of his bayonet to carve Martin Wander's name into the wood. When he reached his year of birth, they looked at each other quizzically. Hülsmann insisted, saying it was undignified not to include it. August's stomach churned as they dug him up. With one hand to his mouth and the other fumbling over Wander's body, Hülsmann finally located his pay book in his breast pocket. The cross now carried the inscription: "Martin Wander 1919-1942."

August's throat ached, and he wheezed whenever he coughed. The fever made him sore and stiff. His head was hot, and the steel helmet—which felt a great deal heavier than it once had—now felt like it had fallen down over his ears. He heard next to nothing. He had retreated into his own world, and when people spoke to him, he frequently had to guess what they were saying.

He watched Gildehaus blowing into his hands and kicking indifferently at a frozen puddle. With his heel he pierced the thin layer of ice under which a pocket of air was trapped.

Just then Reichel barked an order that soon spread through the column like wildfire. The men formed a row along the edge of the woods. August could see the top of a church steeple in the distance. Before them stretched an open field that offered no cover. About 1,300 feet ahead, there was a hedgerow of bushes and small trees, and to his right was a stone dike that bordered it.

"A machine gun sniper in those trees could rip the entire company apart," Carstens said.

Gildehaus nodded. "It'd be safer to lead us up along the dike." He glanced at August, who was studying the terrain ahead. He didn't care. Not one bit. If he had a lung infection, as Wander had said, then he deserved to rest at a field hospital. Soon. And if it meant that he would have to run across that field, so be it. He would run across that field, Russians or not.

Snow had begun to fall. The tiny snowflakes descended gently onto the ground, as if every single one of them knew exactly where to land to form a perfect surface. Why destroy such a picturesque scene? What were they supposed to do when they got to the village? Wasn't it just a village like all the rest? What would happen if they left it alone, if the residents were allowed to live in peace, allowed to stay in their homes instead of being thrown out by freezing-cold Germans? He didn't feel the cold, though. The fever warmed his body from within like an oven. At the signal, they started running.

The soldiers' fear was palpable as the platoon moved away from the edge of the woods. Everyone was waiting for all hell to break loose. August heard his own heavy breathing, and each time his boots crunched the new snow, his head throbbed. He was already out of breath, and his body grew weaker with every step. His legs went out from under him. His chin struck his gun, and he tasted blood in his mouth. He wiped the snow from his face. He could see the others' backs, but a lone figure was moving in the opposite direction, toward him.

"If it were up to me, I would fucking let you lie there." Mertz pulled him to his feet with excessive force. "Can you run?"

"Yes. I think so."

"You damn well need to. I'm not going to carry you."

August's chest hurt as he started running again. His ears popped and he gasped for breath. Several times Mertz slowed down to keep pace with him. The others had reached the hedgerow. August and Mertz still had 150 feet to go when August fell.

This time he had enough foresight to hold his weapon out, away from his body, as he fell. He heard the shot the instant he hit the snow. It didn't sound like a shot, more like an echo, but he knew it was nearby, as if the sniper were right behind him.

Instinctively he looked up at Mertz. Blood was squirting from his temple, and a fine cloud of red mist had formed in the air. Mertz collapsed on the ground. Blood ran from between his yellow teeth, and the snow reddened under his head.

August gaped in terror at the others. Reichel crawled over to the fallen man. He put two fingers to the artery in Mertz's throat, then gestured to August, confirming what he already knew. Mertz was dead.

"Where did the shot come from?" he whispered.

"I don't know."

"Goddamn it." The lieutenant shook his head and called for Gildehaus. Together they dragged Mertz's lifeless body into the bushes that served as cover for the rest of the platoon.

"Sniper?"

Reichel shrugged and gave August, who was shaking with cold, an inquisitive look.

Carstens whispered, "It would have been safer to lead us up along the stone dike."

Two days later August lay in a field hospital in Kramatorsk. His body had been close to giving up, and now it consented to all the rest it could get. He slept for three days straight. The place was a cabinet of horrors. At night the hospital was filled with tears, wailing, shouting, and roars of pain, a nightmarish soundtrack. The man in the bed next to August lamented the pain in one of his legs, which was no longer there. Another man looked as though he had turned to liquid and only the mattress and the bed frame held him together. With their vacant expressions, empty eye sockets, and sunken cheeks, they resembled wax figures, like the ones August had seen at Panoptikum in St. Pauli. He not only heard their screams but sensed their silent shrieks of pain, the ones that never emerged from their mouths. He wondered every day whether he was one of them. Had he already stopped being a human? Did he scream at night without realizing it? Maybe he had yet to recognize that he was already dead. Would he ever be able to go home after the war? Would he ever look at Karin and feel the same desire as before? Would he be capable of enjoying his father's piano playing again?

One day a staff officer appeared. A kind-looking man with a narrow blond mustache, he introduced himself as First Lieutenant Wasner from Stuttgart. He awarded August a black medal. August tried to explain that he hadn't been wounded, but the man insisted there'd been no mistake. He was to deliver the medal to August Friedrich Strangl, and that's what he'd done. Wasner said that he had a similar medal himself, but in silver, because he'd been wounded three times in battle. The first time was in Holland and the second thanks to an indignant Parisian prostitute, he explained, patting his derriere with a grin. August was just about to ask about the episode in Paris when the lieutenant mentioned the Seventh Panzer Division.

"Seventh Panzer Division?" he asked, amazed.

"I was transferred to the division just before it left for Russia. It almost cost me my life." He pulled up his shirt so August could see the long, cigarette-shaped scar next to his navel.

"My father's in that division. Karl Strangl."

"You're Karl Strangl's son?" Wasner said, stuffing his shirt into his pants. He turned his head when a patient hoarsely roared in pain from one of the other beds.

August didn't even notice; he wanted to hear about his father. "Do you know him?'

"No, not really." He glanced back at the bed, where three nurses were trying to push the screaming man down. "I was in the combat troops, and he was in the supply troops." A doctor arrived and gave the patient an injection, after which he relaxed.

"But you've met him?"

Wasner seemed uncomfortable and shifted nervously. To August, he looked like someone who'd had enough of hospitals.

"I have met him, and the only thing I can say about him is that he's tall," Wasner said.

"Yes." August smiled at the thought of his father.

A doctor approached August's bed. Wasner uttered a stiff and dutiful "heil Hitler," then said, "Good luck, August Strangl."

"Thank you."

Wasner stepped uncomfortably past the screaming man's bed. An aide was in the process of covering the now-silent man with a white sheet. A pool of blood underneath the bed was slowly widening, filling the grout between the tiles, and when the grout was full, spilling over onto the white tile and sliding toward the lowest point in the floor: the drain. The aide struggled with one of the dead man's arms, which kept sliding off the bed so that it hung near the floor, swinging back and forth. The aide grew gradually more flushed and finally shoved the man's arm underneath him. August couldn't bear to watch and rolled onto his side. The war had abolished all reason: A dead man mocking a living one, Germans turning into killers, the innocent transformed into soldiers, and other innocents dying—and why? To what end? How could human beings treat each other this way? He didn't understand any of it. He tried his best not to think about it, but he couldn't suppress the ineradicable images that lived inside his head.

The doctor had apparently said something to him, but he hadn't caught a single word. Then he nodded at August and moved on to the next bed.

August got to his feet and shuffled to the window with faltering steps. He peered down at the small courtyard a few stories below, which was crammed with a welter of clotheslines. Had the Germans been victorious, he thought, the courtyard would have been decorated with red flags bearing swastikas, but instead the clotheslines were draped in bloodied sheets. Emblems of the vanquished. He crawled back into bed and pulled the wool blanket over his head.

Seven days later August left the hospital and returned to his unit.

Near Rzhev, Russia, March 14, 1942

They stopped in a small village. They all looked alike. The only things that distinguished them from each other were their names and locations on his map.

A big, burly man appeared in the doorway of one of the houses. A thick beard extended down his cheeks to his unbuttoned shirt. He signaled that he wished to speak with them. Paul made his way toward him cautiously, which made Karl smile. Although the man was big, Karl couldn't imagine that he would take on an entire company of German soldiers. When Paul reached him, he called for Pasek, a German from the Sudetenland who knew a few Russian phrases.

"He wants to invite the commander inside for refreshments," Paul said when he returned to Karl.

"You don't say no to a man of his size, do you?" Karl said, smiling at Paul and adjusting his cap. They'd been in the country for nearly a year, and their relationship with the locals had grown only more tense. Many of the men wanted to tear the head off any Russian they met, but Karl still believed that kindness was the best policy. Everything was easier when they were in good standing with the civilians. He planned to set a good example. He might have been a bit naïve, but he was in good spirits that day. The ground had begun to thaw, and the change in the weather made him feel more energetic than he had in months. He'd never gone through so difficult and merciless a winter, and now they all could see the light at the end of the tunnel. Spring's arrival meant that they could renew their advance on Moscow and be back in Germany before the following winter set in. That was something to be happy about.

The man nodded toward his house, then disappeared inside. Karl studied the squat building for a moment before following. With its thick, untreated outer walls of logs, moss-covered roof, and tiny windows, it looked like all the other houses in the village. He ducked as he entered so that he wouldn't bump his head against the low transom. At first he could see nothing in the pitch darkness, but his eyes soon adjusted, and the room began to take shape. He'd entered into a kitchen. In the middle of the room was the customary oven that served two functions: food preparation and heat. The walls were crude, and in one corner, the usual images of saints hung in gilded frames that had seen better days. Below the holy icons was a spinning wheel. As far as he could tell, the house consisted of just two rooms, and he assumed the other room was where the entire family slept.

An old woman was rummaging with some pots and pans. When she noticed Karl, she put them down, let her arms fall, and stared at the floor. He walked toward her and kindly offered his hand. Without raising her eyes, she wiped her hands on her stained apron and gave his hand a light squeeze with a wizened hand that reminded him of his old nanny, Mrs. Buchholz. When they were children, he and Gerhard agreed that she must have been at least one hundred years old, though she could hardly have been over fifty-five. The woman before him looked to be a great deal closer to one hundred than their former nanny had been. He had never imagined that a human being could be so wrinkled. She had typical Russian features: potato-colored skin, gray-blue eyes, and paper-thin lips. The skin of her neck had lost its battle against gravity and hung like a rooster's, which made her appear slightly grotesque. She peered up at him with deep-set, bloodshot eyes, and her toothless mouth formed a submissive smile. It looked like it hadn't smiled in many years.

Karl was startled when the man put an enormous fist on his shoulder. Without a word he offered Karl a seat at the large table. On the table sat a strange metal device that Karl had never seen before. He sat down, and the man settled across from him. Karl studied the strange contraption, which reminded him of their own field kitchens—the goulash cauldrons—or an urn with a chimney affixed to it. A small pipe extended from the bottom and terminated in a spigot. The old woman set two mugs before them, and the man twisted the spigot. A dark, steamy liquid poured into the mugs. The man dropped a couple of sugar cubes into one of them and set it down before Karl. An indistinct but pleasant aroma blended with the thick smell of the petroleum lamp above the table.

The man raised his cup to his mouth. Karl followed his lead and took a cautious sip so as not to burn himself. The taste was indescribable. The first mouthful was unpleasant, maybe because he wasn't used to it. There was a smoky taste to it, and it was redolent of unfamiliar fruits. He held up his mug, smiling to indicate what he thought of the tea.

That's when he saw the younger man in the corner opposite the holy icons. Half-concealed by the darkness, he rocked soundlessly but intensely back and forth in a rocking chair. He had a wild expression in his eyes, as if it took all his concentration to see just a few feet in front of him. The large man, who noticed Karl watching the cripple, spun his index finger around in circles at his temple. Karl understood. He figured the two men were brothers and that the old woman was their mother.

His host said nothing, just scrutinized Karl while occasionally raising his mug to drink. His eyes radiated a mixture of curiosity and vigilance. From his pants pocket he removed a leather pouch of tobacco, then began to roll a cigarette. When he was done, he offered it to Karl, who politely accepted it. He'd heard rumors about the Russian *mahorka* tobacco but was certain the stories were overblown, just like the ones about the Russians being cannibals. He noticed the cigarette had been rolled in newspaper, probably yesterday's *Pravda* or *Krasnaya Zvezda*; it smelled of sawdust and seemed harmless.

He took one drag on the cigarette and moments later had tears streaming down his cheeks. The man sat impassively while Karl did his best to suppress a coughing fit, but Karl was certain that he was laughing inwardly. The man said something to him then, and Karl gave him an apologetic look. The man pushed back his chair and went to pick up a square plate of some kind that was leaning against the wall. When he set it on the table, Karl saw that it was a chessboard. He shot Karl a questioning glance, and Karl nodded. The man began to set up the pieces, black for Karl and white for himself. A rook was missing, and in its place was a hunk of wood that had been cut so that it would stand. Karl waited patiently for his host to sit down, but to his surprise the man went over to the cripple instead. He put his hand beneath the cripple's arm and guided him to the chessboard. The big man then positioned himself next to the table and crossed his arms. Karl sized up his opponent. He tried in vain to make eye contact, but the young man's eyes darted about restlessly.

With a hard jerk, the cripple moved his king's pawn to D4. Trying to overpower his opponent, Karl shifted his knight to F6. The crudely carved piece was heavy. Pawn to C4. The young man played quickly; he didn't waste time contemplating his moves. Karl's plan was to overtake the middle, so he moved his pawn to C5. The cripple lurched in his chair, then pushed his D-pawn forward one square. There was something apt about their choosing the classic Benoni Defense, Karl thought. The name meant in Hebrew "the son of sadness"—which was telling, given his opponent. Though his protruding teeth caused his mouth to twist into a smile, his face was full of sorrow. His eyes were wet, and drool glistened at the corners of his mouth and chin.

Karl considered himself a skilled chess player, but he was quickly in trouble. No matter what he did, the cripple remained one step ahead of him, forcing him onto the defensive. Karl tried frantically to improve his position, but defeat was inevitable. It seemed he'd underestimated his opponent. The big man appraised Karl, who gave him a strained smile in return. Following an ill-conceived move by Karl, the young man nearly fell out of his chair in excitement. Checkmate. The banging pots fell silent, and the house was still for a moment, the only sound coming from the German soldiers outside. Then the big man began to laugh. His booming laughter shook the walls, and he laughed until his belly jiggled, his deep voice echoing throughout the house. It wasn't malicious, but an unfamiliar sensation began to grow in Karl. He was the object of this peasant's laughter. It was degrading. *He's mocking me,* he thought to himself. His uniform jacket suddenly felt constricting. *He has been waiting for me to lose in order to humiliate me, an officer of the Wehrmacht.*

Karl stood abruptly, and the chair toppled over behind him. He drew his service pistol and shoved the barrel between the man's eyes. The man fell silent. The old woman dropped a bowl behind them, and the clatter of broken glass filled the room. The man breathed heavily through his nose. Karl looked at his hand; his viselike grip on the pistol's shaft made the veins on the back of his hand bulge, and his hand began to shake. It occurred to him that he hadn't considered how this scene would play out. There were two possibilities: he could shoot or he could let it go. Should he shoot this crude peasant? He wondered how he would feel seeing the huge body drop lifelessly to the floor. But what was the man's crime? He'd had a laugh at Karl's expense. But was murder a reasonable punishment for insult? The man wasn't part of the war, after all; he was a random resident of a country at war. He decided that his death could not be justified. It would be the equivalent of SS justice—in which hundreds of civilians paid with their lives for every dead SS soldier. He saw then tension in the man's face. His jaw muscles were stiff beneath his beard, and his forehead was so furrowed that the muzzle of the pistol practically disappeared in his wrinkles. He stared at Karl with a mixture of defiance and wonder, as if fearing death and refusing to fear it at the same time. His mouth gaped, and the tart stink of the man's tobacco breath reached Karl every time the man exhaled.

Suddenly Karl thought there was something wretched about the man, something frightening about how swiftly a pistol could change the balance of power between two people. He glanced at the cripple rocking slowly and sluggishly back and forth, which seemed to underscore the seriousness of the situation. A single squeeze of the trigger, and the old woman would have only one half-son left. He looked at the woman, who stood as if petrified among the shards of broken glass, her over-sized apron wrapped around her waist like a shroud. She was obviously poor. The place showed no sign that anyone else helped feed the little family apart from the man with the pistol at his forehead. No, it wasn't worth it. The man's death would benefit no one. His hotheaded urge for revenge, so strong only a moment before, began to subside. The big man sat stock-still, awaiting his fate. Karl then thought of something else: Would he lose face if he turned and walked out the door?

The man apparently sensed Karl's hesitation, as his defiant expression slowly spread to the rest of his face. Karl tightened his grip on the pistol and pressed the barrel harder against the man's forehead. He was overcome with a sudden fear that the man would fight back, because for some inexplicable reason he sensed the man gathering his courage. Moving quickly, Karl thumped the base of the pistol's shaft against the man's temple. The man raised his hands to his face instinctively as a stream of blood ran down his cheek and through his coarse beard. Karl ran past the woman, who hadn't moved, out the door.

Daylight cut through Karl's eyeballs, causing a murderous pain in his eye sockets, which then spread to his ears as the old woman began to scream. It wasn't so much a scream but a lonely, hollow wail. Seeing Karl's expression, Piroska quickly ordered all the men to their vehicles, and the column drove away from the village.

Piroska sunnily hummed Franz Grothe's "Am nächsten Tag." Karl knew Piroska well enough to understand that he was trying to cheer him up. He leaned against the window and pretended not to notice Piroska eyeing him. He didn't feel good about what had happened back there. Striking the man had been unnecessary. And yet he'd done it anyway. Like a crazy man. Like all the others. The Opel Blitz's shock absorbers were in poor condition, and he let the battered road's jolts and vibrations punish him. He didn't move his cheek away from the window, didn't try to absorb the bouncing, but accepted it like a boxer too tired to put up his hands to block the blows. He deserved it. He cursed the fact that he'd allowed himself to imagine he had a place in this war—that he could make a difference. He shook his head sadly at the sight of a Panzer IV standing on the side of the road.

"Gunpowder is mankind's worst invention," Karl said.

The panzer's caterpillar tracks marked the path it had taken, reminding Karl of a runaway dog dragging its leash behind it. He guessed the tank had been walloped by a T-34. Grass and shrubs had begun to emerge from underneath the melting snow, growing between the heavy belts of manganese steel, as if nature had decided to conceal the war. A hare had apparently accepted the presence of the charred wreckage; it sat contentedly on one of the tracks. At the sound of the convoy, it turned its ears attentively, then darted between the trees.

"I would say that religion is worse," Paul said, his gaze fixed to the road. A pothole jounced him in his seat. "Much worse."

"Do you mean that?" Karl's voice quivered because of the road.

"Isn't that why we hate Jews?" Paul turned to Karl.

Karl studied his next in command, who'd once again directed his attention at the windshield. "Because of religion?"

"Yes."

"I don't think so."

"Why do we hate Jews, then?"

Karl shrugged. "That's just how it is, no one likes the Jews." Both men knew that neither one held the slightest thing against the Jews.

"Religion is a claim, that's all it is," Piroska said following a short pause.

Paul confused him on occasion. His way of thinking was so different, so provocative. To think of religion as a manmade invention along the lines of gunpowder, the wheel, or the telephone—to compare faith with objects—was offensive to most everyone on the planet. But it was typical Paul. He always said what was on his mind, taking every opportunity to curse Hitler and religion in that order.

"My brother is a doctor."

Karl already knew that.

"He's stationed at a military hospital in Kraków." Paul rolled his window down and spat out of it. "He wrote to me about a small city near Kraków, Oświęcim, I think it's called. They're gassing the Jews in a gigantic camp."

"He wrote that?"

"No, not that. The censor would have blotted that out."

"I've heard rumors of the camp. And of others," Karl said.

"Have we lost our minds?"

"Hmm, maybe the rumors are worse than the truth."

"Hitler's crazy."

How things had changed, Karl thought. There was a time when people would have been shot for talking like that. Now, it was common to hear such remarks among the men. And Paul was right. Karl's thoughts circled back to the Court of Honor in Berlin and the time he'd met Adolf Hitler. The man who was responsible for Karl being thousands of miles from his family, the unassuming little man who'd brought the world to the brink of chaos. He'd recently overheard a peculiar conversation between two group leaders. They'd been discussing Hitler's and Stalin's mustaches—whether one could pick the war's victor by looking at them—and they'd agreed that if size was what mattered, Stalin was in the lead. But if originality was the deciding factor, then Hitler had a slight edge over his rival. The thought made him laugh.

Paul made a dry, hoarse noise. He rolled his window down again and spat. Karl scrutinized him, unable to reconcile himself to the fact that Paul was a lawyer. He liked to spit, he enjoyed the front line, and he was generally capable of finding something positive to say about life as a soldier. Karl struggled more and more with that as time went on.

Karl didn't want to believe the rumors about the camps. He sincerely hoped that no one could be as evil as the rumors purported. But the camps existed—deep down he knew it—and the SS was responsible for them. Karl hated the SS. Even though he was a member himself, he felt no kinship with them. They were a bunch of psychopaths, and unfortunately his own son-in-law was among them. As was his brother. It had been some time since he'd thought of Gerhard. They wrote to each other, of course, but it was as though they didn't speak the same language anymore. As though Karl had been in Russia so long that his words had become warped. Gerhard, too, had adopted a new language that Karl didn't understand. Their letters were safe and superficial, always variations on the same template. *I'm well, and I hope you're well.* They were meaningless and irrelevant, but maybe that was what all letters were like these days because of the censors.

Paul leaned over the steering wheel and stared through the pane of glass. "Is that the rebel forests? Or do we only call the woods near Smolensk by that name?"

"They're all filled with rebels."

"Do you feel safer with Morgenroth in the column?"

Emil Morgenroth was a young lieutenant who'd been named column commander. His two platoons were supposed to protect the supply convoy—which now consisted of thirty-two trucks—that was hauling gasoline to the front. On their return trip they would carry wounded men.

"He seems confused about who's in charge, me or him."

The lieutenant had been raised in the Hitler Youth and was the type of man who always saluted officiously. He and Karl had had several run-ins already. The young officer had difficulty accepting Karl's relaxed leadership style. He insisted on strict discipline, and it quickly became clear that he had an itchy buttonhole—which is how they described soldiers eager to get medals clipped to their chests. Morgenroth was twenty-four years old and had been in France for six months, but as a newly appointed lieutenant, he'd requested a transfer to the eastern front. Protecting the supply column was his first real assignment, and he'd now been with Karl's company for fourteen days.

"Why don't you arm wrestle for it?" Piroska said, grinning. He stopped laughing when the truck thumped against something, startling them both. "What the hell did I hit?"

"You can't stop," Karl said.

"It was an animal."

"You can't stop." In Piroska's side mirror Karl saw a white wool pelt splotchy with red stains lying at the edge of the road.

Paul had seen it, too. "Why the hell is there a goat in the middle of the road?"

"It's a trap. They want us to stop."

Just then a spray of bullets pierced the radiator. Piroska jerked the vehicle to the side of the road. It sounded like an animal was dying beneath the hood. Then the motor sputtered out, its suffering over. The big truck rolled over the edge of the ditch and crashed against the other side. Piroska opened the door and leaped into the ditch. Karl's door was jammed against the embankment, so he scrambled out the driver's side just as bullets pelted the passenger's side where he'd been sitting moments before. The glass shattered.

The vehicles behind them came to a stop, and the men followed their lead and dropped to the ground. Karl could see their attackers through the trees. He couldn't tell how many of them there were, but the ones he could see weren't wearing uniforms. They had a Maxim machine gun on a tripod, and he figured that's what killed their Opel. His troops needed to put that machine gun out of commission, but a quick assessment told him they were outnumbered.

Here's Morgenroth's chance to earn some medals for his chest, Karl thought. He'd had his doubts about the conceited officer, but Morgenroth leaped around shouting orders, first to one side, then the other.

The rebels fired, and the Germans fired back. Grenades exploded, men were injured, men died. The machine gun was destroyed by hand grenades, and the rebels panicked. Against Morgenroth's decisive leadership, their lack of organization became catastrophic. Some turned and fled while others fought on. In the confusion Karl had forgotten his pistol in its sheath. He reached for it, but then stopped. Everything was happening so fast. Paul lay in the grass screaming. Remmel, too. There was blood, lots of blood, a river, a sea, an ocean of red. Paul's screams grew fainter, and Remmel fell silent, too, as he tried to concentrate on keeping the wounded man alive.

"Where's the nearest field hospital?" shouted the medical officer. "He won't survive without proper care."

"I don't know," Karl shouted desperately.

Remmel struggled like a man possessed. "Press here," he said, moving Karl's hand to Paul's chest. Karl could feel his friend's crushed rib beneath the slick film of blood. Paul mumbled, gurgled, and began to cough. Karl spoke to him gently. Told him about the Alster, about things Piroska had described to him in Passau, and about Liesel. Though his head and body were about to explode and chaos was erupting all around, he spoke softly, with a steely calm. He hadn't realized it, but he was crying.

Karl stood. Paul Piroska's body lay lifelessly in the damp ditch. Until just a few minutes ago, it had been healthy and vigorous, but now it was bleeding and raw, reduced to flesh, bones, and guts. Remmel gave Karl a look of despair.

Morgenroth and his men had chased the rebels into the trees. Shots rang out from the woods, and the men soon returned, bringing with them eight or ten blank-faced Russians. They were bearded and beardless, young and old. The lieutenant was radiant, and in that moment Karl despised him with all his heart. Not because Morgenroth had taken the prisoners, but because he allowed himself to be happy.

"Gather the troops!" Karl shouted peevishly to the lieutenant.

"What about the prisoners?" Morgenroth asked.

"Tell them to go that way." He pointed without knowing which way was west. "They'll come to one of our prison camps sooner or later."

"But our duty is to—" the lieutenant persisted.

"Do whatever the hell you want with them. They're your prisoners, not mine," Karl cut him off and turned to help maneuver Piroska into one of the vehicles.

Morgenroth pointed at one of the rebels. The Russian blinked, shrugging uncomprehendingly. The lieutenant walked over to him, grabbed his collar, and pulled him toward the woods. He threw the Russian to his knees and drew his service pistol. The other prisoners shifted nervously when he put the weapon to the man's neck.

Shots resounded in the woods, and Morgenroth stood at the edge looking on while the rest of the prisoners were executed.

Karl sat with Piroska on one of the truck beds and puffed agitatedly on a cigarette. He exhaled vigorously, watched two cone-shaped spirals billow from his nose, and demonstratively turned away from the macabre scene. He shouldn't have let Morgenroth decide. He should have insisted, but he'd let the idiot lieutenant take charge. Karl had been weak, he hadn't wanted the confrontation, and now there were Russians scattered among the trees, their brains splattered across the forest floor.

Morgenroth and the others crawled onto the trucks at the back of the convoy, and the column headed out. Karl could see into the cab of the truck behind him and noted Morgenroth's satisfied smile. He had an almost irrepressible urge to draw his pistol from his holster, aim it at the truck's windshield, and empty the magazine into the dumb officer. Karl would make certain that this little incident cost Emil Morgenroth his career. Goddamn upstart. He would report the incident to Major Strunz when they returned to Rzhev. He would see to it that Morgenroth received his proper due. Karl was certain of that.

Piroska's head lay in his lap. With his fingertips, he carefully closed Piroska's eyelids. He would write to Liesel himself.

When the recently promoted First Lieutenant Morgenroth was transferred two months later, an Iron Cross Second Class hung around his neck. It gleamed as he reported to the headquarters of the Panzer Grenadier Regiment Grossdeutschland. Meanwhile, the Seventh Panzer Division was reassigned to France in half as many transport trains as had carried them to East Prussia a year before. Some cried with relief; the thought of putting the Russian hell behind them gave the worn-out soldiers hope that they might yet survive.

Near Maykop, Russia, October 12, 1942

Trees dotted the landscape ahead of August. With their scrawny trunks and bashful crowns towering over the other trees, some looked like gangly schoolboys. A tree with white, heart-shaped flowers strewn across its branches looked as though it had been blanketed with snow. Every hue of green, yellow, gold, and brown was represented among the leaves. Green had always brought out something calm and pleasant in August. The color was harmless. It bore no evil—unlike red with its associations with blood, love, and hate. Blue possessed the same traits as green, because of the sea—which he'd seen all too infrequently. As he pushed farther into the forest, he was calmed by the cloudless sky and the many shades of green.

A ways into the forest, he hiked down his pants. He squatted behind a tall maple next to a young tree that was not yet taller than a man. He trapped one of its thin branches between two fingers and pulled until it snapped. He released it, letting it dangle there. *Like a man on the gallows,* he thought, like one of the bodies they'd passed on the road. Three men and a woman had been hanged from a tree much older and bigger than the one he was squatting next to. They'd been barefoot, with blackened heads. Around their throats they wore signs bearing words written in Russian. He remembered the woman especially; her clothes had been ripped open in the front, exposing her belly and breasts. Her skin, which surely had been soft as silk, was black in death. He looked at the branch. The tree's white pulp oozed out of the open wound, trying to heal itself. He wouldn't allow the branch to become like the people in the tree. He tugged at it, but it struggled against him. The youthful tree was incredibly elastic. The branch refused to release the trunk, bending toward him instead. Though he pulled with all his might, the branch wouldn't let go. Defeated by a tree, he finally gave up.

Just as August finished, he heard the Russians. He couldn't tell how many there were. Slowly, so as not to make any noise, he got to his feet, squeezing his belt buckle in one hand to keep it from jingling. He pressed his spine into the tree and cursed to himself when he realized that he'd leaned his rifle against the other side of the maple. If they spotted him, he wouldn't have the slightest chance. His heart was hammering as though it knew the end had come.

His companions would never find him out here. He hadn't told anyone that he'd gone into the forest to relieve himself. The others just dug holes next to the trench when their need was urgent, but he wanted to be alone, to have peace and quiet, a foolish notion that might now cost him his life. What if his impatient gut was his undoing? His mind worked frantically to figure out how to get away without being seen. He heard them getting closer.

Judging by the noise, there were two of them, at most three. He heard one of them laughing, the unmistakable sound of a woman's airy timbre. He slid down into a squat and leaned against the tree. He could barely discern the outline of the two figures between the trees. They'd apparently stopped walking.

They were about a hundred feet away and stood facing each other a few feet apart. They moved slowly sideways, so that their legs crossed and their movements formed a circle. They danced in this manner for a while, not once taking their eyes off each other. They smiled.

The young soldier appeared to be August's age. He was wearing the kind of fur cap that could be buttoned on his head or fastened under his chin, and his coat was buttoned on one side. He'd leaned his rifle against a tree. The girl, too young to be called a woman, was probably about seventeen or eighteen. Like him she was in uniform, and she wore a soft cap that didn't conceal her shoulder-length blond hair, which was combed back in a tight little ponytail. Over her shoulder she carried a canvas bag emblazoned with a red cross. August couldn't tell whether she was armed or not. With her large and indelicate features and her short legs, she wasn't beautiful, but he still found her strangely charming. Though he didn't understand what she was saying, he could hear the playful tone in her voice.

She kicked at a fallen branch, which struck the soldier in the thigh. She laughed the most beautiful laughter August had ever heard.

"Я иду к тебе," said the Russian soldier.

"Сперва тебе надо меня поймать, Владимир," said the girl.

"Сейчас я тебя поймаю," he replied.

Although August didn't understand Russian, he sensed that the young girl was teasing the soldier, who hungrily devoured her body with his eyes. She winked flirtatiously at him, and he suddenly leaped at her. She tried to evade him but fell with a loud moan, then tried crawling away on all fours. He clutched one of her boots and it slid free with a slurping sound. She threw a handful of leaves in the soldier's direction, covering him with the red-brown foliage. He put the boot in his mouth and shook it like a hungry bear. She rolled onto her back, surrendering, and he crawled toward her, laughing. She pulled herself up on her elbows and drew him close once he lay on top of her. They kissed for a long time.

The soldier slowly unbuttoned her jacket and pulled up her sweater. August trembled when he caught a brief flash of her naked skin. She helped him remove her jacket. August sneaked closer to get a better view.

The soldier had now pushed her sweater so far up that her small breasts were exposed. When the soldier began to caress them, August felt himself getting aroused. An overturned tree trunk partially blocked his view. He crawled soundlessly around it and hid behind a large rock.

The soldier got to his knees and slowly pulled her pants down around her ankles. Then he removed his own jacket and pants. They regarded each other expectantly, then the soldier gingerly climbed on top of her again. August's heart accelerated, and when the soldier penetrated her, it skipped a beat. She let out a short moan.

The soldier slowly thrust up and down, and the couple quickly found a rhythm. She wrapped her short legs around him and buried her fingers in his broad back, making low, repetitive noises, like a sign swaying in the breeze. He'd never witnessed anything like it and was completely absorbed. It aroused him that they didn't know they were being watched. He tried adjusting his pants, which felt tight in the crotch. August crept closer until he was only about thirty feet away.

A pheasant suddenly flew up right in front of August, flapping its wings over his head. The soldier stopped and turned toward the frightened bird. At first he didn't notice August, but his roaming eyes soon settled directly on him. Both men were completely paralyzed.

August was the first to break out of his hypnotized state. He stumbled clumsily to his feet, nearly tripping with his first step. He recovered his balance and ran as fast as he could, his thoughts moving as quickly as his legs. *If he gets to his rifle, I'm a goner,* he thought, but the other man had started running after him. He'd hiked his pants back up and drawn a short knife from his boot. He seemed more agile than he had at first glance, and he was catching up to August, who threw himself sideways over the overturned tree trunk.

Though he'd traversed only a short distance, he already felt winded and his rifle was still thirty feet away. But did he remember the right tree? Had he remembered to load it? Was the safety off? He heard the soldier right behind him. The girl had seized her lover's rifle and now rushed after them.

I'm going to make it, I'm . . . He stopped thinking and hurled himself onto his belly, grabbing the butt of his rifle, which nearly slipped from his hands. He searched feverishly for the trigger and spun around to face the soldier, who was closer than he'd thought; the short knife was raised above his head, ready to be jammed deep into August's skinny body.

The shot caused several birds to fly off from the treetops, but all August heard was the girl hysterically screaming the soldier's name. *Vladimir.*

Vladimir stood stock-still, so close that August could've touched him with the tip of his rifle. He dropped the knife. Like a dart, it penetrated the topsoil between his boots. The bullet had entered his upper chest, and the bloodstain darkening his green shirt quickly widened. He watched August with sad eyes, mumbling softly as if he were recounting a fairy tale to child.

"Vladimir!" The girl was now right beside August. He didn't know what she intended to do with the rifle she carried. He swung the shaft of his weapon at her head, and she dodged it. But the blow struck her hard on the shoulder, and she tumbled onto her back.

August aimed the rifle at the soldier again and, closing his eyes, squeezed the trigger. Vladimir fell heavily. His lifeless body landed on one of the girl's arms, breaking it with a loud crack.

August stared at the two Russians. He loaded his rifle as a reflex. The girl couldn't move. Her arm was pinned underneath the dead soldier, who stared with wide-open eyes into the trees. Lying beside each other, they looked like a couple in their marital bed.

She didn't make a peep but gaped intensely at August. He shifted nervously. What should he do with her? He couldn't shoot her. Why would he?

A strange thought occurred to him. *I have to apologize. I have to tell her I'm sorry. I didn't mean to.*

She was trembling in pain. He watched as she struggled to free her broken arm from under the corpse. It clearly hurt too much, and she gave up. She looked up at him, pleading. She was so beautiful, lying there. Her blond hair was wreathed with red-brown leaves, and her pretty blue eyes were filled with tears that slowly trickled down toward her small ears.

"Отпусти меня," she said.

"I don't understand."

"Пожалуйста, отпусти меня." Her voice was urgent.

"I don't understand you. I wish I could let you go, but I can't. You must understand." August felt sad, but he knew he had to do it. He was a soldier, and it was too risky to let her return to wherever she'd come from before he'd randomly stumbled upon them.

He aimed his rifle at her. Her voice quivered, but she spoke slowly and clearly. Even though he didn't understand a word, he still seemed to grasp what she was saying. He raised his Mauser and prepared to fire. She continued talking to him. Her tone of voice was kind, almost affectionate, like a mother addressing her child. He stood like that for some time, ready to fire the killing shot while she kept talking. He swayed slightly. He closed his eyes and squeezed the trigger halfway down—until he could feel its resistance. All his index finger had to do now was give the smallest tug, and he could forget all about the Russian girl. He'd never seen her before. She meant nothing to him.

She'd fallen silent. He opened his eyes, and only now did he notice that she was holding between her fingers a small silver cross attached to a thin chain around her throat. He felt her fear like a cold blast of air. A small tap on the trigger, and he would never forget her, he knew. Her eyes were closed. She was waiting for him. Waiting for him to shoot.

"I can't," he shrieked, throwing down his weapon. "I won't do it."

He fell back against the tree where the rifle had stood, and slid down the thick trunk until he was seated on the ground. A tear trickled out of the corner of his eye and was soon joined by others.

"I'm sorry, I'm sorry," he said, looking at her.

She stared at him in confusion.

"I'm not an evil person. I'm not evil," he repeated, burying his face in his filthy hands.

He steadied his gaze on her, his face dissolving in tears. "I've always thought of myself as a good person. I didn't mean to kill him. I don't want to kill you."

He fell silent except for the occasional sob.

He stared into the air. "Is someone evil because he's done something evil?" He gave her a questioning glance. "Can a good deed make it right again?" He stood resolutely, then stopped. "Can a good deed make it right again?" He chewed on his own words a moment.

Then he walked resolutely over to her and carefully lifted Vladimir's heavy body off her broken arm. August helped her to sit up. He unhooked his canteen and filled the aluminum cup with water, then held it to her lips. They trembled. He poured too quickly, and part of the cup's contents dripped down her chin and onto her chest. Her name was embroidered on the left chest pocket of her shirt. He pointed at the name, and when she didn't understand, he spun his index finger toward himself and said, "August."

He pointed at her name again, and she stuttered softly, "Nadia."

He helped her to her feet. Her arm hung loosely at her side, and he saw how courageously she swallowed her pain.

"Go now," he said softly, indicating the direction she'd come from with the soldier. "Go."

She understood the meaning of his words and slowly began edging away from him. She glanced at the body of the soldier, who until a few moments ago had been her lover, then lowered her head and walked off unsteadily. Before long she vanished in the trees.

He sat down heavily. He felt exhausted, sick. He emptied his canteen and tilted his head back to gaze into the treetops, which began to spin. They spun faster and faster until he had to close his eyes so that he wouldn't throw up. *I've just killed a man*, he thought, *because I needed to go to the bathroom. I've just taken a girl's lover away from her.* Maybe they were going to get married someday. Maybe they'd known each other since they were children, and everyone in their village had always known they would be man and wife one day. There would be a wedding. Vladimir and Nadia would be married. "We told you so," the old women in the village would say. Nadia would give birth to five children; they would live in a nice little house, which Nadia would turn into a fine, loving home despite their meager resources. The children would never go to bed hungry, and Vladimir would make sure the fire in the fireplace never went out. They would grow old together. Nadia would die of old age, in her sleep, and Vladimir would follow her to the grave a year later, consumed by grief. But then along came a German, and now Vladimir was dead, and Nadia was a cripple. August shook his head despondently.

"You're not thinking of running away, are you Strangl?" Falkendorf was suddenly standing beside him. Despite his size, he had a way of moving soundlessly through the woods, like a predator stirred by its hunting instincts.

"Holy shit, what happened here?" He whistled, impressed. "Did you do this, Strangl?"

August nodded silently.

A satisfied smile emerged on Falkendorf's lips. He held out a cigarette pack for August, who declined with a wave of his hand. "Good work." Falkendorf grinned. "Maybe I was wrong about you after all."

August said nothing.

Neuengamme, Germany, October 15, 1942

"Is this where you'd like me to stop?"

"Yes, thank you. This is fine."

Gerhard watched the car vanish in the direction of Hamburg. Wanting to hold on to the last of his freedom, he'd ask to be dropped off here so he could walk the rest of the way. The flat asphalt road was surrounded by tall trees and fields. The birdsong relaxed him, and he noted how close to the ground the swallows were flying. The gray clouds confirmed what the birds had already told him: rain was on the way.

A red brick watchtower interrupted nature's harmony, and he knew he'd soon be able to see the outline of the camp. He got a whiff of the smell. A putrid, revolting odor that invariably made him think of the fish market in St. Pauli, but this stench was worse, harsher. A blend of chlorine, latrines, and filthy people, it reinforced the images that he'd formed in his mind. He felt an urge to turn around, to spin on his heels and vanish. He paused and put his suitcase down. His good sense stifled this sudden impulse; he picked up his suitcase and went on.

His steps slowed and shortened as he approached his new place of employment. Flowers in every color of the rainbow bloomed beside the main entrance like a multihued welcoming committee, but the camp's stench overwhelmed the aromatic florae. The flowers didn't match the season.

Two columns of around thirty prisoners appeared from the other direction. Their faces were emaciated and sullen, and most of them shuffled bent forward with short, dragging steps. Gerhard started in alarm when a guard—who looked quite like a prisoner himself—shouted at the gray mass. He should have fled, he wasn't at all ready for this, but it was too late to turn around now. He hadn't even entered the camp yet, and he was already overcome with an all-consuming mixture of powerlessness, anxiety, and fear of what awaited him.

A uniformed guard stood at the entrance next to a red-and-white-striped sentry box, a rifle on his shoulder. Behind him was a red brick building, above which loomed the watchtower. The prisoners waddled through the gate and past the guard, but he didn't deign to so much as glance in their direction. Instead, he smiled pleasantly at Gerhard, like a clerk in a haberdashery. Gerhard handed his transfer order to the soldier, who scanned the paper quickly and nodded. The soldier said something to a colleague, who stuck his head out of the sentry box, and Gerhard heard him making a phone call inside the little wooden house. Gerhard watched the prisoners disappear into the camp, and suddenly goose bumps riddled his flesh.

He was asked to wait. He stared at the camp in disbelief. The prisoners looked like corpses. Their striped clothes hung from them as if on clothes hooks. Though he was still outside the camp, the stench filled his nostrils, and he swallowed to prevent himself from throwing up. He couldn't believe he was going to work in a place like this—that he would, in fact, live in a place like this.

An officer came over to greet him. His gait was self-assured, and he didn't pay the walking dead any mind. He was a short man, but his girth made up for his stature. His head seemed pressed onto his shoulders as though he had no neck, and his corpulent body bulged beneath his tight-fitting leather jacket. Underneath his arm he held a riding whip with a carved white ivory shaft.

"Senior Assault Leader Edwin Turek," he said. "Welcome."

Gerhard's anxiety had spread to his palm, which was clammy with sweat as he greeted Turek.

Turek was the camp director. He spoke in curt, concise sentences that he fired off at a brisk clip. Since he was clearly used to being obeyed, even regarding the most trivial matters, his pronunciation had grown lazy and the ends of his words vanished somewhere in his mouth. The aggressive barrage of talk, compounded by the smell, made Gerhard woozy.

They entered the camp, and the camp director gave Gerhard a tour, describing the various buildings and their purpose in an animated tone. The camp was in a low-lying marsh area called Vierlande. It was surrounded by a chain-link fence pumped with enough electricity to kill a person, Turek explained proudly. The barbed wire made a loud, dry crackle as they walked alongside it.

"Well, well. We got a rat in our trap." Turek grinned.

Gerhard wasn't sure if he meant it literally. All he knew was that he would have to get used to this kind of thing, but how was he ever going to do that?

The camp entrance was flanked by the guard building on one side and depots on the other. Just beyond the main gate was a huge, paved courtyard for roll call. The eerily empty space was fenced in with barbed wire that was broken up only by small gates leading to long rows of double barracks. In all there were nine squat, green wooden barracks, which housed around six hundred prisoners per unit. Gerhard could see a gallows with three swaying nooses between some of the barracks. A person was hanging from one of them.

On the other side of the courtyard, there were five sanctuaries, the infirmaries. Vacant faces stared at them from the windows. They looked like mummies—more lifeless even than those he'd just classified as walking corpses. Turek referred to the pale men as *Muselmann*. He pointed at a red brick building behind the infirmaries.

"That's where they're heading. It's the final station."

Gerhard eyed the crematorium. A column of smoke plumed from the smokestack.

Turek stopped and faced Gerhard. He looked at him quizzically. "Do you smell that sweet stench?"

There was no way of avoiding the crematorium's stench. Nausea filled his throat, and he puffed out his cheeks to stifle the unrelenting urge to vomit. He nodded silently.

"It's the smell of burning people." Turek started walking once more. "But it's the right thing to do," he said as if in apology. "You'll get used to it soon enough," he added over his shoulder.

Beyond the crematorium were a number of squat buildings. They made up the Walther-Werke factory, where the prisoners produced pistols and guns for the weapons manufacturer Carl Walther GmbH. Firms like Jastram and Messap also made use of this cheap labor force, loaned to them by the SS. Towering on the camp's northern end was an enormous tile factory complete with presses, a mashing plant, stoves, and drying facilities. Here they produced bricks that were then transported to Hamburg via the waterway on large barges. At first this had required access to the Elbe River, so the prisoners had dug, by hand, a four-mile long canal connecting Neuengamme with the Elbe. Near the tile factory was a large area with greenhouses and vegetable gardens that supplied the SS camp with tomatoes, turnips, and cabbage. Turek made no secret of the fact that gardening was a popular job among the prisoners, as it gave them the opportunity to steal vegetables. But if they were caught, he groused suddenly, they were killed. As he spoke, he ran his index finger in a slicing motion across his thick throat.

Gerhard noticed the same routine every time they passed an inmate. He would lift his cap, then stand as still as a mouse with his cap at his side, staring at the ground in fright. Over his shoulder, Gerhard watched them hurry away once he and Turek had passed by. The same was true of those to whom Turek spoke. Everyone made sure not to make eye contact with the stocky *Obersturmführer*, who explained that new prisoners were shaved from head to toe, then given a number. They were handed a set of clothes without concern for size or the condition of the clothes. A colored triangle was sewn or painted onto the clothes to indicate the prisoner's status in the camp. Red meant political prisoner; green, criminal; black, antisocial; purple, Jehovah's Witness; and pink, homosexual. Jews wore two yellow triangles that formed a Star of David. International prisoners—and over time there were more and more of these in the camp—were assigned a red triangle.

"Streich!" Turek's shout cut through the air.

A man in riding pants, tall boots, and a cap was beating a prostrate prisoner with a whip. The lashes made a drawn-out flicking noise. He paused and turned toward the two men.

"This is Franz Streich. He's the camp senior." Without waiting for Gerhard's question, Turek went on: "He's a prisoner, but he's in charge of all the others. The barracks leader, the servants, the kapos, and everyone else are under his command."

Gerhard studied the sewn-on green triangle on the man's sleeve.

Turek poked the prisoner on the ground with the toe of his boot. "Put him in the chimney when you're done."

Streich shrugged and sauntered away.

"On the outside Streich was a murderer," Turek said, looking Gerhard directly in the eyes. "That's why he's here. He's a murderer in here, too, a real devil. We're angels by comparison." He made the sign of the cross. "Even the subordinate SS officers fear him."

Gerhard closed his eyes for a moment, as though trying to suppress it all. As though his thoughts might somehow find refuge, even if only for a second or two. *This place is insane. Quite simply insane. This fat man prances around here as if it were the most natural thing in the world, even displaying professional pride in his work.*

"But it's good to have self-policing among the prisoners. That way we can just lean back, eat, and be merry." The director patted his belly.

They'd returned to the main entrance, and Turek paused outside the largest of the depots.

"Your office is in there." Turek pointed at the door to the commandant's barracks.

The door opened right then, and an officer emerged.

"Ah, Dr. Borg. Say hello to our new administrative director."

Gerhard dutifully uttered his name as he shook the man's firm hand. He noticed that the doctor, who'd introduced himself as Erwin Borg, had pleasant brown eyes that reminded him of Emma's.

"Borg, do you have time to show Strangl his new quarters?" Turek asked as he dabbed his mouth with a handkerchief.

"Of course," the doctor replied.

Inside the camp, separated from the rest by a fence, was yet another camp inhabited by some five hundred soldiers. The troop barracks, garage, workshops, and a bunker surrounded a courtyard that was used, Erwin Borg explained, for military ceremonies and on the anniversary of the march to Feldherrnhalle. The camp personnel consisted primarily of SS members. The commandant, a recently named *Sturmbannführer* Gerhard had yet to meet, was the camp's commanding officer; his adjutant, who was in charge of his office, made sure that all orders were followed. In addition there was Turek, a head of the camp's security detail, a garrison doctor, and a camp doctor. The job of the administrative director, the position Gerhard was to assume, was to oversee all supplies to the camp.

"Make yourself at home, and I'll come get you when the commandant has returned from Hamburg. Then you can meet him," the doctor said when they'd reached Gerhard's new room.

Gerhard nodded silently.

After Borg left, he set his suitcase beneath the window. When he saw the view, he hurriedly closed the curtains. Then he lay down on the bed and began to think. Why was he in this godforsaken place? He hadn't been forced to come here; it was just that the alternatives had been worse. But how could anything be worse than this? It was impossible to imagine. He had often felt that he didn't belong, but this time the feeling was especially pronounced. He would never get used to this place, that much was certain. As soon as the commandant returned, he would explain to him that he didn't belong here, and then he would immediately request a transfer. Any place would be better than here.

Unfortunately it wasn't possible to return to the transport division because it had been closed. All the unwanted elements—as they'd dubbed the Jews and gypsies—had been eliminated from Hamburg, and the SS no longer needed von Amrath's department. The SS now needed people in the camps and on the front lines. Those were the options Gerhard and his colleagues had been offered. They had deliberated over them—concentration camp versus war, disease, or famine—at length. He remembered the advice Karl had given him in a short letter: avoid the eastern front at all costs. That was why he had ended up here. Seitz-Göppersdorf and a few of the others had been sent to the camp at Sachsenhausen, but someone must have been looking out for Gerhard, because he was sent to Neuengamme just outside the city. He'd felt lucky until he saw the camp. He could think of only one person who deserved to be imprisoned in such a place: Weinhardt.

He didn't know how much time had passed when Borg knocked on his door.

The commandant's house was in the middle of the camp. Surrounded by a well-tended hedge, it looked as if it had gotten lost, as if it had turned down the wrong street and should have taken the turn that led to the nice residential neighborhood.

It was an ordinary white house with a raised brick foundation and windows divided by muntins. The garden consisted of a trimmed lawn, a few trees, and some empty flowerbeds. Smoke billowed softly from the chimney.

Gerhard walked up the steps that led up to the front door. Before he could even knock, a tall, slender woman opened the door. He was struck by how attractive she was, and her scent only heightened that impression. She had shoulder-length blond hair that curled a little at the ends, and he caught himself wondering how soft it was; her facial features were pleasantly symmetrical, apart from a black mole beneath her nose. She smiled warmly, and her eyes sparkled as she invited him inside. They passed through a cozily furnished room where two well-dressed children, a boy and a girl, were playing cards.

She guided him to a double door that led to an office where a man sat behind a desk, bent over some papers. When the woman closed the door, the man laid his fountain pen on the table, looked up, and said, "As you can see, I haven't forgotten you, Mr. Strangl." He stood now and came around to the other side of the table.

Everything Gerhard had once thought about Erich Lorenz's inability to smile turned out to be wrong. For Lorenz was smiling broadly now, revealing his teeth and two large dimples on either side of his wide mouth.

"I heard what a great job you did for von Amrath, so I made certain that you landed with us."

He was beaming with pride. Gerhard shook his hand mechanically.

"You should be proud; it's an honor to work here," Lorenz said, offering him a seat.

As Gerhard slowly overcame his shock, he remembered the last time he'd seen Lorenz. Now he'd been promoted to Sturmbannführer and had been made the master of life and death. The days Gerhard had spent in a cell thanks to Lorenz suddenly seemed like nothing compared to the suffering the prisoners were subjected to in this place. Thousands of people died here each day. And Lorenz was responsible for that.

He gathered his courage. "I'm not interested in working here," Gerhard said hesitantly.

"It's not a question of whether you're interested or not."

"I would like to request an immediate transfer."

"You do that." Lorenz grinned amiably.

Near Tuapse, Russia, October 18, 1942

Seventeen hundred feet, maybe seventeen fifty.

He was at least a thousand feet from the burned-out Bobik, and from there it was another eight hundred to the German observation post.

Seventeen fifty was about right.

Yesterday had been a good day for Dmitri. He'd killed four Germans, including two officers. Makarov called him the snipers' Justitia. He didn't know what that meant, so he wasn't sure whether the commissar was making fun of him or not. He simply felt he was doing his duty. The Germans were going after the oil refineries in Tuapse, and he would defend them tooth and nail. He knew the battle wouldn't determine the outcome of the war, but as the saying went, the only good German was a dead German.

Today was shaping up to be a good day. The two Germans in the advance position—one of whom manned a machine gun, while the other served as an observer—had no inkling he was there.

The armored reconnaissance vehicle BA-64—the Bobik—had been overturned, blackened by the merciless fire that had ripped through every flammable scrap. Around it lay the corpses of three charred Russian soldiers. Russia looked like hell these days. Dmitri recalled the hot summers when villagers used to work the harvest together, reaping the grain with scythes, then threshing it with flails. At the end of the day, they celebrated—and did so every night until the harvest was done. He thought of the girls with their white shawls around their chubby cheeks, and about Lena. Plump, beautiful Lena. Her father considered Dmitri a simpleton, a good-for-nothing whose future was as bleak as the Russian night sky. Back then he'd surely been right, but maybe the 148 dead Germans would change his mind.

He'd been hiding here for hours, having taken his position under cover of darkness, well camouflaged by his *plash-palatka*, a versatile cape that not only provided protection against the rain but served as a good hiding spot for a sniper. He'd wrapped his Tokarev rifle in strips of burlap and tied them down with yarn to ensure that the sun wouldn't reflect off the barrel and give him away. Your chance of success was greater if you eliminated every uncertainty.

To be a good sniper was, for him, a matter of common sense. What's the distance to the target? How will gravity influence the bullet across a given distance? What are the wind conditions? Is the target moving and, if so, at what speed? His brain assessed all of these factors instinctively. Many believed it was all about having the best rifle, but Dmitri believed that being an effective sniper came down to three things. First, the sniper himself. He needed to have the instinct. If he didn't, he would never be a good sniper. Second, the rifle's scope. It must be precise to ensure that he hit his target where he expected to. Third, the rifle. He needed to understand the weapon he held in his hands the way he understood the old Berdan he'd hunted with as a boy, before the army provided him with a slightly better weapon.

Before the war he'd earned his keep as a carpenter—not an especially good one, according to the people in the village—but now he'd found something he excelled at. It was so easy, so logical, so poetic.

I am like the wind: present, then gone the next instant.

I am like sound. By the time you notice it and try to capture it, it's too late, because by then it's already gone.

His job involved making many decisions. Should he go after the machine gunner or the observer first? The gunner was the immediate threat, but once he fired the first shot, he would alert the observer to his position. He'd be vulnerable if the observer had the presence of mind to get behind the machine gun—which, judging by the mouth of the barrel, was an MG 42—before Dmitri fired his second shot.

He saw the world through his rifle's scope. Even when he wasn't looking through it, he could see the black cross, as if it were burned into his cornea. It even appeared in his dreams. Luckily he hadn't been dreaming of late.

August raised the binoculars to his eyes. There were short fir trees scattered across the landscape, with fifty to sixty feet between each one, and he couldn't tell if they'd been planted in any kind of order. They reminded him of small, fat dwarfs. Apart from the dwarfs, he had a clear view of the forest about 1,500 feet ahead. The wreck of a Russian vehicle indicated that they weren't the first German soldiers to set foot here.

They sat behind the remains of a stone dike that had probably withstood wind and weather for centuries. Maybe the dike had been built after a dispute between two farmers who'd disagreed over where the border between their properties was located. It wasn't like that anymore, though, because the state owned everything.

Though it was summer, it had been a cold night and it had rained. Stanislav had insisted they share a cigarette because he claimed it helped them to stay warm. A foolish decision, but luckily no one had seen them. August didn't actually like the taste of tobacco, but he smoked anyway these days.

"Your strap won't do you any good when it's that loose," August said, pointing at Stanislav's helmet.

"It's loose only because I've lost weight."

"Why don't you tighten it?"

"I never thought about it." Stanislav removed his helmet, studied it for a while, and then fumbled a bit with the strap before putting it back on.

"It's easy. You just need to pull on the buckle a little to tighten it up," August said.

Stanislav tried again but discovered that he'd tightened it too much when he put it back on. After several attempts, he finally got it just right. August could tell that it was still too tight, because it made a clear white stripe under his friend's chin, but he didn't say anything.

"I'm looking forward to going home and fattening up." Stanislav smiled. "At night I dream that my family is just sitting down to dinner. It's a Sunday, and my mother has made *rosół, kotlet schabowy,* and cheesecake for dessert. Then I wake up, and my face is wet with drool." He laughed a little sheepishly.

"What are those dishes?" August asked.

"Rosół is chicken soup. Kotlet schabowy is the same as schnitzel, just thicker, with braised potatoes and scalloped cabbage." He closed his eyes, as if trying to transform his daydream into reality. "She makes the most fantastic *sernik*. It's a cheesecake that she makes with *twaróg*, a kind of quark."

"Stop or I'm going to start thinking of steak and some delicious sauce."

It would be several hours before they were relieved and could get some rest and a bite to eat. He wasn't actually hungry. Well, he would be if they were going to be eating proper food, but he knew what was in store for them, so he didn't have much of an appetite. But he'd learned that you had to eat whenever you had the chance because you didn't know when the opportunity would arise again.

Dawn had arrived—that eternal optimist—and the sun had slipped imperceptibly into its customary position, illuminating the once-beautiful landscape. Dmitri's assignment was simple: since the Germans figured that the attack would occur at dawn, the Russians planned to wait until later in the morning, when the Germans would begin to feel more secure. Around noon, when the sun was halfway through its daily arc across the sky, Dmitri was to neutralize the advance position. That would be the signal to attack.

The lice itched in his armpits and the waistband of his pants. Those tiny devils tormented him around the clock, and it was impossible to get used to them. He wanted to tear off his clothes and claw at his entire body with a few handfuls of gravel, but he remained still, quiet as a sleeping animal, and tried to forget his small, faithful companions.

He'd had a dog once, Yerik. It too had been faithful. Yerik had been a mongrel, a mixture of the elegant, long-legged borzoi, the pointy-eared, narrow-eyed West Siberian Laika, and the handsome, powerful Siberian husky. With those breeds running through his blood, it could have been an attractive dog, but it had inherited the least desirable characteristics of the three and had therefore been an object of derision in the village. It didn't help when the dog had developed a limp. Dmitri had found Yerik down by the creek one day, a few hundred yards from his father's farm. The poor animal lay in a thick pool of blood, its pelt soaked through. When Dmitri picked up the dog, he noticed that one of its forelegs was missing from the knee down. Yerik had come upon a ravenous stray wolf that had been driven from its pack. So Yerik had walked with a limp from that day forward. But he'd been a good dog and remained a faithful companion until he grew so old and feeble that Dmitri's father put a bullet in his head while Dmitri pressed his face into his mother's lap in tears.

He scratched gently at an armpit. The night was cold and clammy, and he'd watched the two Germans share a cigarette. Tobacco-hungry soldiers made for easy prey for snipers; the best shooters needed no more than the glow of a cigarette to pinpoint their target.

His fellow soldiers claimed that Dmitri was colder than a Siberian winter, but that wasn't true. He wasn't like that at heart, but he needed to be to do his job. The others didn't understand war. They didn't understand that you had to be cynical to maintain your sanity amid the mad and pointless chaos. He reduced his thoughts to the bare minimum: Am I tired? Am I hungry? Am I cold? Do I have more ammunition?

He was, in fact, hungry. For the past few hours, a large, gaping hole had gnawed at him, growing bigger and bigger, until his growling gut made it impossible for him to ignore what he'd been trying so hard to suppress. Just a few more hours; then he could eat. His bladder had also begun to send urgent signals, though he'd relieved himself before taking his position.

A bird hovered silently in the air above him, instinctively calibrating its tail feathers and wings as it flew into a headwind. To the naked eye, it appeared as though it weren't moving at all, but he knew that—like him—it was straining in every fiber of its being. Because they were hunters, and hunters could never allow themselves the luxury of relaxation. Time had stopped, and like a taut bow and arrow, they remained at the ready.

It was a golden eagle. His father had told him that the older an eagle grew, the more its color faded; this one had vivid dark-brown feathers, so it had to be young. Its gaze was alert, on the prowl for prey just as he was. The only difference was that the eagle's quarry was other birds, rabbits, hares, and squirrels, while his was people. Hares and rabbits had once been his preferred target, too, but now it was German soldiers.

The two in front of him would become his next prey. He watched one remove his helmet and fiddle clumsily with the chin strap. He put it back on his head, removed it again, and fumbled a little more with the strap. After repeated attempts, he finally seemed satisfied and settled it back on his head for good.

Dmitri tried to imagine the two Germans as hares; in his mind he saw himself as a boy in the forest behind his father's small farm, with his old Berdan rifle. The old rifle was crooked, he knew, and for every fifty yards the bullet deviated a half yard from its original course. He also knew that the hares could feed his family for days, so he couldn't miss. If he did, it meant yet another meal of cabbage and potatoes.

He shifted the scope from one eye to the other to give his good eye some rest. Though he was right-handed, he always sighted with his left eye. If he used his right, he always shot wide. He located the Germans again.

Half an hour or so remained until the sun reached the point when he would have to shoot, and his bladder was now about to burst. It felt as if it contained all the water in Lake Baikal, but he didn't dare empty it, and pissing in his pants seemed shameful.

Some time passed, and Dmitri was relieved when he glanced up at the sun. Finally. He listened to his breathing as he tried to quiet his pulse, which knew what was about to happen and had therefore intensified. He emptied his head by focusing on the stillness all around. The silence meant he was ready, ready to do what he was good at. A final deep breath, and then . . . three, two, one. He counted slowly to himself and squeezed the trigger the rest of the way as soon as he reached the end of his count. He exhaled deeply when the rifle gave a terse, sharp report. The bullet traversed the 1,750 feet and penetrated one of the Germans right between his eyes. Dmitri saw the soldier's head jerk backward, but the soldier remained seated—as if trying to defy the reality of what had just happened.

Just another half hour and I can go get some sleep, August thought. They'd been sitting there half the night and most of the morning, too, and it had been as quiet as a cemetery. He knew why he and Stan had been assigned to the advance post and why they'd been forced to stay for so long. It was punishment. They were always the ones sent on hopeless patrols, or to outposts, or to form the rear guard—for the simple reason that Falkendorf detested them. August because he was a bad soldier and Stanislav because he wasn't German.

August closed his eyes. He would count to ten and then open them again. Just rest them a moment. He began to count, but by the time he'd reached the number five, his thoughts had begun to wander the way they usually did before he fell asleep. At seven he opened his eyes again, but he didn't know whether it had taken him two seconds or ten minutes to get from five to seven.

He shook his head and blinked rapidly to chase away the sleep. He hated that he couldn't control his sleeping. Sometimes it was as if his head played no part in the decision. In fact his head might resist with tooth and nail, but his consciousness just switched off like a light. He hadn't even noticed that his eyes had slid shut again, but then he forced them open once more. Out of the corner of his eye, he noticed Stanislav's head jerk back hard, accompanied by a dull thump.

"Are you falling asleep, too?" August asked.

Stanislav didn't respond.

"Stan, are you asleep?"

August looked at his companion, who was leaning his cheek against the butt of his machine gun. A stripe of blood ran from a coin-sized hole in his forehead down his face, split by his nose like a forking river. Another trail of blood trickled out from under his helmet down the nape of his neck. His eyes appeared alert, as though he were still keeping watch for enemies.

If he hadn't tightened his chin strap, Stan's head would have been scattered across a Russian field, August managed to think, before he began screaming uncontrollably. He screamed until his lungs were racked with pain. He screamed until his scream became a howl; he screamed until only a whistling sound remained in him.

He hadn't heard the shot that killed Stanislav, and he didn't hear the next shot, either. It wrenched his entire upper body, knocking him off his feet. Instinctively he crawled to the stone dike and sat with his back against the cold stone. He heard a heavy chuffing and glanced at Stanislav, but discovered the sound was coming from him.

The wound in his chest sizzled and bubbled, and a thin billow of smoke spiraled out of a hollow in his uniform jacket. His body grew warmer, and his head felt heavy, as if it had been hanging upside down for hours. His shins began to sting, just as they had when he ran through nettles as a boy. Then silence.

In a house near the Alster, a boy wakes. It's his birthday. His family is waiting for him down in the living room. He smiles because he knows they have gifts for him. He's turning six. He sneaks soundlessly down the large stairs and sits on the third step from the bottom. From here he can see into the living room, where his mother is setting the table. His father is raising the flag. His big sister is helping, and she laughs at something his father says. She's still wearing her nightgown, so he knows now that it's Sunday.

He's holding a wounded bird as gently he can, just enough to ensure that it doesn't fly out of his hand. He thinks it's one of the cuckoo chicks. He cautiously unfolds one of its wings. It's broken. He can tell that, beneath its layer of down, it's shivering with fear. He puts it carefully down on the ground.

He falls, cracking through ice. A hand clutches him and yanks him up through the hole his skates and his body made in the ice. His lungs celebrate as they are reunited with oxygen. It's his father. They are lying on their backs on the frozen lake, and August gasps like a fish on land. Karl picks him up, and he clings to his father's belly. His father dries him off in front of the villa's big fireplace.

August enjoys hearing and watching his father play the piano. He doesn't want to learn how to play; he wants only to listen. To learn to listen. He hears his father improve, and he learns to love Chopin and Debussy. His father's face is peaceful when he's sitting at the piano, and he looks like someone in another world, a parallel universe of notes.

"Where do you go when you dream, Dad?" asks the ten-year-old August.

"I dream I'm in the very place we are now."

"But that's here," August says after a long pause.

"Exactly," his father says.

***

The Russian soldiers ran right past August. He could almost have touched them if he stretched out his arm, but he couldn't move. Several of them noticed him but continued on toward the German position. They came in waves, gushing over the landscape in great numbers; he figured his companions couldn't hold their position for very long. He dozed off.

A soldier stopped and studied him indifferently. August didn't have the strength to lift his head, and his gaze remained focused on the soldier's tightly laced boots. The Russian just stood there, and August's eyes rolled slowly upward. From the soldier's hip hung a green canvas bag with a red cross, indicating that he was from a medical unit. One arm hung down by the soldier's side, but August fixated his attention on the other, which was bound in a sling. He suddenly recognized the shoulder-length blond hair that was tied in a little ponytail under the soft cap. Nadia. He wasn't hallucinating. It was really Nadia. He'd dreamed of her ever since their encounter in the woods, and now she was suddenly standing before him.

She stared at him without expression. He tried to say something. Tried to let her know that he was still alive, but no sound emerged from his mouth. She didn't budge. He wanted to call out to her, but her musical name turned into a rattling cough that ached in his chest. August looked up at her. She seemed so pretty standing with the sun at her back. An angel who'd come to take him wherever he was meant to go. But he didn't want to go. He wasn't ready!

His eyes slid slowly down to her hips and the green canvas bag. Nadia followed his eyes and saw the first aid kit. She flashed a brief smile before turning and running after the others.

He no longer felt the stinging nettles. Both of his legs were numb now. Despite the heat, he felt as though his body were hardening to ice. Another cough racked his chest. The blood that coursed from his body smeared his hands and arms, and he only just managed to think that a person couldn't possibly contain so much blood. He was helpless. He could do nothing but watch himself cease to exist. His father stood beside him now. He lay in a bed; his mother was there, too, and Hilde, Maximilian, and Sophia. The sunlight blinded him. Where was his canteen?

Dmitri pulled out a couple of slices of bread from the bag he'd cinched to his belt. He'd relieved his bladder next to a tree, and now he would satisfy his hunger. He probably had some sausages left. He stretched his back, which was stiff and aching from so many hours lying in the same position. First his right side, from his toes all the way to his fingertips, and then his left. He cut a sausage in half so he would have enough for another meal. Either you ate all you had and were full and happy for a while, or you ate a little bit at a time. That meant, however, that you were always hungry. That seemed like the best option since he was already used to always being hungry.

He watched the remains of the German defense being beaten back while ingesting his meal beneath a tree. Now he heard only the scattered salvos of machine gun fire. He stood up and began to walk.

Dmitri looked at the two dead Germans behind the dike. The first had been felled by the perfect shot. The one snipers dream of. The shot that makes legends of them. In a split second the German had gone from ignorance to nothingness. He'd been alive and dead in the same instant. He shifted his gaze to the other one, who sat leaning against the dike, his eyes staring vacantly ahead.

Russian officers kept saying that once you've killed a person, it's easier to kill a second time. But what about dying? There's only that one irreversible moment. The other German hadn't had an easy death. Why the hell had he stood up? He was a trained soldier, so why had he exposed himself?

Dmitri lamented the shot. He'd struck the soldier just below his ribs, on the right side of his chest, and it had surely taken a long time for the life to ebb out of him. For a dying man, ten or twenty minutes was probably an eternity. Ten minutes was just ten minutes to a living man, but to the dying man, it was all that remained.

He removed their dog tags as proof that he'd killed two more. In a certain sense he was glad that the German soldiers' names weren't on their dog tags. He didn't want to know their names. Though he hated them, a name would make them human. Then he would see that they were like him. He turned the two metal ovals over in his hand. Then he dropped them in his pocket, where they clinked softly as he walked back toward the forest.

PART THREE

Santa Cruz, Bolivia. July 24, 1975

The wind originated in Patagonia and the Argentinian Pampas, and it was ice cold. The doors had begun to rattle, and the house was drafty. His skin was so paper thin that it no longer served as a shield against the cold gusts. He loathed winter. He felt frozen down to his bones. The temperature had dipped so swiftly in recent days that his body hadn't had a chance to acclimate. All the heat had been sucked from the air, replaced by this icy wind. He pulled his blanket tighter around himself.

The wind seemed to have been created to make lonely people feel even more so. Like a knife, it sliced chasms between people, and every soul had to resist its penetration. In Buenos Aires they called it the *pampero*, but here it went by the name of *surazo*. The Argentinian capital had been the right place for him; the wind hadn't been so brutal there. Every time he remembered Buenos Aires, his chain of thought brought him back to Hamburg, a city that he'd come to think had never really existed. That had originated in his imagination. In his memory it lay enshrouded in mist; soon he would no longer be able to see it at all. The towers were invisible, and he struggled to recall whether they were still standing the last time he saw the city. Hamburg had been in ruins, nothing but a heap of rubble and piles of garbage. With his brother buried somewhere beneath it all.

He couldn't decide whether suicide was the solution of a coward or a final act of wisdom. But his brother had been neither a coward nor particularly wise. He wanted to say that he missed him, but over time his heart had grown too weak to miss anyone. And too tattered to suffer.

The whistling wind gave him goose bumps. Like a wolf, it howled at the moon as it searched for openings. He crawled deeper beneath his blanket.

It was one of those days when he felt guilty. His old heart still had the capacity to feel guilt. Thank god it didn't happen often, but it was the kind of thing the wind did to lonely men. When he was overwhelmed by guilt, there was so much he regretted. So much he shouldn't have done. He found comfort in this thought: if he felt guilty, it meant he was human. Making mistakes was part of human nature, and to regret was to recognize a mistake. And only through compassion and courage could one recognize one's mistakes. If one had reached such a recognition . . . Nonsense, he regretted nothing. He sucked at the cigarette he'd just lit, his teeth clenched.

Maybe he should give up, let himself be captured, maybe even turn himself in. Or was that his mind playing tricks on him? Was he just imagining someone was out to get him? No, Buenos Aires had been real. Hadn't it? Was it a form of megalomania to think that he had, in some bizarre way, made his mark on this world after all—whether good or bad? Was he trying to justify their pursuit of him as evidence of that?

If they came for him, he would no longer resist.

He sat listening to the wind blowing through the streets for a long time. The rain had joined it, drumming rhythmically against the tin roof. He suddenly felt vulnerable. When that happened, it was time to leave, time to depart and start over. He was overwhelmed by a compulsion to survive. With his blanket still wrapped tightly around his shoulders, he found his suitcase under his bed.

Near Isjum, Ukraine, January 15, 1943

A hand—a powerful hand with strong fingers—gripped Karl hard around his neck and squeezed his Adam's apple with brute force. Fingernails bore into his skin as the grip tightened, lifting him up. His toes no longer touched the ground, and he kicked wildly. In a moment he would lose consciousness and die. The hand suddenly released him, and he began to fall. It was as though a mine had cut off his legs below the knees. He continued to fall, then broke through the earth's surface. The crust scraped his arms and legs, and blood began to run down his limbs. Then he came to an abrupt halt and remained hanging in the air, as though held up by an invisible rope. He glimpsed a dot down below. It approached slowly, and he saw that it was August. His eyes were open, and he was smiling. When August was close enough that Karl could reach out and touch him, his body dissolved before his eyes. August vanished. Karl opened his hand; in his palm lay a dented bullet. It began to move, then bore into his temple with great force. His head began pounding intolerably. He came to, blinking. Five, ten minutes, he sat staring blankly into space, until his brain slowly began to function again.

He reread the letter. The same way a child who has just learned to read does. One word at a time in order to comprehend, hoping that a second pass through it would change the meaning of the sentences. The result was the same: August was dead. *August is dead.* At first they were just words in his head. He knew the meaning of each individual word, but could not grasp the sentence they formed. As though to convince himself of their accuracy, he said it aloud.

"August is dead."

The letter had been in transit for three months. It had followed his own route, first to France and then to Russia. He had lost his son three months ago, and he was only learning it now. It was unbearable. How had Ingrid been able to write the words "August is dead"? It must have required preternatural powers. She must have mustered all her strength to form the short sentence, the sentence that meant that he no longer had a son. When it came to letter writing, Ingrid was a true virtuoso. Her letters were practically calligraphic artwork, but the brevity and lack of aesthetic expression in the message he now held in his hands testified to her suffering. In the letter's formulaic composition, he felt her reproaching him, a reproach that whispered how he was the one who'd insisted August become a soldier. It wasn't in the tone of the letter; it was in its absence of tone. But maybe a mother always assigns blame when she loses a child. What about fathers?

He remembered the adage "A man who fears death cannot enjoy life." Had August feared death? Suddenly Karl felt that he'd never really known his son. Who was August? Did Karl know his favorite color or, for that matter, his favorite food? Did he actually know him at all? The answer had to be no. They'd spent so many years together, and yet they had been strangers. He began rubbing his palms against his face, as if trying to erase his thoughts. His rough, dry skin itched beneath his stubble, making him rub even harder. It hurt. He closed his eyes and squeezed his head between his hands.

He understood Gerhard better now. He'd never comprehended what it had been like for his brother when he lost Laura and Emma, but now he felt that crushing sensation, a lingering pain, as if all of his organs had contracted. Gerhard had tried to explain the feeling to him, but he'd never understood. He'd wanted to help Gerhard back then, but he couldn't. He'd just made a halfhearted attempt to appear understanding about something he didn't grasp. Back then he simply didn't know any better. But now he missed his brother, and he missed August.

The letter was still before him when he opened his eyes. Some unlucky party official had had the dubious honor of knocking on the door of his villa by the Alster. He imagined Ingrid receiving the news. Sobbing, leaning against the door frame as the official uncomfortably wished her a good day. Had she sat down immediately to write the letter, or had she been unable to? He could understand if she hadn't been able to, but something inside him believed he had a right to know as soon as possible.

He was scared of himself. How could he think so rationally and be so calm? Did death mean nothing? The crushing sensation that pained him from head to toe provided him with his answer. Death meant everything. It meant his son going from present to past tense. From flesh and blood to memory. From a living embodiment of his and Ingrid's love to a photo album of his recollections. He cried.

He recalled things he and August had done together, but he couldn't think of many. Had he been a good father? He supposed it was only logical to ask that question when you no longer had a chance to change anything. One thing was certain: Karl had never understood his son, had never connected with his sullen temperament.

Petrus Keil entered his tent, and Karl gave him an abject glance. Keil, who'd succeeded Piroska as second in command, nodded and sat down. He lightly patted Karl's leg to let him know that he empathized, that there was no need for Karl to explain. They sat for some time. Slowly, Petrus Keil began to transform. His round, steel-framed glasses disappeared; his short, dark hair grew long, blonder, and began to curl; his skinny face with its prominent cheekbones became longer and stronger, as did his nose. Paul Piroska was with Karl now. He wanted to hug Paul, throw himself around his neck, but right then his skin vanished from his face, torn off as if someone had ripped it from his throat. His skull appeared, and where his eyes had been there now crawled fat, well-nourished maggots. White, sleek larvae that wriggled out of every orifice.

Karl felt as though he no longer had any eyes, only tears, tears large as eggs, and he could no longer see. He was blind. Everyone died, everyone died, and at that moment it struck him how fragile life was.

Keil, who must have seen the terror in Karl's face, stood, looking uncomfortable. He cleared his throat timidly. "Colonel Wolter wishes to speak with you."

Gently, he helped Karl to his feet. Karl smiled apologetically, adjusted his uniform jacket, and dried his eyes with his sleeve.

Near Isjum, Ukraine, January 16, 1943

In May 1942, the Seventh Panzer Division had arrived in France. When Karl had seen the men—or those who were left—he had been amazed that such threadbare men had been capable of holding the Russians at bay. Exhausted, both physically and mentally beaten, they had been allowed to rest. The division was held in reserve for a few months, and the men used those months to recuperate. Then, following the Allies' landing in North Africa, Adolf Hitler decided to occupy all of France, and the panzer division was ordered south. On December 22, 1942, the division left Marseille, and they celebrated Christmas on a train heading back to the eastern front. Most of the men had been there before, and those who'd joined them in France listened in horror to the stories that were told.

And now he sat here, in a canvas tent, while everyone around him was buried. It was insufferable. He missed Paul. In that case, Karl himself had been the shy messenger at the front door, bringing the same news he'd received the day before—only for someone else. His letter to Liesel had been rubbish. Karl had written that Paul died a hero's death for the führer, the people, and his fatherland, but the truth was that his death had been anything but glorious. It had been disgraceful. Paul's bowels had loosened, and Karl had chain-smoked on the truck's tailgate to cover the stench.

Colonel Wolter, the new supply officer who'd replaced the fallen Helmut Strunz, sat at a little table with an adjutant. They drank coffee out of dented metal mugs. Strunz had been a cautious, thorough, and very punctual man, but Wolter was quite different. He was a brusque man who spoke his mind, and the men were afraid of him.

Wolter ordered Karl to go to the depot, get four trucks, and report to Major Kuhlau in Isjum, where a special delivery awaited them. It was to be transported—discreetly—to Kharkov. He blinked at Karl knowingly following his last sentence.

The trip to Isjum was uneventful. He drove with Keil, but they didn't talk on the way. In Isjum they picked up their cargo: seventy-eight Ukrainian and Russian women. Karl guessed that the youngest was fourteen and the oldest between thirty-eight and forty. They helped the women into the truck beds, where they all had to stand since there were no seats or benches. Then the two men climbed back into the cab, and Keil popped the engine into gear.

"I don't like this at all. We can hardly pretend we've been overpowered by seventy-eight women," Karl said, shaking his head.

"What the hell is the army going to do with seventy-eight women in Kharkov?"

"What do you think German soldiers want to do with young women?"

"You're not saying . . ."

Karl lit a cigarette and exhaled a thick column of smoke. "Right now, we're a couple of pimps."

"You're shitting me."

"They're freezing back there." Karl took another drag.

"They'll be warm soon enough."

Karl gave Keil a reproachful glare and snorted. And he snorted at the memory of Wolter's explanation. The colonel had said the assignment was of great importance, that it would have a tremendous impact on the soldiers' morale. The division was being held in reserve at the moment, and the women would make the men happy. He thought of Remmel. Poor Remmel had gone with them to Isjum and examined the terrified women for venereal diseases. With his own eyes, the doctor confirmed that a number of Major Kuhlau's men had already helped themselves to the goods. The men's morale was indeed in need of a boost, but Karl wanted no part in turning innocent women into whores by transporting them to the laps of horny German men. And it would take far more than seventy-eight naked Ukrainian and Russian women to reverse their fortunes.

He often felt that the war was eating him up inside. No longer was it about Germany or victory or defeat, but about Karl—Karl's survival. He began to wish he would be wounded so that he could be sent home. A bullet through the leg would be a blessing. He'd reached the point where a limb seemed a reasonable trade-off for escaping the war. That's why he'd become reckless. It didn't matter anymore, and maybe it would all be over soon.

Near Isjum, Ukraine, February 22, 1943

They emerged from the morning mist. At first they were just silhouettes, but before long the horses galloped past Karl, their hooves pounding the soft earth like small explosions. There was a clear hierarchy among the graceful creatures. A dapple gray seemed to be their leader. Every time it cantered or came to a halt, the others followed suit. A golden-brown mare stopped and looked at Karl, its tail swishing rhythmically back and forth. It trudged toward him trustfully, and he gave its muzzle a friendly pat. The beautiful animal snorted thickly, and he felt its warm breath against his hand. It tilted its head to the side, studying him. Between its pleasantly soft brown eyes was a round white mark that hypnotized him like a third eye. If a woman had looked at him that way, he would have given up everything he owned to follow her to the ends of the earth. He liberated himself from the horse's intense stare and thought of Ingrid. He wasn't the kind of man to leave his family in the lurch. And certainly not for a horse.

The horse turned and trotted after the dapple gray with the others. The warm smell of the horses wafted toward him across the stony ground and the interim fence, the same warm smell as the stagnant air inside the tent he and Gerhard had pitched on their parents' front lawn one summer. He remembered the fresh-cut grass and the light summer rain that had drizzled down on them all morning, intensifying the odor. They were going to sleep outside. That night, they had crawled into their sleeping bags and read about Old Shatterhand and his blood brother Winnetou. They loved the popular German writer Karl May's Wild West stories, which Karl read out loud. Karl quickly realized that Gerhard regretted their little adventure. When it was time to go to sleep, Gerhard lay terrified, staring up at the tent canvas. Karl told jokes to relax him, and Gerhard laughed tensely, but at the first hoot of a horned owl, his little brother bolted upright and rushed into the house. Karl stayed put, but Gerhard's fear soon spread to him. He heard scary noises and saw terrifying shadows on the tent walls. A werewolf howled in the distance, a vampire stood right on the other side of the thin canvas, and he heard a monster stomping through the flowerbeds. The sound drew closer and closer. He refused to be overpowered by his fear; he wouldn't give up. He chased the shadows off with his pocket flashlight and stifled the noises by pulling his sleeping bag over his head. He was eventually so exhausted that sleep overcame his fear. The next morning he strolled triumphantly to the breakfast table.

A shiny black stallion charged across the parched field, swirling up a cloud of dust that soon settled and dissolved to nothing. Free of their burden, their equipment, and their riders, these animals must have felt pure, unadulterated joy. He sensed from their friskiness that they hadn't been with the battalion long. They had a higher calling; they weren't born to pull supply wagons and carts across Russia. But these beautiful creatures belonged to Jan-Carl Tortzen's supply column, and tomorrow they would toil once again.

Only now did Karl notice that all of the vehicles from Tortzen's company stood at the far end of the enclosure. There were several HF.7 Stahlfeldwagens, which were steel-mounted vehicles drawn by two horses, small IF8 infantry carts sheltered by tarpaulins, some double MG Wagen 36s—which had room for three soldiers up front and a machine gun sniper in the back—and a traditional wooden horse-drawn carriage called an HF.1. They all stood together in a neat row; a well-thrown grenade could easily have hacked off one of the company's limbs, leaving it to limp around Russia in the months to come.

"Goddamn Tortzen," Karl cursed. "Doesn't he know the vehicles should be scattered?" That was one of the disadvantages of his promotion to major. He had more responsibility now, and he would be blamed if the inexperienced Tortzen committed a blunder.

Thomas Remmel nervously cleared his throat behind him. Karl and Thomas had gone through quite a bit together, but nothing was the way it had been before Piroska died. Back then they had been able to laugh. They couldn't do that anymore. Thomas had distanced himself from Karl—from everyone, really—and he'd stopped laughing. But what was there to laugh about? Rommel's troops were in retreat in North Africa, Field Marshal Paulus's Sixth Army had surrendered in Stalingrad, Voronezh had fallen, Kursk had fallen, Rostov had fallen, Kharkov had fallen, and with each defeat, the mood among the soldiers had fallen, too.

Remmel picked nervously at his uniform collar. "We're running out of morphine."

"Then talk to Werner." Major Werner was the division's commanding doctor.

"I already have. We're running out of everything."

"Then we'll have to make do with what we have. Do we have enough sulfates?"

"I need morphine, goddamn it!" Remmel now stood very close to him. "Morphine!"

Karl had never seen the easygoing doctor so agitated. Normally Remmel spoke slowly in a flat, slightly nervous tone of voice. Even when blood was flowing in battle and he was fighting to keep entrails and limbs in place, he maintained his stoic calm, but now he seemed completely frayed. Karl had seen him lose his composure only once before. That was when Paul Piroska died.

Karl studied the doctor. Perspiration covered his entire face like a thick film, and tufts of blond hair jutted out from under his cap and clung to his forehead. His pupils were enormous, nearly eclipsing the blue in his eyes.

"Are you all right, Thomas?"

"Fine," he said, pursing his lips. "But we can't get by without morphine." He was practically whimpering.

Karl considered. "Didn't we get a delivery five days ago? We haven't been in battle since."

The doctor shook his head dismissively. Then Karl understood. Thomas Remmel was a morphine addict, and he was using the unit's own supply. He should yell at Thomas, make him understand this was unacceptable. It was Karl's duty as his superior officer and friend to make sure this kind of thing didn't happen. Karl was furious as he thought of the wounded men. But as he studied the doctor's wretched appearance, Karl's anger began to subside. In a way he understood Remmel, who saw only death and mutilation all day long and was rarely able to perform his job successfully. Still, it was unforgivable.

He put a hand on Remmel's shoulder, and the doctor looked up at him with a guilty expression, like a schoolboy who had gotten into mischief. As Karl clasped his shoulder, he felt Remmel's body trembling beneath his touch. Together they headed toward the tents.

A screeching sound, sharp as the edge of a knife and growing louder by the second, stopped them in their tracks. Like a siren it pierced a hole in their hearing, becoming a low whistle. Suddenly everything went quiet. Then the ground vanished. The air was ripped to tatters. The sky was a swirl of dirt and gravel, darkened by shards of metal raining down on them. There was something almost spectacular about it.

Gravel, rocks, and body parts came to rest all around Karl and Remmel, who'd been knocked off their feet by the blast. A canvas tent billowed down slowly from the sky, and like Pegasus—or perhaps more accurately, Icarus—a horse plummeted to the ground with a loud, hollow thud.

Remmel was the first to stand up, and he pulled Karl to his feet. They staggered, holding each other up as they stared at the enormous crater that had suddenly appeared between the tents. Two men crawled from the large, smoking hole, looking like infants who were still uncertain whether their bodies were up to the challenge. A trail of blood followed one of the men, who hadn't realized that the muscle in his left leg was gone.

The smell of cordite and gunpowder spread. Remmel ran toward the wounded men, and Karl admired the doctor's courage and energy. Just then, he felt overcome by a surge of pain, but he couldn't place it, had no idea where it was coming from.

Behind him, a horse expelled a long moan and whickered in pain. Karl turned and stood as still as stone, watching the golden-brown mare writhe in agony. For some reason, the horse's suffering made a greater impression on Karl than all the wounded and dead people he'd seen up until then. Observing the animal's death struggle, hearing its despair, he headed slowly toward it. Maybe by putting a hand on its muzzle he could ease its pain; maybe he could say a few words to calm it down. Just like Remmel, he now felt a calling. He had to help the horse; he had to help it die.

A screeching sound, sharp as the edge of a knife and growing louder by the second, stopped him in his tracks. Like a siren it pierced a hole in his hearing, becoming a low whistle, and suddenly everything went quiet. The ground vanished.

Neuengamme, Germany, March 4, 1943

Gerhard struggled out of bed. His head was pounding. His legs were stiff and uncooperative, and the rest of his body was just as off-kilter. He looked himself over. His belly had expanded and now bulged over the edge of his pants, and he noticed that his skin had grown slack. It startled him. In his mind he was still a slender man. He quickly buttoned his uniform shirt to hide what he didn't want to see. Then he put on pants and a jacket. Beneath one of his boots was a piece of paper, yet another rejected transfer request. He got down and peered under the bed. His hand fumbled across the wooden floorboards and finally located what it was looking for. He lifted the bottle up and eyed it fuzzily.

He didn't do it because he wanted to, but he drained the rest of the contents in one gulp, then grimaced at the aftertaste. He'd long ago realized that the best way to keep his hangovers at bay was to keep drinking the next day, but every day was now the next day. The alcohol muted his thoughts. And that was important because they could make his head pound even worse than his hangovers.

They'd drunk heavily the night before, he, Erwin Borg, Udo Pankow, and a few other officers. Turek had been there, too. Since they didn't have anything else to do in the evening, they'd begun throwing parties every night in what they called the Führer's Lodge. They'd wrapped up a couple hours past midnight, and the last thing Gerhard saw before stumbling to bed was Turek's back as he stood pissing in the little fountain outside the Führer's Lodge.

He felt claustrophobic. The air was like sandpaper. He had to find someplace to breathe where the air reached his lungs. Not the way he breathed in the camp, where he inhaled and exhaled only in small, fitful gasps. There was no fresh air here, just the stench of decay and death. He had to get himself onto the other side of the fence, out where the world wasn't insane. Or at least less so.

To avoid drawing attention to himself, he ran down the stairwell and sauntered briskly through the camp. Beyond the barracks, two prisoners were collecting the night's dead. The corpses were tossed on a flatbed truck, on top of eight to ten others that were already there. A head hung upside down over one side of the flatbed, looking as though it had discovered that the entire world was flipped on its end, and stared vacantly at him. A fly buzzed around its gaping mouth, and the dead man's eyes resembled glass orbs. Gerhard covered his mouth with his hand; he wouldn't vomit. Not that it was anything he hadn't seen before, but every sensation felt stronger, harder, and louder this morning.

He was to blame whenever the emaciated prisoners perished. He was the only one responsible for their dying of hunger. As administrative director he was tasked with purchasing foodstuffs for the kitchen, but his budget was ridiculously low, and they were more or less forced to starve. He was aware that prisoners kept the dead in the top bunks—where the people who distributed food could not see that the bodies no longer required sustenance—so that they could get their food rations as well. In the beginning it had tormented him, kept him awake at night. They didn't die by his hand but by what he didn't put in their mouths. But he soon discovered that there was nothing he could do regardless, and that understanding—combined with alcohol—improved his nights.

The two prisoners had reentered the barracks and now dragged out the body of an elderly man. The one in front complained loudly about the weight of the dead man; the other didn't seem to want to participate in the conversation and bowed his head as if he hadn't heard. The first one nevertheless continued to jabber about why the dead were heavier than the living, since this old man was so small and shrunken.

Gerhard covered his ears and hurried toward the camp's main gate. The cloying reek of the crematorium smokestacks, which billowed day and night, brushed the lining of his nose, filling his cheeks and sinuses. The guard greeted him amiably. Behind him, a kapo shouted at a prisoner, and Gerhard turned his head instinctively. The prisoner had exited one of the barracks and started running. The capo screamed even louder. The man's steps were unsteady and wobbly, without substance or strength.

The prisoner was heading straight toward Gerhard and the guard post. Glancing back over his shoulder in terror, he caught sight of the capo closing in on him. The capo swung his cane threateningly, but the emaciated man clanked on. Gerhard could tell the prisoner was trying to pick up his pace, but his legs wouldn't obey him. The capo's blow struck the man in his lower back, and he nearly fell. When he was only a few yards from Gerhard, he wheeled around abruptly. The capo came to an abrupt halt so as not to knock Gerhard down. There was a loud crackle as the prisoner threw himself against the electric fence. The smell of burned flesh and hair was instantaneous. The guard looked at Gerhard and shrugged apologetically before turning away.

When Gerhard was outside the camp, he began to run. His feet pounded the asphalt, sending jolts up his legs and back, but he kept running in spite of his pain. When he was a good distance from the camp, he fell to his knees in the grass and threw up. His stomach churned, and he felt an urge to cry, but not from the pain. He had an inexplicable desire to open himself up, to let all the horrible things he'd experienced come gushing out of his eyes like rivers; he felt the pressure building within him and knew that it would take so little to let it flow. If he relaxed for even a moment, his body would give in. But he knew he had to suppress those feelings, to pull himself together. He'd succeeded in repressing the facts until now. Before he'd felt like a spectator, but now it was as if everything had suddenly become real. He vomited again. When he was completely empty, he fell on his side.

He walked back toward the camp. In the commandant barracks Gerhard nodded silently to Herbert Asner, his scribe, who sat behind his desk. Behind the reception area was a larger office with a desk, filing cabinets, and shelves. Gerhard sat down and lit a cigarette. He heard Asner shuffling papers on the other side of the door and hoped that the lanky prisoner wouldn't disturb him. Flies circled around a glass that had caught their interest. He waved them away, then poured some schnapps in the glass. He held the first gulp in his mouth, meticulously swishing the liquid into every crevice to rid himself of the awful taste of vomit. He gazed through the window and saw Turek and Erwin Borg talking in the distance. Turek always carried on as though he were a king or tribal god. There wasn't a single prisoner who didn't quiver at the sight of him. Near the factory, a section of the electric fence was missing. If a prisoner drifted outside the observable border, it was the guards' duty to shoot him. Turek had a habit of chasing prisoners he didn't like out into the open area, where the guards had no choice but to shoot them. It had become a form of entertainment, a deviation from the everyday routine in the camp, but Gerhard knew the guards didn't enjoy the game.

He hated Turek. Normally he didn't think of himself as the sort of person who hated others, but Turek had earned his contempt. He didn't hate the others. Erwin Borg, the camp's doctor, was a pleasant man. Although Lorenz kept his distance—he had his family with him, after all—Gerhard had actually come to like him.

Another swig of the schnapps pained his stomach. It happened quite a lot. He would ask Borg about it one of these days. He drained his glass and poured himself another. He picked up a stack of papers from the table and briefly studied the figures in the right column. He quickly calculated the numbers and confirmed that Asner's results were correct. This work was so easy, so straightforward. It was the very core of his profession—a simplification—which had now been reduced to its very essence: numbers. It didn't get any purer than this. He played with the numbers and brought them to life. Subtracted and added at a speed that made him smile. But then he stumbled across the number zero. He didn't like zero because the number created nothing. It was a dead number. If you multiplied something by it, you lost everything. He himself had become the number zero. He was nothing. The pain returned.

The door swung open, and Erwin Borg's cheerful face appeared. Borg was frequently bored because Turek had taken on many of the doctor's tasks. Although Turek had been employed as a construction worker before the war, he was now the one who determined which prisoners were physically capable of doing the work in the subcamps, while Borg was the one who determined who would be sent to the subcamps. Borg could only shake his head at Turek's attempts to master this new profession, but there was nothing he could do, and Lorenz stayed out of it.

"You look like shit. Are you all right, Gerhard?" Borg asked as he entered the room.

Gerhard didn't reply until the doctor closed the door behind him. "I can't handle all the booze." He tried to grin, but Borg held his gaze and studied him closely.

"You're not well, are you?"

He wanted to tell Borg that he was falling apart, but he changed the subject instead. "I'm sorry, Erwin, but I'm busy," he said, rifling around in the stack of papers on his desk.

The doctor left the office looking downcast. Through the half-open door, Gerhard watched Borg give Asner a pack of cigarettes. Cigarettes were the camp's leading currency, worth as much as gold or precious gems. *How typical of the kind doctor,* he thought. Gerhard also tried to treat Asner with respect, even though he was a prisoner—unlike

Schmidt, who could barely write his own name but flogged his scribes all day long. He was now on his fifth.

His headache had evaporated, and Gerhard threw himself into his work. During the night they had cleared an entire barrack in the camp to make room for new prisoners from Holland. The Russian and Polish inhabitants had been sent to Bergen-Belsen. He knew they were heading to their deaths. But he was glad there would be more food for the rest of them until the Dutch arrived.

Konstanz, Germany, March 14, 1943

A barely audible whisper reached him. It came from above, as though uttered from a tower and reduced by the wind to a whistling stream of air. It was a sound so muffled that it could hardly be called a sound, except that right behind it skulked silence. It approached, but slowly, as though it feared him, as though it knew that he and only he could make it disappear.

". . . has sustained *contusio regio thoracis sinistra cum* pneumothorax, and we have performed a thoracentesis. Good, good."

The voice was far away, sealed in, little more than a deep, rumbling bass without treble or pitch. He had no idea whether he was awake, or whether what he'd heard was part of a dream. Everything was dark. He thought his eyes were open. And yet he could not see. So he must be asleep. But a jabbing pain on his left side made him question that. The man's voice spoke again, sounding subdued.

Karl felt the blanket covering his legs being pulled aside, then roughly put back. "Good," the voice said.

He heard a pen against paper and an odd gurgling noise, as when a glass is sucked empty with a straw—a hoarse, bubbling noise that came in brief intervals.

The pain intensified, and fire ravaged his body. The flames consumed his skin, which contracted because of the heat. His muscles burned, and his eyes. A pain of that magnitude must mean that they'd fallen out. That's why he couldn't see. He raised his hand to touch them and found that a rough bandage was stretched across much of his face. As the man droned on, Karl tried to speak, to indicate that he was still alive. When the man didn't respond, he screamed.

"Easy now, easy," the man said, squeezing his arm as he called for a nurse. "Easy, Major."

He heard someone else rush over and felt the stab of a needle into one of his thighs.

"I'm Dr. Johan Kirchbaum," the doctor said, slowly releasing his grip. "Can you hear me?"

"Yes." Karl had difficulty recognizing his own voice, which had lost its strength and was drowning in that odd gurgle that followed each of his breaths. He held his breath and the sound ceased, but when he exhaled again, the noise returned.

"Your lungs have been punctured, Major. We've inserted a drain and connected it to a ventilator, which is the sound you're hearing."

With regard to his leg, Kirchbaum explained that a grenade splinter had sliced a deep gash in his thigh, but that wasn't the worst part. Kirchbaum told him with an apologetic tone in his voice that they couldn't save his vision in his left eye, and the chances that he would regain vision in his right were slim. Bandages covered both eyes. It was the same claustrophobic sensation he'd felt inside the enormous warehouses on the outskirts of Berlin at the beginning of the war. He felt constricted, panic-stricken that he would feel this way for the rest of his life. What if his sight never returned? What if he was blind forever? It was impossible to imagine what that could be like.

"Do you remember anything?" Kirchbaum asked.

"Thomas, where is Thomas?"

"Can you remember anything, Major?"

"No. No, only Thomas. And the horses. Is Thomas alive?"

"I'm afraid I cannot answer that."

Karl sighed, dozing off under the influence of the morphine. When he woke again, Kirchbaum explained that he'd first been transported from Ukraine to a hospital in Kraków, Poland. He recalled nothing of this and wasn't sure whether he'd been conscious at any point during the journey. From Kraków he'd been driven back to Germany in a hospital train. Now he was in a military hospital in Konstanz, on the northwestern shore of the Bodensee. He remembered only snippets of the nearly 750-mile train ride, mostly sounds and smells. He remembered the stench, the constant moaning and groaning, the shrill hiss of the signal whistle when the train departed after resting on a siding to allow troop transports or war materiel to pass by. He remembered the nerve-racking screech of the wheels on the rail joints, mile after mile, but most of all he remembered the pain.

The morphine kept the pain at bay now, and every time one of the nurses gave him a dose, he thought of Thomas Remmel. Karl had been fond of the doctor, whom he was convinced must be dead.

Every day around noon, the same nurse visited him. She was kind and spoke to him in a pleasant voice. A faint lavender scent trailed her whenever she came and went, and he could almost hear her smile. Her name was Helena. He didn't ask her age, but her voice indicated she was young. He heard her shake the thermometer, after which she would ask him to turn his rear toward her, and she would always make some disarming remark that made the otherwise humiliating experience bearable.

They talked whenever she came to care for him. It seemed like years since he'd talked, and it felt like decades since anyone had listened to him. But Helena did. He looked forward to her visits. Her voice was soft and airy, like the strike of his Steinway keys. One day he asked her what she looked like, and she took his hands and guided them to her cheeks, letting him feel her face. He touched her high cheekbones. A pair of long eyelashes tickled his fingertips, and with his index finger he felt the narrow arch of her eyebrow above her eye. Her face ended in a narrow, pointy chin, and above it he traced the line of her lips. He parted them slightly and could feel her faint breath against his fingers. Her face was close to his, and he smelled lavender.

The military hospital was huge. He had no idea how huge, but judging by the constant whimpering and moaning—which mercilessly cut straight into his bones—there were hundreds if not thousands of patients in the place. There were soldiers who'd lost limbs from mines and burned men who'd been victims of grenade splinters and bullets. Those who'd either gone into shell shock or descended into madness were housed in a separate unit. The same was true of officers and privates; they were located in two separate wings.

After a few weeks they removed the bandage from his eyes. He was blind. His left eye didn't respond when the doctor swept a finger in front of it, but just rested in its socket as if pinned in place. With his right eye, though, he registered a faint light. He began blinking in desperation, and as he did so, the film that blocked his vision faded. Everything came slowly into focus, and he started to see contours. The room began to take shape, and he soon saw a man standing before him. The doctor must have known that Karl was able to see him, because he smiled, relieved. Standing behind him was another doctor, and next to him was a pretty woman who was smiling shyly. Instinctively he knew that it was Helena.

A few hours later she rolled his wheelchair out onto the large veranda, from which he could see across the Bodensee. The Rhine ran through the middle of Konstanz, and a bridge bound the numerous residential areas and industrial districts on the northern bank with the old city on the southern side. A skiff was sailing on the lake. He thought of August and was overcome with an overwhelming surge of grief. Now, too, he saw for himself the other soldiers' terrible wounds and amputations he'd only been able to hear of before.

To the doctors' surprise, his leg healed quickly. Before long he could walk without pain, albeit with a slight limp. When spring arrived, he would often head down to the lake, where he put his shoes and socks on the small fingers of grass-covered land that jutted into the lake and ambled out into the clear water with his pants rolled up to his knees.

One evening Helena invited him down to the beach. She'd packed a basket with food, bread, and wine. They lay on a blanket and drank chilled Riesling, and it suddenly seemed as though she were the only person he knew.

Helena had been engaged. Her betrothed, Ernst, had been killed in Poland. They had planned to marry when he returned, but it had been three and a half years since a party member had knocked on her apartment door and given her the news.

Karl rested on his elbow while she studied him. He didn't like being looked at. He'd been more or less satisfied when he'd glanced in the mirror earlier, but now he felt a little grotesque wearing the black leather patch Kirchbaum had given him. Helena was beautiful. The last rays of the evening sun gave her brown, slightly curled hair a reddish tint. The skin around her narrow nose was so fine and youthful, and he recalled how soft it was to touch. Her brown eyes pulled at him in a way he'd never felt, and he thought of the golden-brown mare in the Ukraine. Helena's eyes drew him in, and he felt like a piece of soft iron that she'd heated on the hearth and could now bend and shape to her will. He sipped his wine and tilted his head back. A pair of clouds drifted across the graying sky, forming abstract art, but before long all he saw in the white clouds was a single image: Helena's face. The chilled Riesling was making him a little woozy, and he shook his head so that he could think straight.

Helena shifted closer to him. It was an open invitation, an invitation to take her in his arms and kiss her. It wasn't that he didn't want to, because he did, but he couldn't. It was as if a huge sign suddenly hung in the air, blocking his view of Helena. On the sign was written

"INGRID" in capital letters. He took a deep breath and made a decision. He couldn't do this to Ingrid; he wasn't the kind of man who betrayed his wife.

Karl stood. A little wobbly, he thanked Helena for a wonderful evening, put on his socks and shoes, and headed up to the hospital without looking back.

Neuengamme, Germany, May 7, 1943

"We can talk shop after supper," Lorenz said, offering Gerhard a dish piled with meat and vegetables. Gerhard wondered whether the vegetables had been grown in the SS's gardens. He'd heard that the ground was littered with the ashes of the dead, but it was just a rumor. He scooped up a few carrots and some cauliflower.

"Are you married, Mr. Strangl?" Lorenz's wife, Hannelore, asked, and Gerhard couldn't help but notice Lorenz giving her a reproachful glance.

"My wife is dead."

"I'm sorry to hear that," Hannelore said, giving him a sympathetic look.

They ate in silence, their only accompaniment a piece of classical music that Gerhard assumed was Brahms. He wondered if they always listened to music to drown out the noise of the camp; judging from the size of their record collection, he figured he was probably right.

After finishing the meal, he thanked Hannelore for dinner and followed Lorenz into his office.

The camp commandant closed the double door, and they sat down, Lorenz behind the desk and Gerhard on the opposite side.

Lorenz cleared his throat. "I like you." He paused. "I will be sorry to lose you, but I know that you would like to leave."

Gerhard stared at him, confused. He didn't respond, but waited, curious what would come next.

"You can have my job. Well, not *my* job," Lorenz corrected himself quickly, "but a similar job. On a smaller scale, however."

"I'm not sure I understand."

"Listen," Lorenz said and started to explain. The SS planned to open a new subcamp in Neugraben. They'd begun to build wooden barracks on a patch of land there for some five hundred prisoners who would be arriving soon from Auschwitz-Birkenau. What the commandant said next caught Gerhard completely off guard. The majority of the five hundred prisoners were to work for the Strangl Clothing Factory.

He composed himself for a moment. "At my brother's request?"

"Hans Müller's. The factory quite simply cannot keep up with the demand. All the men have been sent to the front, and the women are working in important branches of the war industry." Lorenz lowered his voice and continued in a kind voice: "And you are the perfect choice for camp commandant. It's your chance to get out of here."

"Why are you letting me go now? You've ignored all my transfer requests."

"Like I said: I like you." Lorenz smiled apologetically.

Gerhard lay down on his bed. He exhaled. He felt a sudden joy, a feeling that had lain dormant in him for some time now. Now it returned at full strength and warmed him from within. Neugraben was a way out; Neugraben was *his* way out. He smiled in the dark. Lorenz had given him what he'd wanted ever since he'd first set foot at Neuengamme.

In some bizarre way he'd grown used to life in the camp, but the only person he would miss was Borg. And yet he wouldn't truly miss him, either. Perhaps he simply liked Borg because he was the least crazy of all the degenerates who worked there. Or was he? No, Gerhard was deceiving himself, because even though he and Borg might have enjoyed a few cultivated conversations, Erwin Borg was and always would be a monster. A psychopath. It was his job to select prisoners for transport to Bergen-Belsen, and Gerhard knew this was tantamount to sending them to their deaths. He signed all death certificates, though the causes of death were never listed as hangings or beatings. And he was responsible for the brothel, too. No, he shouldn't confuse him for a good person.

After some consideration he decided Lorenz was also a horrible person. He was the only one who had the power to change the conditions in the camp; he alone could stop what was happening. But it was obvious that he didn't want to know what went on, even though he lived right in the middle of it all. It was like having an address in the middle of Dante's Inferno. Of course he knew what went on.

Gerhard imagined that he could make a difference. He could make sure that the prisoners at Neugraben were treated better. He would make sure that they were given enough to eat, that they weren't beaten, that they could lead a relatively decent life. He would make sure that they wore clean clothes, could shower, and went to bed with full stomachs. It would be entirely different from Neuengamme. He smiled again. He couldn't wait to get away from Neuengamme.

Konstanz, Germany, July 5, 1943

He was overcome by an intoxicating feeling, and for a moment he thought he might faint. For a few seconds his entire body tensed like a bow. As Karl relaxed, he couldn't control the smile that formed on his lips. The quivering sensation that had just filled every fiber of his being began to recede and was replaced by a surge of well-being. He remained on top of Helena.

He pulled out and rolled onto his side, to look at her. A sudden modesty caused her to pull up the blanket. He tugged on it gently so that her body was slowly revealed again. He studied her. Her breasts were neither small nor large, but round and well formed; her belly bulged slightly, and her hips were narrow, but not in the skinny way he disliked. They'd made love three evenings in a row, and he had already grown accustomed to her body: the tiny mole on her lower back, the scar tissue on her elbow, and the little crack her neck made whenever she stretched. Now her beautiful body was exposed to him again, and for a moment he considered making love to her once more, but then he decided he was too tired and too lazy. He closed his eyes.

"What are you thinking about?"

He shrugged.

"My mother thinks you're too old for me."

He rose up and leaned on his elbows. "You told her about me?"

"She wasn't happy. She probably imagined that I would marry a doctor, since I work in a hospital."

He didn't know how to respond. He kissed her, swung his legs over the edge of the bed, and began putting on his clothes. "Since we're on the subject of the hospital, they're sending me home soon."

The satisfied expression vanished from her face. "Are you going back to your wife?" She pulled up the blanket again.

"I'm going home to Hamburg. I have to."

Helena was silent, and he was annoyed at himself. He'd just ruined the mood. Why had he said it aloud? He should've just kept his mouth shut and, when the day arrived, taken his leave of her. He would miss her, of course, but hopefully he would also forget her. He'd enjoyed their time together, but he knew it was temporary. Ingrid was his wife, and he would simply have to erase Helena from his mind.

He was overcome by a strange feeling as he left her apartment. The previous mornings they'd eaten breakfast together, drunk coffee, and read the newspaper until she had to go to the hospital. He had stayed in her apartment or walked around the city, aimlessly killing time. He'd never had that kind of freedom before, and it was liberating to suddenly get to know a new side of himself. He wasn't the conscientious major here, or the chairman, or a father—he was just Karl.

Karl was released a few weeks later. A day later, he stood at the central train station in Hamburg with a pass for an extended leave in his pocket. Because he hadn't told anyone that he was coming home, no one was there to pick him up at the station. He and Ingrid had exchanged letters while he was in Konstanz, and though she'd wanted to visit him, he'd insisted she remain in Hamburg.

He began walking through the city. He was stunned to discover that the Alster Pavilion had been bombed, and the city had been scarred by several air raids.

An unfamiliar sensation raced through him as he strolled up his graveled driveway. As he ascended the steps to the front door, he wasn't sure whether he should simply go inside or ring the doorbell. He rang the bell as if he were a guest. He heard steps behind the door. Karin opened it, then gaped at him in shock. She put her hand to her mouth and dashed into the house. Unsure of what to do, he remained standing outside. Fast steps now echoed inside the dining room, and Ingrid came running. She threw herself into his arms. They hugged for a long time, and she started to cry, something Karl had never seen her do. She fiddled with his eye patch, and he let her. When she guided him into the hall, she held his waist a little too hard.

"Be quiet!" He'd missed Sophia and Maximilian, but now they seemed noisy and irritating. He retreated into his office and looked around. What had he ever done here? Suddenly he had no idea what to do. Everything seemed trivial, unimportant, utterly meaningless. He'd been home for two weeks now, and he'd felt the same way every day. Would he ever get used to being home again?

One afternoon the telephone rang. Karl answered in the hallway.

"You can't call here. How did you even get my number?" he whispered into the receiver.

"Kirchbaum just gave me an exam. I'm expecting."

He pretended he hadn't heard. "I need to go."

"You can't."

He could tell that Helena was on the verge of tears. "I need to."

He hung up and stood staring blankly at the telephone. He expected it to ring again. The loud noise would resound in the hallway, and he would grab the receiver as if he could hide the call from everyone in the house. But what was he supposed to say? The phone remained silent. When the door opened he turned, startled, and saw Karin rushing down the hallway. He didn't move. How pathetic he was. He'd been a fool, and now he was unable to own up to the desire he'd felt for Helena. He felt despicable. He was despicable.

At the dinner table that evening, he was still in a foul mood. Maximilian and Sophia had left the table, or rather, Ingrid had asked them to leave the table. The remark that followed came as a complete surprise.

"I know you're having an affair with another woman."

Karl slowly patted his mouth with his napkin. "I don't know what you're talking about."

"I know you're having an affair with another woman," Ingrid repeated, this time more loudly. She tried to hold his gaze, but Karl evasively reached for the wine bottle and studied it. He poured some wine into his glass. Several times during the past few weeks he'd considered telling Ingrid about Helena. He'd prepared the story in his mind. "There's something I have to tell you." Then he'd reconsidered: "I've done something foolish." He'd brooded and brooded and brooded on the best way to tell her, reflecting on how the same story could be told many different ways. It was all about finding the right words. He'd come up with a few possibilities, but in the end he'd chosen not to say anything. Now it was too late, and gone were all the mollifying speeches and variants that he'd considered—words meant to make what he'd done seem forgivable.

"Ingrid, I'm not having an affair," he said, his gaze still fixed on his glass. He knew his face was blank as a sheet of paper, and he feared even the slightest flinch or frown would expose him.

"There's no need." She seemed calm, her voice firm. "We're not like that, Karl. We don't do such things."

Resisting her was pointless. He wasn't sure whether he should nod or shake his head, but he settled on giving her a stiff smile. He swallowed a lump in his throat, thinking that the gulping sound must seem like a confession to her.

"I'm taking Maximilian and Sophia to Rügen, and we'll never discuss it again."

He nodded, but felt he needed to say something. "She wasn't—"

She held up her hand to stop him. "I don't want to know anything about her."

They ate the rest of their dinner without saying another word. The food suddenly had no flavor, and he chewed in silence. He felt Ingrid's glare on him, but he avoided her eyes. The silence was filled with contempt, a contempt for him and what he'd done. She stood and left the dining room.

Immediately after dinner she began to pack. She planned to move back with her parents until the war was over. He couldn't object to that. She and the children would be safe on Rügen, but he knew that his stupidity was the real reason she was leaving.

They stood stock-still on the platform.

"I'll return."

Though he heard Ingrid's words, he knew it wasn't the truth. She might return physically, but she would never return to *him*, and their life would not return to what it had been. Their life together was irrevocably finished. He held her tight. She seemed limp in his arms, and he released her clumsily. She kissed him on the cheek, a dry, disinterested kiss, as if her lips were aiming for the least possible contact with his skin. He wanted to take her in his arms again, but she pulled away. He tousled Maximilian's hair.

"I'll miss you three," he said as he patted Sophia on the cheek. When they boarded the train, he walked along the cars and watched them take their seats. As he observed them through the window, he felt burdened by the question of whether or not he would ever see them again.

The train chugged away from the platform. His throat closed up, blocking a lump that could go neither up nor down, but just expanded in his gullet. He turned away and started toward home.

Hamburg, Germany, July 27, 1943

Such incredible news! For the first time in ages, Karl felt alive. It was as if his blood had finally begun to circulate again. He just wished Ingrid were there to share his joy. It was one of those moments in life one shouldn't experience alone. He suddenly felt old. Tomorrow he would turn forty-five, and soon he would be a grandfather.

He hugged Hilde and felt the heat of his daughter's body warm his own. His body and mind had waited so long for something positive to happen. It was a relief to finally feel good again.

Heinz stood behind Hilde, looking a little shy. Karl let go of Hilde and offered him his hand.

"Congratulations. Congratulations to you both."

They sat in the living room. Karl hadn't seen Heinz since before the war, but he recalled the last time they'd been together. Heinz had just joined the SS, and he'd proudly shown off his uniform, demonstrating where his distinctions would go on his pockets. But the man who now sat across from Karl was the exact opposite of the Heinz who'd wanted to take on the world. Although no medals gleamed from his pockets, it seemed that sort of recognition no longer meant anything to him. Instead he appeared taciturn and damaged.

Heinz had been in one of the special task units, and during the past year he'd been stationed in Maly Trostenets, an extermination camp outside of Minsk. Karl could see in his eyes that he was not the same person. His eyes were squinty, and he spoke more softly than he had before.

At the hospital in Konstanz, Karl had met an officer who'd told him about all the gruesome things he'd experienced at a similar camp, in Majdanek. He described the film roll constantly unspooling in his head with images of the camp, like a horror flick or a war movie for madmen. No doubt the same was true for Heinz as well. Karl noticed that he didn't finish his sentences, and he often gazed distractedly into the distance. Hilde excused him by saying that he was tired. And Hilde was happy because it didn't appear that he would be deployed again. Couldn't she see that he was no longer the same person? He'd been sent home. Karl could tell. Like an unstable mental patient, he'd been found unfit, then discarded.

Hilde stood, and the two men looked at her. She excused herself and went to the bathroom.

"She needs to use the bathroom all the time," Heinz said quietly.

For a moment they sat in silence. Karl lit a cigarette.

"Do you know what we did there?" Heinz finally asked, scrutinizing his palms.

"I do."

"We shot them. I shot them. So many. And when I wouldn't do it anymore, they mocked me. They mocked me." Their eyes met, and Karl noticed that Heinz's were wet, glistening.

"They called me weak. But wasn't I the strong one because I said no?"

"Yes," Karl said. "Yes, you were."

Karl tried to find the right words to console Heinz, but he found that he didn't want to console him. The man's eyes were searching for forgiveness, for soothing words, but Karl couldn't bring himself to say them. He simply couldn't, because he hated his son-in-law, and it wasn't until now that he realized it. He'd tried over and over again to convince himself that everything would get better, that Heinz would mature and come around. But he knew what the special task units had done; he'd heard the rumors about Maly Trostenets—and men who'd done what he did were contemptible. Unworthy of his daughter.

Hilde returned.

"Listen. Let's go out to dinner tomorrow, the three of us. It's my birthday, and we'll have a pleasant evening and forget all about the war. Just the three of us," Karl said, to say something.

Hilde embraced him again, and he followed them to the door. Karl watched them go from the large window beside the main entrance. Hilde took Heinz's hand, and they headed down Heilwigstrasse, their fingers braided together.

Karl went to the sunroom, which made him think of Ingrid. Out in the garden, summer had turned everything green. Glancing at the copper beech, he thought of the unbearably dry Russian summers.

Karl recalled an episode when the men in his company had celebrated a passing freight train outside of Minsk. "Hamburg" was written on the cars, and everyone had considered it a greeting from home. Later he learned that the train was filled to the gills with Hamburg's Jews—Jews on their way to Maly Trostenets.

Karl lay in the bed on the first floor, unable to curb his train of thought. It was absurd: Gerhard had sent the Jews from Hamburg, Karl had waved at them en route, and Heinz had met them at the end of their journey. Karl could clearly picture what Heinz had done in the special unit and in the camp, and now Heinz was imprisoned by his own conscience. Karl was disgusted at his son-in-law, but maybe there was a trace of hope after all? Today he'd witnessed signs of another man living inside Heinz, a better man; it was visible in the tenderness he'd shown Hilde, as if he recognized that he needed to change. That only by being a good man could he remedy the things he'd done. No, Karl couldn't delude himself. Heinz had declared his hatred of the Jews and his love for the führer before the war, and all the human lives he had on his conscience could not be removed, not even with kindness. But what was Karl to do? His daughter was married to Heinz, and if the choice was between seeing Hilde—and therefore Heinz as well—or not seeing either of them, then he would be forced to accept him as a part of his life.

He let the thought go and rolled over in bed. He didn't think there was anyone else in the house. It was possible that Karin was in her room, but she usually stayed with her sister on the outskirts of the city. The cook, Mrs. Hanke, was with family, and Albert and Mr. Nikolaus had gone.

All at once his bed seemed enormous, and he felt like a boy who'd sneaked into his parents' double bed. He felt lonely. It was a hot evening, and he knew that between the heat and his ruminations, he'd never fall asleep. He got up.

He pulled on a pair of pants and a shirt. In his office he found an unopened bottle of schnapps. With the bottle in one hand and a glass in the other, he went upstairs. All the furniture and other flammable objects had been removed from the second floor, and all that remained were bare floors and walls with faded squares where pictures had once hung. It was his house, goddamn it, and it vexed him that others—the English and American bombers—had any influence on how it was furnished. That was exactly what he'd told Ingrid, but she'd just shaken her head in resignation and continued carrying things downstairs.

A music box stood on the floor in Sophia's room. A ballerina had paused in the middle of a pirouette. He turned the little key on the back of the box, and she began dancing to some piece of classical music that he recognized but couldn't remember the name of. In Maximilian's room rows of tin soldiers were positioned in formations, ready for battle. A single wooden floorboard divided the two armies, who would attack each other as soon as Maximilian returned. It would be a bloodbath, Karl thought. He was seized by the knowledge that he would never see Maximilian again, or Sophia or Ingrid. But he had only himself to blame. Irritated, he kicked the soldiers, which scattered and fell. There were no survivors.

He went into his old bedroom. It was empty. He opened the door to the balcony and sat in a patio chair. The air was still warm. Slowly, but purposefully, he began draining the contents of the bottle. He gazed across the city and its many towers. It was an impressive sight. The church towers—St. Michael's, St. James's, St. Peter's, and St. Catherine's—and the pointy courthouse tower all bore witness to a city that refused to be broken.

He glanced over at the slender clock tower of St. Michael's Church. *I wonder if Gerhard's home,* he thought, but he knew deep down that he was in Neuengamme. They hadn't spoken since Karl returned. Before the war they'd lived in the same city but inhabited their own little corners of the world. The gulf between them had only widened since the war began. Gerhard would never understand what Karl had experienced on the eastern front, and Karl had no idea how Gerhard wound up in a concentration camp. Gerhard, of all people.

He felt a kind of relief as the schnapps began to take effect. His feet prickled, and a stream of giddiness flushed through him. He decided that he didn't want to think anymore that day, but just go wherever the alcohol took him.

That's why he did nothing when the air raid sirens went off. The oil refineries and the shipyards were usually the targets. So why should he be afraid? He filled his glass to the rim, and some of the liquid sloshed onto his hand. The alarm—a piercing screech with a light vibrato—continued to sound and eventually died out, like a car engine, only to start again, building toward the siren's insistent note. There were two kinds of siren: first a warning and then the full alarm, which meant that it was time to take cover. But in his mind the two merged into one. He could hear the drone of the airplanes now. The noise grew louder and louder in his head. He looked up. The illumined night sky was full of black shadows. They came from the south like migratory birds returning home to breed.

As the bombs began to fall on the other side of the Alster, a voice inside him told him to run. But he didn't want to go to the bomb shelter alone. So he sat there with his eyes wide, spellbound by the spectacle unfolding before him. The sky was illuminated and filled with a sound that rose above the lake with unabated strength, causing the house to tremble. The deafening impacts and the thundering, pounding booms from the city's flak cannons—in tandem with the blinding flashes and missiles racing across the sky—lifted his spirits. There was something extraordinary about this catastrophic scene. He started to laugh. A night fighter crashed into the lake, drawing a tail of fire in its wake. He laughed again but couldn't hear himself above the infernal racket emanating from the harbor and the inner city. He nonetheless managed to hear a thin voice behind him.

Karin was shouting at him, though the thick wall of noise eclipsed her words. She walked across the terrace to him. Fear made her eyes small. She put her mouth close to his ear.

"You can't sit out here, Mr. Strangl," she screamed. He could tell she was terrified.

He tried to stand, but his legs wouldn't budge. He teetered for a moment. Karin helped him up and supported him as best she could. They went inside but stumbled onto the floor. Karin tried to lift him, and he wobbled uncertainly to his feet again. Another tremor that felt as though it came from the center of the earth shook the house. Plaster rained down from the ceiling, blanketing them under a fine, snowlike layer. He looked at her and laughed, and they fell to the floor again just as an enormous boom resounded above the lake.

Neuengamme, Germany, July 28, 1943

The deep, distant rumble of the countless bombers faded, and a strange silence settled over the camp. Gerhard and the others emerged from the bunker, where they'd taken refuge when the wind carried the sound of the first air raid sirens across the marshland. Now it was almost three in the morning. The people, the heat, and the certainty that family members were in the city made it impossible to sleep in the bunker. They went outside and took a few deep breaths before going back to their beds in the barracks.

Gerhard climbed up one of the guard towers to view the city. The sky was illuminated in a radiant orange sheen, and searchlights continued to flicker nervously. The powerful light from the city made several of them think that it was morning, and some of the officers glanced at their watches in confusion. An enormous mushroom cloud of smoke hung above Hamburg. Gerhard guessed that the oil depots on the harbor had been hit.

"Holy shit," Borg said. He'd climbed the tower, too, and now stood wide-eyed, staring at the terrible scene, flames reflected in his pupils. "The city really took a beating this time," he mumbled softly.

They watched the burning city in silence. Gerhard had trouble focusing his mind. He thought of his apartment on Jakobstrasse, of his book, and of course of Karl and Ingrid. Thank god they lived on the Alster's southern bank a good distance from downtown, but it appeared that the entire city may have been bombed. Everything was on fire—at least that's what it looked like—and an acrid stench filled the air.

Borg put a hand on his shoulder. "It's a catastrophe. Nothing less. No one could've survived that."

"Is your family there?" Gerhard asked, uncomfortable with the doctor's touch.

"My old mother."

"What about your wife?"

"She's dead," Borg replied.

"Mine, too."

And maybe my brother's dead now, too, Gerhard thought. He was overwhelmed by a devastating certainty, and he knew of only one way to rid himself of it. A few minutes later, in the Führer's Lodge, he poured himself a tall glass of schnapps.

Hamburg, Germany, July 28, 1943

His mouth was dry, and his eyelids were tacky and opened quite slowly. When Karl forced them all the way open, he was startled by what he saw, then realized it was only one of Maximilian's tin soldiers aiming its gun at him. He looked around. He lay on the floor in Maximilian's room, his cheek wet with drool. He stumbled to his feet and discovered that his fly was open. He glanced down at himself and noted tiny splatters of blood on his pants. A few drops had worked their way into the light gabardine fabric and now rested there raising questions he couldn't answer.

Vague images from the evening before started coming to him—the bombs, the booms, the brilliant flashes of light, the empty bottle of schnapps. The chubby servant girl had been with him. He remembered falling. His knee was filthy. The horrible realization of what must have transpired gradually came to him. He raced downstairs into the kitchen in a panic. He had to find Karin and determine what had happened, or apologize for what had happened. He didn't know which.

The sun had yet to rise, but Mrs. Hanke was already there. The cook told him that Karin had gone. She'd left the house a half hour earlier carrying her suitcase. A smile that might have been masking reproach transformed into one of relief. "I'm glad we made it through the night."

"Yes, me, too," Karl said, disoriented by the realization that it wasn't even five o'clock.

"It's a good thing your wife and children are safe," the cook said, handing him a cup of coffee. "This is one of those days we should have a real cup of coffee," she rambled on, though she didn't pour herself a cup.

Hilde! Why hadn't he thought of Hilde? His behavior had made him forget all about Hilde and Heinz—even his grandchild! They were in the city, and he'd gotten himself drunk. But what should he have done? And what *could* he have done? Nothing. But he could do something now; he could find them, help them. He consoled himself with the thought that he'd already helped them by persuading them to move out of the loft apartment on Brennerstrasse. Though Hamm wasn't among Hamburg's most exciting districts, it was still better than that vulnerable attic apartment. But the move didn't necessarily mean they were safe. He had to find them.

As soon as he was out the front door, he smelled it. A thick and dense smoke wafting off the lake. He started walking through Alster Park. This side of the lake appeared to have been untouched by the bombs, but the opposite shore was a broad latticework of glowing flames. That was his destination. He crossed Lombardsbrücke. The courthouse looked to be intact; the tower, too. The same was true of St. Catherine's Church, though the spire and the roof had splintered just above the clock. The hands had stopped at a quarter to one. As he got closer, his fear of what he'd find in the bombed areas increased.

He headed down Brennerstrasse and paused in front of the house where Hilde and Heinz had once lived. Fires burned quietly there, slowly consuming the entire house. There were flames behind each window, and fiery tongues shot out occasionally as if someone inside was blowing on them. Flames licked the roof's spine and devoured the rafters where the apartment had been.

A gray-black smoke billowed down the deserted street, stinging his nose and throat. He struggled to breathe and was forced to cover his nose and mouth with his hands. A couple of slight gusts punctured the smoke, and he had a clear view of people emerging from a basement farther down the street. They embraced one other, happy to be alive. A gray-bearded man kissed the ground, and the women kissed each other. But just then the house collapsed, and five stories crashed down on top of them like a giant wave.

His first impulse was to help them, but his body didn't move. There was nothing he could do. The spot where they had been standing was now just an inaccessible mountain of rubble and wood. He felt a sharp pain in his chest, as if he were about to explode, or as if his body were incapable of bearing such a burden. At the same time he had an ominous feeling that the worst was yet to come.

He started back, still in shock at what he'd just witnessed. He had to find another way to Hamm. But now it seemed as though he was no longer in a hurry to find Hilde and Heinz. He knew his reluctance was born of fear, a rending terror that they were dead, buried alive under rubble like the people he'd just seen rejoicing. He saw others appear down another street, their eyes red from the burning ash.

"Don't go that way. It's hell that way," called an old man with a voice made hoarse by the fire.

A piece of flaming lumber crashed down from a house a few feet from Karl and sent coals flying. Terrified, he began to run and stopped only when he came to where the Luftwaffe's barracks had been. But they were no longer there.

On one corner, a building smoldered before his very eyes. Only the glowing red fragments bore witness to what had once stood there. Everything was enshrouded in red flames; all of Hamburg was burning. The smoke carried with it large, hot flakes of ash, which stung his cheeks and burned his face. The dead were everywhere. Charred, stiffened corpses lay on the streets and sidewalks, blackened by the heat, their clothing seared. Some had been pulverized, while others looked like empty shells.

The survivors were also empty shells. They sat or lay on the ground with vacant, blackened faces and flame-reddened eyes, some barefoot, others wearing only pajamas or nightgowns. They hadn't even the strength to cry. Screams of horror could be heard from buildings, from basements, but the fire ignored them. It raged on, took a deep breath, then blazed and blustered with renewed vigor.

Karl continued on. The fire made it difficult to get to where he was going, but he still clung to a small thread of hope; he had to. He needed to believe they were alive. He rounded a corner, then stopped in his tracks, dumbstruck. He brought his hands to his ears. Everything was gone. Ahead of him was a wasteland, a huge burning wasteland like the controlled burning of a field, in the middle of the city. A few lonely house façades remained here and there—a wall, a light pole—but Hamm's residential neighborhoods were now nothing more than a pile of ruins enveloped in flame. He could not even differentiate between the streets and where the buildings had stood. Hamm was gone.

The sound of enraged flames was deafening. Weary firemen fought desperately to save people until they threw up their hands in defeat and collapsed, exhausted, right where they stood. Karl saw an emergency vehicle that had melted into a gnarled, blackened lump. A woman rushed toward him, but suddenly her dress ignited, and she fell screaming to the ground. He wanted to help her, but at that instant he was sent flying.

A powerful blaze had knocked him off his feet, and he landed heavily on his back. The flames were everywhere—above him, below him, behind him, ahead of him. He flapped and beat at his arms to knock back the blazes, but it was pointless. Drained of breath, he managed to leap into an entranceway where a man began pounding on him. Confused, Karl tried to wriggle free of the blows raining down on him. Now he was trapped between the omnivorous fire and a madman. He shouted at him, but the man kept at it, and then a woman appeared to help. Karl fell to the ground. Only when they began to roll him around on the hard stone floor did he understand that they were trying to put out his burning clothes.

When the flames had finally been extinguished, he lay on the floor, his head spinning. The man helped him to his feet.

"I'm sorry we had to do that to you."

"It's all right, I was on fire," Karl said, still confused. "I was on fire."

"My name is Dieter," the man said, adding quickly, "We've got to get away from here before the whole thing comes down."

He grabbed Karl's and the woman's hands, and they began to run. Karl knew the man was guiding them to the harbor, but that route was blocked off. They had to find another way. They were surrounded by an enormous sea of flames, and he soon noticed that the soles of his shoes had begun to melt on the scorching asphalt.

The woman was quickly depleted of energy, and the two men had to support her. Their mouths and throats were raw and dry, and it hurt to breathe the scalding air. On a street corner some men tried to tap a fire hydrant to get a drink of water. The three of them stopped to help, but it was soon clear that it wouldn't budge.

They were exhausted by the time they reached the harbor. Dieter dove into the water, and Karl and the woman followed suit. The water soothed the stabbing pain on Karl's parched skin. For a moment he forgot where he was and began to sink. In a panic, he beat the water with his arms and legs, then gasped for breath when he reached the surface.

The woman hadn't emerged, and Dieter screamed miserably, "Lotte! Lotte!" He dove, came up, gasped for breath, dove again, came up, dove.

Karl didn't have the strength to help. Approaching his own limits, he struggled to clutch a large iron ring bolted to the side of the pier; the water he'd swallowed came up in a thin stream of diluted vomit. On land the flames continued to rage, and others leaped into the canal, which was soon more crowded than Alster Lake on a summer day. Several times, his exertions nearly caused him to let go, and his arthritis jolted through his hands. A young woman crying in fear struggled to keep herself afloat. He reached out to grab her, but she flapped her arms wildly. With great difficulty he pulled her to him, and they both clung to the iron ring.

Karl wasn't sure how long they were in the canal. Although the water wasn't cold, he was freezing. The intensity of the fire had abated, and people appeared on the pier to help, including firemen, boys in Hitler Youth uniforms, and ordinary folks. He made sure the woman was the first to get assistance, and that's when he realized she was pregnant. She said nothing but gave him a grateful, sooty smile as a fireman wrapped her in a blanket and led her away.

Shaken to the core, he headed slowly and uncertainly toward home. He was thirsty, tired, and weak. He looked down at himself. His clothes were soaked, tattered, and filthy, but he'd survived; he was alive.

Flames continued to burn everywhere, and where they had already been put out or gone out on their own, blackened, soot-covered buildings bore witness to their visit. People lay all over the streets, half-burned or simply transformed into ashes; it was like walking through a morgue. It was already evening by the time he got home. He remembered that it was his birthday.

After spending a sleepless night in his bed, Karl got up and once again set off to navigate the sooty ruins. He stopped at the end of the block where Hilde and Heinz had lived. The façade was still standing. He could see the blue summer sky through the windows, which no longer held glass. He entered the hole where a door had once stood; all that remained of it were the metal hasps. Behind the façade was a vast open area that looked like a construction site full of trash.

He'd actually expected to fall apart, but instead he just felt empty. Not the kind of emptiness that meant he felt nothing, but rather an emptiness that made him unable to respond. He felt as though he were witnessing his own autopsy. His internal organs had been removed, his heart scooped out, his lungs and kidneys carefully placed on a metal tray. But he couldn't lose hope now; it was his fatherly duty to keep the faith. He would find Hilde, and when he found her he would never let her out of his sight again.

He exited onto what until just a few days ago had been a street. A red-haired woman was writing on the façade of a building with a piece of chalk. She looked up at him with tear-streaked eyes, then handed him the chalk. His hands trembled as he began to write, but his arthritis wouldn't allow him to form the letters. The woman offered to help, and Karl dictated a short message to Hilde, which she wrote for him.

He embraced the woman when they parted. He didn't know her, but they had something in common. On his way back, he noticed that people everywhere had scrawled messages to relatives or friends on walls and on placards mounted on light poles.

Every day Karl strode around the city searching for Hilde. The city's parks and green areas had become living quarters for the newly homeless. Although tents and other temporary shelters had been set up, many families were forced to sleep under the open sky. As he walked through the parks, he saw Hilde everywhere. In a red dress, in a nurses' uniform, or with a ponytail. But he was always disappointed. Every night he aimlessly tramped around his empty house, the echo of his steps following him from room to room.

A week after the bombing, parts of the devastated areas were cordoned off by high walls. Karl watched as people in prison uniforms were trucked into the areas of the city that were closed to the public. Prisoners from a concentration camp, they were forced to clean up the debris and rotting human corpses under surveillance. His search for Hilde began to feel increasingly futile.

Karl felt guilty. And ashamed. He'd sat laughing on his balcony. While people had been trapped in an inferno of fire and death, he'd watched the scene unfold as though it were entertainment. He hated himself for that. How could he have acted that way? Was this the kind of man he was without Ingrid? He missed her terribly, and he missed Hilde, too.

Hamburg, Germany, August 3, 1943

They clattered down another ravaged street, the suspension squealing and the cab shaking every time the car drove over yet another pothole. It had seemed like a morbid suggestion when young Dietmar Pacholz approached Gerhard.

He'd been of two minds. A week had passed, and he hadn't dared learn the truth. He didn't believe Karl was alive, but he would eventually need to know for a fact. On his way through the city, he grew more and more doubtful; it was a tragic sight. Hammerbrook, once a working-class neighborhood packed with people, was now mostly gone, and several other districts were also badly battered. The fires had simply pulverized everything in their path. Gerhard's whole body trembled as he studied the corpse-strewn streets. They'd been transformed from flesh and blood to ash in split seconds. Others had suffocated in the very bunkers that were meant to protect them. At least the dead had been convinced they wouldn't die. A few soldiers had shot themselves when it became clear that the enemy—in the form of fire—was invincible.

There were flies everywhere, large, fat, well-nourished blowflies that thrived on the open-air cemetery. The smell was like that of the camp but with more decomposition. Many corpses had already been removed, but just as many had melted into the asphalt as a continual reminder of that horrific night. Only the skeleton of the city remained; its skin had been peeled off, its innards removed. In a few places there wasn't even a skeleton. It was more like entire districts had been cremated. But the urn hadn't been lowered into the ground yet.

Once upon a time the buildings had stood as symbols of the city's progress, but it was all a desert now. From the cab of the truck, he witnessed hundreds of people in prison suits busy with the insurmountable task of cleaning up. He thought of Sisyphus, whose job suddenly seemed meaningful compared to the prisoners' task.

The procession came to a halt, and the windows stopped clanking. Gerhard looked up toward the sky. A balcony jutted from the façade above them. One half had been yanked loose from the house and now dangled threateningly. The window box was filled with red flowers.

The SS guards began directing the prisoners off the trucks once they'd entered the area surrounded by the newly built wall. The sub-camp's task was to clean up, remove fragments, and clear the roads. Like tiny, busy ants, the men in the black-and-white-striped suits immediately began picking up scraps, wood, and whatever else was scattered on the streets.

On the other side of the wall, the world had ceased to move. Gerhard started walking toward the lake. The once-teeming streets were nearly empty. Only a few lost souls wandered about. Gerhard nearly stumbled over the remains of a person, a woman in a half-charred red dress with small white dots. Pretty, not a nightgown. He turned away quickly. Sometimes he had done that himself: slept in his clothes when he went to bed because he knew he would end up in the bunker some-time during the night along with the other residents of Jakobstrasse. For a fleeting moment he considered heading over to his old apartment. Something in him, an inexplicable feeling, told him the apartment was intact still, and in the apartment was his book. His creation, his work. No. If the apartment was no longer standing, he would rather wait to find out. First he needed to find Karl.

Gerhard paused and gazed across a street littered with thin pieces of foil, the kind bombers hurled down to confuse the radar system. A man came toward him, moving slowly, carrying a suitcase. He was short and hunched, as if an enormous weight were forcing him down or gravity were tugging at him. There was something familiar about him, but Gerhard couldn't place the face at first. He thought he recognized the man's characteristically prominent chin, the cheeks that made him look like a Saint Bernard, and the almost-bald pate. He ruled out all the professors at the university and the residents of his apartment building. Gerhard rifled through the various photo albums in his head. When the man was right beside him, he finally found the image that matched: Detective Superintendent Kögl.

The other man recognized him at the same time: "Gerhard? Gerhard Strangl?" he said in a whisper.

Gerhard wanted to ignore him, but Kögl's pathetic countenance made him suddenly feel a pang of sympathy for the man.

"Detective Superintendent Kögl." Gerhard made sure to contain his voice.

"Not anymore," said Kögl. "The Gestapo kicked me out long ago. Can you believe I wound up sitting in the same cell as you?" He gave off a caustic grunt.

Gerhard was struck by the notion of revenge. Kögl had ripped his life apart. It was all his fault. Kögl's, and no one else's. What would his life have been like without this pitiful man's meddling? Kögl was the one who'd thrown him in the cell. And what had he done to Weinhardt? A single glance at Kögl, though, and Gerhard knew the man couldn't possibly sink any lower. His life hung in tatters. Revenge was superfluous. The detective superintendent was but a shadow of his former self. He'd lost his power; he was nothing.

"Is that what you managed to save?" Gerhard asked, straightening his uniform.

"No, these are the remains of my family." Kögl clamped the suitcase to his chest, sounding confused. "They're in here."

"In the suitcase?"

"Yes," he said. "My son died in Russia, and I have the rest here." He tapped the suitcase lightly with his palm.

They stood for a moment without uttering a word. Kögl stared at the ground, while Gerhard looked directly at Kögl. Then Gerhard cleared his throat, and the former detective superintendent stuttered a tentative good-bye before going on his way. Gerhard turned and watched him. Only then did he notice that Kögl was wearing pajama pants and slippers on his feet.

"Wait."

Kögl stopped.

"Tell me who reported me to the Gestapo."

"Does it even matter now?"

"It does to me." Gerhard stared at him firmly.

"It was Heinz."

"Heinz?" Gerhard eyed Kögl in disbelief.

"He hates you. That's what he said. You and your intellectualism and your arrogant demeanor. And he probably wanted to make a good impression on the Gestapo."

Gerhard stared straight ahead. "It wasn't Weinhardt, then?"

"No, he had nothing to do with it." Kögl started down the street.

Heinz. Dear god, it had been Heinz. He couldn't believe it. Which meant that Gerhard had delivered Weinhardt to Kögl for no reason at all. In reality Gerhard had been the informant. He'd done the Gestapo's bidding, had reported an enemy of the people. Where was Weinhardt now? Was he alive? Dead?

He pressed forward on shaking legs until he came to what had been the Alster Pavilion. All that remained was ruins.

A number of tents were pitched in the park along Alster Lake's eastern bank, and it was crowded with people. He walked across the bridge to get a view of the villa. If it had been bombed, he didn't want to find out as he was heading up the driveway. Relieved to see that it was still standing, he started back over the bridge, covering the last section at a brisk pace.

When he stood at the front door, he suddenly lost his breath. His chest heaved up and down like a bellows. His finger approached the doorbell but stopped in midair, hovering over its target as though blocked from it by an invisible barrier. It was just his brother, just

Karl. But what if they were strangers now? Maybe too much had come between them? Maybe he ought to turn around? He took a deep breath and pressed the button.

The bell chimed noisily, and he heard running footsteps approaching. The door was thrown open.

"Hilde!" Karl stood in the doorway, his eyes wide.

Gerhard saw the surprise in his brother's face. Like the clock on St. Catharine's Church, Karl had gone still. His mouth gaped, and for several seconds he didn't blink. Finally he came to, and his lips formed a smile. The two men shook hands hesitantly.

After searching in vain behind the bar, Karl found a bottle in a corner cabinet. He poured out some of the sweet *Kräuterlikör*, and Gerhard accepted the thick-bottomed glass. They hadn't yet said a word to each other, had just tacitly and—of course happily—confirmed that the other was alive.

"We're lucky," Gerhard said softly, before draining his glass in one gulp.

Karl grunted.

"We're alive." Gerhard raised his glass as if to toast.

A sound like a sigh emerged from Karl, who now stood next to the office's only window. He fingered his eye patch distractedly.

Gerhard's mind fixated on his last sentence. A life for an eye was an expensive but acceptable trade. He didn't know what Karl had experienced, but he was not the same man. Maybe he'd also given up his mind in exchange, because the real Karl was gone, replaced by the taciturn man at the window.

Gerhard stood. He picked up the bottle and refilled his glass, not because he liked the taste of the sticky liquid but because of its effect on him. At the window Karl was quiet. Gerhard could almost see the thoughts circling above his brother's head. The uncertainty of Hilde's fate. Gerhard had seen Hamm with his own eyes. No one could have survived. He tried to think of something to say. Some consoling words that could help Karl, but they didn't exist. He gave up.

"Have you spoken to Müller since you returned?" he said following a long pause.

"No."

"Then you haven't heard about the factory?"

"No, Müller's taking care of it."

So Gerhard told him about the new camp in Neugraben, which was to open in September, and explained that he would be its commandant.

Karl seemed indifferent to the news, and said nothing.

"So we'll be able to maintain production," Gerhard concluded.

"Fine, wonderful."

Gerhard heard in Karl's tone that he wasn't interested. He changed the subject. "Do you know who reported me to the Gestapo?"

Karl didn't respond.

"Heinz. It was Heinz."

"Hilde's Heinz?"

"Yes." *Hilde's goddamned Heinz,* Gerhard thought.

He studied his brother's back for a long time. Though Karl didn't say anything, Gerhard noticed the desperation in his demeanor. He heard his heavy breathing and watched him working his jaw. Karl hadn't moved for several minutes; he stood as if waiting for something. He must've accepted that Hilde wasn't going to turn up, Gerhard thought. Then it occurred to him that perhaps Karl was waiting for him to leave. They hadn't seen each other in years, and yet Karl didn't seem happy to see him. Gerhard became angry. *How disrespectful.* Sure, August and Hilde were no longer alive, but couldn't Karl at least be glad that his own brother had survived? He got to his feet. He had nothing more to say.

"I have to go." He waited for Karl to look his way. But he didn't.

Hamburg, Germany, August 3, 1943

Karl sat at his piano. He placed his fingers on the keys and waited for the familiar, joyful sensation. He hadn't sat on this stool since before Ingrid left. But today he'd gathered his courage. He pressed down on the keys tentatively, but the feeling eluded him. The notes didn't come together; they were just fragments of disconnected sound. Impatiently he moved his hands toward the right. The notes formed rows underneath the lid of the piano, but like lemmings they disappeared over the edge and fell. He didn't have the touch anymore; it was dead, and the notes weren't there. They no longer existed.

With the slow melancholy of defeat, he lowered the lid. He felt the hollow space in his chest filling with pressure from within. A wave of exhaustion rolled through his body. He couldn't do it anymore. *Would this damn war never end?*

The doorbell brought him to his feet, and he dashed through the hallway. He practically stumbled into the door as he pulled down on the handle with all his might, calling Hilde's name.

But it wasn't Hilde. It was Gerhard. Karl felt himself come to a standstill. Disappointment: that's what he felt. The hope that it was Hilde had eclipsed everything else. It hadn't even occurred to him that it might be Gerhard. Finally a kind of relief flooded him. At least Gerhard was alive.

He offered Gerhard a glass. He noticed that his brother drained his drink in one gulp. That wasn't like Gerhard.

"We're lucky."

Karl responded with a grunt. Maybe Gerhard felt lucky, but his definition of luck appeared to be quite different from his own. If only his brother would stop blabbering. If only they could just *be* and not talk. He turned his back to Gerhard and gazed across the lake.

"We're alive," Gerhard said.

Karl sighed. *I'm not alive. I'm living but dead. Maybe you're alive, Gerhard, but I am no longer here. Ingrid is not here, Hilde is not here, August is not here, Maximilian is not here, Sophia is not here. So I am not here, either.*

He heard Gerhard filling his glass behind him. "Have you spoken to Müller since you returned?"

Was Gerhard a fool? The factory meant nothing anymore.

"Then you haven't heard about the factory?"

"No, Müller's taking care of it." Karl hoped that would put an end to the conversation, but Gerhard prattled on about Neugraben instead.

"So we'll be able to maintain production," he concluded.

"Fine, wonderful."

"Do you know who reported me to the Gestapo?"

Karl didn't respond.

"Heinz. It was Heinz."

"Hilde's Heinz?" Karl asked.

"Yes."

It couldn't possibly be true. Heinz had done some terrible things, sure, but betray his own family? Karl didn't believe he would do such a thing. But he didn't have the strength to argue.

Gerhard had stopped talking. To Karl, the silence was suddenly overwhelming. Although he had thought he wanted silence, he no longer did. Gerhard was his last remaining relative—or that's how it felt—and Karl wanted him near. He would turn, embrace him, feel his heat, and just be silent. He began to cry soundlessly.

Gerhard said something.

"We're all we've got now, Gerhard," Karl said finally, but at that moment he heard the front door slam.

Hamburg, Germany, August 4, 1943

Karl weighed the pistol in his hand, then ran the tip of his finger across the cold steel. It felt good in an odd, disconcerting way. He undid the Luger's safety with his thumb. With the thumb and index finger of his other hand, he pulled back the bolt, and a Parabellum cartridge dropped into the chamber with a swift, metallic click.

Forehead, temple, or mouth? He stubbed his cigarette out in the ashtray and resolutely picked up the pistol. It was suddenly heavier. In the short second between decision and action, the pistol suddenly weighed ten times as much as before. He used both hands to lift it. They shook. He put it to his temple, but it was as if the Luger's cold, black steel made his mind race. The pistol's barrel became a funnel, and his thoughts rushed through it.

How was he going to do it? *How did one do this kind of thing?* He could ask no one for advice. Anyone who'd ever had the same objective was, of course, gone. And he didn't have the time. He wanted to die, and he wanted to die now. But what he faced was a titanic battle. It felt like the classic clash between good and evil. A part of him wanted to die, and another part resisted, but which part was the good and which was the evil?

The war had taught him that things were never simply black or white. There were good men and evil men in every army, but most often both attributes could be found within the same person. If there was one thing the last few years had taught him, it was that man was neither good nor evil. People were good *and* evil. Even he was evil. He knew that. But hadn't he been a good father? Hadn't he been a good husband? Hadn't he been a good friend? He didn't want to know the answers.

He looked down at himself. He adjusted his uniform jacket. It seemed like an eternity since he'd donned his uniform. But it felt wrong to exit his life wearing a suit. He had to die as the person he was: a soldier. But who was he, actually? Who was Karl Strangl? One thing was certain: he wasn't the man he'd believed himself to be for a very long time.

He couldn't imagine living without August and Hilde. Hilde, an extension of himself, and August, an extension of Ingrid. Now they were gone, reduced to memories. It was pointless to live in the vacuum that had materialized in the middle of his life. And what about his life with Ingrid? What would that be like? Would she ever forgive him? Or would he always feel the coldness he'd felt before she left? Would they ever be Karl and Ingrid again? He had his doubts. No. He knew better. There was no doubt about it: it would never happen. It was irreparable.

Even the army wanted nothing more to do with him. They'd informed him, via letter, that he'd been sent home due to his age. Forty-five years old and useless. Discarded from the only thing he'd ever been good at. He couldn't imagine returning to the factory. It was simply impossible.

He grew dizzy. He'd lost all control of his life. An insurmountable force was bearing down on him, tearing at his arms, and clawing at his legs. The globe whirled on its axis, and he felt pulled down by the force of the rotation. All his life he'd been pulled down. His father and the clothing factory. The SS and the war. Helena had pulled him to her, as had Karin. He'd ruined everything. But no more. It was over now. The king was one move away from checkmate, having lost its queen, its rook, and its beautiful knight.

His finger curled around the trigger. He ought to be able to manage one final effort. But his entire life swirled before his eyes, alongside the life that might've been. Moral questions floated to the surface like air bubbles in a lake. He popped them all.

A thought took root in his brain: Karl needed to be two people at once, executioner and victim. The victim had to recognize his fate, and his last hope—the only friend who could stay the execution—was his arthritis. The executioner, on the other hand, needed to be hard and cynical and determined. The executioner needed to be active, the victim passive. Somewhere between Karl the victim and Karl the executioner, he would die.

He tightened his grip on the pistol and pressed it harder against his temple. Suddenly a yawning chasm opened between thought and action. It wasn't his thoughts that stopped him because his head was empty, and there was no trace of his arthritis pain. But he couldn't squeeze the trigger. His fingers were simply frozen in place. He put the pistol down on the table.

He couldn't even do that.

Neugraben, Germany, September 19, 1943

Gerhard dabbed his forehead with his handkerchief. He was tired of the heat—today was a September day disguised as midsummer—and he was tired of the way his uniform absorbed the sunlight.

He'd been waiting at the main gate for more than half an hour. Where were they? It was unbecoming for a commandant to walk with his column, so he'd left that to Brunner. He studied himself. One had to be presentable on such an important day. He tried approaching it from a practical point of view: guests were coming, and he was the host. That was a crude oversimplification, of course, but that's how his mind worked best now. The entire world had been simplified. He'd sealed away his grander thoughts until after the war. Then he'd sit down at his typewriter once more. Then he'd once again hear the energetic sound of the swing arms forming letters that became words that became sentences that became paragraphs that became books. His apartment and his university life felt light-years away. But he would return to them.

Gerhard was still full of energy. He'd arrived at Neugraben the day before and was ready to get to work after a good night's sleep. A great deal needed to be done before the Jewish women arrived in the camp. Most of them would be working at the clothing factory; the less fortunate would toil at the cement factory or be put to work building houses and roads. But in the camp they would be treated well. Though he knew it would be difficult, he would make sure of that. He'd made many requests—for a doctor, clothing and shoes, blankets, and mattresses—but all of his applications had been rejected so far. So he'd had to settle for old Hartmut's first-aid kit, a few poorly educated guards, and the loudmouthed Brunner, who was always referring to how things were done at Stutthof or Treblinka.

Gerhard had spent the previous evening memorizing the guards' names. He wanted to make a good impression on them, and the least he could do was know their names. Armin Brunner, who was closest to his rank, was twenty-five and had had three of his fingers shot off near Leningrad. Neugraben was his third camp. The thirteen male guards were customs officials transferred from the free port, and all of them were over fifty years old. The female guards were young. It seemed so wrong, women as guards.

The youngest had instantly caught his attention. Her dark pageboy hair kept falling over her face, even though she continually tucked it behind her ears. She was beautiful in a traditional way, but small and slender. Her name was Anneliese Möhlmann, and she seemed sweet and shy.

The flies were already out. Gerhard slapped at one, but he was too slow. He bent over once more to wipe a little muck from his boots with his handkerchief. He stood, straightened his uniform, and studied the two watchtowers and the short barbed wire fence that surrounded the camp. The camp consisted of five barracks. Two of the long wooden buildings were to house the five hundred women, while the others contained wash facilities, a kitchen, and latrines. It wasn't exactly a welcoming sight. He peered down at himself. What was he doing? What kind of a show was he putting on? He was such an idiot! What a foolish idea. Why should he be standing here as though for a parade when the tattered women arrived in their prison garb? He spat on the ground in disgust, turned, and started toward the guards' residences.

In the office he found a half-empty bottle. He sat down at his desk and poured some of its contents in a tin cup. A half hour and three brimming glasses later, he spotted the column marching toward him. Armin Brunner was in the lead, his chest puffed out and his German shepherd on its leash. The rest of the guards walked alongside the column in case some of the prisoners considered bolting. Judging by their wretched appearance, it wouldn't take much to chase them down.

The courtyard was soon filled. Brunner's dog barked savagely, and the prisoners shifted around nervously until they stood in perfectly straight rows.

"Attention!" shouted Brunner, and all the women removed their scarves.

Gerhard left his office on wobbly legs. His eyes swam a bit before he could focus. He took a deep breath and made his way to the center of the courtyard. His voice quivered, just as it did when he used to begin lectures.

"Anyone here speak German?"

No one moved.

"If anyone here speaks German, step forward."

He scanned the women, whose eyes were fixed on the ground. A woman stepped forward hesitantly, and Gerhard walked up to her.

"You speak German?"

"Yes."

"Please translate the following." He took a step back and began his speech, speaking loudly. His voice grew calmer. He paused, anticipating that the woman would translate what he'd said. She remained silent.

He glanced at her. "So translate, woman."

"But . . . but I don't speak Czech. They're all Czechs," she said, looking frightened.

"Then why did you say yes when I asked? Aren't you Czech?" Gerhard said irritably.

"No, I'm German. From Hamburg."

"Jew?"

"Yes." She replied softly and hesitantly.

"How did you wind up here?'

"They forced me to divorce my husband. He's Aryan." She struggled to say the last few words. "I was sent to . . ."

Gerhard raised his hand. He didn't want to hear anymore. Experience had taught him that the less he knew about the prisoners, the easier it was for him to block out the fate that awaited them.

He stepped away from the woman. "Anyone else speak German?"

"I speak German," said another woman with a thick accent.

"Good. Translate. I will do everything in my power to ensure that you are treated well here."

The woman's lips formed an acerbic smile. He'd expected some form of appreciation in the woman's eyes, but all he saw was contempt.

"I mean it."

She nodded and translated his remarks into Czech.

Montauban, France, April 11, 1944

Karl opened his eyes slowly and peered around the high-ceilinged room. He stretched his long body and yawned. He often imagined that the four-poster bed he slept in had once belonged to a baron or a baroness. Now it belonged to him.

He'd been seconds away from taking his own life. Now he couldn't even comprehend how staggeringly close he'd come to bringing on his own demise. He remembered putting the pistol down and thinking for a while about how close he'd been to death. Then a new thought had popped into his head: his war wasn't over. He could still be put to use, and if the Wehrmacht didn't want anything to do with him, then he'd find someone who did. He'd thought of August, of Hilde. He didn't want their deaths to have been in vain; he didn't want them to have died for a vanquished Germany. He would become active in the SS.

Ernst Grabner had been pleased to hear from him and promised he would make sure Karl didn't wind up back with the supply troops or behind a desk. Ernst had powerful friends and could send Karl wherever he wished. That's how he'd ended up in France.

He swung his legs over the edge of the bed and looked out the tall window. Afternoon was turning into evening, and the others had built a bonfire down on the lawn. His thoughts occasionally turned to all that he'd experienced on the eastern front, but he was far away from Russia now, far from death and danger. He was safe here because the English were cowards and the Americans preferred talk to action. They had nothing to fear. And even if the enemy did try penetrating the Atlantic Wall, they would do so near Calais, and they wouldn't stand a chance.

The eastern front did something to people, something he couldn't explain. People grew wild, primitive, beastly. He'd seen farmers and soldiers lying in ditches, shot in the back of the neck. He'd witnessed a prison transport full of diminished, lethargic, and deadened beings. When one of the prisoners had collapsed, the rest had come alive, tearing the corpse to pieces and devouring it with terrifying swiftness. Germans would never behave like that. Although he'd seen his own countrymen act indecently, he knew they would never eat their own.

He dressed and walked out to join the others. He sat on a wine crate and looked up at the little chateau. The towers on the outside of the building were like small, thick barrels, and the wall was in good shape. He savored the moment and its aromas. He loved those rare flashes when he managed to forget everything.

They sat in the splendid garden among small fruit trees and well-tended shrubbery. As he had done on prior evenings, Laub was squatting down, feeding wood to the bonfire. Everywhere he went, Karl noticed that someone always accepted the role of tending a fire. That person took to the task eagerly, ensuring the perfect distribution of hardwood, sticks, and twigs—as though it were some kind of high art form. This was always accompanied by explanations of how beech and oak burned longer, and disdainful remarks about willow's capacity to burn. With Laub it was no different.

All the men he'd begun to like were sitting around the bonfire: Herbert Malinowski, the tall Schröder, Laub, Danek, Wiessmeier, and the two drivers whose names he didn't remember. Schröder played the accordion, and they sang. A bottle of red wine was passed around, and nobody worried where the next would come from because the basement of the estate housed an abundant collection.

Danek tossed the empty bottle on the fire, and Laub glared at him. "It could explode, you idiot." But he said this without any irritation in his voice as he scooped the bottle out of the fire.

Karl grinned. He felt young and comfortable. He couldn't imagine anything that could burst the joy he felt just then. He was part of a community united in its hatred of Germany's enemies. That seemed a noble cause at the moment.

He reached between his legs and pulled a new bottle from the crate. He examined the label before he tossed the bottle to Danek.

Ralf Burchert joined them.

"Let's see it," shouted Danek impatiently before Burchert had even managed to sit down.

Burchert rolled up his sleeve to reveal his new tattoo. His skin was swollen and red. Karl watched Malinowski pleasurably smoking his pipe. He seemed much older whenever he puffed on the fine piece of wood. Karl frequently forgot about the age difference between them because Malinowski was always calm and measured, and always communicated with beautiful but enigmatic expressions.

"Good work." Danek nodded at Wiessmeier.

"How many does that make?" Danek asked.

"Fifteen," came Burchert's swift reply.

"Including the SS tattoo?"

"Yes."

Malinowski pointed the tip of his pipe at Karl. "Have your append-ages ever been beautified with such a humble splatter?"

"If you mean the blood type tattoo, then no," Karl said.

"Wiessmeier can take care of that in no time," Danek said. "Right?" He glanced at Wiessmeier, who was suddenly attentive.

"No, that's okay. It's not for me," Karl said, hastening to add, "I'm not in the *Kriegsmarine*, you know."

"Come on," Danek insisted. Schröder nodded approvingly.

"I don't know. Do you all have one?"

Everyone nodded.

"No, I can't do it." Karl laughed and glanced at all the faces glisten-ing in the fire's light.

Wiessmeier stood. "Let's get it over with."

Schröder had put his accordion down, and now all they could hear was the crackle of the bonfire. Everyone's attention was focused on Karl, who finally responded.

"Oh, what the hell," he grinned, a tinge of misgiving in his voice. "Let's do it."

Neugraben, Germany, May 16, 1944

He heard Armin Brunner's dog barking in the distance. He must have dozed off. It must have sniffed out some terrified woman and forced her into a corner. He imagined it lunging at her, snapping its jaws, while Brunner did nothing to stop it.

He swung his legs down from the table and lit a cigarette with his table lighter. Judging by the sound, the dog was getting closer. He'd already forgotten its name. He stretched lethargically and glanced at the clock. It was afternoon now. He had nothing to do; he was super-fluous. He was sitting in the office only because someone had to take responsibility for the place.

Gerhard had thought of Neugraben as an opportunity. He'd wanted to make things better. He'd wanted to provide the inmates with food and blankets, give them a little hope, a little dignity. He would be to Neugraben what Lorenz hadn't been for Neuengamme. The difference would be that Gerhard cared about his prisoners. But he'd quickly admitted defeat. It didn't matter that he was the camp commandant; there was nothing he could do. Everything was insufficient: the financial means, the food, the barracks, everything. He'd reproached Lorenz, but in reality they were no different. He'd been so naïve. No matter what he did, they would still die. He couldn't save them, so why try? Why believe that he could make a difference? He sat in his office—waiting, apathetic—but he didn't even know what he was waiting for. For the war to be over? To discover that it was all just a nightmare? For someone to save him?

He heard Brunner's boots against the wooden boards in the reception area. His second in command resembled a film star—with his long nose, square face, and cleft chin, he looked like Cary Grant or Randolph Scott. Gerhard suspected that Brunner and Anneliese Möhlmann were lovers. He had no proof; maybe he just thought that because they were both beautiful. And maybe he just thought they were beautiful because the camp was otherwise devoid of beauty.

A draft carried the stench of the camp beneath his door. The pretty Möhlmann, with her angelic face, was the very personification of evil, and she played a key role in the death stink that hung over the camp. Even in the most macabre corner of Gerhard's mind, he'd never imagined that women could be the most brutal of all.

As usual, Brunner entered without knocking. "One of the prisoners was given food from people in the city," he said, more loudly than necessary.

Gerhard had feared this moment. Though he didn't know Brunner well, he knew he'd be a by-the-book type in such a situation. Gerhard was aware that people in the city gave prisoners food whenever they worked in the clothing factory downtown, but he hadn't planned on doing anything about it. Just as in Neuengamme, the prisoners didn't get enough to eat—despite his best intentions. He'd just hoped that Brunner would never find out.

"And what do you suggest we do?" he asked a little hesitantly, fully aware that it was up to him. He hoped Brunner would handle it.

"It's customary for the commandant to punish the first one to break the rules." Brunner was more familiar with both the written and unwritten rules than Gerhard. Gerhard's impression was that the only thing Brunner liked was his dog, which now sat obediently at his side, following their conversation with interest. It went everywhere with him, and he spoke to it the way one would speak to a lover.

"That's out of the question," Gerhard said evasively.

Brunner was clearly racking his brain to think of something to say because he paused for longer than usual. Gerhard took great pains not to look at him. Finally his subordinate cleared his throat. "Then I'm afraid I must report you. It is your duty."

Like a card player, Brunner had now revealed his trump: the accursed SS law that hung over them all the time like a hungry vulture or constantly prodded them like an admonishing index finger. They'd made a pledge of allegiance to carry out orders, and if they refused, they were shot. It wasn't a direct command, but what was he to do— challenge the entire system? He would lose; he knew that much for certain. Brunner obviously wasn't afraid of Gerhard, and why would he be? What reason had he given Brunner to respect him? He'd done nothing. Everyone could see that he didn't belong here, but Brunner was the only one who dared take advantage of that. Why should Gerhard punish a woman whose only crime was hunger? He looked at the dog, who stared back at Gerhard as though it, too, awaited his response. He swallowed a lump in his throat.

To Brunner, the rules were sacrosanct. People's fates did not concern him, and he didn't suffer from the flaw called compassion. Gerhard had seen many men like Brunner at Neuengamme. Before the war they'd been tram conductors, warehouse foremen, factory workers. They were hardworking and efficient, but only when their work was clearly structured. The war was their opportunity to change their lot, and Brunner understood that.

Brunner stared at Gerhard, who made a dismissive gesture. The subordinate interpreted this as capitulation and nodded.

The silence lay like a mist over the courtyard. The only sounds were the soft rustle of the wind in the treetops behind the camp and the whip's lash against a naked back. Gerhard swung it again. This time with more force. He no longer heard it slice through the air. The first few lashes had been excruciating. The whip had seemed heavy, and he hadn't brought his arm all the way down. Now he moved in a constant rhythm. Every time the leather met flesh, a gasp went through the other prisoners, who were all gathered on the square. He averted his gaze from the woman, who'd stopped screaming. He'd actually believed her screams would get louder the more he struck her.

Thirty lashes; it was simple mathematics. He had to lash her thirty times before he could stop. He needed twenty more. Armin Brunner stood with his back to Gerhard, facing the prisoners, his dog's leash wrapped twice around his hand. The German shepherd sat unperturbed at his side.

Gerhard wished he'd had the courage to say no, to put Brunner in his place. He was the commandant, after all, and yet he'd been humbled and forced to carry out this inhumane act. But he didn't dare disobey SS ordinances. He was a coward. *Goddamn me and goddamn Brunner.*

He whipped Brunner. The lashes grew in strength. He whipped Heinz, he whipped Kögl, Glienicke, Lorenz, Turek. He stopped counting; the numbers were suddenly gone. The woman whimpered. He didn't see the blood. He knew it was there; he just didn't see it. And he didn't see the raw flesh, the long strips crossing her back. He whipped for Karl, his brother whom he no longer knew; he whipped for August; he whipped for Emma, Laura, Hilde. He'd become mechanical; he'd become a machine and nothing more.

That's why he didn't notice when the woman stopped moving. The guards had turned their heads, Brunner's dog barked, Gerhard's uniform was red with splattered blood, and the woman didn't move. He paused. Everyone was silent.

He took a step back. He dried his mouth on his sleeve, which came away white with froth. He slowly turned his head and looked at the female guards, who were standing stock-still. He looked at the prisoners, who were staring at the ground. No one met his gaze. Even the rustle of the wind in the treetops seemed more subdued now. He opened his hand and let the whip fall to the ground. He studied the bloodstained switch. Fresh blood clumped the gravel. He swayed a bit as he started to walk away. He was careful not to look at the dead woman as he stumbled past her on the way back to his office. Behind him the silence was broken only when Brunner began snarling orders. His shouts echoed in Gerhard's head. Before long the courtyard was empty.

Every time he walked through the courtyard, it felt like a crime scene. He'd suddenly become everything he had never wanted to be. He was Dr. Jekyll and Mr. Hyde. Until now he'd been able to tolerate the camp because he'd accepted the absurdity of it. But now everything had been turned on its head, made irreversible. He, Gerhard Strangl, had killed a human being.

He'd been frightened by his own intensity during the incident. He'd felt like someone outside of himself, watching the whip, arm in motion, lashing the woman's back. He hadn't realized he was capable of such a thing. He had believed that he knew himself, his thoughts, his actions, his methods of response. But now he was afraid of himself, afraid of what he might do.

Many prisoners died. New prisoners arrived and they died, too. Illness, malnourishment, work accidents, and beatings were the most common causes of death. Gerhard remembered one prisoner, a tall Czech woman with scarred arms and legs. She'd come from Auschwitz at the beginning of 1944, and he'd noticed her right away. She seemed so strong and indestructible that even Möhlmann couldn't break her. In a way he admired her.

It was around this time that Brunner's dog died. One evening it began vomiting. Then its muscles cramped up, and finally it expired. The dog's death amused Gerhard, but Brunner was beside himself.

Convinced that his dog's death wasn't the result of illness or natural causes, Brunner began to brutally interrogate select prisoners. Many succumbed to his methods and perished. He didn't give up, and after he had for weeks terrorized the prisoners even more than was customary for him, a Czech woman, to save her sister inmates, finally confessed. She'd force-fed the dog dark chocolate, and all the theobromine had killed the animal. They never found out where she'd gotten the chocolate.

Her punishment was for all to see. Tied to a wagon wheel in the center of the courtyard, she reminded Gerhard of Leonardo da Vinci's *Vitruvian Man*. And there she remained until she died of hunger.

Carles, France, June 10, 1944

The truck came to a stop, and Karl jumped down on the cobblestone street. He stood in front of the vehicle, studying the colonel of the regiment, Rudolph, who was leaning against a fountain in the town square. The privates were setting up the headquarters in the town hall, dragging, carrying, and maneuvering equipment into position. A private unfolded a chair next to Rudolph, and the colonel wiped it off with his hand before sitting down and crossing his legs. He tilted his head back a little and caught sight of Karl. The ambitious and arrogant colonel reminded Karl of Emil Morgenroth. There was something overbearing about the way he sat there, like some plantation owner surveying his land while sipping a glass of red wine. The way he carried himself suggested he didn't give a damn about the war. It was just an obstacle to be overcome. Karl headed toward him reluctantly.

"We'll never get to Normandy if these bandits keep delaying us." Rudolph made a frustrated face and studied Karl. "Are you the man for the job, Strangl, or do we need to get one of the younger guys to do it?" He raised his glass of wine to his lips.

Karl didn't respond but managed to nod curtly.

"You're a veteran of the Russian theater. It should be no problem for you." Rudolph gave him a friendly pat on the shoulder, and his wine lapped over the brim. "You know what I expect of you." He licked the wine off his hand. "And remember," he added, "cowardice is infectious."

Karl tried to conceal his irritation. Why the hell did Rudolph think he could talk to him like that? Karl was the head of the battalion now, and yet he had to obey this boy. What did he know about war? Wasn't it his first?

But Karl knew he had no choice. He couldn't refuse it, and if he didn't satisfactorily complete the assignment, he'd end up with another shit job just like it. He had to do it, and effectively, so that he wouldn't have to do it again, because this was the kind of assignment he could only do once.

He agreed that they needed to clamp down hard on the *maquisards*, who'd shot three careless SS soldiers at a railway crossing near Balfour-sur-Roche; the resistance movement's courage had vastly improved following the Normandy landing a few days earlier. He just didn't want to be the one to do it.

He walked to one of the trucks and called for Darrah, one of the forcibly conscripted French soldiers from Alsace. "How many people live in this city?"

"Three hundred to five hundred, I'd say."

Karl took a deep breath, then clenched his jaw. "Find Captain Malinowski. Tell him we're ready for a briefing."

"Yes, sir."

Malinowski, the head of the company, nodded slowly, contemplating his pipe as Karl gave him the command.

"We need to be brutal. They're a bunch of goddamn communist terrorists," Karl said, repeating Rudolph's words. Laub, Danek, and Burchert seemed eager, Schröder and Wiessmeier less so.

Karl watched the soldiers climb into the trucks. They were young, very young, the youngest no more than seventeen. His henchmen were all overgrown kids. They didn't look very brave; in fact they looked a bit anxious. Just like the cuckoo chick August had found once. That bird's wing had been broken, but these boys were still intact—for now, at least.

He climbed in beside the driver, who'd told him his name at least fifty times. He still couldn't remember it. Then they headed toward Balfour-sur-Roche. They drove through the highlands and the affluent villages with their massive stone houses. There was no lack of food here, and flocks of sheep and muscular Limousin cows grazed in fields and small groves that gave off a pleasant scent. A road sign at a T junction indicated that they were about a mile from the village. The column waited for a bus carrying a large charcoal oven and chugging slowly toward Balfour-sur-Roche.

One platoon parked outside the city, while the other two drove up the curving main street past the many small shops. Lieutenant Burchert and his men began herding people out of their houses, then forced them to march ahead of the trucks up the street toward the main square.

It was Saturday, and the square was teeming with people because the tobacco rations had arrived that day. Stalls had been set up with fish, meat, vegetables, and fruit for sale, and Karl immediately sensed the peaceful atmosphere of a place that had never had any contact with an enemy. Until this moment. A newly trimmed man stepped out of a barbershop and ran his hand gently through his dark hair, but his satisfied expression quickly fell away when he spotted the camouflaged trucks.

As people got off the bus, Karl noticed a young blond woman being greeted by an older woman with open arms and a kiss on her cheek. The young woman bore a slight resemblance to Hilde, and Karl swallowed a lump in his throat. He shook his head to rid himself of the feeling. He couldn't be sentimental today. This day would require a lot from him, and he couldn't allow his emotions to get in the way.

The cars stopped next to the mayor's office, whose windows were concealed by colorful shutters. Karl ordered Darrah to find the mayor, and he heard someone shout: "Get Gariol."

Darrah and another soldier accompanied the woman who had been sent to find the mayor. They soon returned.

"He's refusing to come," Darrah said.

"Refusing to come?" Karl shouted, surprised. "Take me to him."

Meanwhile, the soldiers searched every house in the city with brutal thoroughness, and the throngs on the square quickly grew.

The woman guided them into a house and up the stairs to the second floor. She paused at the door, then indicated to Karl that the mayor was inside. He kicked the door open.

Karl looked down at the woman in the bed. Her legs were spread wide, and her fingers were clutching the sheets. The hair on her forehead was curled with sweat, and she released a long moan.

He heard Darrah's guilty voice behind them: "What should we do? She's having a baby."

The man who was leaning over her straightened up angrily. "I am Auguste Gariol. The village doctor . . . and mayor. I protest." The little man's face was beet red. "I . . ."

Karl turned on his heels and exited the room before the man had finished his sentence. Outside, he lit a cigarette. He removed his cap and dried his forehead with his sleeve. This was an impossible situation.

There was a pistol aimed at his head, but this time he wasn't the one holding it. Rudolph was. He grew resentful, and acid filled his throat. He spat on the ground, but the terrible taste in his mouth remained. Was that how guilt felt? But he didn't have a choice. It was an order, and he needed to carry it out. He ran his hand through his hair and sighed. "Shoot him."

Darrah turned reluctantly to go.

"No, wait. Shoot them both."

"But she . . ." He paused in the middle of his sentence, as if he hadn't considered how to end it.

"We're here to shoot them all, so what difference does it make that she's having a baby? We're to shoot everyone, and that means everyone."

Schoolchildren came marching up in two orderly rows, their teacher out in front. The children were wearing wooden clogs, and the clapping of their soles against the cobblestones echoed off the buildings.

Half an hour later, all of the town's residents were gathered on the square. Karl stood in the background, looking on. He sat down on some steps and lit another cigarette. Malinowski knew what to do. Karl had watched the company commander suddenly transform into someone else before. He shouted and screamed now like a man possessed. The relaxed, pipe-smoking commander was nothing like the brutal, efficient officer he became when it was required. The company commanders and the privates were clearly mesmerized by Malinowski's aggressive tactics. The tension mounted. Gun butts slammed into spines and toes of boots against the backs of knees. Orders were barked at the terrified residents, and they were soon divided into two groups: men in one, women and children in the other.

The women and children, including the pupils, were led to the church. A frightened woman pushing a stroller at the head of the procession infected the rest with her fear, and many began to cry. The men were brought to three different warehouses around the town.

Karl went from warehouse to warehouse to make sure that everything was under control. In one of them, the men were ordered to unload the farmers' carts. A broad-shouldered farmer asked in fragmented German: "Where are you taking the women?"

"They're safe . . . in the woods," Karl responded promptly. He heard Danek chuckle behind him, and he turned, glowering at him in reproach. Danek fell silent.

Once all the men were in the warehouses, he went back to the square. He unholstered his Luger, then slowly lifted it out. He removed the safety. What if he didn't shoot? If no one got the signal? He could stroll slowly down the street, out of the town. No one could reprimand him because he wasn't the one who'd started all this. He glanced at his hand holding the Luger, and for the first time he wished that his arthritis would help him. That it would stop what was about to happen. But no, it was his duty.

He pointed the pistol in the air and pulled the trigger. Then an infernal racket erupted. Shots and explosions could be heard from every corner of the city. Fifteen minutes later, the lieutenants reported back to Karl. Those in the first warehouse had been shot and the warehouse set ablaze. The second warehouse, too, and so on.

Karl headed to the front of the church, which smelled of gas and petroleum. Guards were stationed all around the building, and he heard gunfire from their pistols when some of the women tried fleeing through the windows. The fire inside the building was already raging. Laub stared in thrall with his handiwork.

Malinowski rapped his pipe against the cobblestones. Wiessmeier and Schröder stood smoking silently beside him. No one said a word. Malinowski had once again become the relaxed version of himself, though Karl noticed he seemed a bit more tense than normal. Bundles of hand grenades tied together with yarn lay nearby. Judging by the empty boxes, several of them had been used inside the church.

A thick, suffocating smoke billowed from the empty windows, and there was a shrill, penetrating crash when the church's large bell tumbled down onto the flagstones inside.

"God is dead now," Malinowski said drily. The others grinned.

Karl recalled the church outside of Minsk. The injustice he'd felt watching that building go up in flames. What did he feel now, he wondered? Nothing. And what did that mean? He had nothing left inside. Nothing had any meaning anymore. So many of the people he loved had been killed—why shouldn't he in turn kill people loved by others?

He hadn't noticed that evening had arrived. He looked around. The entire town was engulfed in flames. They'd done their duty, but they hadn't found any of the weapons supposedly concealed in the village. Soldiers from the second platoon had found a wine cellar in one house, and the entire company was now drinking heavily. He heard songs and accordion music. Someone handed him a bottle. He put it to his lips.

Neugraben, Germany, February 6, 1945

Snow lay in tall drifts outside Gerhard's window. The heavy snowfall in December and January had nearly buried the camp, and many prisoners had died. Now he was to shut the entire camp down and transfer the remaining inmates to Hamburg-Tiefstack. He wasn't sure whether it was a change for the worse or the better, but he'd stopped expecting anything and now just accepted whatever happened.

Behind him a voice on the radio said that German troops were fighting heroically near Colmar, and that Budapest was refusing to surrender to the Russians. He snapped the radio off. The war would soon be lost. You didn't need to be a university professor to figure that out, though he hadn't thought of himself that way in some time. As a well-educated man. He'd stifled any thought of his future because it was doubtful he even had one. Not in Hamburg, in any case, because the university had been bombed. Only one thing was certain: he had to retrieve his book. It had been lying inside his desk drawer in his apartment on Jakobstrasse for almost four years. He had typed the final period, and he still thought of it with a touch of pride. At least he could be proud of that.

When they reached Tiefstack, the women were immediately tasked with digging antitank ditches. Many more of them died, and on April 7 the surviving prisoners and personnel set off for Bergen-Belsen on foot. As the prisoners stumbled and lurched forward, the guards thrashed them with ritual precision. Brunner had gotten a new dog, a fierce German shepherd, and its leash was always wrapped around his wrist so that the beast was like an extension of his evil. Gerhard's suspicions had been correct. Brunner and Möhlmann were lovers, a fact they no longer even tried to conceal.

They tramped down a country road with ditches on either side. Birds twittered, and the countryside was in bloom. They'd just passed through Soltau, making no attempt to hide what they were doing but herding the prisoners right through the center of the city. All of Germany had grown used to seeing ragged prisoners marching through their towns by then. Though the Germans ought to have thanked them for their incalculable contributions, everyone turned the other way and acted as though the prisoners didn't exist. As if the columns were invisible except to those in SS uniforms.

A woman at the back of the column fainted, and Möhlmann was on her at once. Brunner waited for her patiently as she finished her work. That's when they heard it, first as a low whistle, then louder. Then Gerhard spotted it. A single airplane was approaching. Gerhard commanded everyone into the ditch. Irritated, Möhlmann glanced over her shoulder. Brunner tried to hurry her as the plane opened fire. A barrage of gunfire rained down on the asphalt road, and Gerhard watched from the ditch as Anneliese Möhlmann and Armin Brunner were shredded by bullets. Then all was quiet. He watched the plane fly off, banking to the right and then disappearing out of sight.

Shaking, Gerhard got to his feet. "Gather the prisoners and continue," he shouted at one of the closest SS guards. The subordinate dutifully commanded that everyone get up, and the column continued its slow march.

Gerhard remained standing in the middle of the road, studying the two dead officers. One of Brunner's arms, the one with the hand missing three fingers, clung to his shoulder on thin filaments, and his face was pressed flat against the asphalt. The dog leash was still wound around his wrist, and the dog lay on its side next to him. It raised its head a little, growled, then dropped its head back to the ground. Möhlmann lay a few yards away. Her short pageboy hair was tangled and bloody, her refined features obliterated by a gaping exit wound. Steam rose off her. Gerhard turned and surveyed the column.

He started walking back in the direction of Soltau. He tried to appear natural, but he knew that he was deserting. Heart thumping, he hid in a basement stairwell until nightfall. He found a pair of overalls and a smock in a nearby workshop and set off down the main street in his new clothes. The city was just waking up. A baker said hello to him through a window. He had to get going, had to start walking, but in which direction? If he went south, he'd run into the Brits. To the east, the Russians. And to the west, Americans. So he headed north toward Hamburg. The city hadn't fallen yet, and he had to retrieve his book.

A few days later he heard that Bergen-Belsen had been liberated by the British. He was quietly pleased to learn that some of the women had been saved.

Shortly after reaching Hamburg, he stood studying the remains of the building that had once been Jakobstrasse number 7. He threw himself on the ruins and began to dig with his hands. He worked feverishly, chasing hopefully after every scrap of paper he saw.

An old man came by. He removed his hat, dried his forehead with the sleeve of his coat, and looked at Gerhard sympathetically. "Your wife?"

Gerhard didn't hear him, so the man shouted. Gerhard turned and shook his head slowly. He inspected his hands. They were bleeding. He caught sight of St. Michael's tower between a couple of lonely façades. It was still standing. Uncertain what to do, he sat amid the rubble, staring in disbelief at the stubborn tower. Then he started to cry.

Hamburg, Germany, April 20, 1945

The sun had begun to set as he turned into the driveway. All at once a surge of relief expunged his exhaustion: the villa was still standing. For some time he simply stood there admiring the house, which gleamed pink in the setting sun. He walked around it. The mortar was peeling in some places, and several of the balusters on the balcony were cracked, but otherwise the house was intact. He inspected the yard; there was a crater in the center of it, and the tall willow lay upon the grass like a fallen soldier, its trunk splintered. He recalled the pale-green leaves that turned orange in late summer, until they dropped to the ground, lifeless and bronze colored, every autumn. Now the tree had fallen like the rest of Germany. He strolled down to the lake. Some of the mooring posts were still standing, but the pier was gone.

The lake, in contrast to his emotions, was calm and unperturbed. He'd left his unit in the lurch. He'd deserted them. In France he'd cursed the Alsatians who'd deserted when they reached Normandy. Now he was the deserter. He'd committed the most ignoble act a soldier could: he'd bailed. Like a coward he'd left the others on the battlefield. But his days as a soldier were over. He'd never fit in. He wasn't SS material. He had the tattoo—which like a family's coat of arms connected him to them—but he wasn't one of them. Not him.

Still, his conscience nagged him. But so did thoughts of home. The uncertainty of not knowing whether there would be anyone to return home to. He felt he would perish if he didn't resolve that burning question. He looked up at the house. Deep in his chest was the hope that Ingrid was inside. He knew better, but the hope wouldn't go away.

He opened the door cautiously and switched on the light: the electricity still worked. He cocked his head and listened, but all he heard was the faint crackle of the outlet. He went slowly from room to room in the empty house, which was filled to the brim with memories. The staircase creaked loudly, as if feet hadn't touched it in years. He wondered how long it had been since anyone had been here.

In the living room he snapped on the radio and dropped heavily onto the couch. British troops had reached the Elbe and were now attacking Bremen; American troops were in Nuremberg, Düsseldorf, Leipzig, Halle, and Magdeburg; and the Russian artillery was in the vicinity of Berlin. When Bremen fell, the English would have access to Hamburg. The only thing left, he thought, was self-deception: people's belief that it would all work out, though they already knew everything was lost. He stood up mechanically and switched off the radio.

It had grown dark outside. He could no longer see through the windows. They'd become mirrors, and he was in every reflection. Now he saw himself as he was. Self-deception was also his worst enemy. Delusion was a widespread disease, but he refused to suffer from it any longer. He'd let it happen; he'd been weak. The questions had always been there, inside him, but he'd suppressed them as if he feared what they might lead to. In the same way he'd stifled his imagination as a child, trying not to think about scary things.

He was alone, and now he would forget the Nazis. He'd been their loyal servant; he'd fought their fight; he'd been their henchman, their equal. He'd taken their money; he'd carried out their orders. He should have refused. He should have. But he had been no better than the rest. The only difference was that he'd imagined he was better than the others. But not anymore.

Hamburg, Germany, May 2, 1945

Gerhard gazed across the lawn, then the lake, from Karl's office window. Beyond the lake was downtown, but the painting was incomplete. Several of the towers that had once stretched toward the sky were gone, and he could tell that the harbor had been transformed. His eyes roamed across the once-immaculate lawn—the knee-high grass, the dandelions, the overgrown bushes, and trees. The willow that had always loomed over them like a tall shadow now lay on its side like a beached whale. Mr. Nikolaus would cry if he set eyes on what Gerhard saw. Or maybe he would turn in his grave? What had become of the old gardener?

At least the villa was still standing. He hadn't bothered to knock. He figured that Ingrid and the children were still in Rügen, and that Karl was away defending the fatherland—if he was still alive, that is. The house was empty. Everything was abandoned, unlived in.

He picked a cigarette out of the walnut box on the table. He lit it, then sucked the gray smoke leisurely. He stared across the lake again, enjoying the silence.

"That's where I found him."

Gerhard turned, startled.

Ingrid was leaning against the doorjamb. Her face bore no sign of grief but was steely and calm. She wore a simple pantsuit and appeared relaxed.

He wasn't shocked. So Karl had done it after all. The last time they saw each other, he'd seemed so tired of life. The news seemed more like a confirmation of what he already knew, just like when he had learned of Hitler's death. The broadcaster had explained in a hesitant voice that Adolf Hitler was gone, that the führer had fought against Bolshevism and for Germany until the very end. It had felt more like hearing that someone had died following a long illness than hearing news that someone had died unexpectedly. Years ago he would have been relieved to hear of the führer's death. Such news would have opened up a world of opportunity. Now it closed all opportunity. And now he was alone. Without Karl.

"When did you find him?" He swallowed.

"Ten days ago." Her voice was calm and composed.

"And the children?"

"They're still in Rügen."

"It's good to see you."

"Don't be ridiculous." Her voice sounded tired now. "Take whatever you want and go away. The desk drawer key is hanging on a nail underneath the table." She turned to leave.

"What about you, Ingrid?"

She gave him a terse smile. "I'll survive."

"What about the factory?"

"It'll earn enough that I can get away from this city and this country."

"Where will you go?"

"Switzerland, I think. I'm through with Germany." She looked him in the eye. "And I'm through with you."

"But we can leave together."

"No," she said firmly.

319

"But . . ."

Ingrid turned and left.

Gerhard found the key where Ingrid had said it would be. He looked around the office. There wasn't a trace of what Karl had done. Gerhard found some money in the locked drawer as well as several packs of Gauloises. There was enough money for him to get by for a while.

He walked to the bar. He took a slug from a random bottle, then found Karl's flask squeezed between some cognac and a bottle of vermouth. He read the inscription and fought back his emotions. KS, Karl Strangl, deceased Karl Strangl, his brother Karl Strangl.

He filled the flask and stuffed it in his pocket. In the driveway he turned for one final look at the beautiful home. Behind one of the large windows, a curtain closed.

Coroico, Bolivia, May 6, 1983

Gerhard picked up a glass from the small kitchen table. His arm grew sore before he'd even filled it, and he set the glass on the nightstand indignantly, cursing his deterioration. Today was especially bad. He was completely drained. He'd been too tired to take his daily walk through town. No one would notice, he knew. The feeling that the life inside him was ebbing away grew stronger every day. Not that it would be today, tomorrow, or even next week, but the energy depleted from him would not return.

He went to the window. There was an ashtray on the windowsill. A cigarette had burned out. It still retained its shape, but the tobacco and paper had been reduced to ashes. He didn't recall having lit it. His thoughts slipped back in time. It had been a foolish impulse, but it had seemed like a noble gesture at the time: after the war Gerhard began smoking Gauloises in honor of Karl. But getting his hands on French cigarettes in South America had been difficult, so he'd stopped that silly habit.

He thrust open the window and stood enjoying the sight of Cerro Uchumachi. Gerhard's landlord, Esteban, trundled across the little plaza on his way toward the high point of the day, the siesta. A stray mongrel nearly knocked him over, and Gerhard heard him yell a few obscenities at the dog, which scampered off with its tail between its legs. As always, Esteban's plump wife, Agnes, was sweeping the walk in front of their house across from the small *taberna*. She glanced briefly at Gerhard but didn't say hello. A sense of loneliness washed over him. He'd begun talking to himself. He'd probably done so for a while but had only noticed it recently. He carried on long conversations with himself, and he liked hearing German phrases.

He removed his glasses and put them on the nightstand, then slowly lowered himself into his bed, his bones aching. He sighed as his head dropped onto the pillow. Out of habit he started turning his wedding ring around his finger, and then his thoughts began to flow. The same ones he'd had for the past thirty-eight years. There was nothing new to add. Even though he believed he'd scrutinized them thoroughly, they persisted in resurfacing. They always took the same path. They began with him leaving Hamburg and continued in Buenos Aires, Montevideo, Santa Cruz, or wherever he was at the moment. Then they would work their way through what his life would have been like had he not wound up in the Gestapo and SS—what course his life might have taken. Whenever his chain of thought reached this point, his mind began spinning in circles, if only, if only, if only . . .

A light breeze brushed against his feet and slowly up his body. He was freezing. Down on the plaza a dog barked. Once again he saw the image of the burned-down building on Jakobstrasse. He hadn't written a word since that day. His ability was gone, vanished along with his desire. He had sat before a blank sheet of paper only once. Though his memory had diminished with age, he recalled clearly the few words that he'd managed to write.

When I enter a room, when I meet a person, I'm not just me. I am a whole life. I am my present, but I am much more my past. I am a traveler and I bear a heavy burden.

It was a tragic conclusion to his literary career.

He thought of Karl. They'd always been so different, and yet they were the same. He had always viewed Karl as summer—outgoing, upbeat, radiant—while Gerhard himself was withdrawn and shy, like winter. The thinker consumed by his own thoughts. Karl was light, and he was darkness. Two polar opposites who shared the same blood. That's how it had been once, but then they'd each gone into hibernation in their own minds. They had tried to suppress the world. They had lived in darkness, and like people freezing with cold, they had done everything they could to get warm. But they were still frozen solid. Karl in death, him in life. They felt nothing; they sensed nothing. Karl had found his peace in this state, while Gerhard remained stuck. For him there was only one natural way out. And that was what he was waiting for.

The last time Gerhard saw Karl, he had seemed so lonely, so vulnerable. He'd known his brother well at one time, and he ought to have known that Karl was considering taking his own life. But so much had come between them. He didn't know Karl anymore. He barely recalled his face. He felt the same way when he saw himself in the mirror. He didn't recognize the eyes that stared back at him. He'd become a stranger to himself. And he'd grown cold. It was a measure his mind had taken of its own accord: to become cold and emotionless. He now remembered only vaguely who he had been before the war. There had been no "before the war" for decades. In his mind he saw only the war. What he buried within was terror and destruction, and all that had once been beautiful in his life was now so distant that it was hardly a memory.

He thought of the Alster. The lake was so lonely, utterly abandoned in the wintertime. It was like his life, the summer of his youth and the winter of his old age. He was a winter man. That was what they were, he and Karl: winter men. Deep-frozen winter men. He thought of Emma, and then his head stilled like an old clock that had counted its final seconds. Finally. Stillness. Silence.

ACKNOWLEDGMENTS

An exhaustive amount of research went into this book, and everyone who helped with its genesis deserves a huge thanks. Some provided professional expertise, while others provided subject-specific knowledge. Therefore I would like to thank Ronny Ritschel, photographer; Christoph Awender; Svetlana Karlin; Marcus Wendel; staff members at KZ-Gedenkstätte Neuengamme; the University of Hamburg; Hamburg Museum; Das Bundesarchiv; Maria Mackinney-Valentin, Kunstakademis's Design School; Karsten Skjold Petersen, Tøjhusmuseet; Peter Sorensen, associate professor at Architektskolen; Søren Hjelholt Hansen, lecturer at Vestfyn's Gymnasium; Dr. Lars Kensmark; Anders Beckett; Bjørn Lemming Pedersen; and Jesper Richard Christensen.

In addition, I would like to thank all the people who read the manuscript along the way, fixed my mistakes, suggested improvements, or in some way inspired me to write this story: Karina Bugge Kold, Torben Herrig, Henrik Hagsholm Pedersen, Søren Lind, Jess Dalsgaard, David Becker, Thomas Lyngdorf, Søren Vad Møller, Mads Rangvid, Asbjørn Bourgeat, Tage Kold Jensen, Niels Rosenkvist, Charlotte Hinze Nørup, Anni Jensen, Trine Toft, Allan Gylling Olsen, Mark Linkous, Steven Galloway, Sine Norsahl, and Marie Brocks Larsen.

In memory of the millions of Jews who lost their lives during the war, all the names that appear in the deportation section are names of real persons who were transported from Hamburg to Lodz, Poland, on October 25, 1941. Of the nearly six thousand Jews who were deported from Hamburg during the war, around five hundred survived.

Any mistakes that have found their way into the novel are my own.

Jesper Bugge Kold

ABOUT THE AUTHOR

Photo © 2016 Peter Clausen

Jesper Bugge Kold was born in Copenhagen, Denmark, and worked as a journalist before becoming a librarian and website designer. His deep interest in the Second World War inspired him to write *Winter Men*, which was first published in Danish as *Vintermænd* and nominated for the debutant prize at Denmark's Book Forum in 2014. He now lives in South Funen with his wife and two children.

ABOUT THE TRANSLATOR

Photo © Eric Druxman

K. E. Semmel is a writer and literary translator whose work has appeared in the *Ontario Review*, *Washington Post*, *World Literature Today*, *Southern Review*, *Subtropics*, and elsewhere. His translations include books by Naja Marie Aidt, Karin Fossum, Erik Valeur, Jussi Adler Olsen, and Simon Fruelund. He is a recipient of numerous grants from the Danish Arts Foundation and is a 2016 NEA Literary Translation Fellow.